A Man
Finds His Way

Also by Freddie Lee Johnson III

BITTERSWEET

A Man
Finds His Way

FREDDIE LEE JOHNSON III

One World
Ballantine Books • New York

A One World Book
Published by The Ballantine Publishing Group

Copyright © 2003 by Fred L. Johnson III

ISBN 0-345-44598-8

Text design by Holly Johnson

Manufactured in the United States of America

Dedicated to Rev. Dr. Ronald J. Fowler.
Your love, compassion, and wisdom showed me the way.

A Man
Finds His Way

1

IT'S BEEN ALMOST SIX MONTHS SINCE MARCY AND I started seeing each other, and it's time to take our relationship to the next level. So tonight I'm going to tell her. She needs to know that she's the best thing to come into my life in a long while. She deserves to hear that she's the sun that shines on my face. In her lies the promise of my better, brighter future. She's becoming the center of my world, the joy in my laughter, the sweet contentment filling my heart. And I want to be with her *only*.

Once we've finished dinner, slipped into our comfy clothes, and snuggled together on the couch to kill the last of that gallon of chocolate chip ice cream, I'm going to cut off the TV, look straight into her eyes, and confess the truth of what I'm feeling.

I carefully position a small portion of parsley next to the salmon fillet on Marcy's plate, sprinkle some chives onto the steaming red potatoes, smooth a thin coat of butter onto the asparagus, and set the plate down in front of her.

"My goodness, Darius," she says, looking beautiful behind the burning candle. "Your culinary skills are enough to make a woman swoon."

I place my finger beneath her chin, gently lift her face upward, and brush my lips across hers. "Not just any woman," I say softly. "But *you*."

Right on cue, the DJ on the jazz radio station puts on a classic cut by the late great saxophonist Junior Walker, who belts out a sexy tune that adds more steam to the moment's building romance. I hurry and fix my plate, sit down across from Marcy at the small dinette table, and take hold of her hand. She squeezes mine tenderly and I kiss her palm.

"This is the highlight of my week," I say. "I'm *really* glad to be here with you."

Marcy half smiles, then looks away. I'm disappointed that she doesn't affirm my statement with a similar response of her own, but she said she'd had a rough day at work and is probably just tired. Today was an overloaded Thursday, so I know how she feels.

After giving two lectures at Erie Pointe University this morning, chairing a panel discussion this afternoon, and making a presentation to the Cleveland Black Historical Society this evening, I was whipped. But I wanted to see, smell, and feel Marcy so bad, I persevered through my exhaustion. I sent out an e-mail canceling Friday's classes, fought through the construction forever clogging Ohio's lousy highways, got frisked three times at Cleveland-Hopkins Airport, and endured a claustrophobic sixty-five-minute flight, sitting between a fat man, a bulkhead, and a screaming starboard engine. Minutes after landing at Baltimore-Washington International I plowed through the meandering human herd, rented a car, and tore down 95 South to Marcy's home in Fort Washington.

It was a hectic, stressful journey, but the sensual tigress staring out at me from Marcy's eyes offers strong hope that my efforts will be rewarded with lots of rambunctious lovemaking. I pour us some more wine, and we start eating. Marcy picks at her food, sighing every now and then.

"Is everything all right?" I ask.

She looks up and smiles. "Yes and no," she answers, shrugging.

"Is there anything I can do to help?"

She shrugs again. "Not really. I've just got a lot on my mind. It'll be all right."

I take a swig of wine, dab the corners of my mouth with the cloth napkin, get up, and step quickly over to her stack of CDs. I search through them, find one filled with the smooth, sultry tunes of balladeer Peabo Bryson, put it on, and hurry over to Marcy. I wait till the music begins and extend my hand to her.

"What's this all about?" Marcy asks.

"It's about me trying to bring a smile to your face." I bow slightly and say, "Can I have this dance?"

Marcy's eyes glisten as she smiles. "Yes, Darius. You most certainly can."

I wrap my arms around her and we start moving in slow love circles toward the center of the darkened living room. The two table candles are like distant stars, their pinpricks of light casting our long, willowy shadows onto the walls. Peabo's voice soars as he pleads with heaven to help him resolve his heart's dilemma. Marcy hugs me tight and grinds her pelvis hard into mine, refocusing the desires of my stomach onto the mounting hunger in my crotch.

"Darius, I care so much about you," Marcy says, kissing my neck. "And I never, ever would hurt you on purpose."

"I feel the same way about you, baby." I hug her tight and whisper directly into her ear, "I have a lot to tell you. I was going to wait, but now's as good a time as any."

"I have something to tell you also."

"Okay," I say. "Go ahead."

Marcy stiffens slightly. "No, Darius. You first."

"Okay," I agree, gulping down a knot of fear. "Marcy, you're fast becoming the most important person in my life."

She turns her face into my shoulder and cries softly. I stroke her hair, savoring the warmth slowly spreading through me as my baby cries her tears of joy.

"Go ahead, baby," I say, patting her back. "Just let it flow. I'm right here with you."

She turns her head to the side and speaks in a soggy voice. "Oh, my God," she laments. "I had no idea it would be this hard."

I laugh softly and squeeze her tight. "There's nothing hard about caring for you, Marcy. If anything, it's wonderfully sweet and easy."

"Darius, please don't talk like that."

I hold her shoulders and gaze into her eyes. "But I have to, baby. Don't you understand? For the first time in a long time, I'm feeling alive again. I'm not just lurching from one day to the next, but looking forward to the future. I'm cherishing every breath I take as another moment to be with you."

She shoves me away and bursts into tears. "Why do you have to make this so difficult?" she demands.

"Difficult? What're you talking about?"

"Breaking up!"

For a long moment, I imagine myself being sucked into the whirling blades of a jet turbine and spit in pieces from the exhaust.

"Marcy, I, I don't understand. I'm not breaking up with you."

She stomps over to the CD player, cuts it off, and turns on the lights. "It's not about you, Darius. This concerns me. *I'm breaking up with you!*"

I shuffle back to the table, grab the bottle of wine, fill my glass to the brim, and slosh it down. Marcy crosses her arms tight over her chest as she sobs and paces back and forth in the living room.

"I'm sorry," she says. "I've been trying to find a decent way of telling you, but there just isn't one."

I plop down in my chair, shove aside the now-cold salmon, and try to shake the disbelief from my head. "Marcy, would you mind telling me what's going on?"

"I'm sorry," she offers. "But I just can't do this anymore."

"Can't do *what*?" I nearly shout.

Marcy stops pacing and looks directly at me. "There's no need to raise your voice, Darius. I didn't want it to be this way, but no matter how hard I tried, I couldn't figure out how to let you down easy."

My jaw falls open. "Let me down easy!"

The multiple indignities of my sudden has-been status, realizing that I've been floating in a dreamworld, and angry embarrassment for having stupidly exposed my feelings spin my emotions into a tornado.

"Darius, please don't be mad," Marcy implores. "I tried. I really did. But I can't go on living a lie. I care about you, but I love Stan."

"Stan!" I blurt, springing up and knocking the chair backwards. " 'Just a friend Stan'? The one who I wasn't supposed to worry about? The one who was just a fun colleague?"

She grabs a tissue off her coffee table and honks into it. "Make fun all you want, Darius. No matter what you think, I tried really hard to fight these feelings. But Stan kept persisting. He just wouldn't take no for an answer."

"So what!" I snap. "Did his refusing to accept 'No!' mean that you had to give him a 'Yes!'?"

"It's not that simple. He was our most important client. I spent hours working with him. We got to know each other, and then . . ."

"You knew me too, Marcy!" I shout. "Or didn't that matter?"

She starts to answer, but I cut her off. "Why am I asking that stupid question?" I growl, throwing my hands up in frustration. "If it had mattered, we wouldn't be having this conversation."

I kick aside the toppled chair and storm past Marcy into her bedroom.

"What are you doing?" she asks, her voice tentative and worried.

"Gathering up my stuff so I can leave."

Marcy eases over toward the door and wisely stands off to the side. "Darius, please don't do this. We should at least talk about it."

I stop packing and glare at her so hard, my eyes burn. "You must be out of your mind. There's *nothing* to discuss."

"I'm sorry," she says, sounding more frustrated than remorseful. "I know you won't believe me, but I sincerely thought you'd appreciate being told in person."

"What I'd have appreciated is not having wasted my money on a plane ticket, stressed myself out to get here, and walked into an ambush!"

"Ambush! I resent that!"

"Good!"

"Darius, I'm trying to be up front with you. Doesn't that matter?"

"The only thing that matters to me right now is getting back to Cleveland."

I zip up my garment bag, throw it into the living room, snatch up the phone, and start dialing for a cab.

"I knew you wouldn't understand," Marcy grouses.

"What am I supposed to understand? That you're seeing someone else? Your lame excuse about not knowing how to tell me? Or how I missed seeing that you were a *dawg*?"

Marcy's head snaps up and she locks her narrowed eyes onto me. "Darius, are you calling me a . . ."

"If the leash fits, wear it!"

"I want you to leave," she demands.

"Not as much as I want to go!"

Why is it taking this cab company so long to answer? After several more rings, they do and I give them the address details.

"How long?" I ask.

"About fifteen minutes."

That's fourteen and a half minutes too long, but it'll have to do. I breeze past Marcy out to the front door, lean against the wall, and massage my temples, hoping I can rub away this throbbing headache.

Marcy wanders over to one of her three aquariums and starts feeding her tropical fish, which means she's upset. After I leave, she'll stare into that water world for as long as it takes her emotions to smooth out and sail her to inner peace. I'll have to satisfy myself with watching the clouds on a flight back to Cleveland, assuming one's available.

"Darius, we shouldn't end things like this," Marcy says, her voice calmer already.

She sprinkles fish food into the aquarium, taking care to make sure it spreads evenly across the water's surface.

"I was hoping we could at least remain friends."

There's close to six hundred dollars' worth of fish swimming around in that tank, four hundred of it spent by me for those two rare Burmese kissing fish. Being kissing fish, especially the rare Burmese type (which, according to the fast-talking pet shop guy, would die without their mates), they had to be purchased in pairs. So I bought them. It was Marcy's birthday. I knew she loved fish and I wanted to make her happy. Not to mention that their spectacular colors were guaranteed to turn her tank into the envy of similarly obsessed hobbyists.

"And I'm truly sorry, Darius. But you know that I'd never purposely hurt you."

On the other side of the living room, suspended like a floating brick in Marcy's largest tank, is her evil-looking piranha. When she first bought the predator, it was just slightly larger than a credit card. But after a steady diet of fat goldfish, it swelled to a medium-sized plate. It's always unnerved me to stare at it, those unblinking eyes sizing me up while that powerful mouth grins, displaying rows of sharp teeth.

"Maybe it was fate," Marcy drones. "Momma always said that the heart wants what it wants."

She strolls across the living room to the piranha and kneels down to feed the goldfish, crowded into the small tank on the bottom of the two-tiered aquarium stand. They're the victims whose sole purpose is to feed the fury floating above them. I've always considered fish to be kind of stupid, but some of these goldfish get agitated as Marcy approaches, diving toward the bottom, pushing their slower, less alert kinsmen toward the surface where doom awaits.

"Darius, don't you have anything to say? I'm trying to extend an olive branch."

Two months ago, Marcy woke me out of my sleep with a phone call announcing that she was going to accept her company's offer to transfer her to D.C. I didn't want her to go but was also worried about sounding like a selfish, nonsupportive jerk. Insisting that she stay was made all the more difficult by her constant confident assertions that the move was best for her career, so I encouraged her to pursue her dream.

"Darius, stop ignoring me! Why won't you talk about this?"

She wasn't sure if a long-distance relationship would last. I was certain it could, explaining that there were people living near me I couldn't stand and others a world away whom I considered close friends. The reasoning was sound, Marcy agreed, and we promised to protect our relationship from the wolves who would eventually be on the prowl.

"All right, Darius. If you're going to be childish and refuse to talk, that's your choice."

Marcy's absence created an emptiness in me that was filled only when her voice came through my phone. Our e-mails sizzled with a passion that threatened to leave our computers smoking. And although I sometimes had to scrounge the money, I jetted my way into the D.C. metro area at least three weekends a month, doing whatever it took to be near her as often as possible, as long as possible. The strain and pain of being without her was always hard, but we healed each other on my visits, going on minisafaris, exploring the "wilds" of Maryland, D.C., and Virginia.

"It's too bad," she sighs. "I was really hoping you wouldn't let it end like this."

I glance at my watch. Where's that cab? I need to get out of here before my name gets listed on tonight's Prince George's County police incident blotter. Mercifully, a horn blows outside. I grab my bags and leave, kicking myself for not renting a car. But that wouldn't have made any sense. We were supposed to catch a tour bus to Atlantic City on Saturday morning for a short but intense weekend of casino entertainment, a couple of romantic moonlight beach walks, and fantastically good, unbelievably low-priced food.

"Where to?" the cabbie asks.

"BWI."

The cabbie turns around, his Rottweiler's head twisting the layered rolls of fat on his neck into a fleshy network of Xs.

"Baltimore-Washington International? That's quite a distance. It'll cost ya."

"I've got the money. Let's just go."

The cabbie puts the car in drive, then hits his brakes when I holler, "Wait!"

"What'sa matter?"

"I'll be right back," I say, getting out.

I hurry to Marcy's front door and pound a few times. She answers, the irritation lines in her face smoothing out when she sees me.

"Darius! I thought you were leaving."

I smile. "I was. But you're right, Marcy. We've been through too much to end things on a sour note. If you're still willing, I'd like to talk about it."

Marcy gives me a wary sidelong look, then smiles. "Darius, you don't know how happy this makes me." She glances down at my empty hands. "Where's your bag?"

"Still in the cab. I didn't know if you'd let me back in."

She rolls her eyes. "Don't be silly. Get it and come in. I'm on the phone with Tonya. Give me a few seconds and I'll be right with you."

She heads back into her bedroom and I hurry over to the tropical fish tank, grab the fish net, and scoop out the Burmese kissers. It helps that there's nowhere for them to run.

"Okay, Tonya," Marcy says from the bedroom. "Look, girl. Let me talk to you later. Darius is here."

Her voice drops to a whisper, probably to tell her sister-girlfriend that even though I was being unreasonable, I've accepted reality and we'll be friends after all. I step over to the piranha and hold the net with the flopping kissers over the tank. Marcy comes out of the bedroom, stepping lively and smiling. Until she sees me.

"Darius!" she shrieks. "What're you doing?"

I drop the kissers into the tank, twist the thin-wired net into a mangled mess, and toss it in behind them. Marcy blurs across the room and shoves me aside.

"My fish!" she hollers. "What've you done to my fish?"

I ease over to the door and watch calmly as the aquatic death dance begins. Marcy scrambles around, searching for another fish net while the piranha casually moves toward the frantically swimming kissers. Like the goldfish in the watery ghetto below, they suddenly understand that it's every fish for itself.

The piranha corners one kisser, hovers for a moment, then strikes, sucking it into digestive darkness. I step out the door as the piranha lines up on the second kisser, motionless and resigned to its fate. Another quick strike and it's over. The piranha zooms around in a couple of tight circles, like the victory loops of a fighter pilot.

I'm waiting at the cab when Marcy bursts outside and hurls an encyclopedia of obscenities at me. I get in the cab and tell the smirking cabbie, "Okay. Now we can go."

2

THE CAB ZOOMS DOWN THE BALTIMORE-WASHINGTON
parkway to the airport, and the warm glow from upstaging Marcy is gradually replaced by churning frustration. She's definitely the main source of
my headache, but what's really pissing me off is the miserable certainty of
having to return to the toxic cesspool of dating. It's been just over a year
and a half since Cookie and I filed for divorce, but it feels more like fifty.
Maybe I should've waited before diving into the quagmire of dating. That's
what ever-controlling Cookie suggested.

A week after I'd moved into my apartment she called one night and
said, "Darius, I've been giving this some thought, and suggest that you
wait before getting into another relationship. Especially a serious one."

I didn't know whether to be confused, flattered, or offended. "Cookie,
thanks for the advice," I said, "but my emotional health is no longer any
of your business."

"Poor Darius," she chuckled. "I'm not concerned with your emotional health. I just don't want you to be disillusioned about not finding
someone of my caliber."

Flames shot from my nose. "If it's someone who's just as hard to deal
with, then I sincerely hope that she's *not* of your caliber."

"Oh, stop being such a sore loser," she admonished, talking to me like
some kid who'd been trounced in a marble match. "Just because you
couldn't meet my needs doesn't mean you won't benefit from having a
woman like me."

"And why, Cookie, would I want to replicate in any way, shape, or
form what I've been through with you?"

She was answering before my lips stopped moving. "Darius, you're ca-
pable enough. But ever since you got that doctorate, you've been a low
achiever. You should be glad that I want someone who'll push you to further success."

"I'm already a success!"

"You can do better."

And that was that. According to the gospel of Cookie, I'd voluntarily stunted my growth, settled into the vaporous routines of academe, and angered the gods of fame by loving the muse of history more than political stardom.

It was the usual argument that always went nowhere fast. And since Cookie had again gotten in the last word, I knew she was satisfied. I naturally refused to follow her advice and wandered into the foggy mists of the dating world. It wasn't just to defy her, but more from a determination to not let a spoiled marriage turn me into a hermit.

When I told my best friend, Nash, he said, "Get ready, D. There's a lotta game-playing going on out there."

He grossly understated the case. Years of being off the "market" had left me woefully unprepared for all the maneuvering, smoke blowing, second-guessing, power playing, and subterfuge. The longer I stayed out "there," the more apparent it became that the dating skills of my first bachelorhood were obsolete, irrelevant, and even self-destructive in the second.

I glower at the scenery whizzing past. "At least Cookie was consistent," I grumble.

"You say something?" the cabbie asks.

"No. Just thinking out loud."

His suspicious eyes linger on me. "We don't carry no more than fifty dollars," he says, speeding up.

"My heart pumps piss for you."

He narrows his eyes, then slams shut the sliding window between us. He can grind his teeth into powder for all I care. All he's got to do is drop me off so I can get on a plane, get back to Cleveland, and forget Marcy. Meeting her had been such a relief. We just happened to be standing in the same line at the movie theater. We were both alone, so I asked if she wanted to sit together. She said yes, the movie ended, we went out for a bite, switched numbers, and a whole new world opened up for me. It was just in the nick of time.

A couple of weeks before, I'd had a blind date with the distant cousin of my barber, Blake. He'd sworn on stacks of Bibles that "man, you'n Vondelle will hit it off for sho'!"

The moment Vondelle opened her apartment door, I wanted to beat a flaming trail over the horizon. It was too late to pretend being a lost pizza delivery guy, especially since instead of a pizza, I had a bouquet of roses. And no pizza pusher I'd ever seen made deliveries in a double-breasted suit.

Vondelle looked at the bouquet and, in a voice like nails scratching across a chalkboard said, "For me!"

Light glinted off the gold rimming each of her teeth. She smelled of Eau-de-Cheap perfume and looked like she'd been shopping at Hoochies R' Us. Her incessant gum smacking and popping was worse than anything I'd ever heard from my students. And I spent the entire dinner at the restaurant ducking behind the menu every time she erupted into donkey-braying laughter.

The final straw came when she said, "Ugh! You're a historian! That's *soooo* boring."

Which of course meant that I was, too. "Dat lyin' Blake told me you had an important job," Vondelle complained.

"What I do *is* important," I insisted. "Learning about yesterday's mistakes is the best way to keep from repeating them today."

"The only thang I wanna know 'bout yesterday is the winnin' lotto number."

She sucked food juices and crumbs from her fingers, then said, "I want a man who's a 'zecutive, got a title'n goes to meetin's 'n stuff. Hmph!"

There was no point in lashing back with rude questions about how her junior assistant manager's position at the Glitz-N-Go Car Wash was so much more important than my allegedly dead-end job. And I was thrilled when after dessert Vondelle started hedging about continuing the date. I glanced at my watch, suddenly remembered I had an important early morning meeting, and suggested that we call it a night. The relief on her face was palpable.

I skipped lunch the next day and stopped by Black Heads Barber Shop to harass Blake. Except for the murmuring discussion among the other barbers, Parker, Otis, and Moon, and the lone beautician, Zenobia, the place was silent. I stormed in, grabbed Blake by his elbow, and dragged him to a corner. Parker, Otis, Moon, and Zenobia were all smirking, so I knew that Blake had shared Vondelle's report.

"How did you conclude that we had anything in common?" I asked, irritated.

I noticed that the shop had gotten totally silent, so my "private" discussion was public anyway.

"Don't be like that, D," Blake answered, grinning. "You're always talking about how you want a woman who's gonna be herself and act natural. Vondelle's about as natural-acting as you can get."

Parker was biting his lower lip. Otis was pinching his nostrils. Moon was hiding his face. And Zenobia had pursed her lips so tight together, they looked fused. All of them looked so silly that I finally surrendered, and we all burst into laughter.

"Sorry thangs went rough for ya," Blake said, chuckling. He put his arm around my neck in a loose headlock, led me back in, and slapped the seat of his barber's chair with a towel. "C'mon and lemme give you a trim. On the house."

"It better be," I grumbled.

"Aw, c'mon, man," he said, flipping on his clippers. "Vondelle's single, available, and horny. You wouldn't'a had to marry her just to get some booty."

"Blake, I always appreciate the booty," I said. "But I'm looking for something more."

With Marcy, I thought that I'd found it. My premature return to Cleveland is glaring proof of how wrong I was. The cabbie cruises into BWI's airport traffic and I tap on the sliding glass window.

He cracks it open. "Yeah."

"Drop me off at Great Lakes Airlines."

He slams the window shut, angles over to the curb near the Great Lakes Airlines logo hanging from the door, and parks. I pay the fare, grab my bag, and prepare myself to stand in the line from hell. But I'm in luck. The line moves quickly, so the wait isn't long.

Rearranging my flight plans costs me an extra *hundred-twenty-seven bucks*! It's my latest tuition payment at the University of Lie, Deceive, and Manipulate. And even though the ticket agent's smiling when she says there's room on the flight, her acid tone warns me that I should plan better in the future.

A little while later, I'm staring out the airplane window watching the ground race by as we take off. I settle back into my seat and sigh. It's just like my buddy Ike once said before a book club meeting: "It doesn't matter how talented, smart, or fine the babe is; she's gonna send a brother through changes." I'm tempted to agree but refuse to adopt his sour perspective! There has to be a woman out there, *just for me*. It's just a matter of us finding each other.

Just over an hour later, the plane lands. I take the shuttle to my car, pay the attendant, and leave. Forty minutes later, I pull up to my Shaker Heights apartment building, glad to be on familiar turf. I grab my belongings and go inside, stopping on the way to get my mail. The radio I left playing greets me with a nice jazz tune as soon as I step through the door. Marcy's already fading into the distant past and I'm deciding that it's not such a bad day after all.

I set my garment bag down and sort through my mail. It's the usual junk and bills, and I'm about to toss aside the whole mess when I see the envelope from the Cuyahoga County District Court. I open it and scan down the page, my eyes lingering on the sentence that's the final nail in my and Cookie's marital coffin:

> . . . the divorce proceedings between the parties Darius Collins and Collette "Cookie" Hargrove are hereby finalized and concluded.

I plop down on my couch and let the letter fall free. B. B. King's despondent voice groans out the radio as he laments that "the thrill is gone." And more than ever I feel like a man rowing in circles on a storm-battered sea.

3

THREE BEERS FOLLOWED BY A HALF PINT OF JIM BEAM wasn't the best way to handle yesterday's emotional roller coaster, but it helped me sleep and that's what mattered. Now that I'm awake, the morning isn't looking much better. I'd register a complaint with the cosmic Better Business Bureau, but the practical-joking "ruler" of the cosmos would probably put me on hold.

My father would cringe to know I was thinking such thoughts. So what! Being a preacher's kid didn't obligate me to mimic his beliefs, especially not when it comes to blindly following a deity whose interest in me probably doesn't extend beyond the time, place, and method of my next screwing.

I get up and get in the shower. The hot water feels good, massaging my muscles in a way I was hoping Marcy would. She obviously had other ideas, so the prickly water stings will have to suffice for her strong, slender fingers.

I step out of the shower and dry off. There's a small dry spot on the steamed up bathroom mirror and I take the towel and wipe it into a larger circle. I peer close, examining my face, hair, and body.

A recent lack of diligence in my workouts has resulted in a slight gut expansion, but I can reverse that with thirty days of crunch exercises. At six feet, I'm not a giant, but I'm also not lurking down in mushroom territory. My hair's cut short and has had its natural waviness enhanced by that Night Wave Seven Blake sells me. There are strands of gray here and there, but I've been told by a number of women that they make me look handsome and distinguished. My mostly consistent weight-lifting routine has kept my shoulders, chest, and biceps broad, hard, and well defined. My butt that once caused detractors to call me Bubble Butt is hard-rubber firm. My teeth are all there, straight and white. And my light brown eyes contrast nicely with my rich chocolate skin, adding a nice touch to my close shaven, nicely outlined shadow of a beard.

"So what's wrong with me?" I mutter. "I'm an employed, decent-looking, well-educated, self-directed, non-drug or -alcohol dependent black man and my love life is a train wreck on rewind."

My self-inspection is interrupted by the NPR reporter's voice speaking from my living room radio. He sounds surprised as he shares the dismal results of yet another study on American race relations.

". . . findings show that African-Americans are still routinely discriminated against in housing, education, employment, income, getting loans . . ."

I hurry from the steamy warmth of the bathroom into the chilly living room, turn off the radio, and dash back. I'm forever baffled as to why the researchers conducting these studies are amazed at their bleak findings. The only ones not surprised are the black people who deal daily with the reality of the statistics. What they should do is conduct a study examining why African-Americans aren't routinely driven insane by the constant stupidity thrown at them over the course of a lifetime.

I pull on some well-worn jeans, a baggy T-shirt, and comfortably battered Nikes, grab my keys, and head down to the corner Rapid Shop to buy some papers. I get copies of the *New York Times*, the *Washington Post*, the *Cleveland Plain Dealer*, the *Chicago Tribune*, and the *Los Angeles Times*. With those publications I can get a good feel for the nation's news and editorial pulse, minus the silly commentary and endless commercials.

On my way to the checkout counter, I fix a cup of coffee to drink while I'm reading the papers at the park bench just outside my building. It's a treat I give myself on those weekends when the weather's nice and I've got the time. I hadn't expected that luxury this weekend, but since Marcy's given me a windfall I might as well take advantage.

I grab a pack of Gummy Bears, pay at the checkout, and stroll home. Minutes later, I'm sitting at a park bench, chuckling at an editorial cartoon in the *Post*.

The picture shows an enraged man dressed in surgeon's garb, holding a giant screw in one hand and a large drill in the other. The words "American People" are written across his chest. His smoldering eyes are locked onto a wide-eyed, sweating pig of a patient, lying half-naked on his stomach across an examining table. "IRS" is labeled prominently across the patient's wide, quivering butt, perilously close to the surgeon's screw.

The caption over the patient reads: *"Will it hurt?"*

The one over the doctor answers: *"No more than when you do it to us."*

"Good morning, Darius."

I look up and see Rev. Hezekiah Boxwell, pastor of the New Deliverance Christ Temple, out walking his Great Dane, Preach.

I offer a broad smile. "Good morning," I say. "It's good to see you, Reverend."

"Likewise, son."

Just like when I was a boy, Reverend Boxwell's calling me "son" makes my heart swell with affection for him. Back in Cincinnati, he was the youth pastor at my father's church, Holy Word Faith Tabernacle.

I was fifteen going on fifty and Rev. B, as we called him, was in his early forties, a lean, prematurely balding dynamo who possessed a booming laugh that, according to him, was a testament of the gladness of his spirit. He was one of the few elders I respected since, in my wet-behind-the-ears-know-it-all opinion, most of the others were up to their necks in dirt.

"I can't tell you how glad it makes me knowing you're so close by," Reverend Boxwell says. "It's just like being back in Cincinnati."

I reflect for a moment. "Yeah. Those were good times."

He nods. "Yep. But then all you knuckleheads took off for college and I had to start teaching a whole new crew about the wisdom of the Word."

I smile. "If you taught them the way you taught us, I'm sure some of the lessons stuck."

"Some!" he grunts, puffing up with indignation. His smiling eyes betray the effort. "They *all* stuck. No matter how far y'all traveled, or how long we were out of touch, I *know* God's Word is living in y'all's hearts."

I nod and look away, embarrassed at the memory of my limp efforts to maintain contact. After I started attending Kent State University just outside of Akron, Ohio, Reverend Boxwell and I stayed in sporadic touch. While in grad school at Ohio State, I dropped him an infrequent line, but only to say hello so I could finish my next almost-due paper. By the time I started teaching at Erie Pointe University in Cleveland, Cookie and I were married and the demands of life, love, and career further diminished my letter writing. Becoming a father added pressures that left me gasping to make it through a regular day, never mind scribbling out greetings in a card or letter. And then came e-mail.

It was through e-mail that Reverend Boxwell contacted my sister,

Danielle, who gave him my e-mail address so he could reconnect with me after a few years of silence. We exchanged phone numbers, talked and brought each other up-to-date, and quickly rejuvenated the closeness we'd shared before.

He had retired as pastor of Holy Word Faith Tabernacle, where he'd taken over after Mom and Dad were killed. At the urgent request of an old associate, Reverend Boxwell had come out of retirement, moved to the Cleveland area, and taken over as pastor of New Deliverance. That's when we discovered that, with the church and parsonage being just a few blocks down from me, we were neighbors.

Reverend Boxwell glances at the newspapers on the picnic table. "I see you're catching up on our nation's mischief."

"Yes, sir. It's a guaranteed cure for optimism."

He chuckles. "Can't argue with you there. That's why it's so important for us to place our trust in Jesus."

I maintain a noncommittal silence.

"You know, Darius," Reverend Boxwell begins, "you've been on my mind quite a bit. Can I take a minute of your time?"

I wave him over and move some of the newspapers to make room. I'm hoping with all my might that he's not about to launch into a well-meaning but unwanted lecture about me being on a wayward path, blah, blah.

Reverend Boxwell takes a seat and scans the sky. "God's given us a beautiful morning,"

I glance up, then back at him, and nod. "Yes. It's quite a morning."

Preach tugs at his leash, trying to reach me for a sniff.

"Steady, Preach," the reverend softly commands, patting the canine horse. "Steady, boy."

A dog lover like me can't resist such a beautiful specimen, so I move over and pat Preach, since he can't come to me.

"He's magnificent," I say, stroking Preach's back.

"After the Lord and my wife, he's truly man's best friend."

I nod and scratch behind Preach's ears and his tail goes into hyperwag.

"Anyway," Reverend Boxwell continues, "I'd like your opinion on something."

I shrug. "Okay. Shoot."

He smiles like a fisherman who's gotten a solid tug on his line. He starts to speak but grabs his forehead and winces.

"Are you okay?" I ask.

He nods quickly and, speaking through a strained voice, says, "Yeah, just gimme a sec."

And just about a second later, Reverend Boxwell is okay. "What I'd like to know," he resumes, "is what do you think will be the long-term impact of so many black boys being raised in fatherless homes?"

I stop scratching Preach's ears and look hard into Reverend Boxwell's eyes. "If you want an answer to that question, we'll need more than a minute."

"Actually, I'd just like for you to think about it."

"Is there some purpose to this exercise?"

Reverend Boxwell smiles like he's landed his fish. "Yes. I'm launching a program to address that problem in our community. And since the Lord's work should never be done halfway, I'm enlisting some of the best minds I can get on board."

Reverend Boxwell pats Preach's head, then looks at me. "How's *your* son?"

I stiffen as my jaws tighten. "Jarrod's doing fine." I don't bother adding, "As far as I know."

"He's got a good, strong name."

"Strength is something he's needed."

The truth is that *I'm* the one who's needed strength. Strength to endure missing Jarrod. Strength to endure always being the last and least informed about his life. And the strength to believe that he's not being ruined by all the Romeos slithering through Cookie's romantic revolving door.

"Well then, perhaps when New Deliverance launches its Warrior Passages program, you'll let him participate," Reverend Boxwell suggests.

"Warrior Passages," I say. "Sounds like a good title."

"Yes. I thought it appropriate for the Christian training our boys need as they pass into adulthood."

I consider for a moment and say, "Sounds like a good plan."

He smiles, extends his hand, and we shake. "Thanks. Well, I'd better go now. Preach'll be acting up all day if we don't finish his morning walk."

"Okay, Reverend. Good talking to you."

He turns to leave, then turns back. "Darius, I'd like to invite you over for dinner. Maybe in the next day or two, if you've got time."

"For you, I'll make time."

He smiles. "Okay then. Let me check first with Sister Boxwell and we'll set it up."

Reverend Boxwell steps off quickly as Preach hurries away, dragging him along. I wave good-bye and chuckle to myself, knowing that I just signed on to help Reverend Boxwell and dinner will be his way of not only saying thanks but also putting me to work. That's okay. Anything to help black boys is worth the effort. And maybe I'll take him up on his suggestion to have Jarrod participate. This Warrior Passages program couldn't expose him to anything worse than what Cookie and I have dumped onto him.

An hour later, after finishing most of the major news stories and touring the editorials, I'm back in my apartment, sitting at the computer, and working on the next chapter for my book, *Rails to Freedom: Blacks and the Triumph of Civil War Railroads*.

I arrange my notes in the correct order and have gotten to work when the e-mail alert flashes on my monitor. I click open the message and am pleased to see that it's from Lawrence P. Brockett, president of the Cleveland Black Historical Society:

> Dr. Collins,
>
> Thank you for your wonderful presentation. Your comments were quite compelling. A number of our members were challenged by some issues you raised and would like to meet with you further. A good time would be a few weeks from now when the CBHS executive board meets to finalize plans for the new program year. If that's not good for you, please advise and we'll meet at your convenience. I look forward to hearing from you.
>
> Sincerely,
> L. P. Brockett
> President, CBHS

This is great! I'm next in line to be the new CBHS president and Brockett's satisfaction with my presentation doesn't hurt the likelihood that he'll endorse my candidacy. If he does, I'm a cinch to win the election, since CBHS members usually defer to the nominee choice of the outgoing president. It hasn't always worked that way, but only during those periods when the current president has so thoroughly alienated people that they vote contrary to his or her wishes as a repudiation. Luckily for me, Brockett's been a president who, while not doing much in his three years, hasn't angered anyone.

I e-mail him of the week that'll be best for me, then continue working. Most of the scholarship on Civil War railroads is pretty good, but it's predictably glossed over the contribution of the blacks who built, maintained, and repaired the railroads that were so critical to obtaining Northern victory.

After a couple of hours, my thoughts are flowing, the writing's going, and my points of analysis are gathering into an argument that's certain to withstand refutation. I'm just about to focus upon the 1863 controversy that surrounded the establishment of a training camp for blacks along the line of the Baltimore & Ohio Railroad in West Virginia when the phone rings.

The racket jars my concentration, but I refocus and keep typing. The caller is going to have to leave a message. This project has already taken longer than expected and my publisher's starting to ask questions. On the fourth ring, the answering machine picks up and crazy Nash starts talking.

"Darius! You good-for-nothing lowlife. When you return from your weekend of feasting off Marcy's good loving, call me so I can tell you what happened at . . ."

I pick up the phone and say, "I might be a lowlife, but at least I'm a biped."

Nash laughs. "What're you trying to say, man?"

"That you should stop hiding and turn yourself in as the missing link."

"And what'll you do when I tell 'em that we're twins?"

"DNA testing will prove that while my parents had big feet, yours belonged to a tribe called Big Foot!"

Nash and I laugh and exchange a few more insults. "What're you doing home?" he asks. "I thought you were going to D.C. for some R and R."

"Me too. But my R and R turned into D and K, so I caught an early flight back."

"D and K?"

"Dropped and kicked."

The humor flees from Nash's voice as he says, "Are you serious?"

"As a third-stage heart attack."

"What happened?"

I give Nash the highlights of how Marcy lowered her boom, forging ahead through his frequent interruptions of, "That's cold-blooded!"; "Naw! She didn't!"; and "They've got the nerve to call us dogs!"

When I tell him about the fish, Nash blows out a slow, soft whistle. "Well, brother. If you meant to burn your bridge, I'd say you torched it to the max."

I reflect for a moment, wondering if I should've left at least a portion of the bridge standing.

"So are you really gonna let it go at that?" Nash asks.

"What else can I do? Marcy called it off! It's over!"

"Don't bite my head off, D. I just thought you really cared about her."

Nash's complaint tells me that I might not be recovering from Marcy's flushing as well as I'd like to think. I adjust my tone and speak with more calm.

"I did care about her, Nash. That obviously wasn't good enough, so here I am again, back in the wilderness. Why didn't you tell me?"

"Tell you what?"

"That the dating world stunk so bad."

Nash chuckles. "I *did* tell you. And it depends upon when you're dating. In your twenties and early thirties, it's not so bad. Once you hit thirty-five and into your early forties, it gets ugly. The stakes are high, time is short, the pickings few, everybody's got baggage, and gravity's winning."

"Don't forget about diminished hopes, shaken confidence, and fading dreams."

Nash hesitates, then says, "Yeah. Those too." After a few seconds, he says, "So what now?"

"I don't know. I guess I need to find out where I am and where I'm going. At least until my head clears and . . ."

". . . your heart heals," Nash interjects.

I start to argue the point, then decide, What's the point? Marcy's thrown me for a loop. And along with trying to figure out why I didn't see it coming, I just want to spend some time in an environment free of the turmoil that for the last year and a half has been following me like a cloud.

"You know, I sometimes find myself almost missing Cookie," I say. "She was hell to live with, but she was a familiar hell."

"They'll be there in a few minutes."

"Who?"

"The nut wagon."

I laugh. "Didn't you hear me say 'almost'?"

"I heard you. I also know that if you're having those kinds of thoughts, you should jump off a bridge. It's faster. It's final. And it won't keep hassling you after the *splat!*"

"Okay, okay," I chuckle. "Call it a weak moment of insanity."

"If you have another one, keep it to yourself. I don't even want to joke about you revisiting that torture."

"Trust me, Nash. I'd kick my own butt if I ever seriously considered reconnecting with Cookie, especially now that it's officially over."

"You got the decree?"

"In the mail yesterday."

"Dog, D. Yesterday must've been pretty bad, huh?"

"A regular collector's item."

Nash's voice is an odd mixture of sorrow and celebration when he says, "Man, I know it's been painful, but . . . congratulations."

"Thanks. I think."

Nash has already been through the divorce grind, so he doesn't ask how I'm feeling or other asinine questions equating to asking a double-leg amputee how it feels to be legless.

"Say, D. Can you do something for me?"

"Ask and it *might* be given."

"I need you to watch Player for me."

"For how long?"

"Just a week."

"No way."

"Aw, c'mon, man. I'd leave him next door with Mrs. Carson, but she won't watch him no more after he cussed her out."

"Forget it, Nash. I refuse to have that foulmouthed cockatoo in my apartment for a whole week."

"C'mon, D. Help a brother out. Eileen called and said she might be coming in from Indianapolis soon. There's no telling what kind of in-criminating junk'll come flying out of Player's beak."

"Well, then you should either stop cheating or get rid of that stupid bird!"

"I'm not cheating. I'm just keeping my options open."

"Fine. If you're not cheating, you shouldn't be concerned about Player busting your action!"

"See there, D. You're not right. I'd do it for you."

"You wouldn't have to. I'd never be crazy enough to have that tattling pygmy buzzard for a pet."

Nash pumps dejection into his voice as he says, "So then, you're not gonna do it?"

I grimace and exhale a snort. "I'll think about it."

"I won't forget it, D."

"I said that I'd think about it."

"Good!" Nash exclaims, sounding like I've already said yes. "Just let me know soon. Eileen doesn't know exactly when she'll be coming, but whenever it is, it'll be lots better if Player's not here."

"I repeat: *I'll let you know*."

Nash doesn't press any further, figuring correctly that I'm not going to commit right now.

"Well," Nash says, "I was gonna have you give me a call when you got home so I could tell you about tomorrow's book club meeting. But since you're here, you can come see for yourself."

"It's over at Omar's, right?"

"Yeah. And you'd better bring body armor."

"Why?"

"Both Ike and Kiva will be there."

I smile. "If nothing else, there'll be plenty of fireworks."

"You know it," Nash agrees. He's quiet for a moment, then says, "Hey! Now that you're free, you can make a play for Gina."

My mouth falls open. "Jeez! You don't wait for the body to get cold, do you?"

"Rules of the game, my brother. I don't make 'em. I just play 'em. And after that shafting Marcy just delivered, you know good'n well that being a Mr. Nice Guy doesn't get you squat."

Nash has a point. But my positive (and possibly stupidly naive) side refuses to believe that he's right.

"That remains to be seen," I say. "As for Gina, she's a friend and colleague, which means she's off-limits. I don't mix work with my personal life."

"You ought to rethink that policy. Keeping 'em separate doesn't seem to be working."

A bolt of anger shoots through me. Long seconds of silence get longer and Nash says, "Sorry, D. That was a low blow."

I wait a few more moments before answering. "Apology accepted."

"Seriously, man. It came out without my thinking."

"So what else is new?" I ask, chuckling. The tension slackens and Nash laughs with me.

"Look, man," I say. "I've got eyes and at least a half cup of common sense. So I know Gina's desirable. Under different circumstances, maybe I'd consider going after her. But there's one minor detail you keep overlooking."

"What?"

"She's happily involved with Mr. Bruce Manchester the Fourth."

"Involved, perhaps. Happily, no way."

"Why not?"

"Because, no matter how good the relationship or how deep the dude's pockets, no babe is ever satisfied with her sucker of the moment."

"If you believe that, why are you suggesting that I pursue Gina?"

"Because you're my best friend, and I know you'd someday like to hook up with her. If she's gonna be dissatisfied, it might as well be with you."

"That's ridiculous!" I say, laughing. "And you're crazy."

But even so, I wonder what it would be like to connect with Gina. She listened for long hours when I struggled through my meltdown with Cookie. I did the same for her when Landon, her hotel manager boyfriend of two years, jilted her for a freak in housekeeping.

"You should see her," Gina had complained. "Her butt looks like someone stuffed two watermelons into a GLAD bag."

I got a glimpse of that mighty butt when Erie Pointe University hosted a Sixties Retrospective Civil Rights conference at Landon's hotel. Gina was right. The woman's rear end should've been declared a historic landmark or one of the world's natural wonders.

"Should I take your pause to mean that you're liking the idea?" Nash asks.

"No, you shouldn't. Look, Nash, taking things to a more intimate level with Gina might be nice. But sooner or later, we'd find ourselves staggering around like punch-drunk boxers in a relationship minefield. Rather than jeopardize a good friendship and lose a brilliant colleague, I'll leave things as they are. Besides, after Marcy, I'm not in the mood."

"Suit yourself. But I think you're letting a good one get away."

"According to you, there aren't any more good ones."

"After Gina, there aren't."

I laugh. "If you're so pro-Gina why haven't *you* gone after her?"

Nash is straight-arrow serious when he answers. "If she'd looked at me the way I've seen her looking at you, maybe I would have." He sounds downright grim when he adds, "And D, don't tell me you haven't noticed."

"Nash, I'm not blind. But things have got to be different next time. From here on, I don't care how pretty the face, sweet the voice, or fine the body; there's got to be more."

"More! What more could you want?"

"Don't get me wrong," I caution. "I'm *not* on the Great American Ugly hunt. But what good is it having someone who is mouthwatering attractive but has the personality of a rattlesnake?"

Nash grumbles his agreement, probably remembering his stunning ex-wife, who, besides spending money like it was water, possessed a mean streak as wide as the Sahara.

"Fine and sexy is good," I say. "But I also need someone who's stable, sensible, reliable, and, most of all, gentle and kind."

"And on what planet do you expect to find this woman?"

"Maybe on planet Dream," I sigh. "Either way, that's my position."

"Don't hold that position too long, brother. Even a black man's balls can turn blue."

We make arrangements for Nash to come pick me up so we can ride together over to Omar's, then hang up. I glimpse Marcy's picture on the way back to my computer, her lovely face smiling at me with bright beams of love. I snatch it up, take it into my back room, and shove it into a box of miscellaneous notes labeled: CIVIL WAR.

4

WHO'S GOT THE NERVE TO BE BUZZING ME AT 2:00 A.M.
on a Saturday? I put on my slippers, grab my bat, and pad quickly across
the living room to press the intercom button.

"Who is it?" I bark.

"Buzz me in, Darius. We need to talk."

It's Cookie. I lean against the door and groan. What in the name of all
that's right and good can she want? I activate the lock release, grimly aware
that I might be letting in one of the four horsemen of the apocalypse.

Whatever this is about, I'm ending it quickly. During our last few
months of marriage, Cookie spent all her waking moments telling me,
"Darius, we have nothing to talk about. Darius, we have nothing to talk
about."

The frustration and anxiety produced by that daily pummeling resulted in a twenty-two-pound weight loss and days spent questioning the
walls as to how my world had been blasted apart. Fortunately, Danielle
and Nash were there to pull me through.

Danielle kept my hopes alive early on, encouraging me to focus on
the good things about Cookie, the life we'd built together, and how much
stronger we'd be after all the commotion. That worked for a while. But it
soon became apparent that Danielle's advice to hang in there and love
Cookie was more applicable to situations where reason could still prevail.
In our predicament, the slashing had gone on for too long, leaving cuts
too deep for even love's potent healing powers.

Nash offered no opinion, other than to say that he'd support me no
matter what I decided. That decision came late one evening as I put the
finishing touches on a presentation I was to deliver at a historical conference. The paper examined the desperate efforts of a few Northern and
Southern politicians who, just before the Civil War, came to Washington,
in February 1861, to attempt reaching a compromise. Ultimately, Abra-
ham Lincoln and the North could do nothing to stop Jefferson Davis and

the South from seceding. And likewise, there was nothing I could do to stop Cookie from leaving.

But unlike Lincoln and the North, I didn't intend waging a long, miserable fight to reestablish union. For the heroes of 1861, it was a matter of national cohesion. For me, it was a matter of psychoemotional stability. And since I didn't have the power of the presidency, an armed-to-the-teeth military, and a thoroughly hostile population of former slaves to help battle a court system that had turned marital secession into a growth industry, I quit!

Cookie's footsteps echo down the hallway, getting louder as she approaches. I watch for her through the peephole, opening the door as she reaches for the knocker.

"Hello, Darius," she says, giving me and my rumpled Star Trek T-shirt, Minnesota Vikings gym shorts ensemble a quick scan. "It's been a while."

"So it has been," I reply, looking hard into her eyes.

Cookie's always been attractive. Over time, she's gotten better. But I refuse to let her catch me inventorying her looks. I'm not going to give her mountainous vanity a reason to gloat that I've been kicking myself for letting someone so beautiful get away.

"Cookie, it's two in the morning," I say, keeping my voice low.

"I can tell time, Darius. Do you think I'd be here at this hour if it wasn't important?"

"Cookie, I don't presume to know what you'll do at any time."

Cookie bites her lower lip, closes her eyes, and takes a deep breath. It's probably torturing her to suppress a snide comeback, but she'd better swallow it. This apartment may be rented space, but it's *my* space and I'll decide what toxins will or won't enter.

Speaking slowly, calmly, and respectfully, Cookie says, "Darius, may I come in?"

I let a few seconds pass to emphasize that her entry's at my discretion. Then I step aside, let her pass, and lock the door as she glides into the living room. I hate to admit it, but the woman looks good. She's dressed in a full-length strapless gold gown with a low-cut back, matching purse, and white gloves that cover her forearms to just above the elbow. An elegant gold necklace hangs from her neck, flowing down to her lush cleavage, complemented by sparkling diamond earrings and a gold hair comb. Her hair hangs down in straight, wispy lines, the portion about her face cut slightly shorter and curling up just a bit around her jawline. Her perfume fills my nose with aromatic ecstasy. And even though most of my body follows orders and stays cool, my eyes revolt and follow the undulations of Cookie's rear end as she passes, reviving memories of desire.

But then Cookie says, "I've forgotten how small this place is," killing the memories and fouling my attitude.

I step into the living room and lean against the wall beneath my pictures of Frederick Douglass, Sitting Bull, and Francisco Pancho Villa. "Cookie, my life's basic and my needs simple. But my time is precious. Why are you here?"

"May I sit down?" she asks, sitting before I say yes.

I shake my head, go in the kitchen, and start setting up the coffee brewer. I'm obviously not returning to bed anytime soon, so I might as well be alert for torpedoes.

"Isn't it kind of late for you to be wandering Cleveland's suburbs alone?" I say.

"I'm not alone, Darius. My escort is waiting outside in the Jag. We were about to leave the mayor's reception when I got the call."

I stop and gaze at Cookie, casually flipping through my latest *Ebony* magazine. Did I hear her right? Escort? Jag? Mayor's reception?

During our last few gasps of marriage, Cookie swore she could do better than someone who meant to spend his life communing with dead presidents. And I had no doubt that a ravenous, self-serving, materialistic climber like her would succeed. But this kind of progress is beyond what I thought possible even for her. She lives in a nice new house and her two-door, two-seat Mercedes 230 SLK definitely outclasses my Chevy Cavalier. But even so, she's just a working stiff like me, or so I thought. I was obviously wrong in assuming that the political elite Cookie always salivated after would find her storm-surge ambitions too repugnant for even their Babylonian proclivities.

I turn back to the brewer. "Aren't you being rather formal, referring to Andre as your escort? And won't he get suspicious, wondering what's taking you so long?"

Cookie crinkles her nose and sticks it in the air like someone just passed a mound of dog poop beneath it. "Andre's no longer in my life, Darius. And the person outside is just a friend and entertains no illusions. So it's appropriate to call him my escort."

I bite my tongue to keep from laughing and asking Cookie when she started speaking with a British accent. I'll bet some of her old neighborhood pals back in Cape Charles, Virginia, would just love to hear that! And too bad about poor Andre. Like Bernard, Maxwell, Eric, Montfrey, Phillip, and Hernando, he joins the ranks of us dinosaurs who are now extinct.

"Want some coffee?" I ask.

"Yes."

I was only asking to be polite, assuming that Cookie would decline in consideration of not wanting to keep her "escort" waiting. But why am I surprised? As the imperious Queen of Lake Erie, she probably figures that the schmuck should be grateful he's breathed her air. One complaint and he'll join Andre in the brachiosaurus boneyard.

The brewer starts gurgling as the dark brown liquid drains through the filter into the pot. I fix our cups of coffee, sweetening Cookie's with a hefty teaspoon of honey and a quick plunk of cream just the way she likes it. Just like I remember. I walk slowly into the living room and set hers on the coffee table in front of her. I sit down in my rocking chair diagonally opposite her.

Cookie sips the coffee and closes her eyes. "Mmmm. This is good."

I sip mine and nod. "All right, Cookie. You said something about a call. What's going on?"

"In a minute, Darius. I need to gather my thoughts. Please?"

Please. That's a word I've rarely heard fall from Cookie's lips. Uttering it to a proletarian like me must be a stinging slap of humiliation for her. She looks so tired and deflated, her weariness burning like the mid-morning sun through the misty haze of her posturing, public self, revealing the Cookie I once knew. The Cookie whose eyes sparkled when she saw me speaking on the steps of the U.S. Capitol, protesting with other students to have Martin Luther King Jr.'s birthday declared a national holiday. The Cookie who went door-to-door with me and my fraternity, getting out the black vote to defeat the Klansman who'd changed his looks but not his ideas. The Cookie who cried with me through the movie *Glory*, especially the scene where the black Civil War soldiers who knew they wouldn't survive attacked Fort Wagner anyway. Those memories earn Cookie her minute, so I wait.

She sips her coffee and sighs. "Darius, Jarrod's gone crazy."

I place my coffee cup on the small table beside me. "What do you mean?"

"I mean, your son has gone crazy."

Now he's *my* son. When we split up, Cookie never missed an opportunity to remind me of how I'd never be able to understand the mysterious bond between mother and child since I hadn't carried Jarrod to term. It sounds like she's discovering that the cute little kid who once refused to go to sleep without hearing the antics of the Cat in the Hat or Horton the Elephant isn't the same cute little kid. He's becoming a man whose biology has plunged him into dangerous waters where he risks drowning in his own stupidity.

"You'll need to be more specific," I observe. "Saying that Jarrod's acting crazy is colorful but not informative."

Cookie grimaces. "Darius, must you always be the scholar? This is Jarrod we're talking about."

"Cookie, I *am* a scholar and I know who Jarrod is. I also know that you woke me at two A.M. to tell me he's gone crazy. Having once been sixteen, I could've deduced that for myself. Now unless you've got something more descriptive and to the point, I'll invite you to finish your coffee and leave."

"Please, Darius. I don't want to fight."

Something's definitely wrong. Cookie's saying "please" twice in the same hour is about as improbable as finding an honest car salesman. It's also a sham. This wouldn't be the first time Cookie's blitzkrieg to success stalled into reverse at a Stalingrad that no amount of coercing, cajoling, or lawyer battering could conquer. At such moments of setback, she's like those Nazis who brutalized the Soviets into a vengeful hysteria. And just like those Nazis did as defeat approached, she seeks the compassion she so callously denied.

"Listen, Cookie. By mentioning Jarrod you've got my attention. But I can find all this out on my own. So unless there's something more, good night!"

"He's gotten a girl pregnant."

The coffee I'm swallowing backs up, throwing me into a fit of coughing.

"Her mother called me after she woke up and found her daughter puking in the toilet. The woman's livid, Darius. She's threatening to sue and take this to the press, which will ruin my chances for . . ."

"How far along?" I ask, hacking out my last few coughs.

"How far along what?"

"How far along is she pregnant?"

"I don't know. What difference does it make?"

"If you have to ask the question, you won't understand the answer."

"Don't insult me, Darius. Jarrod's the one who got the girl pregnant. Not me."

It's a painful acknowledgment, but Cookie's right. What she doesn't understand is that knowing how long this girl's been pregnant directly impacts the time Jarrod has left before losing his freedom.

I sit back and groan. Jarrod. Jarrod! *Jarrod!* My precious, one-and-only, used-to-be-innocent son. Don't you understand what you've done? You're a child who's fathered a child. Didn't you hear me say that fatherhood wasn't a game? I told you it wasn't just about diapers, formula, and toys. Fathers are responsible for lives! You'll have to raise a know-nothing, helpless baby into a thinking, independent adult! Something *you* don't yet know how to be! And the law. Oh, my God, Jarrod. It's been waiting for this moment to hound, shackle, and bleed you. Jarrod. Jarrod. *Jarrod!*

"How could he be so stupid?" Cookie mutters.

"How could he not?" I snap. "He's only emulating what he's seen."

Cookie's eyes narrow. "Darius, I'm not here to debate my personal life."

"Is that what you call your circus of monthly boyfriend rotation?"

Cookie slams down her coffee cup, sloshing out some of the brown liquid. "Darius. If you think I've been such a bad mother, why don't you sue for custody?"

"My, oh my. Isn't our memory selective? Well, let me refresh you. I did sue for custody! And was denied on the basis of your allegations of child endangerment through nonsupport."

"And that was the truth! When you left for Denver . . ."

"I thought you didn't remember."

Cookie blinks like she's just been slapped with a wet towel. She sets her jaw and battles back. "So what if I do. It doesn't change the fact that you went off to Denver, abandoning me and Jarrod."

"For Chrissake, Cookie! I'd signed a contract to teach as a visiting professor at Denver University for *one* semester! I couldn't just break the agreement. And with all the trouble we were having, even *you* agreed that we needed some time apart to figure out what we were going to do."

"That's no excuse. How many times did I ask you to come home so we could work on the marriage?"

"You only started asking *after* I'd settled in at Denver when you conveniently decided that I and our marriage might be worth your while after all. How did you put it: 'Darius, I'm only doing this for you, so come home *now*.'"

"That's right! I told you several times to come home. And every time you stalled and made excuses, always putting your career ahead of me and Jarrod."

"Putting my career..."

The rest of the words are blocked by my stunned disbelief that image-obsessed, money-grasping, career carnivore Cookie has the gall to fix her lips and utter such fiction. Never one to miss a last-word-getting opportunity, she exploits my momentary flummoxing.

"It was just like that time you went on that so-called research trip to Washington with Laura," she says.

"I didn't go with anyone. And it *was* a research trip. How was I supposed to know that Laura was working as an intern at the National Archives?"

"Right, Darius," Cookie scoffs. "She just happened to be there and you just happened to need information from the division where she was working."

I throw up my hands in exasperation. "Cookie, that's where the data was located. Where else was I supposed to look?"

Cookie rolls her eyes. "Anywhere but there!"

I grab our cups, go into the kitchen, and rinse them out. We did it again. Always, always, always, no matter what the issue, Cookie and I end up struggling with our unfinished business. During our moments of dé-tente, we've occasionally discussed the absurdity of refighting old arguments. But then something happens and we'll be at it again, proving Nash correct when he observed that no matter how long failed couples have been apart, they'll always have unfinished business.

"Darius, this isn't helping matters," Cookie says. "We've got to discuss what we're going to do about Jarrod."

"Do?" I say, returning to the rocking chair. "What's there to do? The girl's pregnant. For the next few months, it's in the hands of biology. After that, and as Jarrod will have eighteen years to discover, it'll be a matter of the law and economics."

"It's more complicated than that."

"Would you *please* get to the point?"

"The girl is white."

My jaw hangs open. "Oh no."

"Yes. And it gets worse. Her mother's a first-generation PWT escapee working as a secretary down at city hall and . . ."

"PWT?"

"Poor white trash."

"Oh."

"Her name is Bernice Cuppersmith. The girl's name is Bell."

"Bernice and Bell," I grumble. "How quaint."

"The woman wants money, Darius. Lots of it. To keep her from going to the press. If this gets out, it'll be scandalous for the mayor's administration."

I lean forward, elbows on my knees. "Cookie, I'm just a lowly historian. Make me understand how Jarrod's stupidly dipping his wick will scandalize the mayor."

Cookie's voice trembles as she starts explaining. "He just appointed me head of his school reform task force. It's a grand opportunity and something he knew would help me in my run for city council next year. But now that this has . . ."

And like puzzle pieces falling into place, the whole picture comes together. "Wait!" I say, snapping up my palm. "Let me guess. Once it's discovered that the mayor's handpicked crusader has a son who's a teenage father, it'll call your fitness into question and impugn his honor's judgment. People will ask why they should listen to someone criticizing deplorable schools and touting parental responsibility when her own son is out repopulating the Earth?"

Cookie covers her mouth to muffle a sob as I get up and start pacing.

"And imagine the mud that'll be slung as people connect Jarrod's behavior with the home environment that failed to instill into him more wholesome values."

"It's not funny!" Cookie shouts. "This'll reflect as badly on you as it does on me."

"So what, Cookie! My *only* concern is for Jarrod, what this'll do to him, his future, and the welfare of his baby. Our grandchild!"

"Don't you dare!" Cookie hisses. "Don't you dare take that self-righteous tone with me. You don't know what I've been going through. Where are you during Jarrod's moments of defeat, when he needs encouragement? Where are you when . . ."

"I'm right where you put me!" I bellow. "Outside the door of his life, banging to get in. So spare me all the martyrdom crap and stick to the issue!"

Cookie flinches, telling me that my response must've been explosive. But so what! Her kicking me to the curb so she could pursue her destiny lumped me into a social category that assumes all divorced fathers are deadbeats, deadweights, and other species of parental slime. So the *last* thing I want to hear about is her self-imposed misery.

I slip on some trousers, then grab my jacket and keys.

"Where are you going?" Cookie asks.

"Home with you so I can talk to Jarrod. So go and tell Henri, Maximilian, or whoever's in the Jag to stay cool. I'm not in the mood for . . ."

"Jarrod won't be home till this coming Friday."

"Home from where?"

"He's in Aspen with his school ski club."

"Aspen!"

Why would she let him go when Jarrod's last report card showed that his onetime 3.2 average had slid further into darkness with the addition of two Ds? I'd better not ask. Knowing Cookie and those stuck-up nouveau chic buppies she hangs with, she'll answer that some school-trained-life-stupid psychobabbler suggested sending Jarrod off to find his inner Tupac Shakur.

"That explains it," I grumble.

"Explains what?"

"What Chitlins was talking about."

"Chitlins!" she says, frowning in disgust.

Cookie acts like she's never heard of or eaten chitlins, which is a lie. She forgets that I've seen her grandmother's West Virginia cabin where Cookie spent her childhood summers using an outhouse, slopping hogs, chopping wood for a potbellied stove, and weeding a four-acre garden.

"Yeah, Cookie. Remember, he's the campus cafeteria supervisor I hounded to hire Jarrod."

And Chitlins wasn't the only person I hounded. Getting campus administration to divert work-study money from one of our typically destitute undergrads so Jarrod could learn the cause-effect relationship between work and pay took some doing. But I kept lobbying, not only getting him the job but also fixing it so that he was close enough for me to monitor his life lesson.

"What was it 'Chitlins' mentioned?" Cookie asks, still frowning.

"That Jarrod missed work the other day and didn't bother to call."

Cookie ponders for a moment. "Well, he was probably preoccupied with his trip."

"He still should've called. If Chitlins wasn't a friend, he'd have been fired!"

Cookie frowns. "Honestly, Darius. Jarrod's just a child. You can't expect him . . ."

"Yes, I can!" I nearly shout. "And he's not a child anymore! If he's gotten this girl pregnant his playpen days are over!"

Cookie nods and dabs the corners of her eyes with a tissue. "What a horrible mess," she sighs. "Oh, my God, Stovey. I'm so sorry."

I look hard at Cookie. She gasps and covers her mouth, her eyes wide and wary. The only person I know possessing a name from which an odd moniker like Stovey could be pulled is the mayor, Stoverman Tyne.

He's been good for Cleveland, transforming it from a soot-covered eyesore of dingy brick and rusting steel into a relatively safe, sleek, high-tech metropolis of blooming culture. But since when has this loving husband, doting father, and tireless campaigner for decency and character in city government allowed middle-rank players like Cookie such familiarities? Which brings up another question. Why did he bypass so many bright, qualified educators to choose Cookie as his academic guru when she's the deputy transportation commissioner?

"I thought only His Honor's family and closest associates called him Stovey," I say.

Cookie's face smoothly cements into an inscrutable mask, just like those other political chameleons who assume whatever look, posture, or position is needed to win over the crowd of the moment.

She gathers up her purse and gloves and stands to leave. "Jarrod will be home at the end of the week. Why don't you come see him then?"

I study Cookie's face. She's good. But I'm not one of her cronies and don't need to curry her favor for my success. I lived with Cookie, stared into her eyes as we made love, dried them when she lost her father, and saw their light die when she stopped loving me.

"You're having an affair with him, aren't you?"

Cookie's eyes narrow. "I'm not going to dignify that ridiculous accusa . . ."

I shake my head. "Cookie, what were you thinking? What was *he* thinking?"

Cookie's nostrils flare as she clutches her purse so tight the leather groans. Then she drops it, buries her face into her palms, and weeps. I watch silently, savoring this moment of her pain, payback for all the hassle she's caused me. But my gloating's interrupted by memories of the love we shared and the bond we forged that, no matter what, will always make at least a part of her pain mine. I get up and pull her into my arms, stroking her back and inhaling the sweet scent of her soft hair.

"Darius, what am I going to do?" she sobs. "Sooner or later, some reputation-raping reporter will ask the right question and it'll be over. It'll be all over."

There's nothing I can tell Cookie that'll comfort her. Because the sad fact is that after Watergate, Iran-Contra, Filegate, O.J., and Monica, we've been conditioned to feast off of scandal. And the media, ever searching like a swarm of flies for the next pile of human failure, shovels it into our open and waiting gullets.

I lean over to the coffee table, grab a tissue, and dry Cookie's cheeks. "This is so stressful," she says, sniffling. "How'd you have the strength to do it?"

"Do what, Cookie?"

"Cheat on me with Laura."

I exhale a loud sigh, grip Cookie's shoulders, and stare into her eyes. "Cookie, for the last time: I-did-not-cheat-on-you-with-Laura!"

She pulls me close and whispers into my ear, "Yes, Darius. You did."

I pick up her purse and gloves and hand them to her. She takes them and heads for the door, her steps heavy and subdued. Once there, she straightens up and faces me, her jaw firm and eyes filled with renewed confidence.

"This probably makes you happy, doesn't it, Darius?"

"Why should I be happy about Jarrod's becoming a teenage father?"

Cookie blinks. "What? Oh! I was speaking of . . ."

I shake my head and open the door. "Good night, Cookie."

She steps into the hallway. "Afraid to answer my question?"

"No, Cookie. Disappointed that you asked."

She sneers a smile. "Oh, really," she says, a slight British pronunciation seasoning her words. "Why?"

"Because. It shows just how much you really don't know me."

"Oh, c'mon, Darius. You're not going to tell me that . . ."

I close the door and listen for the sound of Cookie's leaving, but there's only silence. Then I hear a sniffle, followed seconds later by the echo of slow, uncertain footsteps that get louder and faster as they approach the building's exit.

5

AFTER COOKIE'S VISIT IN THE WEE HOURS, I SLEPT IN.
That made me start late, a delay compounded by having to read and grade
research papers, calculate and assign midterm scores, and, worst of all,
survive the depression of doing my budget. Now that those chores are finished, I can finally sit down at the computer and work on my book. I've
been typing for just a few minutes when the phone rings. If the caller isn't
Angela Bassett or Vivica Fox, they'll have to try later.

The answering machine picks up and I listen, grabbing the phone
when I hear Reverend Boxwell's voice. I'd still prefer Angela or Vivica, but
Reverend Boxwell's practically family, so he'll do.

"Darius, this is Reverend Boxwell. I . . ."

"I'm here," I interrupt. "I'm screening my calls."

"I understand, son. You're a busy man and busy people have to use
their time wisely, so I'll get to the point. Can you come over for dinner?"

I grimace, remembering that just yesterday I told him I'd make time.
I really need to work on this book, but I've always told Jarrod that if a
man says he's going to do something, he should do it! It's one of the few
lessons my father taught me that I've considered worth passing on to my
son. And speaking of my son, Reverend Boxwell's Warrior Passages program unfortunately applies to him, so I should at least investigate.

I generally have no use for religion, but I'm not so ambivalent about it
that I'm blind to the possibility of its doing some good. And with Reverend Boxwell running the show, this program will certainly be better for
Jarrod than Cookie's coddling, especially given the complications about to
clutter his life.

"What time should I be there?" I ask.

"Everyone'll be here around six. Is that okay?"

Everyone? I'd ask how my dinner date with the Boxwells expanded to
include "everyone," but I can just about guess. The good reverend probably roped "everyone" into this meeting the same way he secured my
voluntarism.

"Six'll be fine, Reverend."

"Good! See you then."

We hang up and I get to work, pounding away on the keyboard. Hours later, I get to a nice break point and force myself to start grading the midterm exams for my African-American history class. It's not that I don't want to do it, but I really hate breaking out of my writing groove. Nevertheless, my students are paying good money for a good education, and I owe them a stellar effort. So I turn to the task of assessing their skills of critical historical analysis.

I've only graded a couple when I realize that I don't have all the exams. I snatch up my briefcase and look through it, my anxiety building as it dawns on me that the rest of the exams aren't there. This is bad.

After I've dragged my students through the labor of reading, studying, and sweating over the outcome of this exam, they'll be ballistic if their efforts are squandered by the professor's stupidly losing their exams.

I do a quick search of the apartment, but no luck. The only place the exams can be is in my office. I glance at my watch. Going on campus isn't my most favorite weekend pastime, but there's no choice. I'd make the trip after dinner with Reverend Boxwell, but I'd be sweating and fretting through the meal and don't need the stress.

I start getting dressed to hurry on down to my office. But wait! Gina's supposed to be on campus this weekend, making final preparations for her trip to that Hemispheric Cooperation Conference in Managua, Nicaragua. If she's there, she can check for me. I grab the phone, dial, and wait through two quick rings.

"Professor Roman speaking. Can I help you?"

My blood rushes at the mere sound of her voice. "Hey, Gina. How's it going?"

"Darius! What a nice surprise."

It's wonderful to talk with someone who's actually glad to hear from me. "Gina, you know the pleasure's all mine," I say, offering my usual half flirt.

"I hope Marcy's nowhere close by," she says, lowering her voice.

I purse my lips before replying. "Have no fear. Marcy's quite out of earshot."

Classy as always, Gina doesn't ask for clarification. "Well, it's good to hear from you. What's going on?"

"I need a favor."

"If it's legal, cheap, close, and quick, it's yours."

We laugh and I say, "Well, then it's lucky for me that all I need is for you to go to my office."

"No problem. What am I looking for?"

"Midterm essay exams for my African-American history class. I've got part of them here and have my fingers crossed that the rest are there."

"Hang on," Gina says. "I'll be right back."

She places the phone down and I slump back against my chair, relieved that I'll soon know about those exams, one way or the other. Part of my relief is in knowing that Gina's doing the checking. Even though professors are strictly forbidden from having keys to the offices of their colleagues, Gina and I had copies made just for such emergencies.

A few months ago, I was scheduled to deliver the keynote address at a two-day conference of the Mid-Atlantic African-American Historical Association in Raleigh-Durham, North Carolina. Everything was great until I discovered that I didn't have my speech. I started to call Marcy but didn't have the time to tell her who to contact for getting into the department, where to look if she did, or how to handle campus security if problems arose. And that was assuming that she'd respond quickly, a gamble, since Marcy was notoriously slow.

I could've called other colleagues but had stupidly left exposed some notes for an in-your-face article on contemporary racism in the academy and wasn't thrilled about someone getting a sneak preview. The obvious person to call was Gina.

The secretary had a master key but kept it locked in her desk drawer. I FedEx'd my key to Gina, who found the speech and faxed it to the Best Western where I was staying. I delivered the keynote as scheduled the next day and immediately contacted Gina upon my return and proposed a key-sharing arrangement. After witnessing my crisis, she was ready to accept.

I hear Gina's footsteps getting close, and she picks up the phone. "They're beside your computer," she says.

I exhale a loud sigh. "Thank goodness all my luck hasn't deserted me."

"Huh?"

"Ah, nothing, Gina. Thanks for looking. Now I can stop worrying about my students mugging me in the parking lot."

"With the way things are these days, they still might."

"Good point."

After a long second, she says, "Marcy's sweet for letting you ignore her to grade exams."

"You'd be surprised at how cooperative Marcy can be."

Gina's voice is flat, almost dejected, when she speaks. "You're fortunate, Darius. It can sometimes be tough maintaining a good relationship."

This sudden downward spike in perspective doesn't sound at all like Gina. If it were someone else, I'd let it pass, but I care about her too much. "What's the matter, Gina?"

"Huh? What do you mean?"

"I don't know. You sound kind of despondent. Is everything all right with you and Bruce?"

"Yes! Everything's fine!"

Gina's acclamation sounds forced, and I'm hesitant to believe her. But then, it could be that the sadness I thought I heard in her voice is nothing more than me projecting my dismal love life onto her.

"Is that all you needed?" she asks.

"Pretty much. How are your preparations for the conference coming along?"

"Wonderful. My travel arrangements are made; I'm putting the final touches on my presentation, and am just about finished with the foundational research I'll need in order to accompany Dr. Sanchez on that archaeological dig."

"Sounds exciting. I almost wish I were going with you."

"You've got a standing invitation."

"I'd take you up on it, Gina. But I'd have to shoot Bruce when he showed up in a jealous rage."

She chuckles. "Darius, Bruce knows that you and I are colleagues. And he definitely knows to not take me through those kinds of juvenile changes. If I cheat, I won't leave the country. I'll do it right here, under his nose, where it's cheaper, more convenient, and the challenge of getting caught is more fun."

All I can do is swallow. I've always known that Gina was strong, but this particular dose of strength catches me off guard. I swallow a second time to clear the lump clogging my throat.

"Anyway," she says, "I'd better get back to work. I don't want to spend the entire weekend on campus."

"Understood."

"Did you want me to drop these exams off?"

I open my mouth to answer but stop, wondering how Gina knows I'm in Cleveland. Who do I think I'm kidding? She knows me well enough to conclude that I wouldn't be grading papers if I were with Marcy. So even if her question's a shot in the dark, it's accurate.

"If it's not too much trouble," I answer.

"No more than it was to see if they were there."

"I've got a din. . . I mean, meeting to attend, but should be back around nine. Ten at the latest."

"Okay. I'll call before coming, just to make sure you're home."

"No need, Gina. Trust me. I'll be here. I've got too much work to do on this book to be staying out all night."

"Okay. See you then."

A long moment passes and I say, "Gina, I really appreciate your doing this."

"You're welcome, Darius. I know you'd do the same for me."

"In a heartbeat."

"And that's why I adore you," she laughs.

We say, "Bye," and hang up. I feel kind of weird for not telling Gina that I had a dinner appointment with Reverend Boxwell, but it's none of her business. No more than it's any of my business what she does with Bruce when she spends the night with him. And since she does that several times a week, I know she's doing a lot!

Later for such quasi-jealous speculation. I've only got twenty minutes before I'm supposed to be at Reverend Boxwell's house, so I wash up, put on some stylish casual trousers, a sweater that Marcy bought me last Christmas, some sturdy but soft casual shoes, hustle out to my car, and get going.

6

I PARK ALONG THE CURB IN FRONT OF REVEREND Boxwell's house and go in. He greets me at the door, all smiles and full of energy. "Darius! I'm so glad you could join us," he says, pumping my hand.

"Hello, Darius," Mrs. Boxwell greets me, extending her slim, delicate hand. "It's good to see you again."

"And you," I answer. I look at Reverend Boxwell and wink. "What does a man have to do in order to find such a wonderful companion?"

Mrs. Boxwell blushes and Reverend Boxwell booms out a hearty laugh. "Son, you keep talking like that and Sister Boxwell's gonna send you home with a plate."

I laugh along with him, but what he doesn't know is that *I'm serious*. He takes my elbow and guides me into the dining room. Three men are already seated at the table and talking among themselves. Reverend Boxwell gets everyone's attention and introduces me.

"My friends, I'd like you to meet Dr. Darius Collins. He teaches history over at Erie Pointe University."

The group says hello; then Reverend Boxwell introduces us individually. He gestures to a familiar-looking thick-necked man sitting closest to me.

"Darius, this is Judge Lucas Newton, director of the Leifler Juvenile Detention Center. Lucas and I go back quite a ways."

"*The* Judge Newton?" I say.

Reverend Boxwell smiles broadly and nods. "The one and only. Also known as Lock'em Up Luke."

"Lock'em Up Luke" is right! Every juvenile thug in Cleveland knows to have his bags packed if he's ever stupid enough to earn himself a meeting with Judge Newton. He hadn't been on the bench long when he made headlines telling a fourteen-year-old smart-mouthed crack dealer, "Son, you've been a pain, a drain, and stain on your community and it's time to clean up the mess!"

Judge Newton half stands, extends his hand, and we shake. "Pleased to meet you."

"I'm honored, ah, Your Honor."

Reverend Boxwell guides me to another familiar-looking person. "This is Wilson 'Willie' Strayhorn, youth services coordinator for the Cleveland Department of Parks and Recreation."

I remember Willie Strayhorn. He was a star linebacker at Ohio State and on his way to the pros when bone cancer forced a below-the-knee amputation of his left leg. Judging from his melon-sized biceps and bowling ball shoulders, that setback hasn't slowed him down one bit.

He pounds his chest a couple of times with his fist. "Pleased to make your acquaintance, my brother."

I nod and smile.

"And this," Reverend Boxwell continues, "is Kingston Garvey, vice president of community development for the Greater Cleveland Chamber of Commerce."

"My pleasure," he says, extending a well-manicured hand.

Mr. Garvey's spiffy suit, neatly styled hair, and precise, almost dainty movements indicate a man who's labored little and rubbed shoulders much with captains of industry. But when we shake, his grip is its own best advice to not mistake his pampered appearance as belonging to a pansy.

Mrs. Boxwell sets a steaming bowl of mashed potatoes on the table with the rest of the magnificent spread and takes her seat at the far opposite end. "Hez, bless the table."

Reverend Boxwell winks at her. "Okay, precious. Come on, Darius," he says, clapping me on the shoulder. "The boss says it's time to eat."

I sit down in the empty chair next to Reverend Boxwell, who takes his seat at the head of the table, and watch and listen as everyone bows their heads to say grace. I feel like a drifter who's returned home and discovered that it's still as warm, loving, and inviting as when I left. But appearances can be deceiving, concealing closets of tragedy where some suffer silently with their pain.

I struggled with mine for years, asking God to help me make sense of losing my parents. He refused to answer, snubbing me when it had been His own force of nature that had taken them. So I freed myself from the obligation to ask Him for anything, including blessing my meals. As God had proven Himself incapable of protecting my parents and unwilling to answer my questions, I had no reason to believe He'd USDA-stamp my food.

After the grace, we dig in. Reverend Boxwell peels back the foil on a pan of beautifully browned rolls and grunts with approval. He looks up at Mrs. Boxwell, who's staring at him with an impish smile and raised eyebrow.

"Precious, I do believe you've outdone yourself." He looks around the table. "Wouldn't y'all agree?"

Judge Newton nods and stuffs his mouth full of greens. Willie wipes rib barbecue sauce from his lips and smiles. Mr. Garvey sounds his approval while using a knife and fork on his fried chicken, taking all the fun out of eating it. I swallow some punch and raise my glass to Mrs. Boxwell.

She gives us a regal nod. "Thank you, gentlemen. I'm glad that everything is to y'all's liking."

She finally helps herself to some food, followed by Reverend Boxwell, whose plate remains empty until hers is filled. For several minutes the only sounds are smacking lips, scraping forks, soft burps, clinking ice, and grunts and sighs of approval.

Mrs. Boxwell motions to get Reverend Boxwell's attention. "Hez, why don't you get started. I'm sure these talented men can listen while they eat."

Reverend Boxwell chuckles. "You're absolutely right, precious. Not to mention that I'm sure they're on tight schedules."

"Now, Hez, you know I am," Judge Newton confirms.

Reverend Boxwell finishes off a last piece of corn bread, wipes his mouth with a cloth napkin, and pushes back from the table. The rest of us take a few last bites or shove in a last forkful of food, but he urges us to continue.

"No, no, now. Y'all go on and eat up. I'm finished," he says, patting his paunch.

He grabs a yellow legal pad off a small table adjacent to him and flips to the desired page. He looks it over for a moment, sets his jaw, and sits up tall, his folksy bumpkinism surrendering to a steeled determination and clarity of purpose.

"My brothers, our future's in crisis and I mean for us to do something about it."

He looks around the table, making eye contact with each of us. "Now I don't have any bunch of statistics, charts, graphs, and warmed-over studies to prove what I'm saying. But what I *do* have is a set of eyes and ears that tell me the problem's real, is getting worse, and is right outside my front door."

"Go on, brother pastor," Willie says. "Make it plain."

Reverend Boxwell scoots close to the table and pushes his dishes aside. "For way too long our sons have been getting set adrift while we stand around waving bye and scratching our heads, not giving 'em any kinda warning or instruction."

"Talk on, Hez," Judge Newton urges. "You're hitting that nail on the head!"

Reverend Boxwell winks at him, then looks at the rest of us. All of our plates have been wiped clean and we're focused on him. He grabs his forehead and winces before continuing. I glance at Mrs. Boxwell. Her face is calm, but her slightly widened eyes are filled with concern.

Reverend Boxwell massages his forehead, clears his throat, and continues. "Every time I visit a fatherless home. Every time I'm called by a principal, expelling some knucklehead. Every time I visit the jails, filled with wasting black talent. Every time I see a brother treating his wife worse than his dog. Every time I enroll a future scientist, college chancellor, or company president into rehab. Every time another link in our future chain is buried, my heart cries out!"

"Lord have mercy," Mrs. Boxwell groans, shaking her head.

"We've got too many boys thinking that peeing standing up makes 'em a man!"

"Say it!" Judge Newton seconds.

"We've got too many men making a living, and forgetting to make a life!"

"Hear, hear!" Mr. Garvey agrees.

"We've got too many men thinking that black women ain't nothing but sperm buckets!"

"Tell the truth, Hez!" Mrs. Boxwell commands.

"Too many of our boys know gangsta rap, and nothing about their history."

"You've got that right!" I shout.

"We raise our boys into adults, without raising 'em into men!"

"Yes!" we answer.

"We've got racist school psychologists putting our prodigies in special ed!"

"Yes!"

"The news media has declared black men to be near extinct!"

"Yes!"

"TV entertainment portrays black men as cave-dwelling fools!"

"Yes!"

"Our sons tempt the law, not knowing it's written for 'Just Us!' "

"Yes!"

"Youngbloods would rather sink a basket, than raise their GPA!"

"Yes!"

"Youngbloods think life's a game, but don't realize it's a full-contact sport!"

"Yes!"

Reverend Boxwell stands, plants his palms flat on the table, and leans forward. "My friends, this world will misuse, accuse, and abuse our sons if we don't train 'em up to be tough-loving, God-fearing, spirit-filled warriors."

I open my mouth to join everyone when they shout, *"Yes!"* but hold back when I hear: "God-fearing."

"Tell 'em your plan, Hez," Mrs. Boxwell urges. "God knows it's time."

Reverend Boxwell glances at his legal pad, then looks back at us. "My brothers, with the Lord's blessing, New Deliverance Christ Temple is launching the Warrior Passages program to rescue our sons. Brothers and sisters from the Ushers' Board, Women's Auxiliary, Men's and Women's Fellowship, and other ministries are mobilized, organized, and ready to work. Parents have been informed and are ready to sign up their sons. Church facilities and funds have been made available. And the time to get started is *now!*"

He looks directly at each of us. "I've talked with each of you privately about this and asked for your ideas and assistance. What I need to know now is, will you help us?"

After a moment of silence, Judge Newton palm slaps the table and says, "Let's get started."

"I'm your man!" Willie seconds.

Mr. Garvey says, "Just tell me what you need me to do."

Reverend Boxwell looks at me and I smirk back at him, irritated, amused, and, in spite of myself, impressed with his orchestration.

I suppress a chuckle and say, "It would be my pleasure."

A broad smile covers Reverend Boxwell's face and he sits down. "May God's blessing be upon each of you. Now here's the way I envision things," he says, his eyes filling with excitement.

For the next few minutes, he outlines the details of his program. It's an impressive, well-thought-out, logically sequenced plan. I chastise myself for assuming it would be some cobbled-together, chicken-'n-biscuits venture. And it's apparent that during all of our previous discussions, including yesterday's, Reverend Boxwell was conducting research, assessing me, my attitude, and my character before inviting me to exert an influence upon the fatherless boys he considers *his* sons.

I wonder if he's aware that I'm a fencesitter when it comes to Christianity. But then again, he's probably cleared it with God, so it's not my worry. What's of major interest to me is his plan. And the more I listen, the more excited I'm getting about being part of something that just might actually do some good.

"Church members are already developing the Warrior Passages program's five main areas of instruction," Reverend Boxwell explains. "We're going to focus on spiritual development; life and work skills; history and heritage; health and self-love; and the law." He pauses and looks briefly at each of us. "What I'd like for you brothers to do is lend your special talents, expertise, and influence to ensure that we're on the right path, have maximum access to resources, and function with a quality and precision that'll leave this effort second to none."

Mrs. Boxwell says, "Hez has told y'all what we want, but there's also some things we'll need."

She glances at Reverend Boxwell, who smiles. "Go on, precious. You can tell 'em better'n me."

Mrs. Boxwell returns the smile and continues. "We'll need y'all's love, for your wives, your children, and your ancestors. Because just like the Lord says at the beginning of First Corinthians Thirteen: *'If I speak with the tongues of men and of angels but do not have love, I have become a noisy gong or a clanging cymbal.'*"

She looks at each of us. "Understand?"

We nod in obedience, like well-trained students sitting before a gentle but firm headmistress.

"Very good," Mrs. Boxwell commends. "We'll also need your labor, dedicating yourselves to helping our sons with the same energy you use to get paid."

We nod again.

"And we'll need your leadership, the bold, brave kind that was exhibited by Frederick, Medgar, Malcolm, and Martin."

We nod once more, then look back at Reverend Boxwell when Mrs. Boxwell gestures to him. He hands us each a packet with WARRIOR PASSAGES printed boldly on the cover.

"My brothers," he says. "Let's get to work."

7

ON THE WAY HOME, THOUGHTS RICOCHET AROUND my head like bullets in a canyon. Reverend Boxwell's goals are ambitious but not unrealistic. He'd save every black boy in the country if he could but is limiting his first effort to his community. And I have no doubt that this dusty down-home preacher is going to become a major force of change in Cleveland.

It's great that something like Warrior Passages will be available to our sons. But what's really great is that it'll be available for *my* son! After that news Cookie delivered last night, it's apparent that neither she nor I have done our jobs right and it's time to get some help.

If I weren't so suspicious of God I'd almost accuse Him of providing a solution. But that would assume that He's actually paying attention to what happens in this mess of creation. Given the hassles penetrating my life and the misery swallowing the planet, that's assuming far too much. Especially since God runs his operation like an intergalactic slot machine with most lever pulls resulting in two lemons and a slap. He might one day get around to lending a hand, but I'm not holding my breath.

My answering machine light is blinking when I get into my apartment. I hit the PLAY button and wait for the first message.

"Darius, this is Marcy. I . . ."

I punch the STOP button, check for other messages, and get back to work on my book. Then the door buzzer rings.

"What now?" I growl. I glance at my watch and remember. "Gina!"

I whiz into motion, straightening up the apartment. I snatch up an empty beer bottle and toss it into the trash. I stuff dirty dishes, pots, and pans into the dishwasher and oven, then blur through the living room and bathroom, grabbing up slippers, dirty underwear, and scattered history books, heave them into my room, and shut the door.

The buzzer rings again and I hurry to answer. "Who is it?"

"Open up, man. I ain't got all night."

Nash! I clench my jaws and stab the intercom button. "Go away! I'm in here knocking boots."

He laughs. "Negro, please! The only boots you're knocking are the ones in your closet."

I punch the building's entry button, open my door, and step into the hallway as Nash gets close. "You've got a lot of balls assuming I wasn't in the middle of some ferocious lovemaking."

"C'mon, D," he says, strolling in. "You're not into that kinda screwing. You're one'a them uppity blacks who pull it out in the dark for a whole twelve seconds of quiet copulation."

I go to slap Nash up'side his head, but he ducks. "Get your lewd self in here," I say, "before my neighbors start blaming me for the property values going down."

I close the door and go sit back at the computer. "So what brings you this way?" I ask, casually reading over some text revisions on the computer screen. "Did some woman show up on your doorstep claiming that you be her baby's daddy?"

"Naw, man," Nash answers, grinning. "That was yesterday." He gets a beer from the fridge, twists off the cap, and takes a long pull. "I just dropped Katrina off and figured that since I was so close, I'd pass through for a quick visit."

"Katrina?" I say. "She's new. Has she already worn out her welcome?"

"Man, why don't you gimme some credit? Tonight was the first date. I took her to Roscoe's down in the Flats on the water."

"The Flats! You went upscale *and* expensive. She must be pretty special."

"She'll do. I'm surprised you haven't seen her. She lives in the building across from you."

I look up from the computer screen into Nash's eyes. "You're kidding."

"Square business, D," Nash says, guzzling some more beer. "She's a nice-enough honey, but not my speed."

"Why? Because she chose to remain upright through the evening?"

Nash smirks and shakes his head. "I know you care. Why do you talk about me so bad?"

"Because one of these mornings, you're going to take a shower and your joint's going to fall off from crotch rot."

Nash jams his thighs together and pretends to shiver. "Naaasty!" He straightens up, waves me off, and finishes the beer. "Take it easy, D. I *always* use protection."

I roll my eyes. "So in what bar did you find this Katrina?"

"It wasn't even like that. She was a temp in the plant front office for a few weeks when Aggie was out for her knee surgery. I was coming out of a meeting one day, saw her, struck up a conversation, and here I am."

"How long has she lived across the way?"

Nash shrugs. "Don't know, man. It can't be too long, though. She said something about still learning her way around this side of town." He winks and says, "You'd be a perfect tour guide."

"What makes you think I want your castoffs?"

"Castoff! Man, one look at Katrina and you'd know I was doing you a favor."

"That's my point, Nash. If she's that hot, why are you being so generous?"

"I told you, D. She's not my speed. Her idea of having a good time is hanging out in art galleries, museums, and going to see live plays. Where's the fun in any of that?"

I laugh softly. "Sometimes I think you were raised by wolves."

Nash answers with a dismissive grunt. "If I had been, I'd be the alpha male. But it wouldn't make no difference, since Katrina's interested in another wolf."

I glance at Nash from the corner of my eye. "What're you talking about?"

"You!"

I push back from the computer and cross my arms. "Nash, I appreciate the help, but no thanks."

"Don't thank me, man. She spent most of the evening talking about you."

"She couldn't have had much to say. I've never even seen or met the woman."

"Doesn't matter. She's seen you plenty of times and has been trying to figure out how to scam together a meeting. I'm telling you, D. The babe's been watching you, but has just been too shy to make a move."

I shake my head. "This is bizarre. Are you telling me that on your first date with her, she spent the evening talking about *me*?"

Nash rolls his eyes. "You oughta stop."

"Stop what?"

"Sitting over there acting like this news is causing you pain. And to answer your question, yes! She's seen you and me coming and going and guessed we were friends. Her only question was if we were sweet on each other. Once I assured her that I was committed one hundred percent to women . . ."

My jaw sags. "She asked you that?"

"Of course she asked," Nash says, shrugging like it's no big deal. "Hey, D. It's a different dating world since you were last in it."

"I guess so."

"Anyway, once I assured her that I liked *only* women, she decided you were okay and made her move."

I shake my head even more slowly. "Well, this takes the cake. I've heard of detailed planning and scheming, but this elevates it to a new level."

"Hey, man. Don't ever underestimate a babe who knows what she wants."

"I was married to Cookie, remember?"

Nash arches an eyebrow. "Oh, yeah. Right."

"Well," I say, exhaling. "Her preoccupation with me couldn't have been fun for you."

"It sucked. Why do you think I'm standing in your living room this early in the evening?"

"Sorry, Nash. Even though it's not really my fault."

"It's *all* your fault," Nash retorts, smirking. "And it's also your fault that I gotta go home and watch a porn tape."

"Whatever floats your boat," I say, turning back to the computer.

"I don't need a boat floated," he grouses. "I need my poker fed."

He gets another beer from the fridge and takes a short guzzle. "Say, man. I know you're feeling pretty bad about ruining my evening, so why don't you pay me back by watching Player?"

"I'm still thinking about it."

"C'mon, D. I wouldn't keep asking if it wasn't important."

I put the computer into sleep mode and go get a beer for myself. "Nash, just what exactly did that feathered flea bag say to Mrs. Carson?"

Nash grins sheepishly. "It's not really funny, but . . ."

"Yes. I can tell how distraught you are."

He ignores me and says, "Player said, 'Dog, baby. Your boobs is droopin' lower than two sacks of concrete.' "

I try not to laugh. But the thought of Player squawking out that insult, the vision of poor old Mrs. Carson's eyes bulging, and Nash's laughter are too much and I join him.

"You're lucky Player didn't end up as a two-piece snack," I say, holding my stomach and wiping laugh tears from my eyes.

"It wasn't like she didn't try," Nash laughs. "When I got there, Player was hugging the ceiling. And Mrs. Carson was armed with a broom and had murder in her eyes."

The door buzzer rings. Nash looks at it, then me. "I hope you ordered pepperoni and sausage."

"It's nothing of the sort, clown. It's Gina."

Nash's face lights up. "Awwww, shucks! What do we got here, y'all? Is Dr. Darius Collins about to *get his freak ON*?"

"Will you shut up?" I say, speaking low and hoarsely. "Even if she can't hear you, the neighbors might."

A toilet flushes, the sound of the gurgling water penetrating the walls loud and clear enough to underscore my point.

"Time for you to go," I say, hurrying to the intercom. "Who is it?"

"It's me, Darius. Gina."

I press the lock release, grab the back of Nash's collar, and hustle him to the door.

"What kinda junk is this, D?" he protests. "Can't I at least say hello to her?"

"Yes! Say it as she's passing you on your way out."

"Hold up, man," he says, pulling out a small square of paper. "Here! Take it! It's Katrina's number."

"I don't want it."

"Look, D. If she'd been interested in anyone else, I'da told her to kiss my split. But since it was you, I don't mind being the messenger. You oughta at least check her out."

I glance at the paper. Nash says, "She's small and petite, has got a tight, juicy butt and big, round knockers that'll leave you drooling."

"Okay, okay," I say, snatching the paper from his hand.

I jam it into my pocket and sling Nash into the hallway, right as Gina gets to the top of the steps. Nash and I both do a double take and lose ourselves in a momentary gawk. Gina's wearing snug-fitting black leather pants, a sheer lavender blouse, and lavender open-toed low heels. Her hair falls elegantly around her face, sweeping back in feathered layers, getting lower and longer as it falls to just below her shoulders. She moves with the strong grace of a lioness.

"Man, she's so fine, I'd kiss the head of her daddy's dong," Nash mutters.

I glare at him. "Leave!"

He steps off slowly. "Don't forget about Player."

"I'll let you know later."

"Seriously, man. I need to know."

"Later!" I rasp.

Nash gives me a thumbs-up and collects himself as Gina approaches. "Hi, Gina. Long time, no see."

"Hi, Nash," she greets him. "It has been a long time."

They hug and Nash glances at me, rolling his eyes back in his head like he's embracing ecstasy. With the way Gina's decked out and emitting sultry sensuality with each hip-swaying step, I can't blame him.

"Are you coming to the book club meeting tomorrow?" Nash asks, releasing Gina.

She lifts her hands in a gesture of uncertainty. "Probably not. I need to finish getting ready for a conference after church."

Church? Since when did Gina attend church? That's what I get for assuming that I knew her so well. I hope she doesn't ever start Bible-thumping me. Like I told Nash earlier, it would be a shame to lose such a good friend and colleague.

Nash waves. "Well, see you there. Maybe."

Gina smiles, waves back, and strides the last few steps toward me. She's *really* attractive. And built! But focusing on pretty faces, firm jutting breasts, long smooth legs, tight rear ends, and cute steamy crotches is what's caused me so much trouble. It was the beginning of my troubles with Cookie. And it played a big part in the confusion with Marcy. I *won't* be duped like that again.

Gina steps to the door and we briefly embrace. Holding her is like melting into velvet, and I savor the feel of her breasts pressing against my chest.

"Thanks for dropping by," I say, smiling as I release her.

She saunters in, pulls the exams from her medium-sized shoulder-strap purse, and hands them to me. "Here's the gold."

I immediately place them on the dining room table with the others. "I hope they're gold," I say. "The ones I've graded so far are more like lead."

"Now, now, Dr. Collins," Gina playfully admonishes. "Remember that it's a privilege to separate the wheat from the chaff."

Gina's lighthearted response contains a potent truth. It is a privilege to teach my students. My frustration stems from not being able to motivate each and every one of them to perform at their highest capacity. I'll have to find the answer some other time. Right now I'm too preoccupied watching Gina's butt as she steps over to the computer.

My eyes linger for long seconds before I remind myself that I'm not interested in physical attributes and start setting up the coffeemaker. "Want some coffee?" I ask.

She glances at her watch. "Just a quick cup."

I nod and finish setting up.

"This is coming along just fine," she says, staring at the computer screen.

"It better be. My editor says it'll help debunk the persisting perception that black people played a minimal role during the Civil War."

Gina nods in silent agreement while she reads. "This part about the 1862 formation of the United States Military Railroads is fascinating," she says, tracing her finger line-by-line down the screen. "Just like you indicate here, the USMRR's creation was a clear example of the expansion of federal power and authority."

I glance at Gina and wonder what in the world she sees in that arrogant bug Bruce Manchester IV. Sure, he owns three car dealerships, is committed to giving back to the black community, and somehow invokes the name of God during his commercials in a manner that doesn't offend the separation-of-church-and-state sensitivities of his audience. But I still can't shake the feeling that lurking behind all his wealth, sophistication, and movie star good looks is a snake-scorpion hybrid.

"He's not all that he advertises himself to be," I once warned Gina. "I can feel it in my gut!"

She smiled and gave my cheek a gentle, condescending pinch. "Oh, come now, Darius. You know that we're trained to trust the facts but believe only the evidence." Then she hugged me and said, "But I think it's sweet of you to be concerned."

I wanted to ask her why she was always so emphatic about me heeding her non-evidence-based relationship warnings but dismissing mine as if they had the validity of a nursery rhyme. I would've argued the point but at the time was too busy fending off Cookie's efforts to financially disembowel me.

The coffee finishes brewing and I fix two cups, give Gina hers, then sit down in the rocking chair across from her. She's sitting on the couch in almost the same place where Cookie sat the other night, her sweet presence a pleasing contrast to the mean-spirited, self-obsessed aura that so recently darkened that spot.

"Mmmm," Gina says, sipping some coffee. "This is good. What is it?"

"It's Kenyan coffee. Dr. Mabuye brought it back for me on his last research trip to the University of Nairobi."

She takes another sip. "I'll have to get him to bring me some on his next visit."

"I've already placed my order."

We both drink some coffee, then look up at the same time. Our eyes lock together for a short but unsettling moment before we quickly cut our eyes away.

"So what're your plans for the rest of the weekend?" Gina asks.

I glance at the exams on the dining room table. "Grading exams, working on my book, and . . ."

"And . . . what?"

"Going through withdrawal from Marcy."

Gina arches her eyebrow and purses her lips. "I'm sorry to hear that, Darius."

"I'm sorry to be able to tell you." I sip some more coffee and sit back in the rocker. "Who knows. Maybe it was all for the best."

Gina doesn't answer, but I know she agrees with me. Just as I warned her about Bruce, she expressed similar misgivings about Marcy the first time I brought her to a book club meeting. I'd told Marcy that I wanted her to meet some dear friends of mine, which was true. What I didn't tell her was that Gina was a *special* dear friend who'd feel at liberty to render an opinion of my latest love interest.

"She's smart and pretty," Gina had commented. "But she strikes me as being *very* high-maintenance."

I, of course, disagreed. Marcy was independent, had forged a successful career as a training consultant, was a heckuva lot more financially savvy than I was, and never left me feeling like I had to apologize for being born with testicles. She loved being a woman and loved me being a man. She enjoyed the finer things, which I considered a plus, figuring that exposure to her would help smooth out the rough edges that Cookie had never tired of criticizing.

Gina sets her coffee cup and saucer on the end table and comes over to me, opening her arms. I set my cup and saucer aside, stand, and greet her embrace with mine.

"This has got to be hard," she says, whispering and patting my back. "Especially after all the turmoil with Cookie."

The turmoil with Cookie has moved into a new, more troublesome phase. Part of me wants to share that news with Gina, but I'm keeping it to myself. Wearing the wound from Marcy on my sleeve is one thing. The difficulties brewing with Jarrod are a matter strictly for family.

Gina releases me, gets our cups, and fixes us new servings. "Breaking up is always hard," she says, stirring some amaretto cream into our brews. "And I don't want to minimize the hurt, Darius, but there is a bright spot."

"If you point it out, I'll be happy to celebrate."

Gina chuckles. "Okay, silly. The bright spot is that breaking up offers an opportunity to start fresh."

"I'll start fresh as soon as the dust settles and the smoke clears."

She hands me my cup and sits back on the couch. "What do you mean?"

I take a sip and shrug. "Something's not right, Gina. Over the last few years, starting with the death of my parents, I've been getting gradually stripped of everything that's precious to me."

Gina merely nods, knowing that right now I need her to listen more than talk.

"My dad and I weren't the best of friends," I continue, "but he was still my father. My mother I loved dearly. Then, just like *that*!" I say, snapping my fingers. "They're gone. My sister, Danielle, and I barely speak anymore since she's decided that I'm as worthless as the scumbag who left her with bills, bad credit, and a screaming kid. My marriage may not have been worth saving, but it was still painful to see it end. And now . . ."

The long silence gets too long and Gina says, "And now, what?"

"Never mind."

She drinks some coffee and sits back. "I know what you mean, Darius. I sometimes feel so disjointed and disconnected from anything that's real. I mean, I know my work is important. I'm just not certain that it matters."

I consider her statement for a moment. "Well, I'm pretty certain that my teaching and research matter. I just need to find out what it'll take to restore some order, stability, and sanity in my world. I need to find a way of holding on to the precious little I've got."

"Your description of what you're going through reminds me of the story of Job."

"Job?"

"Yes. You remember, the rich righteous man who little by little was reduced to nothing."

I roll my eyes. "I know the story all too well. That book and Ecclesiastes were two of my father's favorite Old Testament books."

"Well, is it possible that you're going through a Job experience?"

"I most certainly hope not. From what I remember, things got so bad that Job ended up cursing the day he was born."

"True. But in the end, God not only restored him to his original condition, but gave him more riches than he had at the start."

"That's nice," I quip, my voice heavy with sarcasm. "The question I've always had, which no one's ever answered to my satisfaction, is why God just stood around smoking a joint while brother Job endured all his misery."

Gina stiffens at my irreverence. "Careful, Darius," she says. "If you know the story, then you also know that when Job asked a similar question God said, *'Who is this that darkens my counsel with words without knowledge?'* "

"Yeah, yeah," I rudely interrupt. "I remember the verse. God got an attitude and said, *'Brace yourself like a man; I will question you, and you shall answer me. Where were you when I laid the earth's foundations?'* "

I finish off my coffee and say, "It's the perfect setup. God lets Job get hit with the worst of the worst, then gets pissed when the man asks Him, 'What for?' Job never got a satisfactory response, and I don't expect one either."

"Now, Darius. You know that's not what God meant when . . ."

"It's no different from some kid asking the playground bully for an explanation as to why he's getting thrashed. And even though it wouldn't diminish the bully's power to answer, he instead demands that the wimp explain his own whuping."

Gina stands and gathers her belongings. "It's probably a good time for me to leave."

"Huh? What's wrong? Look, Gina, if I said something that's offended you I'm . . ."

"No, Darius. You haven't. And like I told you, I'm feeling at odds myself. So I understand your anger. You've been through a lot. It's been painful, and you just want it to stop."

I nod and lower my eyes. "That pretty much sums it up."

She exhales, almost despairingly. "I only recently started attending church again. I haven't found all the answers, but there's one thing of which I'm absolutely certain."

"And what's that?"

Gina looks hard into my eyes and says, "God is *not* the problem."

We hug; then she leaves. I watch from the window as she drives away, then return to the computer, gather up the front of my shirt, and spend a few moments inhaling the thinning scent of her perfume. Once I've sniffed out the last traces, I resume typing, using all my mental power to focus upon the black heroes of the Civil War, who keep getting blotted out by thoughts of Gina.

8

IT'S LATE SUNDAY AFTERNOON AND NASH PICKS ME
up in his new SUV Ford Explorer so we can cruise over to Omar's for the
book club meeting. I get in, strap on the seat belt, and check out the
snazzy interior.

"This is nice and fancy," I say.

Nash grins. "Yes, it is, my brother. You oughta try one out."

I settle into the seat as Nash pulls into traffic. "Can't afford it. As
an educator, I'm only supposed to teach the nation's future, not get paid
for it."

Nash shakes his head. "Darius, I can't figure you out. If there's no cash
in what you're doing, then why hang with it?"

"Because, Nash, I'd rather get paid moderately to do something I love
than get paid handsomely for something I hate."

Nash's jaw gets tight. I didn't mean to insult him, but he knows I'm
right. His job as an automotive production supervisor rains more money
on him in six months than I'll see in two years, especially with all his overtime and bonuses. But he pays a high price for it. Stuck between greedy,
shortsighted management and perpetually disgruntled workers, Nash tries
to maintain his balance between a time bomb ulcer and mental exhaustion. If it weren't for his irreverent sense of humor, he'd be a head case
by now.

Nash puts on a tape of Isaac Hayes's greatest hits and adjusts the music so that it's just loud enough to not drown out our conversation. I consider telling him about Cookie's late night visit but decide to wait. Before
cluttering my mind with other opinions, I need to digest what's happened
and figure out the best way to help Jarrod.

"So did you finish the book?" Nash asks.

"Yeah, a couple of weeks ago. I looked it over again last night to refresh myself."

"Whaddya think?"

I slide the book into the passenger door side pocket and say, "It makes me glad I've been given a break from relationships."

Nash glances at me and smirks. "I hear you, man. Once Hollywood turns this book into a movie, there'll be a whole lotta brothers joining you."

We slap each other five and sing along as Isaac Hayes laments the heartache of unrequited love in "I Stand Accused."

After it's over, Nash says, "I read somewhere that this book's based on a true story."

"A lot of good writing is. And the writing in this story is excellent. If there's any truth to her doomsday opinion regarding lasting relationships, I'll be spending more time in solitude than intended."

Nash turns the music down a bit. "You're not joking about being on this quest for the meaning of life, are you?"

"I wouldn't put it like that."

"Well then, how would you put it?"

"I'm just trying to make sense of it all. After the blowout with Cookie, missing Jarrod, nearly losing my shirt in domestic court, and this disaster with Marcy, I've got to be doing something wrong. I just want it fixed so the hassles can stop."

"Too bad you're not close to a solution."

"Why?"

"There's this fox named Yalinda down at the health club. I'd like to take her out, but she won't go unless I bring someone along for her friend, Charisse."

"No!"

"Aw, c'mon, Darius. Now that you're a free man, what's the harm? Why not help a brother out?"

"No! And why are you fooling around with someone who's already taking you through these kinds of changes?"

"Don't go flying off the deep end, man. Yalinda's just trying to hook her sister-girlfriend up with a nice brother."

I smile at Nash. "Thanks for the compliment. And if Marcy hadn't just kicked me in the teeth, I'd think about going. But, Nash, trust me when I tell you that I wouldn't be good company right now."

"If you're saying that your stanky attitude would dim my chances of getting some'a Yalinda's booty, then consider yourself *un*invited."

I look at him as he glances at me with his mischief-filled eyes; then we laugh.

"At least we're clear about where your priorities lie," I chuckle.

Nash grabs a handful of his crotch, jerks a couple of times, and winks. "If you'd ever seen Yalinda in one'a them skimpy outfits she wears to work out, your priorities would be bum rushing mine."

I stare ahead at the road and reflect for a moment. "I haven't lost all interest in matters of the flesh, Nash. But there's got to be more to it. I want someone who'll satisfy my emotional needs just as she does my physical."

Nash looks at me in horror. "Man, why're you trying to complicate things? If a babe's gonna give up some nonbinding booty, that's called a good day."

"No. That's just another day. And at the risk of sounding like a cliché, I've been there and done that."

"You'd best keep on doing it if you don't want your blue balls to blow you into being bowlegged."

"Forget it. I'm sick and tired of wasting time with lunatics, losers, and liars. I have my faults, but I'm not that hard to get along with. I enjoy treating a woman like a lady. I don't demand much and I'm easily satisfied."

"I know whatcha mean," Nash sighs, grinning. "A blow job goes a long way with me too."

I roll my eyes. "You're hopeless."

"Naw, man. I'm horny. And since you fell out with Marcy, you gotta be too."

"Falling out with Marcy has moved me to keep my loins, thoughts, and feelings to myself for a while."

Nash looks at me with sincere concern. "D, if you keep talking like that I'ma have to rush you down to emergency."

"No need to get alarmed. I'm just taking a break to wash off the dirt of dating."

"Man, how do you expect to find the right one with that kinda attitude?"

"At the moment it doesn't matter."

"Oh yeah. Why not?"

"I'm on a quest for the meaning of life. Remember?"

9

THE BOOK FOR THIS MONTH'S DISCUSSION IS *TRAGEDY'S Daughters*, by Xaviera Roubellet. Everyone gathers around Omar's dining room table, filling their paper plates with finger food and snacks. There are no new faces but not to worry. Ike and Kiva are here, so there'll be plenty of entertainment. Neither of them is ever neutral about a book, and they're never in agreement.

I get a few fried chicken wings, some chips-'n-dip, and a diet Dr. Pepper and take my seat at the end of the couch beneath a brooding picture of Malcolm X, watching over us with his penetrating gaze. The room is filled with laughter and the warm din of multiple friendly discussions while Anita Baker's voice floats out from the CD player like rose petals riding a soft breeze.

Ike sits down in the chair opposite me and gets comfortable, setting his food off to the side where it'll be safe from his wild waving hands once he and Kiva lock horns. He bites into a chicken wing and settles into the seat, closing his eyes and rocking his head from side to side to the music's beat.

"Man, that woman can *sing*!" he says.

Phoebe and Egypt sit down beside me, talking low but still loud enough for me to hear the end of their conversation.

". . . your parents feel about you dating a white man?" Phoebe asks.

Egypt dabs the corner of her mouth with a napkin before answering. "They didn't like it at first. Especially Daddy. But once they saw that Riley and I were serious, they adjusted."

Nash sits on a huge beanbag chair Omar's dragged out from storage while Omar takes his seat on the floor next to Phoebe. He looks up at her and they give each other a quick kiss. Kiva marches into the living room and sits down in Omar's recliner. Her eyes are like two dark marbles staring out from a grim hunk of granite. Omar leans over and gives her a soft punch to the knee.

"Don't look so serious," he says, winking. "It's a book club, not an inquisition."

Kiva's lips twitch in what passes for a smile and she scoops up some dip with a chip. After a few more minutes of chatter, Omar gets everyone's attention and we begin.

"So what's y'all's opinion of the book?" he asks.

"Good writing," Ike says. "Too bad she couldn't resist abusing the brothers."

"Since when is telling the truth abuse?" Kiva challenges, looking hard at Ike.

"Here we go," Egypt mutters.

"I thought it was well written and nicely paced," Phoebe observes.

"I'm just glad she didn't waste a lot of time dealing with Charity's meaningless search for lost love," Nash comments.

"I wouldn't call it meaningless," I say. "Finding love is always worth the effort."

Nash and I glance at each other, then focus on Omar. "It's funny you mention that," he says. "I found her not dealing with that aspect of Charity's failed relationships to be a weakness."

"It's almost glaring," Egypt adds.

Ike grunts and says, "It wouldn't have done any good in iceberg Charity's case."

"How can you say that?" Kiva asks. "When she and Melvin broke up, she spent years trying to find the love she *thought* she'd had with him."

"That's bogus!" Ike retorts. "Every dude after Melvin was just fodder for Charity to get a vengeance high. She got even with him by destroying all those other chumps."

With that exchange, the latest Ike-Kiva clash has begun. We munch and marvel as they verbally swat and slash at each other. Whenever their heated exchanges lose some momentum, someone else makes an observation that's analyzed and critically debated, moving Ike and Kiva on to another point of controversy. And that's what I love about this book club. Being in the midst of these gifted, articulate black men and women with their heavily fortified intellects makes me swell with pride.

After listening for a while to Ike's and Kiva's verbal slugfesting, I shift in my seat, squeezing my bladder, which alerts me that it's time for a toilet break. I get up and head for the bathroom. Nash, Omar, Phoebe, and

Egypt ease into the dining room to get more goodies and watch Ike and Kiva duel from a safe distance. Omar's phone rings as I finish my business.

"I'll get it!" Phoebe announces.

"All right, baby," Omar answers. "If it's Grant, tell him to stop worrying. My analysis of those sales figures will be in his hands first thing Monday morning."

I wash my hands, step into the hallway, and am met by Nash, holding Omar's cordless.

"What's'up?" I ask.

Nash covers the phone, leans close, and whispers, "It's Marcy."

"Marcy!" I say her name like an exhaled blast of wind. "What does she want?"

"My guess would be to talk to you," Nash says, the corners of his mouth pinched into a tight smirk.

This is ridiculous. Just two days ago, Marcy handed me my walking papers. Now she wants to talk. *Again!*

Nash extends the phone to me and I shove it away. "Aren't you gonna even say hello?" he asks.

"No! Tell her to be gone and good-bye."

I step around Nash and start toward the living room. He grabs my arm. "C'mon, D. This isn't like you!"

I glance at his hand, then glare into his eyes. He lets me go. "You're right, Nash," I say, my voice rising. "It's not like me. But it should've been!"

From the phone, Marcy yells, "Darius, all I want . . ."

I grab the phone, press the OFF button, and toss it back to Nash. He moves off, grumbling like a bear that's had its nose smacked. I angle toward Omar's goody table, pretending to not notice the averted gazes of everyone pretending to not notice my pretending.

An awkward thick silence fills the room. And Phoebe's not having it! She grabs my hand, pulls me toward Nash, and waggles her finger in our faces.

"I'm ashamed of you boys," she says, her grin betraying her supposed displeasure. "I've warned you about fighting at recess. Now shake hands and make up."

Nash can't resist Phoebe's antics and he plugs into her charade. "But, Ms. Elkins," he whines. "Darius said my momma had big feet."

Phoebe puts her hands on her hips and scowls at me. "Did you say that?"

I try to stay serious, but a smile forces its way onto my face. "No, Ms. Elkins. What I said was that his mother was a Big Foot."

"Forget all that," Kiva grouses. "What I want to know is did his daddy have big hands?"

Phoebe giggles. Egypt, Omar, and Ike, who's joined them at the goody table, snicker. Nash and I laugh, shake hands, and hug.

Omar eases up behind Phoebe and gives her shoulders a tender squeeze. "Thanks, baby."

She strokes his cheek and kisses him.

"Okay, everyone!" he announces. "Back into the living room. Egypt, it's your turn to choose the book we'll be reading for next month."

Fear flashes across Egypt's face. She swallows, glances at Phoebe, then looks at the rest of us.

"Um, well, I think we should read *Forbidden Treasures* by Josette Green."

Ike's left eye narrows into a slit. "Isn't that one of those black-white dating stories?"

"Yes," Egypt answers, wiping her forehead dry with a napkin.

"The reviews have been great," Phoebe says.

"The reviewers loved sister Roubellet's book too," Ike counters. "But after the pummeling she gave the brothers you'll understand if I don't rely upon *their* opinion."

"This oughta be interesting," Nash offers. "It's been a long time since I've read a white-in-the-woodpile story."

Egypt stiffens, looking like a fawn hiding from slobbering timber wolves. Kiva glances at her watch and stands. "A white-in-the-woodpile story is fine with me," she says. "Just so long as the sister finds love."

"How do you know it's not about a brother's finding love?" Nash asks.

"Why're you asking her?" Ike queries. "According to her, a brother's idea of finding love is hanging out a car window and yelling at prostitutes."

Kiva challenges Ike to prove his point and they go at it again. The rest of us watch in amused silence while the verbal battle continues as they gather their belongings and leave. Omar hurries to his front window and waves us over. We look outside and see Kiva and Ike, stopping every few steps to gesture at each other with flailing arms and stabbing index fingers.

"They're unbelievable," Omar says.

The rest of us laugh in agreement. Nash and I escort Egypt to her car, laughing and discussing everything that happened. Once she's safely on her way, we get in the Explorer and head back to our stranger-than-fiction real worlds.

"That was fun," Nash observes.

"Like always."

Nash slips a Sade CD into the player and the SUV fills with the sound of her mellow voice, singing of satin love. I settle into my seat, close my eyes, and indulge myself in the belief that sweet Sade is singing to *me*.

"You're really pissed at Marcy, aren't you?" Nash asks.

"No, Nash. To be pissed, I'd have to care. I don't."

"And you don't want to talk about it?"

"Give that man a cigar."

Sade's sultry voice blows a tender kiss across my lips.

"You've changed," Nash observes.

"How so?"

"I don't know. You just have."

I burrow deeper into the seat. "That may not be such a bad thing."

A soft, low moan rises from Sade's throat like a wispy trail of desire-scented incense.

"Too bad Gina couldn't come today," Nash says. "She sure looked good last night."

"Like always," I say, keeping my voice level and nonchalant.

"Come off it, man," Nash scoffs. "You're not gonna tell me that you weren't nearly blinded by all that fine beaming off 'a Gina."

I yawn. "Big deal! Gina's being gorgeous isn't enough for me to go swimming back into the shark-infested waters of relationship so soon after Marcy."

Nash gives me a lingering look. "Wow, D. You really have changed."

I wink, turn up the volume on the CD player, and drift off to be held in Sade's musically outstretched arms.

10

IT'S A BLAH MONDAY, WHICH MEANS IT'S BACK TO
the salt mines. Despite Erie Pointe University's ethnic balance being 55:45
white-to-black, there are only four black students in my African-American
history class. So thus passes another semester where some of Erie Pointe's
white students have leaped at the opportunity to sponge up knowledge
concerning my people while black students strut around, content to
remain ignorant of the heroes, laborers, and visionaries who sacrificed,
fought, and died so they could get a quality education.

I've got just about ten minutes to wrap up my lecture with some review questions. So I begin. "Mr. Padrewski, state the significance of
Brown versus Board of Education?"

"Uh, is that when the Supreme Court . . ."

"Are you asking me or telling me?"

Padrewski's face reddens. "I'm, ah, I'm telling you."

"Go ahead."

"*Brown versus Board of Education* is the case where the Supreme Court
ruled that school segregation was unconstitutional."

"On the basis of what, Ms. Hanson?"

"It denied children equal protection under the law."

"As stipulated by what, Mr. Edelman?"

"The Fourteenth Amendment."

I zero in on a student staring out the window. "Mr. Arrati, describe
Fannie Lou Hamer's contribution to the Civil Rights Movement."

His head snaps toward me, his eyes blinking into alertness. "Huh?"

"Wrong answer."

"Sorry, Professor Collins. Could you repeat the question?"

"Fannie Lou Hamer. State her contribution to Civil Rights."

"Ms. Hamer was a, um, sharecropper . . ."

"Which was what, Ms. Baylor?"

Augusta Baylor is one of my four black students. And she's brilliant.
During a class debate a few weeks ago she remained calm and dignified

while shredding her opposition into intellectual mulch. It was so smooth and effortless that it could have qualified as art. It also made me glad that I've never been the focus of her disputative surgery.

Augusta's excellent enunciation polishes her response. "Sharecropping was a system of labor and wage payment that developed in the South during Reconstruction. Rather than pay blacks in cash that was in short supply, landowners allowed them to keep a share of the crop they planted."

"What were those crops paying for initially?" I ask.

"The freedmen's labor."

"And later?"

"The freedmen deduced that if they could be paid in shares for their work, they could use those same shares as rent payment for the land."

I turn to LaThomas Patterson. He, Andre Echols, and DeBarron Washington are my three remaining African-American students. LaThomas is the football team's star defensive end. I'm surprised that he bothered showing up today. What's even more surprising is that class is almost over and he hasn't interrupted me about having to leave early and take his gerbil to the vet or rescue the world from alien attack or for some other stupid excuse. Andre and DeBarron are his lapdogs, following LaThomas around and scrapping over the leftover crumbs from his spotlight.

As usual, LaThomas has taken the seat in the back row, slouching low in an absurd attempt to hide his six-foot, four-inch 240 pounds of muscle and sinew behind his smaller classmates. His gimmick for today is gag sunglasses. He's leaning back against the wall, his mouth hanging open slack-jawed, with the glasses perched upon his face. The lenses are painted over with ridiculous wide-open eyes, hiding the real ones in his sockets, which are undoubtedly closed.

I take a deep breath and fortify myself for confrontation. "Mr. Patterson, what was the effect of the sharecropping system on the freedmen?"

Seconds turn into moments. Moments advance toward a minute and he doesn't answer.

"Mr. Patterson!"

He jerks upright with a honking snort. "Yo! Yo, Professor. Sorry 'bout that. Could you, you know, ask that question again?"

Heat waves elevator up my neck. "Explain the effect of the sharecropping system on the freedmen."

"Oh, yeah. Right. Okay. Sharecroppin' was keepin' people down, you

know. Not lettin' 'em do their thang. It let whitey have slaves without calling it slavery."

Some of my white students flush red. Others stir uncomfortably.
LaThomas resumes his slouch.

"Mr. Patterson, this class operates in an environment of mutual respect. Please don't refer to members of the Caucasian race as 'whitey.' "

"Why not? Don't they know they's white?"

On cue and fulfilling their role as loyal stooges, Andre and DeBarron
snicker and slap LaThomas's upturned palms.

"Man, that was schlick!" Andre affirms.

"Yeah! Schlick!" DeBarron parrots.

"Quiet!" I snap.

They shut up and glare, not out of respect but the certainty that
not passing my class will return them to the burger-flipping oblivion
they've managed to temporarily escape.

I focus back on LaThomas. As painful as it was to hear his butchery
of the English language, his answer is essentially correct and deserves
acknowledgment.

"Mr. Patterson, your uniquely stated answer was correct. Well done."

He sneers, waves me off, and slouches lower than before. I clench
my jaw and return my attention to the students who actually care about
learning.

"And so, Mr. Arrati, you assert that Fannie Lou Hamer was part of
the sharecropping system?"

"Er, yeah."

"And her contribution was?"

"She worked to get blacks registered to vote in, ah, Minneapolis. And
she also . . ."

I shake my head. "Hold on, Mr. Arrati. Are you sure it was
Minneapolis?"

He frowns for a second, shakes his head, and shrugs.

"Miss DeFrancis, help him out."

"It was Mississippi."

"Thank you. Continue Mr. Arrati."

"Okay. Um, she also was part of that effort to get whites to let members of the, er, the um . . ."

Augusta raises her hand.

"Go ahead, Ms. Baylor."

"The Mississippi Freedom Democratic Party, an organization created as an alternative to the racist Democratic organization then dominating the state."

"Thank you. And now, Mr. Arrati, how did Ms. Hamer get the nation's attention?"

"She went on TV and told people about how she was beaten and assaulted for her efforts to increase black voting."

I glance at the clock. Only a minute remaining, so I take over. "That's correct, Mr. Arrati. So Ms. Hamer not only symbolized black defiance in the face of police brutality and racist political opposition; she also underscores the contribution of black women during the Civil Rights Movement."

I look around the room. "Are there any questions?" No one raises a hand. "Okay. Remember that you've got another exam next week. Study hard. Do good. See you later."

The students gather up their belongings and leave. I collect my lecture notes and follow them out. LaThomas Patterson is waiting for me in the hallway. Andre and DeBarron, aka Larry and Curly, are hovering nearby.

"Yo! Professor Collins! Can I get wit' you for a hot one?"

"What is it, Mr. Patterson?"

He smirks and sidles up to me, moving like his upper and lower torsos are arguing over which should lead. "Why you always gots'ta be so formal, man? We all part of the same tribe."

"Fate wouldn't be so cruel. What can I do for you?"

He ponders the first part of my response, bewilderment momentarily seizing his face. Then he shrugs and starts talking, using his hands in accompanying gangster rap sign language for emphasis.

"It's like dis, man. I don't know if I can be here for the test because . . ."

"Do you have a game that day?"

"Naw, but . . ."

"Do you plan on being dead between now and then?"

He frowns. "What kinda bugged out question is'zat?"

"About as 'bugged out' as the limp excuse you're concocting."

"Limp! Whutch'you talking about, man? All I'm trying to find out is if I can take the test later so's I can . . ."

I massage my temples, then lock eyes with him. "Mr. Patterson, listen to me closely and hear me well. I've seen you shooting hoops across campus on days you've skipped my class. You insult me by persistently coming to class late and unprepared. You disrespect me with stunts like the one you pulled today with those ridiculous glasses. Your test performance is marginal. And your participation would be zero were it not for my repeated efforts to get you to answer an occasional question."

"Aye, look, man. I know I ain't been . . ."

"Let me finish!" I snap. LaThomas's mouth shuts and his eyes smolder. "In short, Mr. Patterson, you've given me *no* reason to make extraordinary allowances for you."

"But . . ."

"My recommendation is that you show up for this exam on time, prepared, and ready to work."

I step around him and start back to my office. As I pass, he grumbles his response.

"Uncle Tommin' niggah!"

Calmness is an essential virtue in college teaching. As a foot soldier in the war on ignorance, I can't succumb to primal urges like bashing in someone's face for making stupid comments. My job is to try to expose my students to alternative points of view, to challenge and be challenged by them, so we all can grow. So I stop dead in my tracks, slowly face LaThomas, and fulfill my calling.

"I presume," I say, speaking low and slow, "that you're referring to the main character in *Uncle Tom's Cabin*."

His face is blank, as I knew it would be, since he skipped class the two days we discussed the book.

"Tell me, Mr. Patterson. Who wrote *Uncle Tom's Cabin*?"

Blank stare.

"When was it written? What social impact did it have? How did Northerners react to it? What about people in the South? What's the story about? What did you think of Liza? Was Tom weak or strong? What cataclysm did the book help produce?"

Blank stare. Blank stare. Blank stare. Blank stare. Blank stare. Blank stare. Blank stare. Blank stare.

I look hard into his eyes, sizzling with anger. *Just like I am.* "Tell me, Mr. Patterson, do you even know why calling a black man an 'Uncle Tom' is offensive? Or is it truly possible that because of the empty space between your ears, you have no choice other than to mimic your crotch-holding buddies who can't distinguish between a brother who *works* for his pay and one who *waits* for it?"

I narrow my eyes. "How does it feel to mindlessly follow the crowd on a journey to nowhere? How does it feel to be an *intellectual Uncle Tom*?"

He balls his fists. "I oughta . . ."

I step forward. "No! You shouldn't! In fact, you shouldn't even say it. Because then I might think you're threatening me. Then I'd have to report you to campus security, who'd contact Coach Wofford, and then, well, you can fill in the blanks."

He shovels his lower jaw from side to side, wheels around, and stomps away.

11

NOW THAT I'M SITTING AT MY DESK AND MY ANGER'S subsiding, I'm thinking that verbally dismembering LaThomas Patterson probably wasn't the smartest of moves. Especially since he could crush me in a blink. If he ever tries, he'd better bring a lunch. With the absurdities of today's laws, I'd probably be fired for defending myself, but *no one* is going to punk, chump, or disrespect me.

Being called an Uncle Tom was irritating, but what really angers me is LaThomas's squandering the education some other black kid would love to have. What's worse is that I can't get him to understand that as a black man, future husband and father, his education is a survival tool he can ill afford to be without!

"Black folks can't survive America without an education," my dad used to say.

I've tried to pass that message on to Jarrod, but he's so doggone short-sighted! If he truly did get this Bell Cuppersmith pregnant, his education's in jeopardy. He'll still be able to finish high school, but it's going to be much more difficult and maybe take longer than if he'd just kept his pecker in his pants. Keeping him motivated and focused up to now has been tough enough. Once those family court Nazis get hold of him it'll take every resource I've got to get him into and through college. Thank goodness Reverend Boxwell's starting that program.

I pull out the Warrior Passages packet from my briefcase and reexamine the contents. If someone besides Reverend Boxwell were running this, I wouldn't waste my time. But with Rev. B in charge I know he'll bring the same tenacious drive, care, and commitment to it that he brought to the Youth Ministry when I was a kid.

I pick up my phone and call him. Mrs. Boxwell answers. "Hello?"

"Hello, Sister Boxwell. This is Darius Collins."

"Well, hello, Darius. What a pleasant surprise."

"The pleasure's all mine. All the more knowing that I'm talking to such a lovely young woman."

Mrs. Boxwell blushes through the phone. "You behave yourself," she giggles. "What can I do for you?"

"May I speak with Reverend Boxwell?"

"Sorry, Darius. He left just a few minutes ago to take Preach for his walk. I'm telling you, that dog gets right foolish if he doesn't get his walk. And he's just too big to ignore."

I laugh. "I know what you mean. Before I got divorced, I mean, I once had a husky who was the same way about his walk. He'd catch a real attitude if he didn't get it."

"That's our Preach," Mrs. Boxwell laughs. "You wanna leave Hez a message?"

"Sure. Just tell him I'll call back. Do you know how soon before he returns?"

"He'll be gone for at least an hour. Preach takes a lot of walking."

"As big as he is, that's understandable," I chuckle. "Okay. I'll call back in an hour."

Mrs. Boxwell hesitates, then says, "Darius, it's probably better if you just wait till later this afternoon or this evening. We'll be home from the doctor's office by then and Hez will have more time to talk."

I frown and sit up straight. "Doctor's office? Is everything all right?"

"Everything's fine. It's just that I've been after Hez to get a checkup and don't want him to have any excuses for not going."

I listen hard to the tone of her voice. She's calm, confident, and totally reassuring that nothing's wrong, so I relax. After all, besides Reverend Boxwell himself, she'd be the first to know if he was ill. And I'm comfortable in the knowledge that we're close enough so that if something was wrong, she or he would tell me.

"It's really nothing urgent," I say. "I just wanted to tell Reverend Boxwell that I definitely want to enroll my son in the Warrior Passages program."

After an extended pause Mrs. Boxwell says, "But . . . he is enrolled."

"Huh?"

"I'm pretty sure Hez said something about your son being one of the first to enroll, but hold on. I'll check his papers." Another extended pause and she says, "That's right. Jarrod Collins. And listed beside his name is the parental sponsor, Dr. Darius Collins."

This is puzzling. I never said anything definite to Reverend Boxwell about enrolling Jarrod. And I certainly haven't shared why I'd want to.

"Hez did this without telling you, didn't he?" Mrs. Boxwell questions me, her voice filling with iron.

"Well, yes, he did."

She exhales in frustration. "That man! I told him to make sure he talked with you first."

Reverend Boxwell's presumptuousness is irksome, but I don't want to cause him any domestic difficulties and scramble to his defense. "It's okay, Sister Boxwell. I was going to enroll Jarrod anyway, so the reverend saved us both some time."

"Are you sure you don't mind?" she asks, her voice softening.

"Absolutely."

She chuckles softly. "Lord, I love that man. But sometimes after he finishes praying he's just so bullheaded."

"I don't understand."

"Few people do. And I wish I could tell you more, but Hez doesn't always share with me the conversations between him and God. All I know is that he's been in prayer for you and your son."

This is dragging me places I'd rather not go. So I just say, "Okay, Sister Boxwell. Tell him I said thanks and that I'm looking forward to the Warrior Passages kickoff."

"I will. See you there."

We hang up and there's a knock on my door. I stay seated as I roll my chair over to the door, open it, and see Augusta Baylor, my star African-American history student.

"Hi, Augusta," I say, waving her in.

She enters and sits down in one of the chairs I've purposely positioned on the far side of my office. I grab a thick old, battered history text and use it to block the door wide open, then scoot behind my desk. Some students have complained that this arrangement leaves them feeling alienated and weird, having to talk with me from so far away. But the office isn't that big, so it's not too bad. And I wish it didn't have to be this way, but I can't afford to be careless.

All it would take is for one vengeful Barbie or Loqueesha to hint that I'd suggested changing her F or D to an A or B in exchange for a blow job or bounce in the sack. Instead of teaching history, *I'd be history*. By the time the sexual harassment witch-hunters and predator press finished destroying me in the court of public opinion, I wouldn't be able to get a job teaching at the University of Far Side of the Moon. And while I don't think Augusta would ever stoop to such treachery, I can't afford to dismiss the possibility.

"So, Augusta," I say, leaning back in my chair. "What's going on?"

Her eyes fill with tears as she smiles and says, "Thank you, Professor Collins. Thank you so much."

I'm glad to have been so helpful for whatever it is I've done, but I've got to stop her from crying *now*! "Ah, okay, Augusta. You're welcome," I say nervously. "It was my pleasure. Just take it easy. Okay."

I grab the box of Kleenex off my desk, hurry over, and hand it to her. Once she takes it I fly back to the refuge behind my desk.

"I'm sorry for getting emotional," Augusta says, sniffling. "But your letter changed everything."

"Letter?"

"Yes. Your letter of recommendation for the campus housing scholarship."

"Oh! That letter. Well, you're welcome, Augusta. It was an honor and a privilege to write it for you."

"No, Professor Collins," she deflects. "It was an honor and a privilege to have you write it. I just received word that I won."

"That's great!" I exclaim. I start to rush over and hug her but instead extend my hand across the desk. We shake and I say, "That's truly wonderful news."

"It's the best," Augusta agrees. "And so are you."

"I appreciate that. But your grade-point average, campus involvement, and community service work had a lot to do with you winning."

"That's true, Professor Collins. But none of that mattered before. No one else ever supported me the way you did, and I know that's what made the difference. So thank you, thank you, thank you."

"You're welcome, welcome, welcome."

We laugh and Augusta finishes wiping her eyes dry. With the tears gone, the windows to her soul once more reveal the clarity and strength that have propelled her through tragedies and setbacks that would've crushed most people.

A few weeks ago when she asked me to write the letter of recommendation, she shared the whole sad tale. A child of the ghetto, Augusta was one of the roses that broke through the surface of all the crime, chaos, and confusion. But there were challenges. A heroin addict and pregnant at fifteen, she struggled through rehab and school with the help of a loving mother and father, graduating as valedictorian. She applied for and was accepted into the prelaw program at Penn State, moved there, and had a straight A average by the end of her first semester. Then disaster struck.

The Euclid Gardens housing project she'd grown up in—the one that the tenants had forever complained needed this or that repair; the one that the city, the county, the state, and the federal government didn't think was worth the time and effort since, after all, it just housed the working poor—finally gave way during a brutal winter storm. The weight of the snow caused a roof collapse, right on top of her mother, father, and baby girl, Marqueen.

Marqueen survived but sustained brain damage. Augusta, with no knowledge of where her crackhead brother might be or if he was even alive, buried her parents alone. She moved back to Cleveland, got an assembly line job, and was soon unemployed when the factory moved its operations to Chile. A long series of odd jobs couldn't compete with Marqueen's medical bills, and home soon became the streets, then a shelter. During the respite Augusta applied to Erie Pointe University, took advantage of every assistance program available, established her intellectual clout, then zeroed in on the campus housing scholarship. Winning it has granted her a year's free room and board, just in time to finish her senior year and graduate.

"So you see, Professor Collins," Augusta says, "now that Marqueen and I have someplace to stay for a while, I'll truly be able to focus on my schoolwork."

"If you focus any harder, we'll have to invent a new grading system to accommodate your outstanding performance," I chuckle.

She blushes. It gradually fades and is replaced by a troubling trance-like stare. "It'll also give me time to work on my project," she says.

The strong undercurrent of menace in her voice makes me shudder. Augusta's spoken of this "project" before, always with the same intense stare and razor-sharp edge in her otherwise soft and inviting voice. She first mentioned it a few months ago when she was asking about procedures for gaining access to the archival records at the Cleveland Black Historical Society. As I am an active member and presidential hopeful, her question naturally piqued my interest, and I inquired about the nature of her research. Her eyes flashed angrily, her jaws tightened, and lips thinned.

Then in a tone vibrating with rage she said, "I'd rather not say at this time."

I'd been verbally mangled by Cookie enough times to know when to leave good enough alone. When Augusta was ready to talk about her "project" she'd let me know. As we've gotten to know each other, she's spoken of it more often but still keeps it shrouded in mystery. Had I not been connected with the CBHS she might not have mentioned it all, which adds more intrigue to whatever she's doing. But I'm not a complete fool. Augusta's on a mission, and "whoever" or "whatever" is the focal point of her research is in for some major disturbances once she finishes her work.

She stands and says, "That's all I wanted, Professor Collins. Just to say thanks and that, well, you're one helluva black man."

"And you're one helluva black woman," I reply.

She starts over to my desk and I meet her halfway. There's a moment's hesitation and the urge to hug is great. But Augusta and I are both aware of the jackals waiting to pounce, so our hug is a handshake and a sterile but safe good-bye.

I close my office door and finally begin reading the last of the research papers I assigned to my African-American history students. There's only three remaining, the ones written by LaThomas Patterson and his pathetic sidekicks, Andre Echols and DeBarron Washington. I probably should've graded them first but couldn't face reading their usual could-care-less garbage.

LaThomas and DeBarron achieve their standard level of poor performance and are rewarded accordingly. Andre, however, has turned in a paper that's not only well researched and documented but also constructed in a fashion that demonstrates much depth of thought and skillful analysis. And his topic, "America's Reaction to Executive Order 9981," Pres. Harry S Truman's 1948 directive ordering the military's desegregation, is far superior to LaThomas's "The Secret Life of Yo' Homey!" and DeBarron's "Bling! Bling! Gimme My Gold."

Andre's writing skills could use some improvement, but they're a quantum leap ahead of his prior lousy performance. There's something going on with him, and just as soon as I can isolate him from the other two-thrirds of that clown triumvirate, I'm going to find out what it is.

I'm just about finished reading when the phone rings. "Hello?"

"Hi. Can I speak with Dr. Darius Collins?"

"This is Dr. Collins. Who am I speaking with?"

There's a moment's hesitation before she answers. "This is Katrina Sewell."

"Katrina Sewell? I'm sorry, but I don't know of any . . ."

"We're neighbors."

Nash! I'm going to throttle him when I see him.

Katrina says, "Your friend Nash Ayers gave me your number. I hope you don't mind me calling you on your job."

"Not at all," I say, trying to sound cordial through gritting teeth.

"I'm so glad," Katrina says, relieved. "I normally don't call people at their place of employment. But, to be honest, I couldn't think of a better way to introduce myself."

"Ah, well, I'm happy you took the initiative."

"You sound kind of irritated. Believe me, Dr. Collins, I understand. This is unusual for me also, but I've been wanting to meet you for so long and have just been too shy."

My cheeks slowly expand into a smile. There may be some possibilities here after all. "No, no," I say. "I'm not angry. If anything, I'm flattered."

"I'm so glad to hear you say that. And, well, I don't mean to sound forward, but I think you're quite a hunk."

I sit back and put my feet up on my desk. "Well, Nash tells me that you're quite attractive also."

"He's kind. I'm just average."

She's being modest. Nash wouldn't be caught dead with a woman who wasn't magazine-cover quality.

And then there was his description: *"Tight, juicy butt . . . big, round knockers."*

That physical stuff is interesting but is secondary to establishing a good relationship. Even so, it won't hurt to take a look.

Katrina says, "I don't want to take up your time, Dr. Collins, but . . ."

"Please. Call me Darius."

She hesitates, like she's thinking it over. "Okay . . . Darius."

"See. That wasn't so hard. Almost painless."

She giggles softly. "It's a beautiful name."

"Katrina's pretty too."

"Thanks, Darius. But I really don't want to impose on your time. I only called to say hello and introduce myself. Since we live so close."

"Yes, we do, don't we? Maybe we should get together."

"That would be great."

Tight, juicy butt . . . big, round knockers.

The phone call that started as a mild irritation extends into a nice conversation as we share our vitals. Like Nash said, Katrina's new to Shaker Heights. She's working but looking for better employment. She's single. Available. *And has no kids!* It's not that I'm against kids, but the loss of Jarrod and the stresses of raising him have effectively cured me of any desires to procreate.

"Well, if you're up to it, I'd love to go out for coffee sometime," I say. "Just say when."

"When!"

We laugh, make the arrangements to go out this evening, and hang up. That was easy, smooth, and enjoyable. And I'm wondering if the dynamite, dashing Darius of my first bachelorhood has finally returned to rescue me in the second.

I sit back, put my feet on my desk, relax, and replay the conversation's highlights. Katrina said I was "quite a hunk." Which means that she's not only interested but has good taste as well. It's wonderful having someone express a definite desire for me, especially after having had my self-esteem nearly blown to rubble by Cookie.

For years, I tried getting her to want me as badly as I wanted her, but she wouldn't budge. Toward the end, I stopped caring. Whenever I was fortunate enough to catch her willing to give a sexual handout, I'd climb on top, hump my way to climax, roll off, and fall asleep. That naturally made matters worse and all activity soon stopped, except for the close, loving relationship I developed with my palm.

Thoughts of Cookie and the dark times with her remind me that I'm supposed to meet her for lunch, so I leave for our appointment. Like most meetings with her, I'm not looking forward to this one. But there's no getting around it. It's the price I'll keep paying for exercising such poor, shallow judgment when I lay down with Cookie and produced the offspring who'll keep me connected to her for life.

12

I PULL INTO A PARKING SPACE AT THE WIRED TIGHT
Coffee Shop and see Cookie's car. I'll say this much for her. She's always
been punctual. I step inside and see a golden-skinned stalk of a man leaning against the table where Cookie's sitting. She's batting her eyes and has
her legs crossed. It has the effect of hiking her skirt up just enough to give
the guy a visual freebie. That "freebie" was until very recently *mine*. And
even though Cookie might protest, I'm going to tell this beanpole with
the hair that looks like someone waved a wand over it and said, *"Poof!"* to
get lost.

I step purposefully toward the table and interrupt the lanky puffball.
"Do you work here?" I ask.

He scowls and tugs on the apron he's wearing with the big, bright
Wired Tight logo printed on it. "Yes. I do."

"Well, I'd like a large cup of today's house blend."

I glance at Cookie. She's loving this. I look back at the puffball. "Is
the coffee here?"

"Of course it's here," he answers testily, obviously forgetting that even
jerk customers like me are always right.

"No. It's not!" I say, gesturing at his coworkers who are busy waiting
on counter customers. "My coffee's over there, waiting for you to bring it
here." I stab at the spot where I'm standing with a rigid forefinger.

The guy looks at Cookie, almost like he's asking for permission.
"Shoo, shoo," she says, fanning her hand dismissively. "Crusher was just
released from an institution for the criminally insane. We don't want to
upset him."

The guy's eyes balloon. "Y-yo, y-yo, m-m-man," he stammers. "I-I
was just, you know, having some friendly conversa . . ."

"My coffee!"

He scrambles away. I sit down and join Cookie laughing. "Criminally
insane?" I say.

"Yes. That way he won't be tempted to spit in your coffee."

Cookie and I laugh about how we used to play that same trick on guys who'd try to hit on her and the occasional woman who'd hit on me.

"We had fun, didn't we?" she says.

"Yeah, Cookie. We did."

The guy brings my coffee with two muffins. "Here's your coffee and a couple of blueberry muffins," he says, his voice shaky. "On the house."

"Thanks," Cookie responds. She glances at me, then the guy, and says, "Crusher's not so homicidal when he's been fed."

The guy swallows and darts away. Cookie and I laugh. And then, faster than a Florida thundershower ruining a sunny day, Cookie mutates into her werewolf self.

"Okay, Darius. Here's what we're going to do. When Jarrod gets home, you come over to my house, where we'll talk to him together. That way . . ."

"No, Cookie. I want to do this alone."

"What for?" she asks, indignant.

"I need to talk with him man-to-man and I'm not going to have you circling overhead like some vulture waiting to swoop down and interrupt me the moment I depart from your script."

Cookie's face contorts like her muscles are seizing. "Are you crazy? You can't dictate where I'll be in *my* house when you talk to Jarrod."

I sip some coffee. "You're right. I have no authority over you in your home. *But I've got total authority in mine.* I'll just wait and talk to Jarrod there."

Cookie sits back like she's been punched in the chest. "Darius, this isn't just between you and Jarrod. Chances are that when the baby's born, it'll be spending most of its time with me, and I deserve to . . ."

"That's why I don't want you around," I interrupt. "You've already assumed that the baby will be spending more time with you, like it's some immutable natural law."

She thrusts out her chin. "The baby *will* be spending more time with me. You know that I've always been closer to Jarrod than you and . . ."

"This is pointless," I say, grabbing my jacket. I lean forward and struggle to keep my voice low. "I've spent years enduring your know-it-all, super-parent crap in raising Jarrod. I won't go through that with my grandchild."

"There you go again," Cookie says, smirking. "I've never assumed that I was a better parent than you."

"Why should you have?" I retort. "The court decided for both of us. You're the parent. I'm the support check."

Cookie's eyes narrow. "Darius, don't you assume that victim's posture with me. I've never, ever done anything that would've prevented you from being a father to Jarrod."

"Cookie, even though you've compounded the challenge of being Jarrod's dad, you've never had the power to cancel my fatherhood. And while I appreciate the somewhat free access, don't expect slathering gratitude. I'm no happier about being reduced to a cameo bit player in his life than you'd have been if the situation were reversed."

I stand, zip up my jacket, and toss some money onto the table. "One year ago, you, domestic court, and those Children's Services pencilnecks colonized mine and Jarrod's relationship. As of now, that ends!" I say, stabbing the table with my forefinger. "You might still be in charge, but you're no longer in control. A revolution's in progress and *I'm* the one who'll decide upon the new form of government, especially when it comes to explaining to Jarrod what he's imposed upon himself as my grandchild's father."

Cookie opens her mouth and I stride away toward the door, a warm adrenaline glow surging through me. When we were married and I was still interested in compromise, I'd have tried swimming upstream through the river of sewage she might've spewed at such a moment. But that's what's so beautiful about this moment. *We're not married!*

I march outside, grimly aware that getting Jarrod to fully comprehend the scope of his troubles in so short a time is a tall order. But it's also possible. The previous months of marginalized time-sharing with him have taught me a lot about wringing the most out of a moment. Cramming more profound life lessons into a few hours of instruction will just be another opportunity to perfect that skill.

My key is in the ignition when I hear Cookie dashing across the parking lot, calling my name.

"Darius! Wait!" she hollers.

I settle back in the seat but start the car anyway. The instant she fixes her lips to tell me why we should do it her way, she'll be talking to my exhaust.

She charges up to the driver's window and leans against the car. "All right, Darius," she huffs. "I'll let you do it your way."

"Cookie, you're not *letting* me do anything. Like it or not, I'm talking to Jarrod alone."

She clenches her jaw. "Why are you so belligerent? I'm agreeing with you."

I shift the car into drive and press down hard on the brake. "That's the point, Cookie. I don't need your agreement, acknowledgment, endorsement, permission, or anything else. And I won't negotiate with you as if I do."

"Darius, the only reason I wanted us to talk to Jarrod together was so we could make sure he understands the importance of what he's done and the gravity of his responsibility."

"And I'm telling you that those are lessons being taught too late. Jarrod knows about the complications of pregnancy, VD, and so on because we've each discussed them with him. But he's a teenager. And for teenagers, *talk is cheap!* What he's heard us saying isn't nearly as important as what he's seen us doing."

Cookie's eyes flash, then narrow. "What're you implying that he's seen?"

"What's there to imply?" I say. "On different occasions we've bored Jarrod with a lot of highfalutin talk about love, respect, and chastity. Imagine how ridiculous we've sounded, talking to him about such things when we're the jokes whose lifestyles have told him that monogamy, loyalty, and devotion are for losers."

"That makes no sense whatsoever, Darius. We're divorced! What were we supposed to do?"

"Good question. Unfortunately, I don't have a good answer. But believe me when I tell you that somewhere in the hormonal chaos of Jarrod's mind, he concluded that if his parents could fall in love, marry, have a child, and fling it all to the wind, then all that lecturing about the sanctity of life, love, and family was just a river of crap!"

Cookie stands erect and crosses her arms, her stance and posture indicating clearly that my words are having no more effect on her than bounced tennis balls have on a brick wall.

"Darius, I disagree," she says, calm, resolute, and absolutely certain that I'm wrong.

I take my foot off the brake and roll away, saying, "I know, Cookie. Good-bye."

13

I GET BACK ON CAMPUS JUST IN TIME TO TEACH MY
afternoon Twentieth-Century U.S. Foreign Policy class. Now that it's over,
I'm going to enter their quiz grades, then cruise on down to Black Heads
Barber Shop so Blake can tighten me up.

I'm really looking forward to meeting Katrina and seeing if she's got
some character and substance.

"Tight, juicy butt . . . big, round knockers."

I've just about finished entering the quiz grades into my record book
when someone knocks on my door. I open it and see Dr. Avraham Silberberg. He's smiling, but his eyes look troubled.

"Hi, Avi. What's going on?" I ask.

"Got a minute?"

"Sure. Come on in."

Avi's the most gifted historian in the department, turning out articles,
book reviews, and monographs at a rate that's led others to sneer and call
him a machine. I used to bounce back and forth between being envious
and intimidated. Then I got busy. Rather than spending my time in jealous awe, I started cranking out my own publications, earning the notice
and respect of the discipline's heavyweights.

I close the door as Avi sits down. "What's on your mind?" I ask.

He crosses his arms and slumps into his chair. "You're pretty good
friends with Gina Roman, aren't you?"

The question sounds more like an accusation than an inquiry, but I
let it pass. "Yes. What of it?"

"And she's the adviser to the Middle Passage Club?"

"Yes, Avi. She is. What's this about?"

He sighs. "Darius, there's going to be an explosion if they go through
with their plans."

I sit up tall and steeple my fingers. "Avi, I'm at a disadvantage here. I
have no idea what you're talking about."

Avi shakes his head. "They're going to invite that what'shisname, Osmani el Bornu, to come speak on campus."

My steepled fingers collapse. "You're joking!"

Avi's hazel eyes darken. "Darius, the man's an anti-Semite. It's hardly a joking matter."

"No, Avi. It's not!" I say, trying to recover. "When did you find out?"

"Just this morning. One of my students was working in the Center for Holocaust Research . . ."

"Didn't they move that to Frank Hall?"

"Yes. Right where the Middle Passage Club has its office. That's how my student found out. She's pretty good friends with some of the MPC members and learned about this planned disaster in passing conversation."

I exhale a sigh. "For pete's sake!"

"My sentiments exactly."

We sit in silence for a few moments. Then I look at Avi and say, "So what now?"

Avi leans forward, his eyes drilling into me. "Darius, you've got to talk to Gina. Try to get her to understand that this could turn ethnic relations on this campus into a nightmare."

Avi's right. But if it's such a big concern, why isn't he going to Gina *himself*?

"Avi, have you voiced your concerns with Gina?"

He shifts uneasily in his seat. "Yes and no."

"Okay. Help me out. Which is it?"

Avi's brow furrows at my condescension. "What I mean, Darius, is that yes, we went to see her. But she . . ."

"We?"

"Dr. Steinmetz and myself."

"I see."

"Why do you say it in that tone of suspicion? We were only trying to explain . . ."

"Don't get all wound up on me, Avi. I know you and Julian were only trying to head off a disaster. But I also know that if you showed up together, Gina probably gave you a takeout lesson in verbal Kung Fu."

Avi answers with a slow, grim nod. "She allowed us just enough time to state our concerns, then summarily dismissed us."

"She probably thought you were ganging up on her."

"But . . . that's absurd. We were only trying . . ."

"Avi, I repeat: *I'm on your side.* But you've got to understand some things, too. As a black woman, Gina's developed something of a street fighter in her. She's had to in order to survive, especially as a professional academic."

Avi raises an eyebrow. "Honestly, Darius, haven't we all paid our dues?"

"Yes, we have. But the difference between you and her, or me for that matter, is that if you wanted, you could change your name, dress, and beliefs, and disappear into the mainstream as Austin Stevens."

Avi gives no sign of agreement. He also gives no sign of disagreement.

"On the other hand," I continue, "Gina could surgically change her gender, but she'd still be *black.* Society might someday adjust to the weirdness of the first, but it'll never forgive the second."

I give him a playful slap on the knee. "So don't take it personal. Most black men are all too familiar with the kind of machine-gun tongue that just blew you away. It goes with the territory of trying to love people who've traditionally been double-whammied for their color *and* gender."

Avi looks into space for a moment, contemplating. "I guess I can see how she might've interpreted us showing up together as a power play."

"Perhaps you should try again, on your own. I'm certain Gina will hear you out and come to the right decision."

"And what if she doesn't?"

"Then I think we're in for one of those discomforting moments that often occur in an environment promoting the free and open expression of ideas."

Avi folds his hands and leans forward, looking hard into my eyes. "Darius, do you really think this el Bornu will say something the university should be seen as promoting?"

"No, Avi. I don't. But I'm not the one you need to convince. As I said, if you feel that strongly, you should talk to Gina. She's the MPC adviser and . . ."

I stop in mid-sentence as the full meaning and impact of my unfinished statement hit home. Avi raises an eyebrow, a victorious gesture confirming that I finally understand.

"Exactly," he says. "She's advising them. And you know as well as I that even though it's *their* plan, *she'll* take the professional hit. As their adviser, she's accountable."

Avi's concern for Gina's career is touching, but it suddenly strikes me that there's something else at work here.

"What else is this about, Avi?"

"C'mon, Darius. The man's anti-Semitic. Don't you think there's something tragically ironic about the MPC students inviting a racist to deliver the keynote at their annual forum?"

I nod. "It's not only tragically ironic; it's offensive. But, Avi, you know that as soon as someone tries to put the clamps on this it's going to be a First Amendment issue."

Avi rolls his eyes. "Look, Darius. I'm as familiar with the First Amendment as you are. But this is larger. This is about right and wrong. This is about a persecuted people being put at odds with a group with whom we should be allies."

"I agree. But, Avi, pardon me for asking this, and I don't want you to think I'm insensitive, but where was all your outspokenness last year when the Future Americans League invited that bigot Marshall Prescott to speak at their political awareness rally?"

Avi's face turns deep red. Having struck the nerve, I tweak it again. "Do you recall how upset black students were? Remember all the warnings about unrest? How it would tarnish the university's image? How black student enrollment might drop? All that was on the line and nobody, not a single white person from the faculty or the administration, stood behind those kids."

Avi sits back and sighs. "Touché, Darius. Touché."

I'm glad Avi understands. But so do I. Even though the MPC students have as much right as any other group to bring whomever they want on campus, there's always the fallout afterward. First Amendment or not, heads will role for bringing that pseudointellectual, posturing windbag here to spout invective against a people with whom, just as Avi says, we should be closely allied.

And I'm both puzzled and surprised that Gina's not opposing this. Whatever the reason, she's sharp enough to know that being associated with an effort that'll coat the university with el Bornu's slime might possibly tarnish her career, maybe even ruin it.

I also have to believe that she's thought this through, weighed the consequences, and prepared for the inevitable question of how the Middle Passage Club, formed to consistently research the horrors of the transatlantic slave trade and impact of the African diaspora, could sanction inviting to its annual forum someone who routinely berates a people who've suffered unspeakable calamity.

I extend my hand to Avi. "I'll talk to her and see if I can find out what's going on."

Avi smiles, takes my hand, and we shake. "Thanks, Darius. I'd appreciate it. As will the six million who died in the camps."

He gets up and leaves. As he departs, I want to tell him that I, my ancestors, and the millions who suffered and died during slavery and segregation, would've appreciated his standing up for us last year.

14

I LEAVE CAMPUS AND HEAD STRAIGHT FOR BLACK
Heads Barber Shop. I need to be trimmed, clean, and smelling good when
I meet Katrina for coffee this evening. I open the shop's door and am almost run over by a wide-eyed mouse of a man, doing his best to hold on
to a soggy box as he flees Blake, who's chasing him with a wicked-looking
straight razor.

"Felix, I told you I wanted steaks, not patties!" Blake shouts. "And I
want 'em froze and free of dirt!"

Felix scampers into the street and safety, gets a better hold of his soggy
box of melting burgers, and starts wolfing. "Screw you, man! This here's
high-quality cow."

"I'ma 'high-quality' your ten-miles-a-ugly self into pieces-of-darkie if
you don't bring my steaks," Blake threatens.

"And it better not have none'a that hand-'n-feet disease!" Parker
shouts from over the head of his customer.

"That's foot-and-mouth," Otis corrects, adding, "ya non-CNN-
watchin' unedumacated fool."

That starts them on another round of their endless dozens. Zenobia
rolls her eyes and finishes setting up a hair dryer over a large blob of
chocolate that blinks every few seconds. Moon grins from his barber's
chair, pulls a barbecued rib from the Styrofoam box perched on his belly,
and begins stripping off the meat.

Felix flips Blake the bird and sidles off, stopping every few steps to
readjust the disintegrating box.

"Up yours too!" Blake shouts. "But you'd better bring my steaks or
I'ma whup you into punk pudding."

Blake snorts through his flared nostrils, looks at me, and smiles. "Darius! What's'up, doc?"

"Nothing, compared to all your confusion."

He scowls at the departing Felix, then looks back at me. "C'mon inside and lemme hook you up," he says.

"Do me right," I say. "Tonight's important."

Blake's smile widens. He puts his arm around my neck and drags me in. "Guess what, y'all," he announces. "Darius has got a date!"

"Well, good for you," Zenobia says, smiling.

Moon holds up a newly stripped bone, salutes, and grabs another. Parker winks and Otis gives a quick thumbs-up.

Then Parker says to Otis, "Your head's so fat, it caused a solar eclipse."

"And you're so ugly, you were King Kong's stunt double."

"You're so black, night got pissed and quit his job."

"You're skin's so greasy, it sweats mayonnaise."

I sit down in Blake's barber's chair and look back at him. "What's the longest they've ever done the dozens?" I ask, speaking low.

"Two days."

"No!" shouts Moon, sitting up and pointing a rib bone at the TV sitting on a tall crate. "The Browns traded Kendall Jefferson to the Steelers. What'sa matter with them fools up in that front office?"

"So what'll it be?" Blake asks.

"Make me look good."

"Darius, I'ma barber. Not God."

"Quit talking junk and just give me a good trim."

"Now *that* I can handle."

He turns on his clippers, presses the PLAY button on his CD player, and sings along with India.Arie.

"Blake! Why you turn that on when I'm watchin' the sports?" Moon shouts.

"You oughta be cleanin' up that mess around your chair," Zenobia admonishes him.

Otis jerks the head of his customer to the side to better insult Parker. "You're so stupid, you think rap music comes in aluminum foil."

"Your butt's so big, you rent it as a movie screen."

"You're so triflin', you fry chicken with the feathers."

"Hey!" Blake shouts. "Don't be insultin' the heavenly bird."

The phone rings and Zenobia answers. She scowls and holds it out to Blake.

"Blake! Come get this!"

"Who is it?" he shouts.

She turns the phone so the caller can hear. "It's that Tawana heifer who don't know you're two-timin' her *and* my girlfriend."

Blake sputters and curses, then races to the phone. I settle back, close my eyes, and soak up the sweet noise of my people. A little while later, Blake brushes the zillions of hair clippings from my shirt and hands me a mirror.

"Check it out," he says.

I stand up, move closer to the big mirror, and, using both it and the handheld one, inspect the front, sides, and back of Blake's handiwork.

"Perfect," I say.

Blake winks. "Like always. That'll be fifteen dollars."

"Fifteen dollars! It was only ten the last time."

"What can I say?" Blake defends himself, shrugging. "Times is hard. Looking good costs money."

"For that amount, I'd better be irresistible."

The door opens and Parker and Otis, still hurling insults at each other, shut up and stare sallow-eyed and slack-jawed as an absolutely gorgeous dark-skinned sister steps inside.

"Hello, everyone," she says.

She's dressed in a conservative but sexy peach-colored business suit. Her hair's cut short and styled sassy. Her body reminds me of Pam Grier; her voice, Loretta Devine; and her glowing presence is Josephine Baker reincarnated.

"Hey, girlfriend," Zenobia responds.

"'Zup, Ms. Fine," Moon answers, his eyes traveling slowly up and down the woman's brick-house body.

"Hello, Chloe!" Blake calls. "Got some good products for me today?"

"Now, Blake. Would I disappoint you?"

"Naw, baby. You never do."

Blake's staring so hard, his eyes might go brittle and shatter at any moment. Chloe glides across the shop, reminding me of the low-lying mist that hugs the ground in early morning.

"We're running a special this month," Chloe says, pulling some brochures from her slim briefcase.

Blake takes the brochures, flips through a few, then tosses them onto the cluttered counter behind him. "I'll take some," he says.

Chloe pulls out an elegant pad and pen, both looking like they were designed especially for her by Super Fine, Inc.

"Okay," she says. "Which ones?"

Blake leans against his counter and lets his eyes mosey along Chloe's many curves and indentations.

"Which ones what?" he asks.

Chloe smiles stiffly. "C'mon, Blake. Which hair care products are you interested in?"

Bowwow Blake is so busy visually undressing Chloe that he doesn't even hear the stress tones in her voice. And rightfully so. It's apparent from her speech, carriage, and demeanor that she's not just another semi-literate street hoochie. She appears organized and full of purpose, hinting strongly at her being a professional. And her attractive but not overbearing self-assurance indicates a woman of stature, class, and accomplishment.

"Why don't you suggest something," Blake says. "Like the restaurant you want me to take you to."

Chloe offers Blake a stiffer but still-tolerant smile. "Now, Blake. You know I don't mix work with pleasure."

"But that's just it, baby. My work *is* my pleasure. So ya see, if we went out, it would be some'a one, a little of the other, and neither of both."

"Don't trust 'em, girlfriend," Zenobia cautions. "Blake is the original woof!"

He glares her into silence, then refocuses softer eyes onto Chloe. "How about it, sweet thang?"

She doesn't bother smiling this time. I step in and say, "Blake, buy some more of that Night Wave Seven. That stuff does wonders for me."

Chloe looks directly at me and my knees buckle. "Do you really like it?" she asks.

"Er, yeah. It's better than anything I've ever used for keeping my hair moist and shiny."

Chloe looks back at Blake. "Shall I put you down for an order?"

He yawns. "Yeah. Two boxes. Doc D is right. I ain't had a customer yet who wasn't satisfied with it."

"Blake, get me some'a them new thin curlers," Zenobia says.

"And some better razors, man," Parker complains. "The sample that other rep gave us leaves the customers lookin' like one'a them Piccolo paintings."

Otis rolls his eyes. "It's Picasso, *fool*. That's what you get for dropping out'a kindergarten."

The battle of the dozens resumes and Chloe smiles. It's soft and genuine, like the one she wore upon entering the shop.

"How long have they been at it this time?" she asks, glancing at Blake.

"Going on forty minutes," he growls.

FREDDIE LEE JOHNSON III

"With no sign of letting up," I add.

Chloe looks at me again and I extend my hand. "Darius Collins. Blake's tortured customer."

"Chloe Brown. Blake's tortured beauty-and-barber-supply rep."

"And I'm Blake Barnes, tortured boss of those two clowns," Blake says, gesturing toward the sniping Parker and Otis.

The three of us laugh and I say, "Well, I've got to go. Thanks for the rip-off haircut, Blake."

"It's only a rip-off if you don't look good," Blake says. "And ugly as you are, I let you off cheap."

I wave him off, but he doesn't see me, since he's on his way to jump Parker and Otis.

I look at Chloe and say, "It was nice meeting you, Ms. Brown."

"It was good meeting you also."

"Maybe I'll see you again sometime. I come in here every so often for a trim."

She doesn't answer one way or the other. And this is already feeling too much like work, so I turn away to leave. But wait! This is a nice woman, with a decent personality and strong evidence that there's more in her head than just air. Why should I turn away and let some other sucker get what could be *mine*?

I turn back and look directly into her eyes. She locks hers with mine and smiles.

"Do you have a card?" I ask.

She hands me the one already in her hand. "My work, cellular, pager, and fax numbers are all on it."

I chuckle. "Don't you sometimes wonder how our parents got together without all this technology?"

"I wonder about it all the time," she answers, laughing softly. "If anything, all those gadgets have done more to separate us than bring us closer."

"Agreed."

"Do you have a card?"

I stiffen. The moment she looks at my card and sees DARIUS COLLINS, PH.D., ASSOCIATE PROFESSOR OF HISTORY, her eyes will roll and we'll be finished before we get started.

From across the shop, Blake hollers, "And I'm getting tired of listening to y'all running them dozens every day!"

"Well, then get on *his* case," Parker demands, pointing at Otis. "He thinks just cuz he watches CNN twenty-four/seven he's some college professor like Darius."

I grimace. Chloe glances at Parker, then looks back at me. There's no point holding back now. So I pull out my wallet and give her one of my cards.

"Hmmm," she says, looking at it. "You're a historian?"

"Yes," I answer, stifling a groan.

"I love history."

"Huh? I mean, you do!"

"Absolutely. I almost majored in it as an undergrad, but my dad wanted me to work in the family business, so I majored in marketing instead."

"You don't know how glad I am to hear you say that," I tell her, relieved.

"I think I have an idea," she says, smiling slyly. "I used to get some pretty awful looks when I told people I wanted to major in history."

Zenobia gathers up her purse and jacket and stomps to the front door. "I'll see y'all tomorrow."

"Where do you think you're going?" Blake asks, indignant.

"Home! Where there ain't no foulmouthed little boys pretendin' to be men."

"What about your customers?"

"Moon can finish up with Connie as soon as her hair's dry. I ain't got no more appointments, so bye!"

She storms out. Chloe and I follow her. We talk a little longer, write our home phone numbers on the cards we gave each other, and shake hands bye. She goes back into Blake's shop and I get in my car and drive off.

I cruise through Cleveland's traffic on the way to my apartment, singing along with the radio as the disc jockey plays some old-school Teddy Pendergrass, urging his woman to *"turn off the lights."* And rivers of satisfaction spread through me as I'm more convinced than ever that the dashing, dynamite Darius of old has finally returned.

15

I DROP MY BRIEFCASE AND MAIL ONTO MY DINING room table and hurry into the bathroom, stripping off my clothes along the way. Now that Blake's helped me out in the looking good department, it's time to shower so I can get clean, then splash on some cologne and smell good. I'll wear some of that *Vibrant Passions* Marcy bought me. If anything comes of this date with Katrina, it'll be such sweet irony knowing that Marcy's money, excellent sense of smell, and extravagant taste helped me find her replacement.

I quickly shower, pick out some nice casual clothes, and get dressed. My wardrobe's dated, but with the monthly mugging imposed by Beelzebub's domestic court minions, I have no choice but to be fashionably out-of-date.

I've given up openly lamenting the insanity of a system that's making me pay Cookie such whopping child support when she makes more than twice my salary. I once made the mistake of complaining to Danielle and was blasted by a tirade of accusations ranging from being merely selfish to swimming in the slime with "those other worthless good-for-nothings who don't mind being a daddy but don't want to be a father."

I'd somehow forgotten that Danielle *my sister* was also Danielle the *single mother* who'd just been dumped by a guy who, quite frankly, was a worthless good-for-nothing who didn't mind being a daddy but didn't want to be a father. Needless to say, we never had *that* conversation again. In fact, we've barely talked since then.

Lesser encounters convinced me that it was pointless to try to get understanding. In the years I'd been married, I'd missed the moment when men had been declared the enemy. Our apparent crime: *birth!* When I heard that other guys were paying so much that they couldn't even afford my frequent haircuts, an occasional date, and certainly not the phone and travel bills of a long-distance relationship like the one I had with Marcy, I swallowed my complaints and shut up!

I get dressed and check the time. I'm early, which is good. It's also bad. Now I'll have to sit around and dwell upon the suspense, expectations, and hopes for the evening. I sit down on the couch and try to relax, but my thoughts stray to Jarrod.

"Son, there's nothing that could make me stop loving you," I mutter. "But you have no idea of the mess you've gotten us into."

It was so much simpler when he was small. But that's not true. Jarrod's always been a handful, like the time he called Cookie after I tanned his butt for peeing off our apartment balcony.

Cookie was away in Houston on business and was livid when she was pulled out of an important meeting and told by Jarrod that I'd just administered some good old-fashioned Baptist laying on of hands.

Jarrod's butt was still glowing red when he hollered, "Mommy wants to talk to you, *now!*"

As soon as I stepped into the bedroom, he threw the phone onto the bed, flew out of the apartment, and dived into the bushes. I said, "Hello?" and thunder blasted from the phone as Cookie railed and carried on about child abuse, my incompetent parenting, and ruining her meeting. I held the phone from my ear until she expended her fury, then scorched her with my own response.

"I don't care what you think!" I exploded. "That boy's butt needed spanking and I spanked it. If he does it again, he'll get more of the same."

That threw her off guard, but only for a moment. Combative as always, Cookie fired right back. "Darius, I swear if you hurt *my* son, there'll be hell to pay."

"Not as much hell as he's going to catch if he pees on his playmates again."

"If he does *what?*"

By the time I finished explaining, we both were chuckling at the image of Jarrod standing on the balcony, his pants gathered down around his ankles and hips arched forward for maximum dispersal as he literally rained on his friends' parade.

Later that evening, after darkness, cold, hunger, and fear drove him inside, he listened quietly on the cordless as Cookie from Houston and I from the kitchen bent his ears about playing both ends against the middle. Then I ensured that he'd think long and hard before ever again trying to undercut my authority, not to mention hiking up our long-distance bill.

"And if you ever run away or call nine-one-one," I growled between butt whacks, "you'd better stay gone, because it'll be twice as bad when you get back!"

That wasn't the end of Jarrod's attempts to divide and conquer, but he at least had the good sense to try to be more subtle. For all the clashing Cookie and I did over disciplining strategies, all he had to do was sit back and ultimately enjoy getting his way.

Cookie insisted upon raising Jarrod using a lot of fluffy, coddling, New Age psychojunk.

"Darius, he needs room to grow and express himself," she'd always say. "Spanking and punishment will stunt the development of his self-esteem and leave him alienated and questioning our love."

I wanted to raise Jarrod with an omnipresent appreciation for the rod of reality. The rod called *life*, which would destroy him if he wasn't prepared.

"Cookie! This black boy is going to someday be a black man. If we want him to succeed we need to prepare him for survival in a society that'll be busy trying to kill him when it's not trying to lock him up!"

We never did agree. And now Jarrod, my son who still has so much to learn, is allegedly the father of a child he's not prepared to have, teach, or nurture.

The phone rings and I grab it. "Hello?"

"Hello, Darius."

It's Cookie. I close my eyes and grit my teeth. "What now?"

"Why are you being rude? I only said hello."

"Maybe I'm trying to get a head start on the rest of the conversation."

Silence answers back and I'm suddenly feeling bad. Cookie's right. There was no need to attack her.

"You're right, Cookie," I say. "Sorry for being such a grouch."

"No apologies necessary. I'm used to your rudeness."

Everything in me wants to respond, but being caught off guard has the words clogging my throat.

"Now," Cookie says, satisfied that she's recaptured the upper hand. "Jarrod will be back around two tomorrow afternoon."

"I thought you said he wouldn't be home till Friday."

"That was the original plan. Some of the kids were caught with marijuana and the trip was cut short."

"Please don't tell me that Jarrod was one of the violators."

"Don't be ridiculous. Jarrod knows better."

"Yeah, right. Just like he knew better than to get a girl pregnant."
Cookie's voice is as cold as it's ever been when she says, "Good-bye!"
I hang up, glance at my watch, and spring to my feet. I've gone from having extra time before getting Katrina to almost being late. I hustle to the door but stop when the phone rings again. I'll let the answering machine get it but want to hear who's calling.

"Darius, it's Marcy. I don't know why you're not taking my calls, but I want . . ."

What Marcy wants is the last, least of my concerns. I march over to the phone, pick up, hang up, shut off the answering machine, and leave.

16

I DRIVE THE SHORT DISTANCE OVER TO KATRINA'S building, go inside to her apartment, and knock. I'm really looking forward to spending a nice, relaxing time and engaging in some intelligent, meaningful conversation.

"Tight, juicy butt . . . big, round knockers."

She answers the door and my heart leaps into my throat. Nash was right. This woman's hardly a castoff. To tell the truth, I'm wondering why her face isn't smiling from some advertisement along the highway. She's dressed in tastefully snug jeans, a pleasingly tight-fitting sweater, and wearing heels that are just shy of being stiletto.

"Hi, Darius," she greets me, opening her arms for a hug.

It takes all my strength to keep my eyes from lowering and locking onto her—be still, my heart—*big, round knockers.* I happily oblige and give her a hug.

"Just a second," she says, releasing me. "I have to put out some water for my cat and then I'll be ready."

"No problem," I say, stepping inside. She hurries off to finish her chore, the sweet motion of her rear end launching a Fourth of July party in my crotch. If the rest of the evening is as good as this, I'll gladly repay Nash by watching Player.

"Okay," Katrina says. "I'm ready."

We head out to the car. I open her door and she says, "Oh, my. A gentleman. Such a rarity these days."

"It's a rarity finding someone who appreciates such gestures."

She blushes and gets in. I hurry around, get in, and we're off. "Where would you like to go?" I ask.

"Your choice. I'm just glad to be going."

"Okay. Let's try Café Brazilia," I suggest. "They're new and supposed to have some really good blends."

"That's fine with me."

We laugh and talk along the way, the radio playing soft music as a nice backdrop. The DJ puts on Marvin Gaye's sultry oldie "Distant Lover," adding to the sexy mood filling up the car. I turn the volume up slightly and sing softly along.

"This brings back some memories," I say.

"Memories like what?" Katrina asks, smiling broadly and batting her eyes. It's a chore keeping my eyes off her boobs.

I say, "Memories like cruising around in my '79 Firebird, listening to Marvin, Barry White, Isaac Hayes, and Funkadelic."

Katrina frowns. "You were driving back in 1979?"

"Yeah. That's the year I got my license."

The furrows in her forehead deepen. "My goodness," she says, her voice reeking with disgust. "You're old."

I tighten my grip on the steering wheel. "Yes," I say, my voice tighter than a strained cable. "I suppose to some people I would be. How old are you?"

"Thirty-four."

I look hard at her. I'm glaring but don't care. "Give it time, Katrina. Someday you'll be 'old,' too."

She bites her lower lip and offers a cutsie smile. "I hurt your feelings. I'm sorry. I didn't mean that you're decrepit. Just that you've been around awhile. It must've been a blast growing up in the fashion-gagging seventies. I'll bet . . ."

"I understand!" I snap.

I pull over to a Rapid Shop. "I'll be right back," I say, getting out.

Moments later, I get back in the car with two cups of coffee, hand one to her, and head back to the apartments.

"Where are we going?" Katrina asks, bewildered.

"I forgot something."

"Oh."

We ride along in silence. Katrina grabs the door handle as I swerve through traffic, pushing the speed limit as fast as I dare. We're finally back at the apartments and I whip over to Katrina's building and brake to a hard stop.

"Can you wait here for a moment?" I ask.

"Ah, yes. Of course," Katrina answers, looking puzzled. She gets out and says, "What's going on? I thought you forgot something."

I start rolling away and say, "I did. I forgot to *leave you here*!"

Her face ignites into shock, then fury. She starts cussing, hurls her coffee at my car, and storms into her building. The cup hits my rear window with a soggy *thunk*! Coffee splatters everywhere, covering the rear window in a dark filmy haze, just like the one I've been in for months.

17

THE SENSIBLE THING TO DO IS FORGET KATRINA AND
this latest dating abortion, get back to my computer, and resume working
on my book. But I'm so pissed, I'd probably hurl the computer through a
wall. I know I shouldn't let the rude comments of that uncouth she-goat
get to me, but she stomped on an exposed nerve that over the last year and
a half has been plucked, tweaked, and trampled once too often. The last
thing it needed was for some insensitive tramp to point out that the dynamic, dashing Darius of my second bachelorhood is neither dynamic nor
dashing. *He's just old!*

I swing the car toward the parking lot exit, jet out into traffic, and
drive down to the self-serve car wash and blast the grit, grime, and sticky
coffee from my car with a high-powered spray wand. I wash and rinse,
wash and rinse, and wash and rinse the car, taking my sweet time so as to
delay the moment when I finally return to the cavernous silence of my
apartment. But in all honesty, it's not the silence I'm avoiding but the
hissing snickers. The walls are still laughing about me and Cookie crum-
bling and have new comic material after my demise with Marcy. This latest dating disaster will have them howling.

Three car washings is more than enough indulgence of my avoidance
strategy, and I dry the car off and head for the mall movie theater. There's
nothing playing that I'm particularly interested in seeing, so I drive down
to the bookstore. I'm not exactly in the mood for reading, either, but there
just might be something in the history section that'll catch my interest.

I've always escaped into history when things have gotten too rough in
my present. I cross a time bridge to visit people like Frederick Douglass,
Ida B. Wells, Thurgood Marshall, Barbara Jordan, and other luminaries
from my extended African-American family. Reading their words and
learning about their struggles reminds me that my problems are *nothing*
compared to the racism and brutality they endured. They gently but
firmly admonish me to keep striving, excelling, and building up black

people. They plead with me to live a life that won't mock or defile the blood, sweat, and tears of the sacrifices they made for me.

I get out and stroll into the Afrikka Rising bookstore and head straight for the history section. On display is a history of the Black Legion, a 1930s ultraviolent paramilitary offshoot of the Ku Klux Klan that made life miserable for people in Ohio, Michigan, and Indiana. Also displayed is a new history of blacks who served in the Union Navy during the Civil War, and the wartime recollections of Sergeant Major Edgar Huff, one of the first blacks to join the Marine Corps when it finally opened its ranks to African-Americans during World War II.

Almost an hour later I've spent way more than I can afford, but I feel better and that's what counts. I get back in the car and head for home, change my mind, swing around, and head for West Branch State Park. There's only a few hours before it closes, but that's still enough time for me to drive through and gaze at the lake. While I'm gazing I can fantasize about where I'll dump Nash's body if he ever again sets me up with a shrew like Katrina. And speaking of Nash, I'm going to call him and bend his ear.

I grab my cellular, dial his number, and wait through several rings. He's probably not home, but no matter. When his answering machine picks up, I'll leave a message that'll be the first punch of many. But much to my surprise, he answers.

"Hello!" Nash is breathing hard and sounds irritated. I know him well enough to guess that I've interrupted some energetic screwing.

"It's me, you jerk!"

"Darius! Ah, look, man. I'd like to talk, but . . ."

"But nothing!" I snap. "Why'd you give Katrina my work number?"

"Why're you so pissed off? I thought you wanted the hookup. She sure did."

"What she wants is somebody who's not . . . old."

"Old? What are you talking . . ." He pauses and speaks in rushed urgent tones to someone in the background. "Listen, D," he says, returning to the phone. "Can't we talk about this later?"

"No! Do me a favor and don't help me anymore in the dating department."

"Okay, man. Anything you say. I've gotta go."

In the background, a bird squawks and says, "Slam it in there, big daddy."

"Shut up, Player!" Nash yells. Then talking back to me he says, "D, I've *really* gotta go."

"All right, all right," I answer, rolling my eyes. "Get in a good stroke for me."

He chuckles. "It'll be my pleasure."

"Baby, I'm gonna make that booty *snap!*"

"Player! I told you to shut up!" Nash hollers. There's some clattering and rustling, followed by Nash's snarling and growling; then Player squawks, "You lucky I'm in this birdcage."

Then Nash hangs up. I get to West Branch, turn down a narrow tree-lined hard-packed dirt road, and drive for just over a mile toward the lake. The sky is slate blue with long wispy strands of clouds spiraling off toward the eastern horizon that's dappled with the first purple traces of dusk. I get to the parking area, find a space, cut off the car, and gaze through the trees at the water off in the distance. Its surface shimmers in the late afternoon/early evening light.

This is the kind of beautiful scene that would be a romantic utopia if I were viewing it with someone special. It's the kind of scene Gina would appreciate. She's told me that she enjoys quiet strolls along the beach, standing silent in the fall woods, and sitting on a huge rock in the desert, watching the night take slow command of the sky.

Getting Cookie to enjoy such experiences usually required me listening to an avalanche of complaints. Marcy loved the outdoors, just so long as I could assure her that she wouldn't break a nail, encounter a single bug, or be no more than fifteen minutes from downtown Cleveland. But Gina! She's an archaeologist who thrives on being outdoors, a pleasing trait that's balanced by her soft but potent femininity.

I grab my cell phone, walk a few hundred feet through the woods to a high spot overlooking the lake, and sit down next to a thick oak tree. A blue egret flies by, just skimming the water's edge. The wind rustles the leaves above and I close my eyes and inhale deep, savoring the rich scents of earth, water, and evergreen. Maybe someday Gina will come here with me. And even though she's not physically here with me now, it doesn't mean she can't be here with me in voice, so I flip open my cellular and dial. She answers quickly.

"Hello?"

"Hi, Gina. It's your favorite, Dr. Collins."

"Ah, Darius. How are you?"

There's a distant hesitancy in Gina's tone. It's a hesitancy that I've heard more times than I care to remember, and it adds up to one thing: she's got company.

Even though I know this, I ask anyway. "You sound busy. Did I catch you at a bad time?"

"Well, no, not exactly. I can talk. But not for long."

"Gina!" a male voice calls. "Come and try on this Victoria's Secret bra I bought for you."

Gina gasps and covers the phone. There's a muffled exchange between her and three-car-dealership-owning Bruce Manchester IV. I know it's him because even through the muffled exchange I hear her rasping his name as she scolds him for blaring out their intimate business.

When she uncovers the phone, Bruce says, "Sorry about that. Tell your cousin I said hello."

"Okay," Gina answers. And then, "Hold on, Darius. Let me close this door all the way."

She leaves for a few moments, and I can't decide which is the greater disappointment: knowing that Gina lied or knowing that she lied so quickly.

Gina picks up the phone and says, "Sorry about that, Darius. I hope you don't . . ."

"Gina, you don't owe me an explanation. And I don't want one."

"Why are you being like that?" she asks defensively.

"I'm not being like anything. Let's talk about Avi Silberberg."

Gina's defensiveness transforms into a clarified offense. "All right," she says matter-of-factly. "What's on your mind?"

"Avi stopped by to see me today. He's worried about . . ."

"He and Julian Steinmetz are griping about Osmani el Bornu's speaking at the MPC's annual forum."

"So you know what their concerns are?"

"Yes. And I told them that while I appreciate their position, I'm not changing my mind."

"But, Gina. They've got a point. You know what Osmani el Bornu preaches. Bigotry is bigotry no matter what color the face espousing it."

The warm voice that answered the phone gets frosty. "Darius, not everything Osmani el Bornu says is bigoted. In fact, he has a lot of valid points. And beyond that, since when has the university adopted the policy of screening and censoring guest speakers? I don't recall anybody trying to stop that racist Marshall Prescott from speaking to the Future Americans League last year. And the university even paid his expenses!"

"You're right, Gina. And I mentioned that. But it still doesn't change the fact that this will be a disaster. Prescott's venom polarized the campus. And there wasn't an administrator I spoke to afterwards who wished they hadn't prevented his coming."

"And there's probably just as many that you *didn't* speak to who were ecstatic that he did."

"Gina . . ."

"No, Darius. We're not going to resolve anything right now. It's too complicated. I'm too close to leaving for Nicaragua. And I'm, ah, preoccupied at the moment."

"Bruce is there with you, *isn't he?*" I ask, demanding an answer.

Gina doesn't respond right away, and the long frigid silence between us gets longer and arctic cold.

"Darius, I'm going to hang up now," Gina says, her voice flat and absolutely devoid of emotion.

"Wait!"

"What is it, Darius?"

Gina's calm, controlled demeanor is so different from Cookie's mean-spirited histrionics that I'm not exactly sure how to respond.

"Gina, I, I'm sorry."

"Is that all?"

I swallow several times, trying to clear my clogged throat. "Well, yeah. Except, ah, I know you're leaving for Nicaragua tomorrow morning and, ah, just be careful, okay? Maybe when you get back we can . . ."

And then, with quiet, calm control, Gina hangs up.

18

LAST NIGHT, I SAT ON MY COUCH, NURSING A GLASS of wine and watching the wall clock as Monday turned into Tuesday, kicking myself for having been such a jerk with Gina. I desperately wanted to call her back and make things right, but that would've only made things worse. I also don't know if I could've stood knowing that Bruce was lurking in the background, anxiously waiting for her to try on her new Victoria's Secret bra so he could take it off and show her how much he'll miss her.

It's only mid-morning, but I know she's already on her way to Nicaragua. I'll be on pins and needles until she gets back. It's not that I'm worried, but Gina's a good friend and with all the turmoil being caused by these terrorist scumbags, it's appropriate to be concerned.

I can at least celebrate the fact that I don't have any classes today. I'll use the extra time to get some writing done and also decide how I'm going to tell Jarrod about the pregnancy problem that'll soon be his new best friend. It's probably best to just come out with it, explain the harsh realities of his new world, and reassure him that I still love him, am proud of him, and will always be there for him. I'll do all that in just a little while. For the moment, I'm going to finish wolfing down this bacon-and-egg sandwich while going through yesterday's mail. The only item of real interest is the monthly newsletter from the Cleveland Black Historical Society. The main story is disturbing:

CBHS WELCOMES EL BORNU GIFT

I need to get some more work done on my book, but this story demands my immediate attention. Especially since el Bornu's giving gifts to the organization I'm about to head. I grab the newsletter, sit down at the computer, and start reading.

Osmani el Bornu, one of America's most charismatic black leaders, has ensured that the Cleveland Black Historical Society will become a force within the historical community. New Black Movement spokesman Rashid Dakar recently announced that the CBHS would receive a $1.2 million gift. With this donation, the CBHS will be able to more aggressively pursue restoration projects and sponsor exhibits demonstrating the longevity, commitment, and contributions of African-Americans to the city of Cleveland. CBHS president Lawrence P. Brockett offered his thanks to Mr. el Bornu, praising him for his work in helping African-Americans maintain their ancestral conciousness. "He's a great leader," said Brockett. "I can think of no one more capable of articulating the concerns and perspective of the black community . . ."

Larry's not thinking too hard if he considers el Bornu the best person to speak for African-Americans. Like so many others, Larry's apparently swallowed the tele-manipulated bait offered by the media. It's infuriating watching the cameras, microphones, and satellite dishes that pop up from nowhere every time el Bornu clears his throat. And the media kings know there are thousands of black people who not only disagree with el Bornu but also possess opinions variable enough to disqualify their lumping us into a monolithic uni-mind.

But it's not all their fault. Blacks' staying quiet and letting that camera junkie tell us what we're thinking is as much to blame as el Bornu's messianic posturing. I'm certain that if white America's opinions were condensed into the yammerings of a podium-pounding poltroon, the reaction would be swift and the media kings would need backhoes to dig themselves from beneath the avalanche of hostile mail.

I'll be interested to find out how much of the Cleveland Black Historical Society's soul el Bornu's $1.2 million purchased. Whatever it bought, Larry needs to close the deal before his tenure of office is over. Once I'm elected CBHS president, I'm imposing a scrutinizing filter that'll tell contributors like el Bornu thanks, but no thanks!

I toss aside the newsletter, check the organization of my research notes, then get to work. Except for a few bathroom breaks, lunch, and a quick trip down to the Rapid Shop to buy a jumbo bag of Gummy Bears, I spend the greater part of the day pounding the keyboard as my brain transfers the data from my notes into narrative explanation. My skin tingles as hundreds of ancestors crowd around, looking over my shoulder, whispering their encouragement. I'm sailing along in my writing groove when I glance at my watch and realize that I have to stop. It's time to go and confront Jarrod.

I make double sure that my latest revisions are saved, grab my keys, and get on the road to Cookie's mansion. Her home is one of the more obvious reasons that I'm baffled by the court's monthly pillaging of my pocket. A few days after Cookie moved in, I came to pick Jarrod up for his usual weekend stay. Cookie wasn't home and Jarrod wasn't ready to go, so I helped myself to a casual tour.

I was impressed by the elegant beauty of the place but perplexed as to how Cookie's Jacuzzi, Japanese garden, five televisions, king-sized water bed, three overhead fans, room full of exercise gadgets, walk-in closet full of shoes, Italian drapes, and whoknowswhatelse had escaped the notice of the judge who rejected my petition for reduction of monthly child support.

"That money's needed for the welfare of your son, *Mister* Collins," he'd said, saying "Mister" like the word had been soaked in hyena spit. "And you've got some gall coming into my courtroom trying to weasel out of your parental responsibilities."

I should've kept quiet, but the arrogant presumptiveness of that juridical martinet blasted my temper into the red zone.

"Weasel!" I blurted, standing up and slamming my fist onto the table. "How's that worse than being a pompous pontificating pickpocket?"

The judge's head turned tomato-ripe red as his mouth dropped open and half-lens glasses fell off his aquiline nose.

"Mr. Collins!" he yelled. "Say another word and I'll hold you in contempt!"

My lawyer, Oliver Brady, grabbed my elbow to yank me behind him, but not before I fired off another volley.

"And how dare you!" I shouted. "How dare you diminish my parental role into being just a human ATM."

Oliver slapped the back of my head, wrestled me into my chair, then turned to the judge, his arms outstretched in supplication.

"Your Honor, please forgive this outburst!" he begged. "My client's been under tremendous emotional stress since being diagnosed with erectile dysfunction."

"Erectile dysfunction!" I blurted. "Oliver, are you nuts?"

"Probably not!" the judge answered. "But yours will be in a vise if you don't be quiet!"

Snickers and chuckles rippled through the courtroom. A U.S. marshal laughed into his palm while the court stenographer wiped laugh tears from her eyes.

"Mr. Brady!" the judge shouted. "Approach the bench!"

Oliver scampered forward and stood quiet and submissive as the judge snarled his displeasure, pointing his gavel at me with one hand and pounding the bench with the other.

". . . and make him understand that if he says one more word, his tool won't be the only thing left dangling. Understood!"

Oliver kowtowed in classic "yassah, boss!" fashion, then zipped back to our table, glaring at me the whole way.

"Sorry, Oliver," I whispered.

"Darius, will you *please* shut up! Before we both lose our skins."

Judge Plunder recomposed himself, commanded the court to return to order, then proceeded to pound me into obedience with his hammer of humiliation.

"So tell me, *Mister* Collins," he began, leaning forward and drilling his eyes into me, "is your Tourette's syndrome a side effect of erectile dysfunction or were you making rude, uncontrolled outbursts before going limp?"

The courtroom exploded with laughter and I shrank several inches. Oliver's eyes snapped tightly shut as he curled his lips inward to keep from laughing.

"Well, *Mister* Collins?" the judge pressed.

"It's a side effect, Your Honor."

The judge looked toward the ceiling, opening his arms in appeal. "Great Maker, it's just not right that a man in the prime of his life should be cursed with a paralyzed piston."

Then in a voice dripping with concern and empathized shame, he said, "You should seek counseling for your flaccid frustrations, *Mister* Collins."

People in the courtroom fell over themselves with laughter, including Oliver, who finally succumbed to the giggles dribbling from his lips. The stenographer stopped typing completely and held her stomach while the bailiff steadied himself against the wall to keep from toppling over with his Santa Claus–like "ho-ho-hos." It was a humiliating but grimly effective reminder that I stood a better chance of seeing pigs fly than getting a fair, just hearing in domestic court.

———

I PULL INTO COOKIE'S CIRCULAR DRIVEWAY, PARK, AND stroll to the front door. Just as I'm about to knock, it whips open and Cookie shoves a suitcase at me.

"Darius, put this in that minivan, would you?"

I shove the suitcase back at her. "No!"

"Darius, please!"

"No! There's nothing in my ex-husband job description that includes being a bellhop."

She glares at me, grabs a smaller suitcase, and wrestles them out to the minivan. She opens the back hatch, heaves them in, and hurries into the house.

"Going somewhere?" I ask.

Cookie runs up the steps and drags a huge suitcase down, stopping in front of me, huffing and puffing.

"Jarrod's going to have to stay with you for a while."

"What! Why? I mean, I'm glad to have him, but why are you so suddenly for it?"

"I'm going to Munich to negotiate purchasing some new buses for the city."

"Munich!" I blurt, stepping aside as Cookie drags her burden by. "What's the matter with Ford, Chrysler, or GM? And why so sudden?"

"It's complicated," Cookie answers.

"No, Cookie. What's complicated are all the people who keep getting laid off when their leaders send their jobs and businesses out of the country."

Cookie stops and jams her hands hard down on her hips. "Darius, I don't have time for this. And neither do you."

"Me! What're you talking about?"

"The youknowwhat's hitting the fan," Cookie answers, hauling the bulging suitcase through the front door and out to the minivan.

"What exactly are you talking about?" I ask.

"No time to explain."

She dashes back inside and over to the door leading downstairs. "Lowell, hurry up! I've got more stuff to load."

"Okay, sweetness," Cookie's latest pigeon answers from downstairs.

Lowell bounces up the steps, sees me in the living room, and looks me up and down. I look him over also, surveying his wanna-be-a-Rastafarian dreadlocks, the emaciated body in his muscleman T-shirt, the brown khakis drooping off his rear, and clunky boots that only infantrymen, inmates, construction workers, and telephone linemen used to wear.

"Who're you?" he asks, swelling up like he's protector of the realm.

I ignore him and head upstairs to Cookie. "Hey! Where do you think you're going?" Lowell challenges me, hurrying toward the steps.

"To speak with my ex-wife. And I don't need your help!"

He steps forward like he's going to teach me some manners, stopping when I face him.

"Listen, hero. Before you get stupid, you should know that I've been in a bad mood for a long time and need an excuse to release my frustrations."

Cookie staggers out of her bedroom and wobbles toward the steps with an armload of clothes. She peers around the cloth mountain and sees me and Lowell, our expressions indicating clearly that we're not making friends.

"Darius! Lowell! What're you two doing?" she asks, lurching past me.

Lowell says, "I was about to . . ." but is smothered into silence when Cookie dumps the clothes onto him.

"Take those outside," she orders. "Wait for me there. I'll be out in a moment."

Lowell weaves his way outside, another one of Cookie's dromedaries laboring for her favor. She wipes her forehead with the back of her hand, then glances at her watch.

"Good," she sighs. "I've still got time to make my flight."

"Cookie, what's going on? Where's Jarrod? And who's the Bob Marley impersonator?" I ask, pointing at Lowell.

Cookie's light skin flushes when she glances outside at Lowell, listening to the booming car stereo.

"Oh, him. He's just a friend," Cookie says.

Fat chance. If I had a dollar for every guy who's been buffaloed by a girlfriend's or wife's camouflaging a lover as "just a friend" or "play brother" I'd be a black Donald Trump.

"He must've caused quite a stir at the mayor's reception the other night," I say.

Cookie frowns. "What?" She flicks her wrist at Lowell and starts rifling through her purse. "Don't be silly, Darius. I wouldn't be caught dead with him at such a gathering."

The ex-husband historian in me wants to research the details of how and why someone Cookie "wouldn't be caught dead with" in public is calling her sweetness at home. But on second thought, maybe not. There are some facts an ex-husband historian shouldn't know.

"Is Jarrod asleep?" I ask.

Cookie dumps out one purse and starts transferring its contents to another. "Okay. I've got my credit cards, license, tickets, reservation confirmation numbers, and . . ."

"Cookie, is Jarrod asleep?"

". . . bankcard, electronic calendar, and . . ."

"Cookie!"

"What is it, Darius? Can't you see I'm busy?"

"What I see is someone who looks like she's rushing to catch the last train north to freedom."

A wistful smile creases Cookie's lips. "For all your faults, Darius, you could always turn a phrase."

I throw up my hands in frustration and head for Jarrod's room.

"He's not here," Cookie says.

"Where is he? And why didn't you tell me before I drove over here?"

"Why didn't you call? You know better than to show up unannounced."

"Forget this," I say, hurrying toward the door. "I'll see Jarrod later. And consider this my announced intent to return."

"Hold on, Darius," Cookie says. "You need to know what's going on."

"No, I don't! My life's crazy enough without your clutter. I'll talk to Jarrod later."

"That's what I'm trying to tell you," she says, rushing to the door. "He won't be back till around midnight."

I palm-slap my forehead. "Why, Cookie?"

"Denver's snowed in. The next flight won't put him at Cleveland-Hopkins till then."

"So I'll talk to him tomorrow."

Lowell blurts an expletive when the whumping bass beat from the minivan stereo is interrupted. He listens for a moment, then runs toward us, standing in the doorway.

"Cookie! Cookie! You've got to hear this," he says, sliding between us and into the living room. He cuts on the TV, flips a few channels, points, and says, "Look!"

A reporter in the foreground speaks softly into her microphone. ". . . this breaking story from city hall. In just a moment we'll be hearing from

Cleveland mayor Stoverman Tyne, who will respond to allegations concerning his acceptance of campaign contributions from underworld crime figures during his reelection campaign."

Cookie plops onto the couch behind us and groans. "Oh . . . my . . . God," she says, fanning herself. "I knew it would be bad but not like *this*."

"Ssh!" I say, turning up the volume.

The reporter touches her earpiece, listens for a moment, then continues. "There are also allegations of influence peddling, misuse of city government property and monies, electoral fraud, and charges that Deputy Mayor Sarah-Lynn Sheehy has engaged in repeated acts of blatant sexual harassment."

Cookie gasps and covers her mouth with both hands. I glance at her, look back at the TV, and shake my head.

"This is going to get real ugly real fast," I say.

Cookie reaches from behind and takes my hand. Lowell glowers at the gesture, sees me watching him, and looks back at the TV.

Cookie squeezes my hand. "Darius, I didn't know. Not about all this."

Cookie knows better than to feed me that line of baloney. She might not have known about "all this," but her connections and closeness to the mayor suggest that she knew something, which at least makes her a dotted line abettor.

The reporter keeps talking. ". . . and City Council President Milton Fields demanded that an investigation be opened into the appointment of Deputy Transportation Commissioner Collette 'Cookie' Hargrove as head of the educational reform task force, a high-profile assignment that stood to put her in a strong position to unseat the four-time incumbent in next year's city council elections."

When we were first married, Cookie and I went round and round about her insistence that her last name remain Hargrove, not Collins or even Hargrove-Collins, which, frankly, I didn't like much better but could've dealt with.

"Darius, I'm your wife, not your property," she told me. "What difference does it make if I'm wearing your name just so long as we know that we're married and conduct ourselves accordingly?"

It always amazed me how Cookie could be so clear on that issue and so mystified when I offered a similar rationale for not wearing my ring.

"We both know we're married," I reasoned. "What difference does it make as long as we conduct ourselves accordingly?"

Losing that struggle left me puzzled and resentful. But now that I've heard Cookie's name uttered along with the rest of those snake-oil sellers, I'm glad she fought so hard. I don't mind having my name in bright lights, but I don't want it illuminated by the beams of a grand jury.

Lowell sits down beside Cookie and wrings his hands. "Does this mean I won't get to co-emcee the next induction ceremony at the Rock 'n' Roll Hall of Fame like you promised?" he whines.

Cookie snatches her hand from mine and whacks him up'side his head. "Get out!"

Lowell tumbles onto the floor. "Hey! What's the matter with you?"

Cookie hurls a vase at him as he struggles to his feet and scrambles out the front door.

"And don't come back!" she hollers, throwing his jacket out after him.

Lowell runs to the end of the driveway, flips up his middle finger, smooths out his dreadlocks, and cusses Cookie out as he weeble-wobbles down the street.

I bite my lower lip to stifle a laugh and turn back to the TV as Mayor Stoverman "Stovey" Tyne walks briskly to the podium. He's dressed in dark colors, wearing a tailored double-breasted suit, every strand of his iron gray hair in place and his Nordic blue eyes staring out like twin oceans from his ruddy tanned face.

Cameras whir, buzz, and click as the mayor clears his throat to make his opening remarks. He takes a quick swallow of water, sets his jaw, looks directly into the cameras, and begins.

"Late this afternoon, information was leaked regarding alleged improprieties concerning contributions during my reelection campaign. I categorically deny all charges and hope that my friends in the press will exercise caution in reporting such hallway fiction."

"Look at them," Cookie sneers. "A room full of sharks circling for the kill."

"Perhaps," I say. "But let's be honest, Cookie. It's not like they're about to rip apart some innocent baby seal. It's more a case of the sharks ganging up on barracudas."

Cookie ignores the comment and we pay attention as the hunt begins. We listen till the end of the press conference and I cut off the TV. She sniffles as tears stream down her cheeks, her hands pressed together into a tight ball.

"Well," she begins, her voice warbling. "At least they didn't ask anything that would suggest something between me and the mayor."

"Not yet," I say. "But if they do their jobs, they will."

Cookie scowls. "Thanks for brightening my day, Darius."

"That wasn't meant as a slam, Cookie. But it's like *you* said the other night: All it'll take is for one of them to ask the right question."

Cookie nods and sighs. "You're right, Darius. And with Councilman Fields pushing to launch his investigation, that question will probably come sooner rather than later."

She snatches a tissue from the box on the coffee table, cleans her eyes and nose, then finishes her purse-to-purse junk transfer.

"What're you doing?"

"Getting ready to leave. What does it look like?"

"You can't be serious," I say. "Leaving now will play right into their hands. It'll look like you've got something to hide."

Cookie yanks her hand out of the purse and points at the TV. "Darius! Didn't you see what just happened? I have to leave. Maybe by the time I get back, things will have settled down."

"C'mon, Cookie. You're smarter than that. By the time you get back, they'll be waiting with knives, whips, and clubs."

Cookie huffs in exasperation. "Darius, Stovey and I discussed this and he thinks . . ."

"Screw what he thinks!" I say loudly. I grip her shoulders. "Why don't you use some of that formidable political savvy and manage the crisis. The mayor's a big boy. Let him put out his own fire."

"But . . ."

"Don't let him do this to you, Cookie. It'll be tough, but not half as bad as it'll be if you let him shove you into an accomplice closet."

Cookie shakes herself free, then slaps me so hard, I'm seeing double. She grips my shoulders and shakes. "Stop loving me, Darius! Stop loving me and looking out for me! That's not your job! It never was!"

Before I can respond, she covers my mouth with hers, kissing me with a passion beyond an intent to merely keep me quiet. She breaks off the kiss and shoves me outside.

"Cookie, listen to me," I say.

"No! You listen to me. Jarrod arrives at eleven forty-six P.M. on Venture Airlines flight sixteen-twenty-eight. Please try and explain this to him."

"Explain! Just what do you suggest I tell him?"

Cookie swallows a sob. "Tell him I'll call later. And also that . . ."

" 'And also that' *what*?"

Cookie looks hard at me, strokes my cheek, and says, "I'm sorry."

Then she slams the door in my face.

19

I'VE BEEN CRUISING ALONG THE HIGHWAY FOR HOURS, trying to make sense of the chaos swallowing my life. Just yesterday, Cookie and I were arguing about me talking to Jarrod alone. Now she's delivered him into my care. I'm glad for the result but am thoroughly pissed that it's taken a scandal to accomplish what *never* could've been achieved through the lousy system.

I glance at the dash clock. In a little while, I'm going to have to grab Jarrod by the nose and make him understand that his world has changed forever. That's what becoming a father means. Priorities shift from self to offspring. Life becomes more precious with the realization that it is truly fragile. Sacrifice stops being an abstract concept and becomes a daily reality. Responsibility stops being just a good idea and becomes an imperative. The wise words of elders are finally understood. And there's no more doubt that everyone's on borrowed time.

I could use a tender, loving hug right now. If Marcy were here, I'd go to her, release my fears, frustrations, and anxieties, then take refuge in her arms. It would be a sensual but *not* sexual moment. She'd hold me tight, rocking from side to side until my confidence returned and my will to fight was renewed. Then I'd rise and go do what I had to do, being stronger than a titan and certain to conquer the problems afflicting me. That's the way it was with us. I miss those times. I miss that Marcy.

I especially miss the man I was before my divorce detour. The man who knew where he was going, how he'd get there, and wasn't afraid of making the journey. But enough of this mawkish hindsight fixating. Jarrod's plane will be here soon and I need to focus on him. I don't know what I'm going to say, but somehow, someway, I'll have to prepare him for the barbarians that'll soon be crashing at his gate.

I already know that when I get to Cleveland-Hopkins I'm going straight to the observation deck. It's what I did years before when Mom and Dad were killed by the hurricane that swept through Alabama when they were visiting relatives. That was a bad time. Weeks slipped by in a blur until one night I found myself cruising along the turnpike, going east and west, back and forth, over and over, until I came within earshot of jet engines filling the sky.

I still don't know why I was drawn toward them. Maybe it was the idea that those engines were rocketing people away, from their past and their pain. They were going someplace where they could forget and start over. As my eyes followed those metallic Valkyries into the starlit sky, I drew away from God. I needed to nurture my anger against Him for killing my parents. But I didn't completely reject Him. Out of respect for the love they'd had for Him and the lives they'd lived serving Him, I moved to the periphery of God's kingdom. I wasn't certain how long I'd stay but knew I'd someday leave for good if He couldn't demonstrate more than a power to inflict loss.

Danielle swung in the opposite direction. She went from being a wild party girl and dived off a cliff of guilt into the Bible. She convinced herself that Mom and Dad had paid the price for her heathen ways, battering herself with Old Testament Scriptures where God's justice had been swift and indiscriminate against the generation deserving the celestial hit.

While Danielle sank into the Bible, I worked out my anxieties on the Cleveland-Hopkins observation deck, mostly alone, sometimes with Nash. It's where I came to terms with Cookie's divorcing me, let the wind dry my tears when I missed Jarrod, will bury my frustration toward Marcy, and will find a way to resolve Jarrod's mess.

I take the airport exit, slow down as I approach a yellow-turning-red light, and look in the direction of roaring jet engines. A plane rises up from behind the airport, angling higher and higher into the dark purple sky. Part of me wants to be on it, zooming off to someplace where the hardest decision I'll have to make is between Michelob and Bud Light. Someplace where saying, "I love you," isn't interpreted as an invitation to wreak havoc. Someplace where my dear son will call for reasons other than money and . . . a horn blasts from behind. I step on the gas and shoot through the green light, forced by an irate driver to stop fantasizing and move forward into my grim reality.

20

I CHECK THE TIME, THEN SCAN THE HORIZON. THE
aerial activity has slowed considerably, but off in the distance I see landing
lights, descending in a steady, smooth glide. I'll bet that's Jarrod's flight.
He's probably sitting among his friends, tickling their funny bones with
his quick wit while soaking up the attention of female eyes, drinking in
his handsome features.

At five feet, ten inches, Jarrod's almost looking me in the eye, his 185
pounds distributed in a well-developed, sharply defined network of muscles across a frame he employed with silk agility when he won last year's
county wrestling championship. The facial peach fuzz I used to kid him
about is now real hair, requiring a real shaving regimen, sometimes pro-
ducing real problems like the shaving bumps that often plague black men.

Sometimes when he moves a certain way, tilts his head at a certain angle, or talks in a certain tone, I'll flash back to the shrimp who struggled
to throw me a football. I'll recall the amazement that filled his eyes the
first time we went to the Cleveland Zoo. I'll chuckle at the time his pa-
jama bottoms fell off his butt when he dashed to get his gifts from beneath our Christmas tree. I'll recall his utter surprise when the fish he
almost pulled from Lake Erie yanked his rod from his hands and dragged
it into murky oblivion.

But then, there are other times, like when he's brooding or in a foul
mood and I'll wonder, Is it because I haven't been there? Is he struggling
with that Oedipus thing, a man-child loving his mother who's given herself to others? Is he angry about my involvement with other women, di-
minishing a secret hope that Cookie and I will reunite?

I've vacillated on whether or not to address such things with Jarrod.
We've always had open and honest communications, so it wouldn't have
been a problem. But I've always let him lead us into those areas. That way,
rather than forcing the burdens of his parents onto his shoulders, he could
choose his own time for carrying the load. So I've stuck to the standard

speeches about grades, guns, shoplifting, drugs, and sex. Given his behavior concerning the last, I have little confidence that he's adhered faithfully to my advice about the others.

The descending plane lands with the lumbering beauty of a winged prehistoric behemoth. The night is shredded by thrust reversers howling into action, then whining down into a steady hum as the plane taxis to the jet way. It rolls past floodlights, illuminating its blue-and-white tail, painted with the Venture Airlines logo. I wipe my eyes dry and go to meet the shrimp who once struggled to handle a football and tonight will have to begin handling manhood.

Holly Sheridan is the first ski club member I see entering the passenger pickup area. She's a smart, sweet girl from a two-parent home, the star of her debate team, with aspirations of being valedictorian and attending Spellman to major in German and international law. Time has turned her into a lovely young woman, even though her beauty's currently submerged beneath stylish glasses, a juvenile ponytail, an Ohio State sweatshirt, and sneakers tied with multicolored shoestrings.

Holly's had a crush on Jarrod since middle school, which, much to my disappointment, has escaped his cartoon-watching, video-game-preoccupied mind. Even though he's mostly treated her like a cheap wall painting, I still entertain hopes of their becoming high school sweethearts, getting married after college, and building a family. It'll help redeem the mess Cookie and I have made of things. But Jarrod's proven that he's truly Cookie's son, sidelining Holly for glitzy airheaded, hip-throwing troublemakers. When Holly's outer shell matches her inner glory, he'll have plenty of time to remember how he blew his chance, just like I did with Laura in the summer of '80.

We met during Kent State's Freshman Orientation. I adored the shy uncut diamond who didn't mind being friends but made it clear she was in college for academics, not romance. As the youngest of her Cleveland steelworker father's eight children, none of whom had gone to college, some of whom hadn't finished high school, Laura was his last best hope for seeing one of his kids liberate themselves from the certainty of a drudgery-filled future.

She mesmerized me not just because of her potent intellect but for the loving, respectful way she spoke of and to her father. Standing by her at a pay phone one day, I heard Laura say, "Daddy, all I am or will ever be is because of you."

I almost passed out. It was such a refreshing departure from the mothers of my friends or my girlfriends who routinely spoke of their husbands and fathers with liberal sprinklings of "That no-good nigger!" and "He's a worthless fool!" Even Danielle, who had no cause to mimic such talk, sometimes joined in the mass trashing, as if babbling such slanders were a fashion trend.

I would've loved Laura completely, but her focused dedication frustrated my sinister carnal motivations, suddenly freed from parental oversight. Then I met Cookie, who was as interested in me as Laura was in fulfilling her father's dream. Cookie also wasn't bashful about giving up the booty. Her academic program included landing a "man," and since I talked a good game about one day going into politics, being president of a university, and raking in cash off the lecture circuit, she judged me a good investment risk and we got married.

Holly smiles and waves excitedly when she spots me through the crisscrossing human traffic. She weaves her way through, stopping and starting like a squirrel crossing an interstate.

"Hi, Dr. Collins," she says as we give each other a brief hug.

"Hey, Holly. How's my favorite debutante?"

Holly blushes. "Fine. It's good to see you."

"You too. Did you have fun?"

"It was great! You should've come along as a chaperone. Do you ski?"

"Not since I nearly broke my neck learning how."

Holly bites her lower lip and allows a nervous chuckle. More arrivals stream into the main terminal, the next wave followed by loud, raucous laughter. A young woman emerges, dragging a lumpy carry-on, and Holly rushes to help her.

"Bye, Dr. Collins!" she calls through the throng.

Another burst of laughter from the crowd draws my attention and I see him. Jarrod's surrounded by an entourage of five or six students, his arm wrapped around a young woman whose ample offerings are covered by just enough cloth to keep her from getting arrested.

"Finish telling us, Jarrod!" shouts some guy in the back, his head weighed down by rings hanging along the outer rims of his ears.

"Naw," Jarrod says. "How do I know you guys won't squeal?"

"C'mon, baby. Tell us," the near-naked girl urges, stroking Jarrod's cheek with a hand covered with so much jewelry, lifting it probably qualifies as a biceps workout.

Jarrod looks into her slitted bedroom eyes and raises a lusty eyebrow. "Okay, Reesie, just for you."

Then they kiss, their mouths opening wide enough to swallow each other's heads. It's time to put a stop to this! It's bad enough that Jarrod's been off skiing the slopes like one of the rich and famous, leaving the girl he impregnated alone to manage *his* mess. But what's really infuriating is the apparent totality of his ignorance and indifference, carrying himself like a media darling before his disciples. And the arrogance of it all!

Bell Cuppersmith's being pregnant means that he wasn't using any protection. He probably gave her some ancient lame excuse about it not feeling the same, blah, blah, convincing her to let him have his way just before plunging himself into ruining his and her futures. Then he heaved himself into a cheap orgasm, sating *his* desire, rolled off, and called it a day. And after a lifetime of exposure to Cookie's crowd with their army of minions whose sole purpose is to cover up mistakes, it probably never struck him that developments would demand his accountability!

I walk straight to the center of this teen gathering and give his shoulder a hard tap. He looks up with angry eyes.

"Who the . . ."

He swallows the "f" forming on lips when he sees me and says, "Dad!"

"Hello, Son."

"I wasn't expecting *you*. Where's Mom?"

I'm happy to see you too, Son, I say to myself. And yes, I've missed you. And my gosh, you're looking good. I'm so proud of the way you're turning out, no matter what troubles we're going to face. And I want you to know that I'll do whatever it takes to help you make it through. You're my son and I love you and will be there for you.

"Your mother's away on business," I say, forcing a smile. "So I guess that means you're stuck with me."

Jarrod looks around nervously at his questioning admirers who're probably wondering how he'll restore his dimmed glory. Then he smiles, just the way Cookie does when she's about to shish kebob me with a zinger.

"Yo! Listen up, y'all. This be my pops! He's one'a them eggheads over at Erie U."

It's not that I haven't heard Jarrod talking like this, but even so, the sound of him mangling the English language makes me cringe. It's reminiscent of LaThomas Patterson. I can't help wondering if he, like Jarrod, is actually in possession of the intellectual tools for superior academic performance but simply chooses to communicate like an imbecile.

Jarrod's crew bursts into the exaggerated laughter of people who haven't developed the sophistication to not expend so much energy on such lame humor.

"Jarrod, c'mon, Son. We've got things to do."

"Hold up, Pops," he answers. "Lemme say bye to my homeys."

I look around the gathering. "Okay. But why don't you kids move off to the side so we're not in the way of these other deplaning passengers."

"Kids!" blurts a dark, round rebel. "Who's he callin' a kid?"

There are other murmured protests, but we meander out of the way, much to the relief of the acne-battered white security guard who's been shooting us nasty glances.

"Jarrod, are you gonna tell us or not?" asks a gum-popping girl who must've applied her makeup with a mop.

"All right, all right," Jarrod chuckles. "I'll tell y'all."

They gather in close and get quiet. Jarrod scans each face, making sure he has their complete attention. "Okay," he begins. "I put some of the chemicals in her chair."

A roar of laughter erupts. "No wonder Ms. Dolson was walking around with her fat butt hanging out," crows a narrow-faced cackler.

"I'll bet that's the last time she embarrasses you in front of class," another chortles.

"My baby don't take *no* stuff!" Reesie declares, stroking Jarrod's cheek.

"Jarrod, we really need to get going," I say. "We have a lot to . . ."

"Okay!" he snaps.

My nostrils flare, but I stay quiet, remembering that for teens image is everything and that humiliation, especially by a parent, is a fate surpassing death. Jarrod bids his buddies farewell, saving the last for Reesie. But rather than telling her bye, he takes her hand, glowers at me, and starts for baggage claim.

"Ah, excuse me," I say, taking several long strides to catch up. "Is there something I need to know?"

"Naw, Pops. It's under control."

"Jarrod, don't call me Pops. And what're you talking about?"

He huffs and faces me. "Reesie's spending the night with me. I already asked Moms and she said it was okay."

"Look at that face," Reesie snickers.

And I can just imagine how my face must look, mouth gaping and eyes bulging with stun. I can't believe Cookie agreed to this! We've argued before about this kind of permissiveness, most of the time with me repeating the cautions of elders who warned that black girls were usually better prepared for life since mothers routinely "loved their sons but raised their daughters."

Cookie's permissiveness has always been irritating, but this amounts to parental abdication. I've constantly tried to get her to understand that Jarrod hasn't been oblivious to the pantie-chasing jerks she's been inviting into their space. I've also told her that just because those jerks were driving Mercedes, Porsches, and Beamers didn't mean they weren't lowlifes. The argument was always the same.

"Darius, you can't tell me who to date!" she'd say.

"Cookie, I don't care who you date. But if it's someone who's negatively affecting Jarrod, I'm taking you to task."

"Suit yourself! I'm not changing!"

"I'm not asking you to. Just so long as you understand that whenever I suspect something rotten in Jarrod's environment, I'm going to come crashing down on you like a truckload of bricks!"

I've gotten used to Cookie's telling me to "shove it!" since my protests obstruct her mission to be swept off her feet by some Lexus-driving Lancelot. But this business of girls spending the night with Jarrod, that's new. And of course he wouldn't have mentioned it to me, knowing I'd react just as I'm about to.

"Jarrod, you're staying with me tonight!"

The smirk on Reesie's face is snatched off like a bad stage act. She jams her hands down onto her hips, narrows her eyes, and faces Jarrod.

"Tell me this is a joke," she demands, stepping toward him.

Jarrod steps back, glares at me, then looks at Reesie. "C'mon, girl. Don't even think about breakin' bad. I told you I had it hooked up."

"You've been hooked all right," I say. "And you're being reeled in as we speak."

Reesie looks at me quizzically, then dismisses me with a blink. "Jarrod, am I spending the night or not?"

"No! You're not!" I answer, cutting Jarrod off as he opens his mouth.

"Look, man," he says, puffing up. "This ain't funny. Moms said I could . . ."

"You'd better watch yourself, *boy*," I say evenly. "Before Reesie sees 'Pops' squash your cool."

"Your pops is a jerk," Reesie says, curling her upper lip.

I smile at her. "Thanks. That means I'm doing my job."

Jarrod waves me off and grabs Reesie's hand. "C'mon! I'ma call Moms on her cellular. She'll take care of 'em."

In a clear, calm voice, I say, "We need to talk about Bell Cuppersmith."

Jarrod freezes like he's looked on the face of Medusa. Reesie snatches her hand from his and socks him in the gut. Luckily, he's in good-enough shape to withstand the punch.

"Ain't she that white *ho* you was messin' with?" Reesie demands.

Seeing Jarrod struggle for words, I can see why black women get such a kick out of watching the brothers babble.

"Ah, she, she, I mean, that's over with, girl! Why're you trippin'?"

Jarrod glances at me, his expression filled with alarm and his eyes pleading for *help*!

"Well, if it's over with, why's your pops wanna talk about her?" Reesie persists.

Jarrod swallows, rolls his eyes and forces a laugh. "Reesie, I told you it ain't nothin'. Bell probably told some lie to jack me up after we had that fallin'-out. It ain't no thang."

Jarrod looks at me for confirmation, but I stay silent. Reesie follows his gaze toward me, staring straight into my eyes. He's way out of his league with this girl, no, woman! She may be only a teenager, but she already possesses most of the radars, intuition, lie detectors, cheater alarms, and tactical brilliance that'll help her outthink, outtalk, and outsmart her male counterparts. Her stare sharpens, searching my face for the slightest twitch. After a few moments, she breaks off her scan and recaptures Jarrod with her inquiring eyes, still smoldering with suspicion.

"Okay, Jarrod. But don't play me. You know how jealous I get."

Jarrod sighs and takes Reesie's hand. "Quit trippin', girl. You're the only one I want."

I step off and head toward baggage claim. "C'mon, Jarrod. There's much to do."

He follows quickly, this time without protest. We get their luggage and haul it to the door, where I hail a cab. Jarrod eases up behind me and talks low.

"What're you doing now?"

"Getting Reesie a cab."

"But . . ."

"I might've given her a ride home. But everything I've seen since you got off the plane tells me there's not a moment to spare."

"Not a moment to spare about what?"

I look hard into Jarrod's eyes, the eyes of the shrimp who will have to learn his lessons quick.

"Jarrod, go tell Reesie good night."

He slinks over to Reesie, bids her farewell, then stands quietly while she delivers a verbal vivisection. She jabs her finger in his chest, stomps her foot, and accents her words with jerky side-to-side head movements, like she's a spastic cobra.

A cab pulls up and she shoves Jarrod away when he tries to help her with her luggage. She gets in, slams the door, turns around, and flips up her middle finger at me when the cab rolls away.

21

JARROD STARES SULLENLY OUT HIS WINDOW AS WE
barrel down the interstate.

"How long have you been seeing Reesie?" I ask.

He keeps staring out his window, shifting his body so that he's turned
away from me.

"Jarrod, I'm talking to you. How long have you . . ."

"Four months!" he barks.

I take a deep breath to maintain my calm. I don't know where Jarrod's
gotten this nasty attitude, but I'm getting tired of it. My introducing him
to the realities of his new world will have to include a refresher course on
basic respect.

For the next few miles, we ride in silence, Jarrod leaning back and
closing his eyes while I piece together more of his playboy puzzle. Cookie's
commented that she thinks Bell is two months pregnant. Which means
that she and Jarrod did the wild thing during the time he's been with
Reesie. That also means he cheated on Reesie, which presents some ugly
scenarios for his health once the little vixen discovers his treachery. And
again, I'm struck by his towering arrogance. Bell must've felt like a snotty
rag once he finished with her and swaggered back to Reesie, giving her his
heart and attention while banishing Bell into hurt and solitude. He
probably never called her, spoke to her, checked on her, or even had a
flashing thought that something might've resulted from their mating.

In a cruel sparing kind of way, he's lucky it's only pregnancy and not
herpes, AIDS, or some other killer VD that'll suck the life from him. But
what am I thinking? He could still be infected. *He could be a carrier!*

The thought drills a flaming dagger into my chest. If it's true, it
would mean that Jarrod's been sexually active long enough to have committed biological suicide, condemned someone else to die, cut short the
life of his baby, and delivered a cruel blow to Reesie, whom he's probably
slept with. And it's anybody's guess as to how many others he's "shared"
himself with.

I glance at him, sitting there pretending to sleep, his body language communicating that His Majesty doesn't wish to be disturbed. I ought to slug the spoiled brat, throwing off vibes like some Wall Street tycoon who's been offended by an unruly chauffeur.

My cellular rings and I almost growl when I say, "Hello!" There's no immediate answer and I say, "Who's calling?" in a demanding tone.

"Ah . . . is this Darius Collins?"

The voice is female. It's soft, sexy, and close to hanging up, so I adjust my attitude. *Quick!*

"Yes. This is he."

"Oh," she says, relieved. "I thought I had the wrong number. This is Chloe Brown."

I almost swerve off the road. "Chloe! Hi! What a nice surprise."

"Are you sure? It sounded like you were in the middle of an argument."

"You might say that," I answer, forcing a chuckle. "I'm dueling with these clowns on the highway."

"That'll give you an attitude," she laughs. "Anyway, you crossed my mind, so I thought I'd call and say a quick hello."

I crossed her mind! This sounds promising. Very promising. I glance at Jarrod and choose my words to Chloe carefully. He looks to be sound asleep, but I still need to be careful. I haven't quite adjusted to having my son know that I'm consorting with women other than his mother.

"It's great hearing from you," I say. "We'll have to follow this up with a nice outing."

"I'd like that," Chloe answers, sounding sweet and excited.

"Maybe sometime in the next few days?"

"That's fine with me."

"Okay. Let's talk later and set it up."

"All right. Just let me know. My schedule's not too bad right now, but it changes pretty quick sometimes."

"Believe me," I laugh, "I understand."

"Well, Darius. I don't want your talking to me to distract you from the road."

"That's very thoughtful of you."

"Take it easy."

"You too. I'll call soon."

We hang up and I glance at Jarrod. His head is lolling all over the place with the car's movements, so he's actually asleep. Get your rest now,

Son. In a few short months you're going to join the rest of us tillers of soil, hewers of wood, and drawers of water in the rat race that the rats are winning.

I get off the interstate, head for the twenty-four-hour Farmer's Freshest megasupermarket, and park in its stadium-sized lot. Jarrod stirs, sits up, and rubs his eyes.

"Here we go again," he says, his voice full of disgust.

He's talking about my bad habit of last-minute grocery shopping on his weekend visits. It's not that I forget, but I hate grocery shopping! And being my son, Jarrod hates it too.

"C'mon," I say, getting out. "Let's see what they've got."

"That's okay. I'll wait here."

"No, Jarrod. I want you to come with me."

"Dad, it's a food store. I know what's there."

"Jarrod, this isn't a debate. Now, *get out!*"

He grumbles as I close my door. I stroll toward the entrance, checking behind every few steps as he plods along, his shoulders hunched and hands jammed deep in his pockets. I navigate my way to the appropriate aisle, turn down it, and march to the center.

It feels like we're walking through a well-supplied cave. There's hardly anyone here, except for the graveyard-shift stock clerks and maintenance crews. And it's oddly quiet, enough for us to hear the soft hum of a floor scrubber several aisles over.

Jarrod shambles up behind me and looks around. "This is all baby stuff. What do we need here?"

I walk up on him until we're inches apart. "Not *we*, Jarrod. You!"

"Huh?"

" 'Huh?' nothing!" I snap. "Take a good look around. This is your future."

"But . . ."

"Bell Cuppersmith's pregnant!"

Jarrod's jaw falls open as he staggers back into a shelf of diapers. "But, but she said she was on the pill," he mutters, his voice small and trembling.

My heart falls to the floor. Even if it had been a lie, I was hoping that Jarrod would've denied his connection. It would've been Bell's word against his, at least until blood and DNA testing proved otherwise. I could've fought Bell's mother with my own parental indignation, forcing the burden of proof onto her daughter just as she's forced it onto my son.

I could've returned to the fantasy where, aside from some steamy necking, Jarrod wasn't sexually active. But he's not denying anything. He's just stunned.

Jarrod looks at me with angry eyes. "I'm not the only one she's had!"

"So what!" I snap, struggling to keep my voice low. "Whether you're *the* one or one of hundreds, you were there. Which means *you* could be the father."

Jarrod slams his fist down onto the diaper shelf. "She said she was on the pill!"

Everything in me wants to comfort him and tell him it'll be all right and that we'll find a way out of this. But my inner self holds me back, like an anchor restraining a high-powered speedboat, churning the water into froth as it struggles to break free.

Jarrod needs this moment, this convergence of time, space, and reality to smack him into comprehending life's consistently unforgiving equation, which states that stupidity plus recklessness equals disaster. This is the moment when he steps into the light of understanding how results of actions demand actions of accountability. From here on he'll know that a pebble tossed into today's ocean can ripple into tomorrow's tidal wave.

He wipes his eyes and says, "That lying, stinking whore!"

I grab his collar and jerk him close till we're nose-to-nose. "She may be a lying, stinking whore, but you lay down with her. So what does that make you? Huh!"

"But we only did it once."

"Dammit, Jarrod!" I shout. I look around to make sure we're still alone, then whisper hoarsely, "All it takes is once!"

Looking into Jarrod's face, I see my own; young, inexperienced, and frightened. He should be frightened, because the accusers are out there. All of society's ready to condemn him as just another irresponsible black bastard, making more black bastards to suckle at the federal breast. It's been hard enough running the gauntlet of my own mistakes. I'd wanted so desperately for Jarrod to avoid similar ones. Life would've clobbered him with plenty-enough setbacks without his help. But it didn't have to be this one, not like this, not this way, not at this time!

I release Jarrod and shake my head. "Jarrod, this changes everything."

He looks down at his feet. "Dad, I'm sorry," he says, his tone finally devoid of hip-hop insolence. "I'm really and truly sorry."

I grip his shoulder and squeeze. "I know, Son. But it's too late for that."

His shoulders heave as he chokes down a sob. "It was only supposed to be a bet," he whimpers. "Just a lousy stinking bet."

"A bet?" I say. I start to ask him to explain what he means but choke on the question when I consider the myriad crazy things I did on the way to adulthood.

"Jarrod, are you saying that you screwed this girl to win a bet with your fathead friends?"

Tears stream down his cheeks as he looks into my eyes and nods. He can't hold the gaze and looks away. I know why he's averted his eyes. I can feel in my expression the profound anger and disappointment ripping my insides apart. I try to keep it from washing over my face, but this revelation from my son who *I know* has better sense is threatening to drown me in despair.

"What am I gonna do?" Jarrod mumbles.

I take a deep breath, clench my teeth, and speak my answer slowly. "You're going to be a man and do the right thing."

"But . . . but how? I don't even know . . ."

I don't have a clue. But rather than tell him that, I pull him in to me, and we hug.

22

IT'S WEDNESDAY. IT'S A FRESH NEW DAY AND ONE THAT I hope won't contain any of Tuesday's drama. But things are looking up. My son is with me. I'm running ahead of schedule. And since I don't have class until ten this morning, I've got time to meet Chloe for breakfast. Everything is near perfect, until the phone rings. I keep getting dressed while answering it.

"Hello?"

"Is Jarrod okay?" Cookie asks.

"He's fine."

"Let me talk with him."

I'd chastise Cookie for her lack of manners, but why bother? She lives in a world where problems are big enough to grab headlines and potent enough to threaten a big-city mayor. Me hassling her about not saying "Hello," would be like an ant shaking its fist at a stampeding elephant.

I call Jarrod, who's out in the living room. "Jarrod, pick up the phone. It's your mother."

I close my cracked bedroom door so Jarrod will have some privacy. But he must not want any, since he's talking loud enough for me to hear. And it's apparent that he's using the conversation with Cookie to take some cheap shots at me.

"How long do I have to stay here?" he asks. "This sofa bed is like a bag of rocks. He hurt Reesie's feelings. . . . Huh? What about Bell? It's been months since I even talked to her. I wouldn't make such a mistake. . . . Well, *he* doesn't believe me. He never believes me. Tell him to buy some decent food. Please can't I stay at our house? I feel like a sardine here. I can barely see anything on this little TV. . . . Okay," he sighs. "Just come home quick."

"Dad!" Jarrod calls. "Mom wants to talk to you."

"Just a second," I answer.

I take a few moments to compose myself and wipe my misting eyes.

Even though Jarrod's complaining was nothing more than the bellyaching of an overindulged brat, his words still hurt.

I pick up the phone and say, "Okay, Cookie. I'm here."

"Darius, I don't want you stressing Jarrod out about this Bell Cuppersmith business."

"Cookie, don't give me orders. I'm not your son."

"That's right. You're just an ex-husband who's making me wish that I'd left Jarrod with someone else."

"Good-bye, Cookie."

I've almost slammed the phone down when Cookie's voice blasts from the receiver, "Darius! Wait!"

"What do you want?" I growl.

"Darius, I'm sorry. I'm just worried about him. That's all."

"Well, I'm worried about him too. And just for the record, your leaving him with someone else would violate the joint custody provisions of our divorce decree. Something for which I'd gladly take you back to court."

"Darius, how can you be so petty with all that's happening right now?"

I roll my eyes and exhale an exasperated huff. "Cookie, say what you're going to say. I have to leave."

I can almost see her smiling with accomplishment. "Okay," she begins. "Before leaving I made a few phone calls to see what options were available. Trudy couldn't tell me anything right away, but . . ."

"Trudy!" I blurt. "The same Trudy who was your lawyer during our divorce?"

"Why . . . yes. She's competent, well connected, and has a track record of success."

"I'm well aware of her successes," I say, fuming. "I'm also aware that she hates men. Why would you entrust Jarrod's fate to her?"

"I just told you. She's competent . . ."

"Forget it, Cookie. Jarrod would find more objectivity from a skinhead than that estrogen storm trooper."

"Now listen, Darius. I can make this problem go away, but not if you're going to let your wounded pride be an obstacle."

"Pride has nothing to do with it. Common sense dictates that I not let you put my son into the hands of someone who'd like to add his balls to her collection."

Cookie snorts. "Darius! I don't have time for this. Now I want you . . ."

"I don't have time for this either. So good-bye."

"But . . ."

"I have to get Jarrod to school, Cookie."

"Okay. Okay. I'll call later when I get to Munich."

"Where are you now?"

"Amsterdam. Our connecting flight's been delayed."

"We'll be home this evening. Call then if you want."

"You're not going to cooperate, are you?"

"Not if it means going to Trudy."

She slams down the phone and I hang up.

I finish getting dressed, then grab my briefcase and keys. "Come on, Jarrod. Dropping you off will take me twenty minutes out of the way, but if we leave now I can still avoid the worst traffic."

He mumbles something probably not worth hearing, and I urge, prod, and coax him along like a Border collie nipping at the heels of a stubborn sheep. Moments later we pull out of the parking lot and are just about to pass the Rapid Shop when Jarrod snaps his fingers.

"Oops! I almost forgot. Can we stop here for a minute?"

"What's the matter? What do you need?"

"Ah, I've gotta get some paper."

"I've got paper in my briefcase. Take what you need."

Jarrod glances nervously ahead as we speed toward the Rapid Shop. "I, I, um, need to get a pack of vitamins too!"

"What?"

"It's Mom," Jarrod explains quickly. "She makes me take 'em every morning. And I, um, I forgot to ask if you had any and . . ."

"Say no more," I interrupt, glancing at my watch and slowing down. "And just so you'll know, I've got vitamins. Okay."

Jarrod nods and exhales relief. Cookie must have ridden him like a Montana mule to have produced this kind of anxiety over missing a daily dose of vitamins. But I can imagine the gauntlet he probably had to run before she finally shut her mouth, so I gladly pull over.

I park and Jarrod gets out. "Don't take too long," I say. "I can still beat the traffic."

He nods, gets out, and trots into the store. I pull out my cellular and dial Gina's home number. After two short rings her answering machine kicks in and I leave a message.

"Gina, this is Darius. I know you're gone but wanted to apologize for the other night. I don't know what got into me. I would never, ever want to do anything that made you unhappy. Take care of yourself and hurry back. You're sorely missed."

I hang up and wish for the umpteenth time that Gina wasn't hooked on Bruce Manchester IV. She possesses so much of what I'm looking for in a companion, and I suspect strongly that we could work. But maybe it's just wishful thinking. We get along great as friends and that would surely change once we became something more, and I don't want to lose Gina to a situation suddenly polluted by emotion.

I turn on the radio and laugh along as Tom Joyner, Miz Dupree, and crazy Jay whoop it up on the Tom Joyner morning show. Minutes later Jarrod slouches out of the store, carrying a plastic bag and looking puzzled and troubled.

He gets in and I say, "Got what you need?"

He shrugs. In teen language, that translates into a yes, so I start the car and get back on the road. And then, out of nowhere, Jarrod says, "Why's the paper making it sound like something shady is going on between Mom and the mayor?"

"Where did you read that?" I ask.

"At the Rapid Shop. It's all over the front page of the Cleveland paper."

The one time that I hoped Jarrod wouldn't care about what's happening outside his narrow, self-focused world of rap music, he said-she said pseudolove, and overpriced sneakers, he decides to pay attention to the headlines.

I take a deep breath and hope my explanation comes out right. "Jarrod, the paper's reporting an allegation. And that's nothing more than . . ."

"I know what it is, Dad. It still doesn't explain why they're doing it."

"It's complicated, Son. From what I can gather, Councilman Fields is discrediting your mother to ruin her chances in next year's election."

Jarrod looks truly puzzled and hurt. "But . . . she said that Uncle Milton was stepping aside and would help her run."

"Uncle Milton?" I cough. "Since when is he 'Uncle Milton'?"

"Um, well, it's just a play name I was using when he and Mom were, ah, close."

Well, isn't this a rip! All this time I've been under the impression that Cookie and Milton Fields were bitter opponents. The real humiliation is learning of their onetime closeness from *my son*. It's a miracle that some reporter hasn't sniffed out the connection between Cookie and Fields. And it's proof of just how slippery Cookie can be. I'm no expert on city government, but it's apparent that my ex-wife has been getting as much accomplished between the sheets as she has at conference tables.

I clear my throat and continue. "Well, Jarrod. Your mother and 'Uncle Milton' apparently had a difference of opinion and he's out for her political blood."

Jarrod shakes his head. "That's not right."

"What's not right?"

"For him to trash her like that, just because they're not agreeing."

I nod, wondering myself why "Uncle Milton" wants Cookie's scalp. Fields is the most powerful member of the city council and doesn't have to resort to such trench warfare. Most opponents give him a wide berth, not because of what he's done to them but based on what he *could* do. For him to come out swinging like this, Cookie, the mayor, or somebody close must've really pissed Fields off.

"I just don't get it," Jarrod says. "If Mom's not wrong, why'd she run?"

"Jarrod, have you ever known your mother to run from anything?"

"No."

I prefer an answer of, "No, sir," but we're talking with civility, so I let it pass. "Okay, then," I say. "No matter how it looks, I doubt that she's running. Somebody in the press has simply decided to sell a few more papers by making it look like your mother's business trip is somehow connected with the mayor's scandal."

Jarrod ponders for a moment until I ask, "What're you thinking?"

"I'm just trying to make it fit."

"Make what fit?"

"Some things you told me."

"What? When?"

"I don't remember when. But I do remember what."

"Go ahead."

"Well, you always said that if you're not doing anything wrong, there's no need to run."

"Jarrod, I told you. Your mother's not . . ."

"And you said that for black people especially, it wasn't good enough just to *be* innocent. We have to *look* innocent."

"That's right, Jarrod," I sigh. "I said that."

"The paper makes it look like Mom's running."

"Touché, Jarrod. But just remember, it only looks that way. We have a Constitution that guarantees citizens the right to a fair trial in a court of law, not the papers."

"But what about slavery?"

"Huh?"

"You've always said that even though the Constitution's a great document, it's an imperfect document because it didn't outlaw slavery until after the Civil War."

I stare at Jarrod in amazement. I'm ecstatic that he's remembered so much of what I've said but befuddled by what's made him retain these particular lessons. I'm also irritated that he failed to employ his good memory when it came to having sex.

I make a sharp turn and the contents of Jarrod's bag fall out. There's three chocolate bars and some lip balm but no vitamins. He scrambles to stuff them in the bag, but it's too late.

"What happened to the vitamins?" I ask. "And aren't you allergic to chocolate?"

A weak nervous laugh escapes from Jarrod's lips. "I didn't have enough money for the vitamins and my lips were dry," he lamely explains.

"Well, Jarrod. If you hadn't bought the candy and lip balm, you might've had enough for the vitamins. What's going on?"

He turns up the radio and mumbles along with the lurid lyrics of some guy singing about "ba-ba-bumpin' it *all* night long!" That's the *last* thing Jarrod needs to be listening to, so I cut the radio off.

"Jarrod! The candy. What's the deal?"

He grimaces. "It's for Reesie."

"Reesie!"

"Yeah. She called and asked me to bring her some."

"You gave her the number to my apartment?"

"Yeah. What's the problem?"

His superior, condescending tone makes me want to relocate his lips to the far side of his head.

"The problem is that it's *my* home and you need to let me know when you're giving out my number. Especially to people like her!"

"What do you mean, 'people like her'?"

"Never mind," I deflect. "You lied to me, didn't you?"

"About what?"

"About needing vitamins."

"No. Mom really gets on my case if . . ."

"I'm sure she does. So I'm wondering why you chose chocolate for Reesie over fulfilling your mother's wishes."

Jarrod looks ahead in silence, taking the fifth rather than incriminating himself.

"That girl is trouble," I say.

His head snaps toward me. "How can you say that? You don't even know her!"

"I know what I saw at the airport. And I'm telling you, that mean little heifer is more trouble than she's worth."

"She was just disappointed that we couldn't be together."

I shake my head. Jarrod's statement adds emphatic proof that he's oblivious of the seriousness of his predicament. So I make the announcement. "I've enrolled you in a program called Warrior Passages."

"A program called what?"

"Warrior Passages. It's designed to help black male youths transition into manhood."

"Isn't that handled by growing up?"

"Jarrod, becoming a man involves more than growing into the body of one. There are things you have to learn about yourself, people, life, and love."

Jarrod glowers and slouches down in his seat. "I already know about that stuff."

"I disagree. And don't get me wrong. I'm not saying that you haven't or can't learn on your own, but that's doing it the hard way. This program will . . ."

"Dad, I'm not some ignorant kid. In case you haven't noticed, I'm the man of the house now."

"No, Jarrod! You're the male *in* the house. There's a difference."

His glower deepens into a scowl. "I don't wanna go."

"Did you hear me ask for your permission?"

"How're you gonna make me?"

"That's the point, isn't it? The mere fact that I *can* make you is assurance that you *will*."

He stares angrily out his window. "You could've at least asked how I felt about it."

"The same way you asked how I felt about you giving out my home number?"

I take a deep breath and soften my voice. "Jarrod, just trust me on this one, okay? Do you honestly think I'd sign you up for something that . . ."

"This isn't fair!" he says, getting loud. "I don't need someone giving me boring lectures on sex and . . ."

"Boring lectures on sex are exactly what you need!" I blast. "Especially the part about getting someone pregnant and accepting responsibility."

"I didn't do it!" Jarrod retorts. "Why won't you believe me?"

"Why should I? After that vitamin flimflamming you just pulled, how do you figure you're deserving of my blind trust?"

I pull up in front of Vesey High and see a sight that makes my stomach lurch. Reesie's standing outside with a group of hard-looking thugettes, all of them wearing the same hairstyle and black leather jackets.

Jarrod gets out, holding his door open when I call him. "Jarrod!"

He looks back at me, his lips jutting out in a prominent pout and eyes narrowed in anger. It's about as close to a formal response as I'm going to get, so I continue.

"Don't forget about our meeting with Bell and her mother this afternoon."

Jarrod glances over at Reesie, tapping her foot impatiently. He looks back at me and nods slightly, the smile he gave Reesie melting from his face. He closes the door and I watch as Reesie shoves her books into Jarrod's chest, links elbows with him, and drags him inside.

23

THERE ARE TWO GOOD REASONS FOR ME STROLLING into the history department with a glide in my stride and a whistle on my lips. First, even though my breakfast meeting at Bob Evans with Chloe was cut short, it was fantastic. And second, my students just demonstrated what happens when the right mix of energy, dedication, and intellectual prowess boils to the surface.

"You're in a good mood," Diane, the departmental secretary, smilingly observes.

I lean against the bookcase by her desk. "You should've seen the students in my ten o'clock Civil War and Reconstruction class. They were superb."

"Was this the day of their debate?"

I nod. "And they performed wonderfully. It was lively and dynamic, people were informed, and the students supported their points with robust, factually-based arguments."

"It sounds wonderful," she says, handing me a small stack of message slips.

"What's all this?" I ask.

Diane cuts her eyes away and focuses on her computer screen. "They're all from the same person. They said they intend to keep calling until you talk to them."

I don't need to ask if the "they" is Marcy. I tear the stack of messages in half and drop them in the trash. "Thanks, Diane," I say.

She nods and starts typing. I head for my office, my steps heavier and the whistle gone from my lips. Diane only gets my messages if my voice mailbox is full and automatically switches over to the departmental line. I've already cleared my line twice of Marcy's messages and it's full again. I just might have to talk to her after all.

Either way, Marcy's attempt to intrude upon my life can't displace my good feelings about Chloe. We had a wonderful time at breakfast, laughing and talking, and getting a real strong vibe that we've probably got a lot in common.

She stayed long enough to drink a glass of juice and finish off her toast before rushing off to take care of business. I couldn't stop gazing into her big soft brown eyes and had to apologize several times when she blushed and chided me for staring. She's definitely beautiful, but what's really attractive about her is that she's hardworking and smart! She graduated magna cum laude from Case Western Reserve University here in Cleveland, finished in the top fifth of her MBA class at Georgetown, and even though her title is vice president of field operations, she's working as a sales rep at her father's company, Motherland Hair Care & Beauty Supply.

"That's why I was at Blake's shop the other day," she said. "Daddy says that if I'm going to someday run the business, I've got to learn all sides of it."

Her attitude, class, and work ethic were a refreshing departure from that agonizing encounter with Vondelle. I'll have to indulge in comparisons later. Two students are standing outside my office and I shift back into professor mode.

One of the students is Garland Poole, aka Mubarak Kwanju, as he's recently begun calling himself. He's chairman of the Middle Passage Club and has been doing a wonderful job generating interest and transforming it into an organization of some considerable influence.

His face breaks into a full-toothed smile when he sees me. "There he is!" he says, pointing at me. "The keeper of historical truth."

I laugh and wave him off. "Keep talking, Gar, er, Mubarak. Flattery will get you everywhere."

I stifle a groan when I see his companion and co-chair, Julie Cranshaw. "Hello, Julie," I say.

She acknowledges me with a cool nod. Julie's politically to the left of Karl Marx and a cause-a-holic. The semester she took my American Military History course, she tried repeatedly to use it as a forum to lambaste the sinister plot of the U.S. government, which since Plymouth Rock had conspired to impoverish the world.

That continued until the day I pointed out that the U.S. government hadn't been in existence when the Pilgrims landed at Plymouth. Then I asked her to explain why, if America was so corrupt, decadent, and repulsive, so many people were risking life and limb to get here. Her answer that it was part of a big secret plan drew so much laughter and derision that she promptly dropped the class.

Garland and Julie step aside so I can unlock my office door. "What can I do for you two?" I ask, going inside.

Julie sits down in the chair farthest from my desk while Garland stares at my posters of Angela Davis, Nelson Mandela, Sojourner Truth, Eldridge Cleaver, and an artist's rendition of Nat Turner. He turns his attention to the bust of Frederick Douglass sitting on a chest-high Doric statue stand in the corner and blows out a slow, soft whistle.

"Professor Collins, this is tight!" he says. "You've definitely got your history groove on."

"From what I hear, so do you."

"C'mon, Mubarak," Julie says, her tone impatient. "This was your idea, so go ahead."

Garland sits down in the chair next to my bookcase and smiles. "Professor, we've got a problem."

I straighten up and cross my arms over my chest. "I'm listening."

"I guess you've heard about the MPC inviting Osmani el Bornu to speak at the annual forum."

I nod. "It's been brought to my attention."

"Well, then you've also probably heard that not everyone is happy with our choice."

"That's putting it mildly, but yes, I'd heard as much."

"What do you mean, 'putting it mildly'?" Julie attacks. "We've got the right to choose whomever we want!"

Garland takes Julie's hand and gives it a gentle squeeze. "Hold on, Julie. Professor Collins knows all about the Constitution and rights," he says, glancing at me. "He won't let anything shaky go down."

"Hmph!" Julie grunts, rolling her eyes.

"Anyway, Professor," Garland continues, "we haven't been able to get in touch with Dr. Roman, not even by e-mail, and . . ."

"As I recall," I say, interrupting, "Dr. Roman's first going to an archaeological dig in the Nicaraguan highlands before her conference starts."

"Mubarak, this is a waste of time," Julie sneers. "Dr. Roman said she'd be back in three days, four at the most. We can manage till then."

A deep shadow of irritation passes over Garland's face. "Do you really want to sit around for three or four days doing nothing while the Future Americans League gets the administration in their back pocket?"

Julie doesn't answer and Garland turns back to me. "Like I was saying, Professor Collins, we couldn't contact Dr. Roman, so we decided to come see you."

"Come see me about what?"

"Getting faculty support. We've heard the administration's gonna try and stop brother el Bornu from coming."

I shake my head. "I doubt that, Gar, I mean, Mubarak. That would put them in a real bind, especially after that fiasco with Marshall Prescott."

Garland smiles, extends his hand, palm up, and we slap five. "My man, Pro-fes-sor Col-*lins*! I knew we could count on you."

"Now hold on, Mu . . ."

"You see, Dr. Roman said something like this might happen. So she told us that if there was any trouble, you'd be a good person to contact."

I clench my teeth. "Dr. Roman never informed me of this."

Garland shrugs. "All I know is that when she mentioned your name, almost everyone at the MPC meeting was relieved."

"Will you help us?" Julie queries, asking like I'd better answer correctly.

I force a laugh to try to ease the mounting tension. "Whoa, slow down, young people. This issue's got some explosive potential and needs to be handled with care."

Garland smiles. "That's why you're our man, Professor. You've got the inside track, the knowledge, the moves, and the authority. When we talk, they'll hear. But when *you* talk, they'll listen."

"But . . ."

"And we know you're not afraid to take 'em on. Just like when you and Dr. Roman argued them into a box when they gave those sheetless Klansmen from the Future Americans League a student senate seat, but were gonna deny us."

"That's true, but . . ."

"And Dr. Roman said that it was you who wrote the grant that got us our computers and office equipment, so we know you support what we're doing."

I quickly interrupt before Garland can cut me off. "What I support is the research you're doing that'll help quantify and document the horrific human costs of the transatlantic slave trade."

"Can we *please* get to the issue of Osmani el Bornu?" Julie asks.

The chill in Garland's eyes threatens to freeze over his warm smile. "C'mon, Julie. Give the professor a break. He'll help us, but like he says, we've got to be careful."

For a moment, I envision Garland on a future campaign trail, shaking hands, kissing babies, and making promises he can't keep. But for right now, I need to stop his campaign to draft me.

"Mubarak, listen to me," I say, taking a deep breath. "I've already talked with Dr. Roman and expressed my misgivings about the el Bornu invitation."

Garland's smile fades. "Misgivings? What misgivings?"

Julie sits up tall in her chair and sneers. "I told you," she says.

Garland shoots her an admonishing glance, then looks at me. "Professor, what're your concerns?"

I lean forward, placing my elbows on my knees and interlacing my fingers. "Mubarak, Osmani el Bornu's an anti-Semite."

Garland stares at me blankly, as if waiting for me to make my point. I screw up my courage and continue. "Given his repugnant views, I'm worried that the MPC's inviting him to speak will do more harm than good."

Garland's eyes harden into almonds of ice. "Professor, no offense, but it sounds like you're working for the opposition."

"No offense taken. But speaking of the opposition, try to imagine the field day they're going to have with this. They'll be overjoyed to point out that the blacks who are constantly moaning about racism invited a bigot to keynote their annual headliner."

"Professor, I hear what you're saying. And I'll admit that el Bornu hasn't always been kind to our Jewish brothers, but that doesn't mean he has nothing to contribute."

"The only contributions he's interested in are the checks people write him."

"This is pointless!" Julie spits, standing quickly.

"Hold on, Julie," Garland urges. "We need to hear the professor out."

"What more do you need?" she asks, exasperated. "He's not going to help us."

"I didn't say that," I interject.

"So then . . . will you?" Garland asks.

"What I'd like to do is help you find another speaker."

"What if we don't want another one?" Julie demands. "We chose Osmani el Bornu for the message he brings."

"And what message is that?" I challenge her.

"He doesn't take any mess! And he believes in standing up for the people!"

"Julie, believing in standing up for the people and *doing* it are two different things."

Good cop Garland motions for Julie to take her seat. She sits in a huff and grinds her teeth. He looks at me and smiles so smoothly, it's like oil sliding onto his face.

"Now, c'mon, Professor," he says. "I can see that you feel kind of strong about the brother, but he's really not saying anything different from our other so-called leaders."

"Mubarak, there's an old church saying that asserts even the devil believes in God."

"Meaning?"

" 'Meaning' that just because some of el Bornu's beliefs and ideas may accidentally intersect with ours doesn't mean we should adopt or be associated with his agenda."

"You're not going to help us, are you?" he asks, dropping all pretenses of diplomacy.

"On the contrary. I'm going to help you find a speaker who'll be just as 'in your face!' about injustice, racism, and inequality but will deliver the message without trashing our Jewish brothers who've also suffered too long, too often."

"Is that your last word on the matter?"

"That depends upon you, Mubarak. I'm willing to help. But I won't endorse, nor will I assist, an effort that'll tear people apart when our history has been focused on bringing people together."

"Our history's been focused on the struggle for freedom!" Julie says.

I level my gaze at her. "I couldn't agree more. That includes the freedom to say *no*!"

She gets up and stomps out of my office. Garland stands slowly, saunters to the doorway, and looks at me, shaking his head in pity.

"LaThomas Patterson said you were an Uncle Tom. I didn't want to believe him. But he was right. He was stone-cold right."

He glares at me with profound contempt, shakes his head, and leaves.

24

I'VE CUT SHORT MY LAST CLASS SO I CAN PICK UP
Jarrod after school and go meet with Bernice Cuppersmith. I gather up
my materials, stuff my briefcase, and head out to the parking lot. Avi Silberberg sees me on the way out and hurries to catch up.

"Darius!" he calls, trotting over.

I slow my pace but not much.

Avi extends his hand as he approaches. "Thanks," he says.

I take hold of his hand and ask, "For what?"

His face reddens. "For what you did during your MPC encounter."

I start to pull my hand from his. "Were you eavesdropping?"

Avi tightens his grip and shakes my hand anyway. "C'mon, Darius.
It's a small campus. Word travels fast." He smiles and gives me a soft
punch to the shoulder. "Not to mention that the walls are thin and my office is only one over from yours."

"And I forgot to close my door."

Avi offers a sheepish smile and walks with me to my car. "So what
now?" he asks.

I open the door and toss my briefcase onto the passenger seat. "I don't
know, Avi. But it's obvious that battle lines are being drawn. I'm afraid it's
going to get worse before it gets better."

Avi shakes his head. "If only we could make them understand that . . ."

"Avi, we shouldn't *make* them do anything. Forcing an alternative
down their throats will only further entrench them."

Avi's jaw hardens. "Darius, I agree with you one hundred percent. But
how's my suggestion any different from your attempt last year to block
Marshall Prescott?"

"Good question," I answer. "Let me explain. The Future Americans
League invited him. We resisted. It was debated in the faculty and student
senates. The Black Student Union protested. The League counter-
protested. In the end, some people won, some lost, but everybody had a

chance to air their grievances consistent with the principles and spirit of our constitutional system."

"Come now, Darius," Avi postures, his voice filling with professorial authority. "History is littered with atrocities committed within the boundaries of malfunctioning systems. It was such an environment that unleashed bloodthirsty Nazis to slaughter Jews, Slavs, and anyone else deemed *Untermensch*."

"And it was such an environment that permitted slavery and segregation. But try to understand what I'm saying, Avi. I'm not suggesting that we don't fight, only that we do so in a manner that'll preserve the mechanism that makes resistance possible. Forcing a solution onto the MPC compromises their freedom to choose, assemble, and speak."

Avi looks at me with grave intensity. "Darius, your patience is admirable, but it risks yielding too much, too late. For many German Jews, by the time they waited for the government to enforce justice, justice had been murdered."

"And black people have always known that when it came to us, the government was more prone to perpetrate injustice rather than guard against it. That's why we've fought continuously to see the government live up to the ideals of freedom and democracy it claims to cherish." I take gentle hold of Avi's shoulder and look hard into his eyes. "Avi, you've seen the front of the National Archives building, right?"

"Yes," Avi answers, his brow bunching in confusion. "What of it?"

"There's an inscription. It reads: 'Eternal vigilance is the price of liberty.' "

Avi nods, his eyes still searching for my point. I squeeze his shoulder.

"We've got to watch for the enemies of freedom from without *and* within. That includes being careful to not compromise freedom, even in its defense."

Avi ponders for a moment. "You're a good man, Darius. But you're also a historian! With what you know of the human record, how can you be satisfied to merely watch disaster encroach?"

I drop my hands to my sides and stand tall. "Avi, you get that insult for free. Don't do it again."

Avi gulps and forces a nervous laugh. "I'm sorry, Darius. I didn't mean to . . ."

"I'm sure you didn't. But know this! Like your people, African-Americans are well aware that winning freedom has often demanded payment in blood!"

Avi purses his lips and nods slowly. "You're right. Forgive my presumption."

"Forgiven and forgotten."

We shake hands and close out our conversation with statements of excitement about an upcoming regional history conference that'll feature some of the discipline's superstars. Then I get in my car and drive over to Vesey High, park out front, and wait for Jarrod. And wait. And wait.

I grab my cell phone, call the apartment, and get nothing. I call Cookie's house and get the same. I glance at my watch. There's no time to traipse through this giant building to find him. Not to mention that with all the shootings that have turned schools into battle fortresses, I'm not anxious to set myself up for some security guy to get his first bust.

Holly Sheridan and a group of pom-pom-waving girls step from a side door and I toot my horn and call her. She says something to the rest of the chattering group and hurries over as they herd toward the football field. My heart skips a beat the closer she gets.

Without her glasses and with her hair more maturely styled, Holly looks like Laura when I first saw her that freshman summer. She moves with the same poise, each step full of blooming womanhood. Watching her, I flash back to my moment of supreme stupidity.

It was late. Snow was falling. And I waited under a streetlight in a secluded corner of Kent State's campus where no one, especially Cookie or her friends, would know. I hadn't talked to Laura in days, not wanting to drown in her hurt when I confirmed what Cookie's bigmouthed friends had been hinting to anyone with ears.

Minutes passed and I wondered if Laura would show, my trembles smoothing out with the thought that maybe she'd deduced for herself that we were through. But then she stepped into the light, her eyelashes covered with snow, her lips pouting with cold, and her arms wrapped around herself for warmth. Time slowed its march, prolonging each flake's fall. Winter's muffling blanket cocooned us into a warm hollow, echoing the sounds of our exhaling breath.

I thought I could tell Laura, walk away, and forget. But as I gazed into her eyes, already brimming with tears, my resolve melted. And yet I had no choice. I'd made so many promises to Cookie during our wild bouts of lovemaking, I had to follow through.

I took Laura's face into my palms and kissed her moist cheeks. "I'll always love you," I whispered.

She smiled softly and spoke in a voice filled with pity. "My poor, sweet Darius. You don't even know the meaning of love."

She stroked my cheek and backed into the crystalline night, her face turned toward me so that it was forever imprinted on my mind. And I watched like a pride-anchored fool as my future faded into another man's arms.

"Hi, Dr. Collins," Holly greets me. "What're you doing here?"

"Hi, Holly. I'm looking for Jarrod. Have you seen him?"

The corners of her smile droop. "No, sir. I don't see much of Jarrod since he started dating what'shername."

"Reesie?"

Holly nods, looks around nervously, and lowers her voice. "She's part of that girl gang, the Mantises."

"The Mantises? Why would they call themselves . . ."

The question catches in my throat when I remember that those are the predator insects whose females tear off the heads of the males after mating.

"They're pretty scary," Holly says.

"No doubt," I answer, imagining Reesie tearing Jarrod's empty head from his shoulders.

A young woman trots to the edge of the football field. "Holly!" she yells. "Ms. Keckley says c'mon so we can start practice!"

"Okay!"

Holly smiles and waves. "Bye, Dr. Collins. It was good seeing you again."

"You too, Holly."

I call my apartment and Cookie's house again. Nothing. I wait a few more minutes, glance at my watch, and take off, stomping on the gas and jetting into traffic.

Jarrod must be out of his mind, disobeying me like this. This is *his* mess! It's *his* life on the verge of collapse! It's *his* responsibility to confront the results of his actions. And it's *his* job to manage the consequences! Him blowing off this meeting is grim confirmation of his immaturity and unpreparedness. *But that's too bad!* He wanted the pleasures of a man; now he's going to pay the price. He wanted to pound his chest in conquest; now he's going to pound the pavement looking for a job. He wanted to plant his seed; now he'll tend to the harvest.

I zip across town into Fairplane and understand again why black Clevelanders call this the Hillbilly Hood. It's a bleak-looking burg, offering an eye-opening survey of how common white people live. It also makes me wonder where they get off badmouthing blacks.

With each passing block the sparkle of futuristic glass-enclosed buildings, outdoor cafés, and eye-candy strip malls devolves into a dingy post-industrial landscape of dirt and grime. Security gates hang from the tops of stores, waiting to be snatched down and locked when the proprietors escape for the night. Battered BEWARE OF DOG signs hang lopsided from mangled front yard fences. Clumps of white teens sidle down the sidewalk, their pants drooping off their butts in imitation of their black counterparts. At intersections, carloads of low-riding white thug wannabes pull up, the pulsing bass of their rap and heavy metal music easily penetrating my rolled-up windows. I quickly check to make sure my doors are locked, then zip away.

I finally find the street and house I'm looking for, park, and hurry from my car to the front door and ring the doorbell. There's no immediate answer, so I ring again. The noise from a blasting TV or radio is cut and replaced by an irritated hollering voice.

"Who is it?"

I lean close to the door so I won't have to talk loud. The last thing I need is some nosy neighbor calling the cops, reporting a strange black man yelling outside a white woman's door.

"It's Darius Collins, Mrs. Cuppersmith. We had an appointment."

"Just a second!" she shouts. "I'll be right there."

Next door, two elderly white women laugh and talk to each other across the fence separating their yards. They're speaking some Slavic language, their conversation filled with the warmth and energy of longtime friends. A man working beneath a car parked in front of his house, half of it in the street, the other half on the curb, hollers and scrambles from beneath the vehicle, holding his bleeding hand. He kicks the car, cusses it out, then hurries inside, wiping his hand on his grease-stained overalls. Down the street, five city workers fill in potholes, four of them leaning against the repair truck, smoking, talking, and laughing while the fifth shovels gravel.

Two beer-bellied, stringy-haired men amble toward the house. One is dressed in work boots, grubby jeans, and a jacket that barely covers his bulbous belly. His partner's wearing torn sneakers, high-water polyester trousers, and a dingy sweatshirt with a shabby Confederate flag stitched to the front. They're laughing, talking loud, and yelling at passing cars until the Rebel spots me. He elbows his buddy, points at me, and they glare, their scowls deepening when I maintain defiant eye contact.

"This neighborhood's goin' to the dogs!" the Rebel says, his voice sounding like gravel swishing in a bucket.

"Gettin' filled with all kinds'a trash," Work Boots seconds.

A sudden gust of wind rearranges their hair into an unruly mess of spaghetti as I look them over, tenderly clutching the bottles in their brown paper bags. A police cruiser with a black cop at the wheel and a white cop passenger rolls by. As Rebel elbows Work Boots into motion, it slows down and keeps pace with the two dregs, following them around the corner.

Heavy, clomping footsteps from inside approach the front door. Several locks click open, a chain slides across its channel, the doorknob jiggles, and the door opens. The pungent odor of paint and turpentine slaps me in the nose and stings my eyes.

"Mrs. Cuppersmith?" I say, extending my hand.

"*Miss* Cuppersmith," she corrects me, holding the bristle end of a paintbrush up so it doesn't drip.

She's a mildly attractive mid-fortyish woman, dressed in soiled sneakers, a T-shirt, and paint-splattered bib overalls that, although baggy, don't hide the enticing, well-exercised body in them. Strands of her brunette hair have worked their way from beneath a canary yellow bandanna covering her head. The overall pant legs are rolled up to just beneath her knees, revealing a pair of delicate ankles, contrasted by the hard, crusty heels of her feet, hanging out of the sneakers.

"I'm Darius Collins."

"I figured as much," she says, ignoring my hand. She points to the living room. "Have a seat. I'll be right with you."

I take shallow breaths, trying to adjust to the odor while sitting down on the couch. I look around the rough-ordered chaos, trying to size up the woman who lives here by the things she's surrounded herself with.

A huge fake tree is standing in the corner, next to the couch where I'm sitting. Silk flowers line the inside window flower box. The chipped wood coffee table is covered with true romance magazines. Staring down from the wall by the front door is a picture of Clark Gable, dressed as Capt. Rhett Butler from *Gone with the Wind*. On a lamp table in a corner across the room there's a wooden frame with an old, slightly faded black-and-white photo of a gaunt, hollow-eyed man in miner's clothes. A pile of dog-eared crossword puzzle books is stacked next to the table. The gold minishag carpet blends with the tan furniture that reeks of cigarette smoke.

I search for a book, any book! Fiction. Nonfiction. Biography. Philosophy. History. Science fiction. But there's nothing except a dusty Bible sitting atop a stack of lunatic-fringe newspapers, the type that run stories on alien abductions and Elvis sightings.

If two weeks ago someone had told me that my *GQ*-dressing, ski-vacationing, credit-card-carrying, $110.00-an-ounce-cologne-wearing son would've even thought to set foot in here—*even to win a stupid bet!*—I'd have called them a liar. Cookie's raised Jarrod with the best money could buy and cultivated his tastes to expect nothing less. And while I'm glad he's been so well cultured, that breeding has sometimes caused friction. Especially during his weekend visits when he's turned up his nose at my blue-collar cuisine or copped an attitude when we couldn't go someplace or buy some new gadget.

I can't count the number of times I've wanted to shake him and make him understand that my salary gets mugged by the IRS, bled by the courts, and eroded by the cost of living before I ever see a cent! Trying to explain that reality before would've been an exercise in futility. Depending upon what happens in the next few minutes, he might soon get the opportunity to find out for himself.

A toilet flushes and Bernice Cuppersmith shambles into the living room carrying a beer in her left hand and a cigarette in the right. She takes a long drag off the cigarette, sucking its remaining vitality down to the filter, then mashes it into a mound of butts filling an ashtray. She grabs a *TV Guide* off the chair across from me, tosses it onto the coffee table, and sits down.

"Where's the boy?" she asks. "I thought he was coming too."

The way she says "boy" makes my skin crawl. "If you're referring to *Jarrod*," I say, keeping my voice smooth and even, "something came up."

She chuckles and takes a swig of beer. "Some*thing* came up all right. Some*thing* he should've kept to himself."

I shake my head in frustration. "You'll get no argument here."

A movement from near the steps draws our attention. Bernice's eyes narrow and she grabs a magazine off the coffee table.

"Brittany! What're you doin'? Come out from behind there, ya little urchin!"

A scared, wide-eyed little freckle-faced redhead inches out from behind the steps and shuffles toward Bernice.

"Why're you sneakin' like that?" she hollers. She moves quickly, cranking her arm like she's about to throw the magazine. "Get out'a here and stop sneakin'!"

Brittany dashes from sight into the kitchen and out a back door. Bernice tosses the magazine back onto the table, then locks her smoldering eyes onto me.

"Where were we?" she says, tapping her chin. "Oh, okay! There's no point in arguin'. Bell's pregnant. That boy's responsible. It's time to pay."

I take a deep breath and choose my words carefully. "Perhaps we should focus on the issue of responsibility before rushing into discussions of payment."

Her lips tighten into a grim thin line. "And what's that supposed to mean?"

I clear my throat and speak slowly. "Look, Bernice, I'm . . ."

"Miss Cuppersmith!" she snaps.

"As you wish," I say, resisting the urge to roll my eyes. "As I was saying, I'm committed to making Jarrod fulfill his obligations, but, well, to be quite honest, he says that your daughter's had, er, relations with others."

Her mouth twists into a disconcerting smug smile. "Gimme a break, Mr. Collins. What did you . . ."

"That's Dr. Collins, if you please."

The smile straightens. "Whatever. And what did you expect him to say: 'Guess what, Dad! I've just ruined a young woman's life'?"

"Look!" I say, my voice tightening. "I hate to quibble over details, but your daughter's life couldn't have been ruined without her willing participation."

"Who says she was willing?"

The question hits me like a brick to the chin. My heart races to keep pace with my rapid shallow breaths as thoughts zing and ping through my mind.

"That's right, *Doctor*," she says, sneering.

Bernice chugs down the rest of her beer and brings her thumb and index finger together till they're barely touching. "I'm this close to filing rape charges against that boy."

I sit back hard against the couch and try to shake the dizziness from my head. "Please, Miss Cuppersmith. Jarrod, he, he's not that kind of person. He'd never . . ."

"Maybe he would. Maybe he wouldn't. All I know is that my Bell is pregnant and she says the baby's his."

"But, but it's her word against his. Aren't you even interested in finding out who the real father might be?"

She scoots forward in her chair, slams the beer bottle down onto the coffee table, and looks over her shoulder toward the stairs.

"Bell!"

"Yes, Momma!" answers a strained, mousy voice.

"Get down here, ya little slut!"

Bernice snatches a pack of cigarettes from the chair side pocket, lights up, and blows the smoke from the corner of her mouth with the skilled indifference of a mobster. She takes another drag and yells back upstairs.

"Hurry up!"

"I'm coming, Momma!"

Bernice takes a mighty drag off the cigarette, smashes it into the ashtray's growing mound of butts, and lights up another.

" 'I'm coming!' " she mutters, grumbling to herself. "That's the problem. If that boy hadn't been coming, she wouldn't be in this mess."

She takes a drag off the cigarette, wipes her eyes, and continues snarling to herself like I'm not even present.

"How many times did I tell her? 'Bell, don't make my mistake.' 'Bell, have some fun before you get tied down.' But *noooo!* The little tramp spreads her legs for some bastard who'll walk off like her father."

The ceiling groans as heavy footsteps tromp toward the stairs. I look in their direction and my insides collapse as Bell Cuppersmith waddles down the steps into view.

She's dressed in a faded undershirt, oversized sweatpants, and shower slippers, with her hair parted down the center into two thick braids. Beneath the shame-tortured face, disheveled appearance, and chubby body hides an essentially pretty girl. But much of that prettiness has surrendered to Bernice's abuse and these drab surroundings.

"Get over here!" Bernice commands, jabbing her rigid index finger to a spot beside her chair.

Bell shuffles over to where she's been ordered to stand, her eyes gazing at the floor and lips trembling.

"Turn around, fatso!" Bernice orders.

Bell does a slow three-sixty, displaying the global roundness of her protruding belly and the continental spread of her hips. Cookie estimated that Bell was only a couple of months pregnant, but she looks much further along. Jarrod-the-irresponsible-and-absent has less time than he realizes.

Bernice locks her hostile eyes onto me. "This," she says, pointing at Bell, the girl's face awash in tears, "is what that *boy* did!" She springs up from the chair and slaps Bell so hard, the girl spins into a crumpled, crying lump of flesh.

"Hey!" I say. "There's no need for . . ."

"Shut up!" Bernice shouts, jabbing the two rigid fingers imprisoning her cigarette at me. "What do *you* know about what I need?"

She sucks the cigarette into a horizontal column of ash and pounds it into the ashtray.

"I'll tell you what I didn't need," she growls. "I didn't need her pushing out some half-breed baby to make life harder on me!"

"I'm sorry, Momma," Bell whimpers.

"Get upstairs, you sorry tub of lard!"

Bell struggles to her feet, casts a quick glance at me, and waddles back up the steps. Bernice stomps into the kitchen, then comes out swigging on another beer and smoking a cigarette from another strategically placed pack.

"Here's the way we're gonna do this, *Doctor,*" she says. "I don't care if it's you or that stuck-up ex-wife of yours, but I want two hundred grand. That's two hundred thousand dollars, just in case you egghead types aren't familiar with regular language."

"Two hundred!" I gasp. "That's insane! I don't have . . ."

"I want it by the time Bell's bastard is born or your precious son will get a chance to experience jailhouse love. Got it?"

I wipe my sweat-soaked forehead and struggle for words. "Miss Cuppersmith, I can see why you're upset. But this request, I don't have that kind of money. And Cookie, well, she's not even in the country and . . ."

"Good-bye, *Doctor*," she says, swaggering to the front door and snatching it open.

I stand and take a moment to steady myself until my legs strengthen. Once the wobbles subside, I move gingerly across the room and join Bernice in the doorway. We both look toward the street as a powerful-sounding pickup truck roars around the corner and pulls into her drive-way. A thin, leather-faced man wearing jeans and a jean jacket, steel-toed boots, and a sweat-stained baseball cap slides out of the vehicle, his eyes riveted on me and Bernice.

"Ev'ry-thang all right, Bernice?" he asks in a thick-tongued drawl.

Bernice smiles, adding a dimension of sunshine to her face that's a stark contrast to the darkness within.

"It's okay, Lane," she answers. "He's the father of that boy who knocked up Bell."

Lane nods, spits a long, thin stream of tobacco juice onto the ground, some of it splattering onto his boots. He grabs a couple of grocery bags from the pickup, slams the door, and comes up the steps toward the house, glaring at me the whole way.

"You tell 'em what we want?" he asks, keeping his eyes on me.

Bernice takes a drag off her cigarette, exhales, and smiles. "He knows."

Lane looks me up and down, scowling. "Why can't you jigs stay with your own kind?" he rumbles.

I'm asking myself that same question. Lane glances inside and yells, "Brittany! Get'chure cute little butt cheeks out here and grab these groceries!"

Bernice frowns at Lane's comment but wipes it from her face when he looks her way.

"We ain't run out'a beer, have we? Cuz I forgot to get some."

"Naw, honey," Bernice answers. "Go on inside, get yourself one, and relax while I get rid of 'em," she says, jerking her head at me.

Lane shoves past me and into the house. "Brittany! Where are you, girl?"

I look hard into Bernice's eyes, trying to find a glint, a glimmer, any-thing that'll give me a sign that she might be persuaded to back off. But there's only anger, pulsing from the windows of her soul. Even so, I have to try.

"Miss Cuppersmith, please. Can't we . . ."

She grabs my arm with a grip confirming a workout routine and shoves me out the door.

"Two hundred grand!" she snarls. "Or else sweet Jarrod gets the rod he gave my Bell."

25

NASH SITS ON MY COUCH IN STUNNED SILENCE AS I
pace back and forth across my living room, explaining everything that's
happened since Cookie broke the news about Jarrod.

"And now this!" I say. "I'm telling you, Nash. I've studied wars, revo-
lutions, economic chaos, and famine. But I've never truly understood fear
until now!"

I grab my glass of wine and gulp it down. "And I know this isn't as
horrifying as any of that. But it comes close. Like the possibility of seeing
my son caged like some animal while the system takes its sweet time finding him innocent."

A sob geysers up my throat, but I choke it down. Now is not the time
for dramatics. I need to figure out what to do. I need to find Jarrod. I need
to find out if that's his baby. I need to call my lawyer, Oliver.

I grab the phone and dial. It rings and rings, finally switching over to
his answering machine. "Oliver! This is Darius! Call me right away!"

I slam the phone down and resume pacing. "This can't be happening," I babble. "It's like I pissed off some foreign god and now it's payback
time."

"Man, quit talking stupid," Nash says. "You know there ain't nobody
but the one true God."

"I know that!" I snap. "There's only one true God and instead of being on His *j-o-b*, He's off on some Caribbean beach chasing women."

Nash frowns and moves to a chair farther away from me. "You stay on
that side of the room," he says.

"Huh?"

"I'm serious, man. I don't want God mistaking me for you when He
sends that lightning bolt through the ceiling."

I wave him off and keep pacing. The phone rings and I stop cold.
Nash snatches up the cordless and answers.

"Hello? . . . Yes, he's here, but he can't talk. . . . No. Because it's not a good time, that's why. So! If it's that important, call back later. . . . Well, since you broke up with him, that doesn't matter anymore, does it?"

Nash punches the OFF button and jams the phone back into its recharging cradle.

"Marcy?" I ask.

He nods.

I glare at the phone and keep pacing. "She's unreal. You'd think that by now she'd understand that I'm not giving her the time of day."

Nash sips his wine. "Forget her, man. We've gotta handle this thing with Jarrod."

"Nash, trust me. Jarrod and what he's done with his *thing* are uppermost in my mind."

Nash picks up today's paper and reads the headline:

Mayor Denies Wrongdoing. Fields Heads Investigation.

"With stories like this, Cookie's in for one heckuva homecoming," he says. "Assuming she knows."

"Of course she knows," I assert. "Somewhere down there in that Byzantine sewer is a lackey keeping her abreast in the hope he'll get a chance to squeeze hers."

Nash tosses the paper off to the side. "She's one of a kind."

"Yes, Nash. She is. But what's scary are all the variations of her."

"C'mon, D. Don't get loopy on me. I don't hang out with Socrates, Plato, and Apollo, so . . ."

"Aristotle."

"Who?"

"Aristotle. You said Socrates, Plato, and Apollo. The third person's name is Aristotle."

Nash rolls his eyes. "Apollo, Abner, Aphrodisiac. Who cares? What were you about to say?"

I slow my pacing, then speed up the more I talk. "I've been so afraid for Jarrod. I *didn't* want him to end up as just another black man paying child support."

I start to pour myself some more wine, but Nash gets up and snatches the bottle from me. "That's enough!" he orders. "Jarrod'll probably be home soon and you'll need a clear head." He sits back down on the couch and sets the bottle on the end table beside him. "I guess it's a good thing that that Warrior Passages program is about to start," he observes.

I stop pacing and slap my forehead. "That's right! The kickoff banquet's only a few days from now."

I start pacing again, faster. "I can't do it. Not now. Not with all that's going on."

"Can't do what?"

"Reverend Boxwell wants me to deliver an overview of the purpose, goals, and objectives for the history and heritage segment."

"Man, who're you trying to fool? You're perfect for the job. And with Jarrod working overtime to ruin himself, how can you consider *not* doing it?"

I shake my head. "I hear what you're saying, Nash. And I thought the same thing at first. But Jarrod's troubles are way beyond the scope of a Warrior Passages Band-Aiding."

"See! Now you're talking stupid."

I stop and face Nash directly. "Go ahead, Nash. Don't let my troubles deter you from speaking your mind."

Nash dismisses the comment with an eye blink. "Leave the joking to me, Darius. You're no good at it."

"What's your point?"

"The *point*, you spazzing blockhead, is that this Warrior Passages gig sounds like a slick opportunity for you to drill some sense into Jarrod's thick skull."

"What do you think I'm talking about?" I ask, getting loud.

"Blowing a chance to help your son!"

Nash gets up, grips my shoulders, and looks straight into my eyes. "D, listen to me. In less than two years, Jarrod's gonna be eighteen. That's not much time for you to teach 'em whatever lessons you've got left."

"Nash, I . . ."

"Let me finish!" he shouts. "You've got to make the most of this moment. For the first time in a long time you've got total access to Jarrod. Cookie's not around to stonewall or sabotage you. And there's none of her hero-masquerading, snake-in-the-grass boyfriends to steal your thunder and keep you benched."

Nash's gaze intensifies. "Man, you're always dropping pearls of knowledge on me. Now it's my turn. You like to poke fun at my job, but, D, we do a lot of things right!"

"C'mon, Nash. I never really meant . . ."

"Yes, you did! But forget all that. One of the things we do best is teamwork. It's called synergy, Darius, where the sum of the total is greater than the individual parts. And that's what Warrior Passages'll be. If that many brothers and sisters have lined up to pour out their love, Jarrod can't help but get swept toward something good."

He relaxes his grip. "Don't get me wrong, D. Nobody can be Jarrod's daddy like you. But Cookie's seriously pinched your playing time. *Until now.* This is the goal line stand. For the first time in a long time you have to suit *all* the way up. You've been shoved into the game without a warm-up and told to cover a hundred yards in less than a minute. Don't you want some people blocking for you instead'a handling all those tacklers all by yourself?"

I lower my eyes. "Yes."

Nash squeezes my shoulders. "Good answer! Now we're making progress."

"We?" I say, locking my eyes back onto Nash.

He smiles. "That's right, man. As Jarrod's godfather, I'm reserving the right to put my boot in his butt right alongside yours."

Nash and I slap each other five and shake, right as the doorknob rattles with the sound of a key slipping into it.

Nash rushes back to the couch. I stand directly in front of the opening door, my arms crossed tight over my chest, watching as Jarrod staggers in. He gasps, his eyes widening with surprise.

"Heeeey, Pops!" he slurs. "Whuz'zup!"

I lean forward and sniff. "Jarrod! You've been drinking!"

"Yup! Just like you!" he says, pointing at the nearly empty wine bottle on the end table.

My mounting anger must be evident, because Nash says, "Stay cool, D. Just keep it cool."

I glance at him, then refocus onto Jarrod. He gives Nash a wobbly wave and a lopsided smile. "Heeeey, Uncle Nash. How you be?"

"Never mind that!" I snap, grabbing Jarrod's chin and jerking his face to me. "Where have you been? And why didn't you meet me for our appointment?"

"Let go!" Jarrod orders, pulling my hand from his chin. He rubs his lower jaw and says, "Something came up. Isn't that your favorite line?"

I grab Jarrod's collar and yank him till we're nose-to-nose. "Boy! Don't play with me."

"Who's playing?" he shouts, wriggling free. "Some girls were gonna jump Reesie and I went to protect her. Isn't that what you've always said: 'It's okay fighting *for* a girl, but never fight *over* one.' "

"So you're going to run this game, huh? You're going to use my words as the excuse for your disobedience."

"I'm not using nothing. I'm telling the truth. I told Reesie I'd be there for her and kept my word. Isn't that what you've always . . ."

"Jarrod, you know good'n well that when I told you . . ." I sniff, frown, and glance at Nash.

He nods and says, "I smell it too."

My anger boils over and I slap Jarrod with every molecule of energy I can summon. "Negro! Are you crazy, *smoking pot?* Don't you know there's a universe of politicians out there waiting for hardheads like you to help them justify building another prison?"

He staggers sideways and falls across the end table, knocking the wine bottle and Nash's glass onto the floor, where they shatter. I stomp across the room to grab Jarrod, but Nash blocks me.

"No, D!" he shouts. "That's enough!"

Jarrod grabs Nash from behind, shoves him aside, and flies into me with a wrestling takedown.

"Nobody hits me!" he hollers. "Especially some punk part-time father!"

We tumble into the dining room set, knocking over chairs and flipping the cheap table onto its side. Jarrod's wrestling skills have improved tremendously, giving me a run for my money and confirming the excellence that let him conquer last year's county championships. But he's forgotten that even though I'm rusty and out of shape, my wrestling skills once conquered the state!

I do a quick reversal, snake my legs through Jarrod's for a cross-body ride, loop my arms around his head, clasp my fingers, and pull. And just as my wrestling coach promised, Jarrod's body follows his head, pretzeling in toward his crotch.

Nash runs over and pries us apart. "C'mon, D!" he growls. "What'sa matter with y'all?"

Jarrod jumps to his feet and charges again but is body-blocked by Nash. He chicken-wings Jarrod's arms, drags him over to the couch, and shoves him face-first into the pillows. Jarrod spins around and springs to his feet until Nash palm-whacks his chest, shoves him back onto the couch, and holds him in place.

"You're lucky Uncle Nash is here!" Jarrod mouths off. "Or else I'd be . . ."

"Jarrod! That's enough!" Nash shouts.

Jarrod glares at him, then me, then back at Nash, who says, "Don't you get it, youngblood? Your dad wouldn't be trying to stuff your head where the sun don't shine if he didn't care. He loves you, little brother."

"Bump his love!" Jarrod barks. "He'd better not put his hands on me again. I'll put him in his place just like I did Mom."

"What?" I holler. "Did you hit your mother?"

Jarrod just glares. I walk slowly toward him, narrowing my eyes when his hands ball into fists.

"That's close enough," Nash warns.

I speak low and slow. "That's your mother, boy. How dare you raise your hand to her."

"According to you, she's *that woman.*"

"So what! She's also your mother, who deserves your love and respect."

Jarrod's eyes fill with tears as he laughs a soggy chuckle. "She's got my love. But that's all she's getting."

I know better than to ask the next question but do so anyway. "What're you talking about?"

Jarrod's voice warbles with pain. "Now who's playing games?" he says. "You know she's been knocking boots. She never thought I heard her. But I did!"

Nash closes his eyes and shakes his head. I plop down into my rocking chair as it all floods back, every warning I gave Cookie in the early days after our divorce when she was so absolutely determined to shed me through the embrace of other men.

"Jarrod's doing more than playing video games!" I had cautioned her. "How you let men treat you will impact his treatment of women," I admonished. "He's genetically programmed to be a protector, and that includes you," I asserted.

And always there was the refrain: "Darius, it's my life! You can't tell me what to do."

Cookie never understood that, had it not been for Jarrod, I'd have gladly vanished from *her* life.

I wipe my eyes and gasp for breath as my lungs exhale the disgust building for Cookie.

"I don't have'ta listen to either one of you two-faced hypocrites," Jarrod sniffles.

Nash releases Jarrod and hands him a tissue. "C'mon, y'all," he says, glancing at both of us. "This ain't right."

I look past Nash and at Jarrod. "You'll listen for as long you're under our roofs."

Jarrod tosses his tissue into the small garbage can near the end table and grabs another.

"Listen to what? More of your 'Do as I say, not as I do' double-talk?"

"Please, you guys!" Nash begs. "Stop now before somebody says something that . . ."

"No!" I snap, boring my eyes into Jarrod. "My know-it-all son has something he wants to get off his chest and I'd like to hear it."

"D, I don't think that's such a good . . ."

"Go ahead!" I roar. "Before I come over there and choke it out of you!"

"No problem!" Jarrod hollers back.

"Jarrod! Don't do this!" Nash orders.

Jarrod ignores him and focuses hard onto me. "You talk a good game about right and wrong, being abstinent, obeying the law, and whatnot. But what about you and your Honey Mellons porn video collection?"

"Shut up!" I bellow, springing to my feet.

Nash's eyes bulge. "You've got those?" he asks.

"That and some," Jarrod answers. "Always hassling me about staying in the books when you're over here beating off to *Bouncing Black Boobs* and *Big Brown Bottoms!*"

Nash leaps across the room to hold me back while Jarrod keeps wolfing.

"As far as I'm concerned, neither of you can tell me what to do. You oughta be glad I'm not following in your footsteps."

I struggle with Nash for a few more seconds, until all my drive, motivation, and energy collapses. I fall into the rocking chair, cradle my head in my hands, and let the tears flow. For several long moments, the only sound in the apartment is my sobbing.

But then I realize, there's no point in crying. Everything Jarrod said was filled with brutal truth. That's why it hurts so much. I look up at him and wipe my eyes. Nash kneels down on one knee beside me and massages the back of my neck.

"D, are you okay?"

I nod, grab the cordless, and start dialing. Jarrod's cocky, defiant expression shape-shifts into one of concern and uncertainty.

"Uncle Nash," he says, his voice filling with worry. "What's he doing? What's going on?"

Nash scowls. "I don't know. But I think your mouth has run up a bill your narrow butt can't pay."

I punch a wrong number, hang up, and redial. "You're right, Jarrod," I say, pounding the numbers. "Your mother and I have far too many skeletons in our closets to tell a man of your stellar caliber what to do."

The phone at the other end starts ringing. "With us being so imperfect, our love for you must be equally imperfect. And if not imperfect, then definitely too shameful for you to want to follow in our footsteps."

A groggy voice answers at the other end. "Hello?"

"Hello. This is Dr. Collins."

"Who?"

"Dr. Collins."

"You! Whaddya want? It's late."

"I know, Miss Cuppersmith. But I've reached a decision about our problem. Can you hold for a second, please?"

Jarrod's eyes widen with fright. "Dad, what're you doing?" he asks in a rasping whisper. "Look, I'm sorry. I didn't mean what . . ."

With calm dignity and total authority I hold up my palm, commanding his silence.

"You win, Son. From now on, you'll get the adult treatment you've been craving."

I get up and walk slowly toward him. "As your imperfect father who's always wanted to do right by you, I feel obligated to introduce you to one of the hard lessons of not only adulthood, but *manhood*."

Jarrod's lower lip trembles. "Dad, please. I was just angry. I would never do or say anything to hurt you and Mom."

I chuckle softly. "See, Son. That's where you're wrong. You've been acting stupid and reckless, trying to hurt yourself. What you don't realize is that if you hurt yourself, then you've hurt me and your mother. Your hurt *is* our pain."

"Hey! Hurry it up, will ya!" Bernice crabs from the phone.

"I'll be right with you," I answer. I look at Jarrod and cover the phone. "So now it's time to give you that lesson. Most adults refer to it as: 'Be careful what you wish for because you just might get it.'"

I uncover the phone and talk to Bernice Cuppersmith: "Okay, I'm back."

"Make it quick! I've got an early day tomorrow."

"I understand, Miss Cuppersmith. I just wanted to tell you that I *will not* be paying you two hundred thousand, two hundred, or even two dollars. Not now. Not in the future. Not ever!"

"What! Why, you black sonofa . . ."

"If you have a problem with that, you can discuss the matter with my son, who's now handling his own affairs."

A barrage of expletives explodes from the phone as I hand it to Jarrod. He stares at it like I'm handing him a cup of liquid cancer.

"Take it!" I command. "She wants to share her thoughts with you."

Jarrod gulps and takes the phone. He brings it slowly to his ear, and speaking in a voice weaker than that of a wounded sparrow, he says, "Hello?"

I watch closely as Bernice Cuppersmith's tongue batters Jarrod into a quivering blob. He looks from me to Nash and back to me, his eyes pleading. I go gather up his belongings, toss them by the front door, and wait for the call to end.

After a minute or so, Jarrod flinches, most likely in response to Bernice slamming her phone down as she hangs up.

"All done?" I ask.

He nods, the phone hanging loose in his limp hand. Nash gently removes it and places it in the recharging cradle. Jarrod lowers his chin onto his chest and sobs.

"Dad, she, she said that . . ."

I pull him to his feet and hug him. "I know what she said, Jarrod. She told me all about it while you were out with Reesie, fighting, drinking, and smoking pot."

Jarrod throws his arms around me and weeps into my shoulder. "Dad! I'm sorry! Please! I didn't mean it!"

I speak softly into his ear: "Yes, Son. You meant every word of it. And now, just as a man has to do, you're going to live with the consequences of your words and deeds."

I look over at Nash. "Take his stuff out to the car."

"Wanna take my Explorer?"

I nod. "Yeah, let's."

Nash and I exchange knowing glances, both of us understanding that at the end of this evolution I probably won't be in too good a shape to drive. I make a mental note to somehow make this up to my friend.

I peel Jarrod away from me, grab my keys, lock up, and walk with him out to Nash's SUV. We get in and Nash waits till we're both strapped in and ready.

"Where to?" he asks.

"Cookie's."

He shifts into drive and takes off. I can hear Cookie now: "You couldn't handle it, could you? You had him for just a few days and put him out. That's why they gave *me* custody!"

We pull up in front of Cookie's house and park. The night is soft and quiet, as if nature's holding its breath to see what will happen next. I get out with Jarrod and watch him grab his bags from the truck. Nash pulls off a little distance, leaving me and Jarrod alone.

I look up into the clear, crisp night sky. Jarrod follows my gaze. "Your grandmother and grandfather are up there," I say.

"I know."

I sigh. "God, how I do miss them."

"I thought you didn't believe in God."

I keep looking up. "I never said I didn't believe in Him. We've just been having a disagreement."

Jarrod's voice tightens. "Like you and me."

"Kind of. But the major difference is that I've always made sure you knew I was there for you. I can't say the same about Him."

"Dad, are you with me now?"

"More than you know, Son." I take hold of his shoulders. "And that's why I'm going to leave."

"Dad, please don't go. I don't know what to do."

I hug him, kiss him, and whisper in his ear. "Jarrod, a man finds his way."

I hurry to Nash's SUV and we drive off, leaving Jarrod standing forlornly in the circular driveway. I look in the side-view mirror, see the heaving shoulders of his silhouette, and turn away from Nash.

26

NASH AND I ARE BARELY OUT OF COOKIE'S DRIVEWAY
when I start second-guessing myself. Did I do the right thing? Have I
tried every option? Should I agree to Cookie's plan to use Trudy? Will this
finally get Jarrod's attention?

"I promised to show him the way," I mutter. "I promised to be there
for him."

Nash gives me a soft punch to the shoulder. "You are there for
him, D. You've put Jarrod on a path he's destined to walk. But you've
done it with love, my brother."

"Nash, how can you say that? He's my son and I kicked him into the
streets."

"Darius! Get real! He's at home in Cookie's castle. You try selling that
line to someone who's *really* homeless and they'll beat you with a soup
bone."

"Is that supposed to make me feel better? Is abandoning him to familiar surroundings supposed to cushion the impact?"

Nash tightens his grip on the steering wheel. "If you feel that guilty
about it, let's go back and get him."

I sit in smoldering silence, wanting to take Nash up on his dare but
keeping my mouth clamped shut.

"I thought so," he says, shaking his head with disdain. "Man, you're
so full of . . ."

"Full of what?" I challenge him. "Love, care, and concern for my
son."

"In a pig's eye! Admit it, man. Deep down inside, you're doing back-
flips that Jarrod's finally getting his wake-up call."

"Is that right? Well, tell me, O Nash-the-insightful. How are you
suddenly such an expert on my feelings?"

Nash glares at me, holding his gaze so long that I almost start to caution him about keeping his eyes on the road.

"So you wanna get raw, is that it, D?"

"Huh?"

"I'll tell you how I'm suddenly such an expert!" Nash rumbles. "After listening to all your pissing and moaning about what you'd do with Jarrod if you ever got the chance, *anybody* would be an expert!"

"What! I ought to . . ."

"You'd better shut up!" Nash explodes. "Before I drop you someplace where you'll stand out like a MUG ME! sign."

"You're pushing your luck, Nash!"

"Whatcha gonna do?" he asks, belting out a scornful laugh. "Are you gonna send me to my momma's house that's got more room than five of your apartments? Are you gonna whine about feeling guilty for making me see that I'm destroying myself? Or are you gonna bore me with warnings that this Cuppersmith babe is hell-on-a-broomstick serious?"

I flip up my middle finger, turn toward the window, and fume. We ride along for the next few minutes in crackling silence, Nash whipping the Explorer around corners and zipping through yellow-turning-red lights. The image of Jarrod's silhouette, standing alone in the dark as Nash and I drove off, plays over and over in my mind, misting my eyes with tears drawn from wells of anger, confusion, and guilt.

I want so desperately for Jarrod to step back from the cliff edge along which he's dancing. I'm struggling to find the logic that will give me access to his heart of reason. I'm terrified that he's taken his once-in-a-lifetime youth and flung it like ashes into the wind.

"A man finds his way."

My father's words echo down from years before when I told him I was leaving the church, him, and his suffocating rules. He hounded me. We argued. He threatened me. I moved out. He appealed through my mother. I moved away. I knew his heart was breaking. And because Momma loved him so, hers was too. But arrogance stuffed my ears, muffling his voice that never tired of saying he loved me. Then finally, after a while when I'd proved I could make it on my own, he set me free.

I pulled in from work one evening and he was there, waiting in his car. We walked silently toward each other, his eyes filling with love while mine hardened for combat. We stood face-to-face, him looking me up and down and his chest swelling with pride.

"You're looking well, Son."

I nodded and maintained my stony silence, determined to make him pay for his parental heavy-handedness.

"Your mother's worried, Darius. You should call. It'll set her mind at ease."

"I've been busy!" I answered in a tone intended to cut.

Dad sighed, lowered his eyes, then stared hard into mine. He stepped forward, wrapped his arms around my rigid, unforgiving body, and whispered into my ear.

"Son, a man finds his way, if he lets God light his path."

Then he turned and left, walking into a future where the God of his fathers who'd always lighted his path waited in the eye of a hurricane to whisk him into their presence.

Nash and I are about twenty minutes away from my apartment complex when he lightly taps me up'side my head.

"What now?" I snap.

He reaches over into his glove compartment, pulls out some napkins, and presses them into my face.

"Here!" he says, his tone filled with mischief. "Don't be snotting up my vehicle, man. Boogers drag down the trade-in value."

I snap my head around, look into Nash's grinning face, and have to chuckle.

"You know," he says, tossing the napkins into my lap, "if you and I keep arguing like this, we'll have'ta get married."

That finishes thawing us out and we drive the rest of the way in laughter, accusing each other of hurling the first insult, apologizing, then theorizing about whose butt would've been kicked to the moon if things had escalated.

Nash drops me off, pulls away, then slams on his brakes and zooms backwards. He skids to a stop, rolls down the power passenger window, and yells across the Explorer.

"Darius!"

I stroll back, lean against the door, and yawn. "Nash, it's late and I've had a long day. Don't say something that'll make me have to hurt you."

He laughs. "You should be in bed before you start dreaming."

We laugh and trade another volley of insults before I finally ask Nash what he wants. He crosses his arms tight over his chest, arches an eyebrow, and purses his lips into a skeptical lopsided grin.

"You're going back there to get Jarrod first thing in the morning, aren't you?"

I stand in silence, neither confirming nor denying.

Nash loosens up and smiles. "Well, at least let 'em finish his corn-flakes before you rush in to rescue him."

He shifts the Explorer into drive.

"How'd you know?" I ask.

"Know what?"

"That I'd go back and get him."

Nash's smile relaxes into a soft line of compassion. "Man, are you kidding? With the way you love that boy, I half expected you to go back tonight!"

I nod, extend my hand to Nash, and we shake. "Thanks for understanding."

"No problem. Besides, now that I know you're going, it'll save me the trip."

I tighten my grip. "Nash, I owe you."

"You'd better believe it!" he agrees, winking and grinning. "And I know just how you're gonna pay."

He jets away and I know that I'll be bird-sitting Player in the very near future.

27

IT'S 4:20 A.M. ON A DAWNING THURSDAY AND I SHOULD be asleep, but I'm too wound up. I get up and go see what's piled up in my e-mail since I last looked in what seems like an aeon ago.

Reverend Boxwell sent me a revised schedule of events for the Warrior Passages kickoff the day after tomorrow. I'm slotted to make my presentation near the middle of the program, which is fine, since it puts me before him. From what I recall of his oratory, I'd hate to follow him to the podium.

My jaw hangs open when I read the fearful words of Avi Silberberg's "I told you so" message:

> . . . came out to my car after my evening Twentieth-Century Europe class and saw a swastika spray-painted on my windshield. This is what I was talking about, Darius. For the love of God, I appeal to you as a man of reason, compassion, and member of a race that's also spent centuries battling oppression to help stop the further spread of . . .

Avi's already informed our department chairperson, Dr. Esther Kurozawa, and asked her to call an emergency department meeting as soon as possible. Esther's certain to follow through. As the child and grandchild of elders who spent World War II in an American internment camp, then endured postwar yellow peril harassment, she won't blow this off. And I'll definitely be there, since the same scum who trashed Avi's car will undoubtedly be targeting blacks next.

Larry Brockett's announcing a special session of the Cleveland Black Historical Society's executive board. He doesn't say why, but it's obviously connected with our earlier communication:

> Dr. Collins, in your last e-mail you indicated that next month would be best for you to meet with CBHS board members. Cir-

cumstances compel me to ask your cooperation in meeting with them next week. If you could give this the utmost priority, I and the presidential nominating committee would be most appreciative . . .

With an ending like that, Larry can't expect me to turn him down, so I tell him to let me know when I'm supposed to be there.

Ike from the book club has sent an e-mail. There's been so much happening that I'd almost forgotten about that supremely enjoyable part of my life. Which means I've been stressed to the max. I need to make sure I'm at the next meeting so I can plug into the potent intellectual power of those sharp black men and women and recharge my batteries.

Ike's supposed to host the next meeting but asks me to do it, since his condo will still be getting remodeled. With all that's been happening in my home, I should decline. But then I'd have to delay surrounding myself with those witty black people, so I volunteer.

The next message is from Marcy, which I delete without reading. Chloe's sent one and, just as fast as I deleted Marcy's, I open this e-mail:

Darius, this morning's breakfast was wonderful. Sorry I had to rush off, but there are some days when that doggone pager runs my life. Anyway, please know that I really enjoyed myself and look forward to getting together with you again. Soon.

So she wants to get together again. Me too! The sooner the better. I sit back and take a few moments to daydream and remember her soft voice, those luscious lips, her deep eyes, and the bolts of electricity that snaked up my arms the few times our hands touched.

I write her back, confirming that I'm willing to do breakfast, lunch, or dinner anytime she wants, then send the message. Seconds later, I'm pleasantly surprised to get an answer from her: "Would you like to meet for breakfast this morning?"

"Sure," I type. "I don't have class till late, so I'm open."

"Wonderful! Let's meet down at the Soul Stroll diner."

"Good choice. What time?"

"Nine-ish."

"See you there."

"Looking forward to it."

We sign off and I sit back, stretch, and smile. Things with Chloe are sailing smoothly along, and it's about time. After all the relationship crap I've been wading through, it's nice to finally be connecting with someone decent who wants to be with me as much as I want to be with her. All I have to do is check on Jarrod in the morning, make sure he's up and on his way to school, and then I can go and enjoy Chloe.

I check my last e-mail and am slightly surprised. It's from Phoebe, who has written only once before to relay book club news. Surprise becomes suspicion when I read that she just returned from the National Black Trainers Institute in Washington, D.C., the same organization to which Marcy belongs. The vagueness of the message doesn't help:

> . . . when you get some free time, let's meet for lunch. I'll be doing some training down near Erie Pointe over the next couple of days, so I can meet you on or near campus. It's nothing urgent, but I think you'll find it of interest.

Meeting Phoebe tomorrow is too soon, but the day after shouldn't present a problem. Especially since it'll be the noon lunch hour, which will still give me plenty of time to hear her news "of interest" and still make the Warrior Passages kickoff. So I suggest the day, time, and place and tell her to let me know if it'll work for her. Then I sign off and yawn, glad that I'm finally relaxed enough to fall asleep, even though I'm getting up in less than two hours.

I crawl into bed and surrender to merciful oblivion. Then the phone rings. I groan. I'm not about to answer this phone when I'm finally tired enough to . . . *Jarrod!*

I grab the phone and gasp into the night, "Hello!"

"How could you?" Cookie rails.

I jerk the phone from my head to protect my eardrum. "How could I what?"

"Hit Jarrod! And why isn't he there with you? I told you to watch him until I got back. Couldn't you even do *that?*"

My blood's boiling, but I'm too tired to fly off the handle, so I engage Cookie with vigorous calm.

"Cookie, you've mistaken me for someone who can be intimidated, so good-bye!"

"You wouldn't dare!"

"Wouldn't dare what? Hang up on you? Normally, you'd be right, because I hate that. But unless you want to talk with a dial tone, you'd better watch your mouth!"

"Darius, I'm only . . ."

"Bye!"

"Darius! Wait!"

I hold the phone over its cradle, my hand lowering slowly as sleep seeks conquest.

Cookie's voice echoes through my fogging mind. "Darius, I'm only trying to find out about Jarrod."

I yawn and bring the phone back to my ear. "That's touching, Cookie. But if that's your goal, you'll need to enlarge your civility."

A long pause fills up the miles between us until Cookie finally speaks, her voice softer but barely masking her grudging respect.

"If you don't mind," she says, "I'd like to know what's been happening with Jarrod."

"No problem," I answer, slouching deep into my pillow. "How'd you know we'd had some, er, difficulties?"

"He paged me."

"Paged you? Why'd you even bother taking the thing if your intent was to disappear?"

"Not that one, Darius. I have another, for use just between him and me. The telephone lines have been horrible. I'm lucky to have gotten through, since these people in Paris are on strike again!"

Cookie says "these people" with the haughty dismissiveness blacks used to accuse only whites of dispensing.

"What people?" I ask. "And how'd you end up in Paris? When we last talked you were headed for Munich."

"And Munich is where I'd be right now if they hadn't rerouted the plane for some mechanical problem."

"Oh. Well, I suppose it's fortunate that you're safe."

"You suppose!" Cookie exclaims. She sputters and burbles, finally saying, "Just tell me what's going on with Jarrod."

I bring her up-to-date on the highlights, editing out the part about Jarrod's drinking and drugging. She doesn't need the added tension, and I don't need the added lip service.

"I don't approve of your abusing him," she criticizes.

"I didn't abuse him. I slapped the piss out of him, then tried to connect his head to his bowels."

"That's not funny!"

"I'm not joking. Little has happened around here that inspires humor."

"You had no right to hit him. When I get back I'm going to . . ."

"Going to do what, Cookie! Divorce me? Take my son from me? Screw men where he says he heard you?"

Cookie gasps. "You're a liar."

I chuckle. "Cookie, it doesn't matter. Jarrod's seen us for what we are and is acting out the script we wrote for him. We should be glad that all he's done is get someone pregnant, drink, and smoke pot."

Now that it's slipped out, I'm glad. At least now she'll know what sent me up'side Jarrod's head.

"Drink and smoke pot?" Cookie mumbles, her voice laden with sad surprise. "But, but he never showed any signs of . . ."

"What did you think he'd do? Roll a joint and offer you a hit?"

"Why're you making jokes?" Cookie asks desperately. "Jarrod's losing his mind and you're acting like . . ."

"I'm acting like his father who's *here* keeping him from self-destructing."

"Now who's playing the suffering parent?" Cookie accuses. "Don't think you're special, Darius. You're getting only a small taste of what I've been putting up with."

"Yes, Cookie. It's quite apparent that you've been putting up with it rather than *doing* something about it."

Cookie answers with icy calm. "I'd bother being offended, except that it doesn't sound like you're doing such a hot job either. So much for all your better-parent assumptions."

"Actually," I respond, yawning, "I've been doing a fantastically piss-poor job. And like you've said so often: 'I never assumed I was the better parent.' "

After a long second, Cookie says, "Darius, you can't let that Cuppersmith woman hurt Jarrod."

"I have no intention of letting that happen."

"*Please* contact Trudy tomorrow and . . ."

"No, Cookie. I will not."

"For God's sake, Darius! Why not?"

"I've got my own legal contact. Someone who's working with me on this Warrior Passages pro . . ."

"Not your lawyer!" she nearly shrieks. "Oliver's terrible."

"You're telling me," I agree. "But it's not Oliver. It's Judge Lucas Newton. And I know he's got enough clout to . . ."

"Judge Newton! He's a monster. Why can't you just do what I ask?"

"Because, Cookie, it's not the best course of action."

"No!" she hollers. "You're just getting back at me! You're using this situation to make my life harder!"

My voice comes out low, even, and sincere. "Cookie, why should I bother making your life hard when you're doing such a wonderful job yourself?"

"Liar! You're enjoying this, doing what you want with Jarrod, taking advantage of my absence, ignoring my wishes, and rubbing your control in my nose. *You bastard!*"

I sit up straight, tall, and rigid. "I won't dignify that with rebuttal. But since you mention it, how does it feel?"

"You make me sick!" she hisses.

"Yes, Cookie. So you've told me."

She slams the phone down, rattling my eardrum after all. I hang up, toss and turn, then grab Josette Green's *Forbidden Treasures* and read until I fall asleep.

28

MY EYES SLIT OPEN TO A THURSDAY MORNING THAT
has come too early and . . . *what was I thinking?*

My eyes pop all the way open as the question bolts through my brain.
Jarrod's done nothing to show me that he can be trusted with independence. So I shouldn't have left him unsupervised!

I cut on the light, grab the phone, and dial. It rings only twice before
being picked up, and I'm relieved until I hear the female voice that answers.

"Hello!"

"Who is this?" I demand.

"None'a your business! Who wants to know?"

"Jarrod's father!" I snap.

"Hmph!"

She drops the phone and laughs as it clatters and rattles in my ear. I
position the phone firmly between my ear and shoulder so I can talk while
hustling to get dressed and over to Cookie's.

"Jarrod! It's your pops!"

The attitude, rudeness, and ghetto-slaughtered pronunciation add up
to Reesie. I'm half expecting Jarrod to not even come to the phone when
he picks up.

"What?" he barks.

"Don't 'what' me! What's she doing there?"

"Helping me pack."

"Pack! For what?"

"I'm leaving."

My heart skips a beat. "Jarrod! Wait, Son! You don't have to run away.
Wait for me to get there, okay? We'll talk it out."

There's a long silence and I cross my fingers. "Don't get hyper," Jarrod
says, his voice suddenly softer. "I'm not running away."

I plop down onto the bed, one leg in my trousers, one leg out. "Jarrod,
what's going on? Why're you acting like this? Tell me what's bothering you
and we'll work it out. Don't you realize that I'm only trying to help?"

Jarrod speaks low, almost whispering. "Then why'd you'd abandon me when you knew what Bell's mother was threatening?"

"Jarrod, you weren't abandoned and you know it!"

A long silence and then, "Well . . . it felt that way."

I massage my forehead. "Jarrod, I'm only trying to get you to realize the seriousness of your predicament. That woman needs to be stopped! But I can't do it alone. I *had* to get your attention and that's all I could think of at that moment."

Reesie hollers in the background, "C'mon, Jarrod! We gotta pick up Nadine, Noreen, and Glodine."

"Okay!" Jarrod snaps. "I told you I'd be there!"

"Who you think you talkin' to?" Reesie demands, her voice getting closer.

I imagine her head whipping and jerking from side to side like some malfunctioning serpentine carnival ride.

"Chill out!" Jarrod orders. "Can't you see I'm talkin' to my pops?"

"So!" she yells, her voice loud and clear. "You'd better check that attitude, cuz I ain't havin' it!"

"Okay, Reesie," Jarrod responds gently. "You ain't gots'ta go off. I'm feelin' ya."

"Hmph! You talk to me like that again and you gonna feel somethin' all right."

She stomps away so hard, I can hear the clomp of each angry step. I speak slowly and carefully, knowing I'm trodding onto shaky ground. "Jarrod, how can you tolerate that? People who care about each other don't speak that way."

"You and Mom do."

My mouth falls open, stunned and checkmated. If I say I don't care about Cookie, it'll leave him questioning what business I've got commenting upon him and Reesie. If I say I do care about Cookie, it'll call into question months of not practicing what I just preached.

"Jarrod!" Reesie hollers.

"Okay! I'm coming!"

"Hurry!"

Jarrod turns his attention to me, speaking with an urgency that leaves me envious of Reesie's power.

"Dad, I've gotta go!"

"Hold on, Jarrod. You said you were packing to leave but didn't say for where."

"Uncle Milton's."

"Councilman Fields?"

"Yeah. He told me that if I ever needed a favor to come see him."

"But, Jarrod! He's crucifying your mother in the press!"

"He says they're misquoting him."

"Jarrod, this doesn't sound right. And why do you have to go stay with him? I've got more than enough . . ."

"You threw me out!" he asserts. "And besides, Uncle Milton's got the connections to help me."

"Son, I've got connections too. And more than that, I'm your father! Doesn't it make more sense to trust *me* rather than some fork-tongued politician?"

"Jarrod!" Reesie screams.

"On the way, baby!" Jarrod speaks low and fast: "It's funny you mention trust, Dad."

"If there's something funny about all this, please enlighten me."

"What I mean is that I know you don't trust me. But I can't trust you either."

"What're you talking about? Of course you can . . ."

"No, I can't!" he cuts in hoarsely. "You see, Dad, Uncle Milton may be a fork-tongued politician, but when I told him about Bell he did something *you* didn't."

"And what was that?"

"He believed me."

Jarrod's expanding ability to shove those zingers down my throat is proof positive of his prolonged exposure to Cookie. And his refusal to respond to the love of his father is proof positive that he's my son.

"Jarrod, will you at least call me and let me know you're all right?"

"Yeah."

"And don't forget the Warrior Passages kickoff."

"I'll think about it."

My throat tightens, but I force out words that need to be spoken: "I love you, Son. No matter what you might think, I love you with all my heart."

Jarrod's voice is just as tight when he says, "I know."

We hang up and I fall back on the bed, staring at the ceiling and wondering if all this is some weird payback for what I put my dad through.

29

THE PHONE RINGS AND I SNATCH IT UP, CERTAIN THAT
it's Jarrod.

"Hello?"

No answer. "Hello?"

There's a click followed by the dial tone. I call Vesey High and check
to make sure that Jarrod's actually there. He is. I at least know where he'll
be for the next few hours, but since I can't assume he'll stay, I ask the attendance secretary to call me if anyone reports him missing. I don't know
what I'll do if he cuts school, but knowing what's going on with him—
even if it's negative—is better than being kept in the dark.

I finish getting dressed while listening to the last of an NPR interview
with an anonymous physician alleging that black people are routinely
shoved to the bottom of organ donation waiting lists. This is the kind of
information Jarrod needs to hear so he'll understand the lethality of the
racism that's suppressed, shackled, and killed black people ever since New
World settlers land-jacked the Native Americans.

I cut off the radio, grab my briefcase, open my front door, and see
Nash. He's wearing the widest sheepish grin I've ever seen, and for good
reason. Player is with him.

"Tell me you're joking," I say through a groan.

"I wish it was a joke," Nash responds, sounding truly remorseful.

"You're the one who called and hung up, aren't you?"

He nods. "I'm sorry, D. But I knew that if I asked, you'd probably say
no. So I decided to corner you."

His honesty is so naked and direct, I'm momentarily thrown off
guard.

"Eileen called a little while ago," Nash says, his voice filled with
worry. "She'll be at my crib in about a half hour."

"A half hour! Why is she just now calling?"

He grimaces. "It's her way of trying to catch me with my hand in the
cookie jar."

"Don't you mean with your hand down the wrong woman's panties?"

He glances at Player, then scowls at me. "Sshh! You know this fool repeats everything he hears."

"Fool!" Player screeches. "Who you callin' a fool?"

"You! Fool!" Nash snaps.

"Least I ain't runnin' scared of my woman."

Nash shakes the cage, toppling Player off his perch. I look hard at Player, wondering again if this glorified crow is merely repeating what he's heard or actually carrying on a conversation.

"D, I'm sorry to bum-rush you like this," Nash apologizes. "So please, man. *Don't say no.*"

I look past Nash and at Player. He's sitting on his perch, preening one of his wings. He stops, looks up at me, and says, "What're you lookin' at, fathead?"

Nash shakes the cage angrily, making Player squawk in protest and madly flap his wings. "Player! Behave!" he commands.

"I ain't sweatin' you," Player retorts.

I roll my eyes and grit my teeth, knowing I'll regret this. "How long do I have to keep him?"

Nash's mouth explodes into a smile. "Just a couple of days," he answers, shoving Player's cage and stand toward me. "Eileen's gotta be back in Indianapolis by the end of the week to attend some weekend company retreat."

I step aside and point to the corner by my bookcases. "Put him over there."

Nash rushes in, positions the bird stand, then hangs Player's cage from the hook. "You be good," he says softly, sticking his finger through the cage bars and stroking Player's head.

"Why's you kickin' me to the curb?" Player asks.

Nash keeps stroking Player's head. "Don't be like that! You know you're my number-one Player. Now be a good cockatoo and keep Darius company."

"I'll bet this sucker doesn't even listen to rap," Player complains.

"That's right, homey," I say. "Over here we do Patti LaBelle, Miles Davis, and B. B. King."

Player cusses and turns his back. Nash rolls his eyes and hurries to the door. "Thanks, D. Thanks a million."

"No problem. Go handle your business."

He grabs me, hugs me, and is gone. Moments later, I stroll outside and see Katrina just as she's leaving her building. If her eyes were cannon, I'd be a smoking crater right now.

"You're old."

My jaw tightens at the memory of her insult. I'd love to be a fly on the wall the morning she stands in front of her mirror and notices that her big, round knockers have drooped into flat, sagging jugs and that her hips qualify as a "Wide Load." I'd love to see the anxiety on her face when she realizes that the laugh lines around her eyes no longer disappear when she's finished laughing. That would be one sweet moment, and it's too bad I won't see it. But that's okay. Right now, it's good just knowing it'll happen.

I drive across town to the Soul Stroll diner, go inside, ask for two menus, order some coffee, and wait for Chloe. I'm halfway through my first cup when she pulls in. She was driving a compact company station wagon when we last met for breakfast. Today she pulls up in a sparkling late-model candy apple red Corvette and I'm thankful that she hasn't seen my gonna-be-a-clunker-soon Chevy.

She parks and hurries in and I can tell that this will probably be another short breakfast. I stand when she enters and wave her over to our table. She opens her arms when she gets close and we hug, giving each other a quick kiss on the cheek. Gina's face flashes across my mind, piercing me with a stab of guilt. Bruce's face flashes alongside hers and the stab wound heals.

"You won't believe this," Chloe says, sitting down.

"Let me guess. You have to leave shortly."

Chloe's eyes fill with concern. "You're not upset, are you?"

I take her hand and caress it. "Of course not. Believe me, Chloe, I've been on the receiving end of too many complaints about spending too much time at the National Archives or Library of Congress to not empathize with someone's doing what she's got to do."

"I'll make it up to you with a home-cooked dinner."

"Whenever you're ready to cook, I'm ready to eat."

She smiles and covers my hand with hers. "Thanks for being so understanding."

"How can I help it after being hypnotized by those eyes?"

She blushes, looks away, and squeezes my hand. "You're sweet, Darius."

"It must be *you* rubbing off."

Her blush deepens. "Stop," she whispers with a soft giggle. "I'm getting warm over here."

"I'd apologize, but then I'd be lying."

She laughs. "You're crazy."

"And you're wonderful."

She looks hard at me, the smile slowly fading from her lips. Our eyes are locked, and the magnetism that's been working between us pulls us closer and closer. The soft din of customer conversations, cooking food, clanking dishes and silverware and the raucous antics of Tom Joyner's morning show coming from overhead speakers get more distant and quiet as my face draws closer to Chloe's.

The moment's sweet serenity is shattered when a thickset smiling waitress says, "How're y'all doing this morning?"

Chloe and I quickly draw back from each other and sit up straight. "We're doing great," Chloe answers, smiling back at the cheerful waitress.

I hide a glower behind a forced smile, irritated that my first kiss with Chloe has been interrupted by a bacon-and-egg inquiry.

"Are y'all ready to order?" the waitress asks.

Chloe glances quickly at the menu. "I'll just have some juice and toast."

The waitress takes the order, then looks at me. "I'll have the same," I say.

"I'ma let y'all get away with ordering light this time," says the smiling waitress. "But the next time y'all pass through, you need to order a real breakfast. Don'tcha know that's the most important meal of the day?"

Chloe lowers her eyes and nods as if agreeing with the reproach. "You're right," she says. "The next time, we'll order breakfast, lunch, and dinner. Will you join us?"

The waitress beams. "Honey chile, you must not ever had none'a my Rhino's cookin. You'd best believe I'll be joining you."

They laugh and the thickset waitress waddles away. I smile at Chloe and shake my head. "You've got a great sense of humor."

She shrugs. "When you work with the public, it helps."

"Especially when that public consists of people like Blake and his crew down at Black Heads."

Chloe laughs. "Truer words were never spoken."

"How about these words?" I say, leaning toward her. "You're a testament to the beauty, excellence, and elegance of black women."

Chloe's eyes soften into warm pools. She leans toward me and we kiss. It's not long, but what it lacks in duration it makes up for in tenderness. We pull back, look at each other for a long moment, hold hands, and sail smoothly into the next level of our evolving relationship.

30

GETTING TO KNOW CHLOE BETTER IS TAKING A LOT OF
the sting out of all the challenges confronting me right now. We finish off
our small breakfasts, talk for a couple of minutes in the Soul Stroll's parking lot, then hug and kiss before going on our way.

"So when am I going to get this home-cooked dinner?" I ask.

"Sooner than you think, Dr. Collins." Chloe smiles, winks, and gets
into her Corvette. "Would you prefer it cooked at your home or mine?"

"Tell you what," I begin. "You cook the food and I'll provide the atmosphere. My place is small, but it's got character."

"That sounds like a fair trade."

She starts the 'Vette and says, "It might help if I have your address."

I smack my forehead, not even having realized that I had not yet
given her that information. I scribble out my address on the back of one
of my cards and give it to her. She glances at it, smiles, then does the same
for me on one of her cards.

"Be prepared," she warns, backing out of her parking space.

"For what?"

"One of the best meals you've ever had."

"I can't wait. When?"

She smiles and takes off, leaving me standing in the parking lot
watching her with a wide grin on my face. She stops just before pulling
into traffic, waves, and is gone. I stuff her card into my wallet and drive to
Erie Pointe, arriving with time to spare before giving my African-American
history class their exam.

I park on the far side of campus and start the long walk to the history
department in Roosevelt Hall. I need the exercise and can use the extra
time to focus on what to do next about Jarrod. Whatever I decide, I've got
to get in touch with Judge Newton. He's hard as nails, but Reverend
Boxwell says that he's fair and more inclined to help young people if they
come to him before becoming penal statistics.

There's got to be some way of penetrating Jarrod's cranial granite so that he understands the correlation between today's actions and tomorrow's problems. That understanding has to include the warning that every Reesie he invites into his life is dragging behind her a family history.

Momma always told Danielle, "A woman can tell how a man will treat his future wife by watching how he relates to his mother." And she considered it gospel that "like father, like son," the implication being that seeing the elder provided a preview of the junior's older self. What she almost never mentioned, though, was that a man could tell how a woman would treat her future husband by watching how she related to her father. And it was equally true that "like mother, like daughter."

If I'd paid even scant attention to those two maxims upon meeting Cookie's family, I'd have beat feet. But I was in lust, and my throbbing little head choked the blood supply to my big one, blinding me to the obvious evidence.

Cookie's mother, Cozette, ruled her roost with the totalitarian authority of a Stalinist dictator. She'd grown up watching her own mother battle a husband whose anger was routinely ignited into rage by the poverty, southern racism, and terror crippling his ability to provide. The battles wounded Cozette's heart and she passed the hurt on to Cookie and her older sister, Candace. Cozette's getting pregnant by two different "men" worsened matters, especially since they were scoundrels and predisposed to flight, both eventually departing for younger, childless bosoms.

Over and over as Candace and Cookie matured, they were admonished to "let *no* man rule you!" By the time they'd become young women, the message had spawned permutations like: "Do unto them before they get *into* you!"; "Never love them as much as they love you"; and "Men are like dogs on buses—only to be trusted that another one will come along."

Candace learned her lessons well, rejecting the idea of love with *one* man, "finding" it instead through four kids by four different bums. Cookie went on the offense, constructing a bunkered, steel-reinforced life where Cozette's rules weren't needed since Cozette's catastrophes weren't allowed. Cookie was so full of drive, self-direction, and strength, an intoxicating mixture that left my head spinning after being raised in a household content to "let go and let God." She pursued her goals with a certainty of success that yielded results far more immediate, tangible, and satisfying than my parents' exhortations to "wait upon the Lord." And Cookie liked sex, which suited me fine, an ignorant young jerk exploring carnal adventure.

So I casually assumed that Cookie had transcended her poisonous past. I overlooked the obvious in that in order for her to escape *from* it, she had to have been *in* it! I confidently concluded that she'd have related to her father as well she did to me, dismissing the persistent logic that screamed: *"She ain't got no daddy!"* I didn't bother analyzing why *none* of the scoundrels and good-for-nothings who'd splurged on, then sponged off Cozette and Candace had ever asked either to marry. And although Cozette was Cookie's mother, Cookie seemed far too different to truly be Cozette's daughter.

Nash later told me that only a retarded jackass could've missed all the flashing danger signals. He blushed and offered profuse apologies when I reminded him that that jackass looked a lot like me!

"Good morning, Professor Collins," a female voice off to the side greets me.

It's Augusta Baylor, my star African-American history student, approaching quickly and wearing a somber face.

"Hi, Augusta. How are you this morning?"

She catches up and we walk side by side. "I'm all right. I just got my results back from the LSAT."

I stop and look hard at her. "Well! Don't keep the professor in suspense. How'd you do?"

She keeps a straight face for as long as possible, then bursts into a smile. "I kicked butt!"

"That's great, Augusta!" I say, extending my hand. "Congratulations!"

She ignores my hand, hugs me around my neck, and gives me a quick peck on the cheek. "Thanks for encouraging me, Professor Collins. I almost decided not to take it, thinking I needed more preparation. Now I can start law school a whole semester ahead of my original plan."

"You're welcome, Augusta," I say, checking quickly to see who might be watching our close contact.

I move a couple of safe steps back from Augusta and say, "I knew you were prepared. You've got an amazing mind that should be refined into a weapon to serve the black community."

She beams. "I will, Professor Collins. I promise. As soon as I'm finished with my project."

Her eyes glaze over again at the mention of her "project," and my curiosity gets the better of me.

"How's work on the mysterious 'project' going?"

Augusta's looking at me, but she's staring into the great beyond. "I'll have something soon," she answers evenly. "I *won't* be denied my justice."

I have no idea what Augusta's talking about, but it sounds like more than I want to know. I've got enough problems without adding a student's complications to my own, even if she is an academic star.

"Well, Augusta," I say, checking my watch, "I've got to move along. See you in the P.M."

"Okay, Professor," she says, walking off and waving. "See you at test time."

I hurry off, passing the student cafeteria. Chitlins is on the side of the building with a few employees, taking a smoking break.

"Professor Collins! Wait up!" he calls.

I turn toward Chitlins, hustling from the cafeteria. "What's up?" I ask, extending my hand for one of our wrist-twisting, hip-bumping, finger-snapping soul brothers' greetings. Chitlins isn't in the mood and gives me a regular handshake, his grim formality matching his grim expression.

"Why the long face?" I ask.

He looks down and away. "Dr. Collins, I hates to bring this up, but . . ."

"It's about Jarrod, right?"

He nods and his shoulders droop, like he's deflating. "He missed work again. No call, no nothin'. It ain't right, Doc. Not when I got students wantin' a job so's they can eat."

I bite my lower lip and consider the situation. "Chitlins, do what you think is best."

"You understand, Doc. Nothin' against Jarrod, but I gotta run a cafeteria. When folks is hongry, they don't wanna hear no 'scuses 'bout the food ain't ready."

I shake my head and sigh. "The decision's yours. I found Jarrod the job. You gave it to him. He was supposed to keep it. If you feel he hasn't upheld his end of the bargain, I won't have any hard feelings."

Chitlins smiles, his face awash in relief. "Doc, you's one cool dude. I don't care what them protestors is sayin'."

"Protestors? Who? Where?"

Chitlins' eyes shift nervously from side to side. "You mean you ain't heard?"

"No!" I answer, a pronounced edge in my voice. "What's going on?"

Chitlins steps close, looks around quickly, and whispers, "It's them Middle Passage kids. Not all of 'em, but some of 'em's outside the administration building, walkin' to'n fro with signs claimin' theys First Amendment rights is bein' violated."

He glances around again and speaks even lower. "A couple of 'em says you's workin' for the man. They say you's fightin' to keep that el Bornu from speakin' on campus. Say it ain't so, Doc."

I'd answer Chitlins, but my jaw is jammed so tight it'd take dynamite to unlock it. I wheel around and march toward the administration building, located directly across from Roosevelt Hall. I complete the fifteen-minute walk in five and enter a scene too surreal to immediately comprehend.

Mubarak Kwanju, Julie Cranshaw, and several other MPC students are walking in a circle, shouting out the slogans written on the placards they're carrying: *"Free the First Amendment!" "Prescott, the bigot, allowed! El Bornu, the freedom fighter, denied!" "Erie Pointe U equals apartheid!"* and finally, *"Wanted: a real black in the history department!"*

LaThomas Patterson is off on the side, pointing and giving orders to DeBarron Washington, who's busy spray-painting skewed slogans and half truths on other placards. Andre Echols is nowhere in sight, but he's undoubtedly hovering nearby. I reread the messages on the signs, noting that the words are spelled correctly. They can't possibly be DeBarron's handiwork. If they are, he's demonstrated a greater proficiency in spelling than he's ever shown in my class.

He sees me, sneers, gestures to LaThomas, and points. LaThomas grabs a megaphone and aims his big mouth in my direction.

"All right, y'all!" he booms. "We got us a traitor in the house!"

Heads turn and eyes narrow. An ugly murmur ripples through the growing crowd.

"That *punk* flunked me!" someone hollers, his identity hidden in the mass.

It sounds like Dale Buelfren, a worm who skipped half my Civil War class last semester, slept through the other half, then went crying to the dean after I gave him an F! From the foggy, trash-splattered landscape of his perspective, it's payback time. That's undoubtedly the view shared by LaThomas Patterson. But I've got news for him. He'd better show up this afternoon for my test or this "traitor's" going to flunk him too!

In the administration building behind the marching students, small groups of whites gather at second-floor windows, some pointing, some shaking their heads, one hiding behind a curtain and flipping up a middle finger. I grit my teeth and stomp off into Roosevelt Hall.

31

BEFORE I GET TO MY OFFICE, THE DEPARTMENT CHAIR-
person, Dr. Kurozawa, intercepts me. "Darius, come down to my office
for a moment, would you?"

She walks off before I can ask what for, how long, or can it wait? I
toss my briefcase onto my desk, then hurry down to Esther's professional
home. Unlike the sterile, managed chaos of my office, Esther's pulses with
warmth and scholarly pride, indicating the touch of someone who's
clearly not as organizationally challenged as I am.

"Okay, Esther," I say, entering. "Let's make it snappy. I'm giving a test
in a little . . ."

Esther's eyes shift quickly to a couple of stern-faced, official-looking
visitors. They both stand as I cross the threshhold. He reminds me of
straitlaced, humorless, "Just the facts, ma'am" Sgt. Joe Friday off the old
Dragnet series. She reminds me of photos I've seen of plain but stately
nineteenth-century frontier women.

"Darius, this is Ms. Zoe Watsburg from Cleveland Children's Protective Services."

Children's Protective Services. After all the headaches they've caused
me and other single dads they should be renamed the Department of
Meddling-and-Don't-Give-a-Damn.

Ms. Watsburg offers a curt nod. I swallow a groan and return the
gesture.

"And this," Esther continues, "is Detective Sergeant Jim Pullen of the
Cleveland PD Juvenile Crimes Unit."

My head swims with the possibilities of bad news. Whatever Jarrod's
done since I last talked with him, it's beyond me now. If he'd only waited
for me to contact Judge Newton, I might've been able to get at least part
of the soulless bureaucracy on his side. But now he belongs to the system,
and it's certain that he'll learn some things of which I've been glad to remain ignorant.

Detective Pullen and I give each other a perfunctory handshake; then he looks at Esther. "Is there some place we can talk privately?"

"The history conference room is open," Esther answers.

I give her a *thanks-a-lot!* glare. She answers with a *watch-your-face!* scowl. Detective Pullen gestures to the door. "After you, Dr. Collins."

I lead them to the conference room, trying to not fall flat on my face as my imagination serves up visions of the worst possible scenarios for Jarrod's future.

"Would you like some coffee?" I ask, once we're inside.

"I'll have some," Ms. Watsburg answers.

"Cream and jail, er, I mean, cream and sugar?"

She and Detective Pullen exchange knowing glances. "Cream and sugar's fine," Ms. Watsburg responds. "And, Dr. Collins, try to relax. We only want to ask some questions."

I nod, fix our coffee, and take a seat opposite them. Detective Pullen opens a folder and pulls out a photo. "Dr. Collins, have you ever seen this man?"

I stare at it for a few seconds. "No. I can't say I have."

Detective Pullen slides the picture closer. "Try again, Dr. Collins. This is extremely important."

I pick up the picture and stare longer, harder. "Yes! As a matter of fact I have!" I look closer. "Just yesterday! At . . ."

"Bernice Cuppersmith's home?" Ms. Watsburg fills in.

Rather than answer a question that's too closely connected with Jarrod, I say, "What's this about?"

Detective Pullen and Ms. Watsburg exchange another glance. "I'm afraid we can't say. But we'd appreciate it if you'd tell us what you know about this man."

Appreciation. With the way things are going, Jarrod will need all the appreciation and favors he can get. And I wonder again why the fallout from his misadventures keeps raining onto *me.*

"His last name is Younkin," Ms. Watsburg offers.

I shrug. "I just heard her call him Lane."

"Her?" Detective Pullen questions. "Her who?"

"Bernice Cuppersmith."

Another exchanged glance. "Were both girls home?" Detective Pullen asks.

I nod.

"You saw them both?"

"Just for a moment."

Ms. Watsburg moves her coffee cup aside and leans forward. "Dr. Collins, please tell us anything you can remember. Anything at all about the girls, how they looked, how they were acting, dressed, their emotional state, *anything*."

For a moment, I recall a cartoon of a police dog taking a mug shot of a pigeon sitting on a stool. Like that pigeon, I start talking, skewing my comments to lead these two as far away as possible from Jarrod, at least until I can get to Judge Newton.

The questions come faster and with greater intensity: "Dr. Collins, are you sure he used the phrase 'butt cheeks' in reference to the little girl?" "What did the mother do?" "Was there any physical violence?" "Is he living there, or was he just visiting?" "Is the older daughter still in contact with your son?"

Alarms scream inside me. "What do you mean?"

"Are your son and the older Cuppersmith girl still dating?" Detective Pullen asks.

"Dating?" I ask, caught off guard. "That's what it might've looked like, but . . ."

Detective Pullen and Ms. Watsburg lean forward. "Go on," he encourages.

I shrug and try to laugh it off. "Well, what I mean is that, er, no, I didn't know about the dating. That's too serious a step for Jarrod," I chuckle.

My interrogators aren't smiling, so I wipe mine from my face. "Did you notice that the girl was pregnant?" Ms. Watsburg presses.

"No! Maybe. I mean, yes! What's that got to do with Jarrod?"

"We were hoping you'd tell us," Ms. Watsburg answers, stealing a glance at Detective Pullen. "But only if there's something to tell."

I gulp. "There's nothing to tell. As far as I know, Jarrod's not sexually active."

Slight smirks pop onto their faces. They gather up their materials and hand me their cards.

"If you think of anything else, please give us a call," Detective Pullen urges.

I "promise" to do just that and hurry them out the door, glancing at my watch and making apologies about having to end our "conversation" so quickly. After all, I'll soon have a classroom full of customers who have paid good money for me to challenge their intellectual acumen with another test.

I hurry back to my office, worries clanging around my head about just exactly why Detective Pullen and Ms. Watsburg are interested in Jarrod. I hope with all my might that that scurrilous Cuppersmith wench hasn't already gone to the cops. Speaking of cops and the law, Oliver had better call soon. He's a good friend, but if he doesn't contact me, I'll have no choice but to get another attorney.

I force myself to focus on my students and their upcoming test. The exam's already written, but I want to review the questions once more. The quality of the questions directly impacts the quality of the answers, so I always check, recheck, and triple-check to ensure excellence.

I get closer to my office and am floored to see Andre Echols, the missing one-third of the LaThomas Patterson clown show. He's lurking outside my door like a beggar waiting for a handout.

"What is it, Mr. Echols?" I ask sternly, passing him on the way into my office.

"You said you wanted to see me."

"Now why would I inflict such punishment upon myself?"

I should check my contempt for Andre, but the truth of the matter is that I want him to feel every pulse of my disdain.

He scowls, spins around, and stomps off a few steps. I start to let him go when I remember that *I did* e-mail him to come see me today at this time.

"Get back here!" I order.

He stops and stands rigidly erect for a few seconds. He turns slowly around, his nostrils flared, jaws clenched, and eyes aflame.

"Take a seat!" I command. "You're not happy about being here and, just so everything's in the open, the feeling's mutual."

"If you feel that way, then why'd you ask to see me?"

I sit down and drill my eyes into him. "Because, Mr. Echols, I want to know why you're choosing to be an intellectual liar?"

"An intellectual liar?"

"You heard me!" I snap. I hold up his research paper. "This is one of the best-written papers in the class." I slap it down on my desk. "It's thoughtful, well analyzed, easy to read, logically ordered, and generally outstanding."

Andre keeps his eyes locked with mine for a few seconds but slowly lowers them. As his eyes lower, so does my voice.

"So what I'm trying to understand," I continue, "is why you're choosing to perform far below your superior talent and ability. In my opinion, Mr. Echols, *that* makes you an intellectual liar."

After several long seconds of silence he mutters, "You wouldn't understand."

I snort. "Maybe. But whether or not I understand is irrelevant. The larger question for you is would *they* understand?" I point to the many pictures and posters on my walls.

He follows my finger, aimed at ruggedly beautiful Harriet Tubman, courageous conductor of the Underground Railroad; noble Richard Allen, founder of the African Methodist Episcopal Church; Henry O. Flipper, first black graduate from West Point; Marcus Garvey, black entrepreneur and nationalist; W. E. B. DuBois, intellectual giant of the twentieth century; magnificent Frederick Douglass, abolitionist and renaissance man; an unknown black man, lynched naked and hanging from a tree; visionary Shirley Chisholm, first African-American woman presidential candidate; and Dr. Martin Luther King Jr., already hurtling toward eternity after delivering his 1963 "I Have a Dream" speech.

I stab at the pictures and posters and say, "How would you explain to *them* that you're wasting all you've been given when they did so much, with so little, at the risk of their lives and livelihoods?"

He looks into his lap. "It's not what you think," he answers softly. "I can't let people think I'm a sucker. I got harassed for being too brainy in high school, and I, I . . ."

"Look at me," I say.

Andre keeps staring into his lap. "Look at me!" I command. He looks up, his eyes red and watery.

"Andre, you're a black man in America. We don't have the luxury of being weak and uneducated. Our children, women, and elders are expecting us to pursue victory until the next generation's ready to lead. Every black man in our ethnic village has that responsibility."

I recall the words from a sermon my father bellowed years before.

"Andre, we must possess the vision, *for where there is no vision, the people perish.*"

"I hear you, Dr. Collins," Andre sniffles. "But things are different now."

"No! Society's different, but our enemy's still with us. It's gone underground, mutated, and lulled us into a false sense of security. We have to be vigilant and . . ."

"No!" he snaps. He glances at Frederick Douglass, DuBois, and Dr. King. "You just don't understand!" he growls.

Then he springs up from his chair and leaves.

32

I'M JUST ABOUT TO GO TEST MY STUDENTS WHEN THE phone rings. "Hello?"

"Dr. Collins? Hi. This is Larry Brockett, CBHS."

My mouth blooms into a smile. "Why, yes! Hello, Dr. Brockett! What can I do for you?"

He talks with someone in the background for a moment, then addresses me: "Sorry about intruding upon your workday."

"Think nothing of it," I fawn. "I'm pleased to hear from you."

"Well, I hope you maintain that attitude after hearing my request."

"Go ahead, Dr. Brockett. I'm sure it'll be no problem."

Brockett's probably rolling his eyes at this shameless butt kissing. "As you're aware from the latest newsletter and my last e-mail, there are a number of changes taking place at the Cleveland Black Historical Society."

"Well, yes, I'd figured as much. But I didn't think it was anything serious. Is something wrong?"

Brockett tries the same hollow laugh-off that I inflicted upon my interrogators. It's not working any better now than when I tried it.

"No, no. Everything's just fine," Brockett says. "It's just that, well, I know this is sudden and I can't blame you if you consider it even somewhat rude, but . . ."

"Please, Dr. Brockett. I'm at your disposal."

"I was hoping you would be, Darius," he affirms, his tone full of fatherly tenderness. "Would you mind meeting with the CBHS executive board tomorrow?"

I'm speechless. He's right. This is *very* sudden. "Er, I mean, yes! If you really need me that soon."

"You're needed that soon," he confirms. "And thanks so much, Darius. I know this is inconvenient, but the presidential nominating committee was somewhat adamant. I appreciate it and, of course, you'll have my full support."

It feels like a cold, clammy hand has just clapped me on the shoulder while its winking owner picks my pocket. But the idea of meeting with the nominating board and getting my presidential show on the road is too big a bait to ignore, so I rationalize the cold, clammy hand into a warm, sincere hug and ask what time.

"Around two. Is that okay? We can make it later if necessary. It just has to be tomorrow."

"That's fine, Dr. Brockett. That'll still give me enough time to get spruced up for the Warrior Passages kickoff," I say, just happening to mention it.

"You're connected with Hez Boxwell's program?" Dr. Brockett asks, obviously pleased.

"Yes, I am. I'm overseeing the history and heritage portion."

"Well, that's wonderful. That's sure to score some big points when it comes time for you to take over."

I'm smiling so hard and wide, I could use an extra face to accommodate the grin. I always knew Brockett would back me, but that statement's as good as an in-hand endorsement.

"Thanks, Larry," I say, allowing myself the familiarity. "But you know what they say: each one reach one, each one teach one."

"Right on, brother. See you tomorrow."

I hang up and light-step down to my waiting students. Uplifting events like meeting Chloe and Brockett's phone call give me hope that on the twilight side of my current hassles there'll be peace, harmony, and good times.

All my students, except LaThomas Patterson and his crew, are present. My heart breaks at not seeing Andre Echols. I sigh and resign myself to the fact that he'll simply be one of the ones I won't reach. No one will reach Andre, not as long as others want him to succeed more than *he* does.

I turn my attention to the rest of my students and say, "Hello, scholars."

"Hello, Dr. Collins."

They're wearing the oddest expressions, like they're hiding a secret they can't wait to share.

"What's going on?" I ask, dreading yet another surprise.

"Look behind you!" Augusta Baylor says, pointing at the board.

I glance, do a double take, and step back a little to better read the writing: WE SUPPORT YOU, PROFESSOR COLLINS!

The class breaks into applause and cheers, and I keep my back to my students until I've regained my composure and laughed my misting eyes clear.

"Thanks, everyone," I say, raising my voice. "Thanks. C'mon now, settle down."

Several curious people cruise by the door, their strides slowing as they glance inside. I gesture for the students to settle down, and the noise slowly subsides. Once I'm back on firm emotional ground, I look around the room and smile.

"Nice try," I say. "But you all still have to take this test."

The students laugh and Dex Padrewski says, "Bring it on, Professor!"

"Yeah!" several others challenge. "Let's have it, Professor Collins."

"And quickly!" Chris Arrati urges. "Before I wet myself."

The class roars and I distribute the test. Pens start scribbling away as the students give back the information I've poured into them, some grimacing as they struggle to remember the facts, details, causalities, and consequences of the events we've discussed.

I walk over to the window, glance outside, and see a small contingent of MPC students walking slowly in a circle, one of their placards saying GIVE US FREEDOM! My insides churn with disgust at their slave mentality, asking Ole Marse to grant them a freedom that was *never* his to take!

33

I COME FROM CLASS AND DISCOVER THAT JARROD'S
left a message indicating that he again plans to spend the night with "Uncle Milton." Jarrod has surprised me by leaving the number, and I reach for the phone to call him. It rings just as I'm grabbing it.

"Hello?"

"Hi, Darius."

It's Gina! I take a moment to calm my racing heart. Warmth, relief, and ecstasy surge through me, and I want to tell Gina how much I've missed her. But that might be pushing matters and after our last phone conversation I'm already on shaky ground, so I put myself in check.

"Gina, it's really great to hear from you," I say, keeping my tone calm and even.

"It's good to hear your voice too, Darius. I've . . . missed you."

I'm caught completely off guard. It's good knowing that I haven't been pining away in solitude, but Gina sounds upset. Which means that once I find out what's bothering her, I will be also.

After a few seconds, I say, "Er, I've missed you too, Gina."

I hear something sounding like a sniffle. It's soft and almost imperceptible but a sniffle nonetheless. "Gina, what's wrong?"

"Huh? Oh, nothing. Listen, could you do me a favor?"

"Sure! You know our agreement. If it's legal, cheap, close, and quick, it's yours."

She chuckles halfheartedly. "Could you pick me up from the airport when I get back?"

I hesitate before answering. Bruce usually shuttles her to and from the airport, except on those occasions when he absolutely can't accommodate her. Either way, I'm her ride of last resort, which pisses me off but at least affords me an occasional opportunity to be close to her. One of these days, I'm going to stop panting after her like some pathetic puppy. Today's not that day.

"What time do you arrive?" I ask.

She tells me. She has at least once before, but I only half listened, figuring that since she'd most likely be meeting Bruce before seeing me, it didn't much matter.

"Okay, Gina," I say. "I'll be there with bells."

"Thanks, Darius. I really appreciate it."

Another long pause. "Gina, tell me what's wrong?"

Her voice is tight when she answers, "Not now, okay?"

"Okay. Just know that I'm here for you."

She sniffles again, this time not bothering to muffle it. "I'll explain everything tomorrow. I promise."

I offer some gentle but generic words of comfort, hoping they'll help alleviate the stress of whatever she's dealing with. Then we hang up.

I have started to call Jarrod when the phone rings again. "Hello?"

"I don't have much time, so listen close," Cookie orders.

The warmth, relief, and ecstasy that filled me less than a nanosecond ago are crushed beneath an avalanche of cold anxiety and grinding frustration.

"My sister, Candace, is driving up from Shreveport," Cookie continues. "She's going to stay at my house with Jarrod, and should be arriving tonight."

A shiver races back and forth along my spine at the mention of Candace's name. Besides being Cookie's older sister, she's a walking environmental hazard. It could only be sisterly love, desperation, or both that led Cookie to ask Candace to come and turn her home into a model of urban blight.

"Does Jarrod know?" I ask, suspecting strongly that he does.

"Yes! I've had a conference call with him, Candace, and Trudy, trying to handle long-distance what you can't manage under your nose."

"Cookie, you can take a flying leap!" I retort.

She bulldozes right through my rebuff, instructing me on what Jarrod and I are to do next.

"Cookie, you can save your guidance for Jarrod," I say. "I'm going to handle matters as I see fit."

"No, you won't!" she declares. "Trudy's amended my power-of-attorney papers, faxed them to me, and I've signed off. So Candace is officially taking care of my affairs where Jarrod's concerned. If you interfere, she's been instructed to swear out a restraining order against you."

My jaw drops. "Restraining order! Are you nuts? What for?"

"To protect *my son!*" she hollers. "I can't depend upon you to do what I ask, so I, as usual, have taken care of it."

The rage boiling in me is so potent, a sour-tasting bile fills my mouth.

"It's your own fault," Cookie continues. "I told you to contact Trudy so that . . ."

"I've got news for you, Cookie. No one, not you, Candace, Trudy, or anyone else, is going to block my access to Jarrod."

"No one's blocking anything! But you're not abusing Jarrod anymore."

My mouth fills with so many obscenities that my tongue gets tied, reducing me to grunts and sputters.

Cookie exploits the moment with expert skill. "Now that the situation's been handled, can you at least try and keep that Cuppersmith woman from Jarrod until I get back?" she asks mockingly.

"How is Bernice Cuppersmith any worse an influence than you?"

Cookie hurls a number of creative suggestions for me to engage in self-sex, then hangs up. The phone rings again and I snatch it up, still hoping to talk to Jarrod.

"Hello?"

"Finally!" Marcy says.

I slam the phone down and leave.

34

I SWEATED ALL THROUGH YESTERDAY WONDERING ABOUT Phoebe's mysterious e-mail, but now it's time for the revelation. I step into the Liberation Station restaurant, see Phoebe waving at me from a table, make my way across the room, and we exchange a brief hug.

"Glad you could make it," she says.

"Not as glad as I am."

Marvin Gaye's classic song "What's Going On" floats through the restaurant, setting a perfect mood for the occasion. The Liberation Station's a cozy, forever-busy establishment, located several blocks from campus in a section where Cleveland stops being so much a collection of many different people and becomes a hub for *black!* people.

The restaurant's owner, Eli Strothers, a street hood activist turned lawyer-businessman, ensures that the sixties Revolution of his youth is kept alive. Posters of Huey Newton, Jomo Kenyatta, Bobby Seale, Kwame Nkrumah, and Muhammad Ali adorn the restaurant's perimeter walls. Malcolm X commands a center column position, his gaze beaming out from the picture, admonishing his black people to stay on guard. Beside him is a large photo of Stokely Carmichael (aka Kwame Toure), forever frozen by the camera in a raised-fist pose, his mouth and eyes wide open as he exhorts his people to action.

The smell of southern cooking fills the air, making nostrils flare and palates expectant. Marvin Gaye's song goes off and is replaced by Curtis Mayfield's "Choice of Colors." He's followed by Gil Scott Heron, who warns that "the Revolution will not be televised."

Phoebe snaps her fingers to the beat and sips her wine. "Are you sure you won't have a glass, Darius?" she asks. "This is excellent."

"No thanks. I've got a CBHS meeting shortly afterwards and I want to make sure that I'm uptight and irritable."

She chuckles and shakes her head. "Now why do you want to be like that?"

"Negative stress can produce positive results. Grad school and divorce taught me how to channel my anxiety into output."

She ponders that for a moment, then nods, her expression communicating that my weird perspective makes sense, in a weird sort of way.

The server takes our order, all of us bopping our heads and smiling as Aretha Franklin tells her man and the world that she wants some *respect*. I sit back and cross my arms over my chest, smiling as Phoebe looks around and absorbs the essence of the Civil Rights victories won by a previous generation.

"I've been working much too hard," Phoebe observes. "There's no excuse for my not having heard about this place."

"Consider it information sharing," I say, seizing the opportunity to segue. "I've shown you one of Cleveland's finest dining establishments and now you can decode your e-mail."

Phoebe stares slyly from behind her glass of wine. "C'mon, Darius. You can't be as in the dark as you're pretending."

I shrug. "Okay. I'm not."

She finishes her wine, places her elbows on the table, and crosses her arms. "Marcy told me about the fish."

Satisfying memories rebloom within as I recall that sweet moment of victory. The corners of Phoebe's mouth curve slightly upward into a cute impish smile.

"That was, shall we say, a unique response," she chuckles.

"You know me. I strive to set the standard."

Phoebe smirks, then gets serious. "Darius, I think she misses you."

I sit statue-still and silent.

"What's the matter?" Phoebe asks.

"Nothing. Why?"

"Well, you're sitting there like you didn't hear what I said."

"I heard you. Marcy might be missing me. Thanks for the update, but so what!"

Phoebe blinks and clears her throat. "I see."

"Okay. I'll nibble at the bait. What is it you see?"

"Nothing, Darius. I'm sorry I brought it up."

I reach across the table and take gentle hold of Phoebe's hand. "I apologize, Phoebe. If it sounds like I'm directing any lingering hostility at you, I don't mean to."

She ponders for a moment. "You're forgiven, Darius. And I understand. I've been dumped before and know it can be hard."

I smile. "I prefer to think of myself as being recycled rather than dumped."

"You're nuts!" Phoebe laughs.

I squeeze her hand and let go. I could probably hold on to it longer, milking the most from my role as the rejected boyfriend needing a little female comfort. But Phoebe's with Omar and he loves her like nobody's business. Just once, though, I wish I had the guts to be the jerk pursuing another guy's girlfriend. I wish I could shrug off Omar's subsequent pain with the thought that "he'll get over it." But I'm not like that. Even when I've tried to be a dog, I couldn't sustain the act. And so I get to sit here, just another hapless schnook, finishing *last* while Stan fills up the space that was once mine!

"So, Phoebe, what did Marcy say that convinced you she might be missing me?"

"It's nothing she said, Darius. My conclusion's based on simple observation."

"Okay. What did you observe?"

"Well, it's kind of strange. She explained why the two of you couldn't go on and how this Stanley character was so much more compatible with her. And I've got to admit, the man's a dream. He's attentive, romantic, sensitive, and appears to have no higher priority than her happiness. All things considered, it's easy to see how she fell for him."

I sit back and cross my arms over my chest. "Is this the part where you're making me feel better?"

Phoebe blushes. "Sorry, Darius. I didn't mean to imply that . . ."

"That's okay. I've been told by more than one woman that I'm inattentive, unromantic, callous, and distant. It's the price I pay for studying dead guys."

Phoebe's blush deepens. "Anyway, she invited me to dinner and to meet this Stan."

"What's he look like?"

Phoebe purses her lips and looks away.

"Never mind," I say. "Just focus on those parts where I'm better than him."

Phoebe sips her water. "On the surface, it seemed so perfect. But he was thoroughly irritating Marcy."

"How's that possible with someone so apparently wonderful?"

Phoebe slides her glass to the side and leans forward. "For one thing, he was smothering her. She couldn't turn around without bumping into him. And he wouldn't let her do anything for herself. The only place she got some privacy was in the bathroom."

The server sets some bread and butter on our table and leaves, his mellow voice joining the Four Tops as they plead their case to "Bernadette."

Phoebe waits until he's out of earshot, then continues. "I lost count of the number of times Marcy rolled her eyes every time he called her sweetheart, sugar, darling, or some other syrupy pet name. It was enough to cause tooth decay."

I slowly massage my temples so that understanding can better penetrate my brain.

"But I think it was the flowers that took the cake," Phoebe continues.

"What about the flowers?"

"Just as we were sitting down to eat, some guy arrives with this big arrangement of roses. And I'm talking huge!"

"And you're saying this was a bad thing?" I ask. "Were the roses some kind of camouflaged poison ivy?"

Phoebe smiles. "No, silly. It was the overkill. The roses were the third delivery that day." Phoebe's eyes fill with concern. "Darius, are you all right?"

"Yes. I'm fine. Please go on."

"Well, he makes this big deal out of how there's nothing too good for her, and how it wasn't until meeting her that he understood the meaning of being wealthy, and . . ."

I stop massaging my temples. "Wait! Are you saying this guy's rich?"

Phoebe nods gravely. "As in loaded."

I chuckle and shake my head. Phoebe frowns. "Darius, what in the world is going on with your head?"

"I'm just trying to piece it all together. Because it sounds like you're telling me that after trading me for a suave hunk whose personality and wallet weight are superior to mine, Marcy's still not satisfied."

"I didn't say she wasn't satisfied, Darius. I just think she misses you."

"Whatever!" I retort. "If she's so happy and satisfied, why bother missing me?"

"Because you're real, Darius. And with you, Marcy could be herself. She never worried about whether or not you were judging her."

These are most certainly the things Marcy once said she adored about me. And I'm perturbed that she shared them with Phoebe (and therefore Omar). But I'm also chastised with silent reminders of me sharing such secrets with Nash along with all those macho lies of male conquest.

I brush off the memory and resume discussion. "Phoebe, that's all wonderful to hear, but why should I care?"

"I'm not saying you should. I'm only pointing out that it seems as though Marcy's missing what she had with you and that, well, maybe you should think about it."

"You can't be serious. What's there to think about?"

Phoebe looks hard at me. "Darius, listen. What Marcy did was a mistake. The minute I found out, I told her so. For the most part, you're a good man and . . ."

"For the most part!"

Phoebe offers a devilish smile. "C'mon, Darius. After all, you are just a man."

I flex my mediocre biceps like I'm competing in a Mr. Universe contest. "I'm not 'just a man.' I'm a love machine. I'm *the* stud muffin of Cleveland, Ohio."

Phoebe rolls her eyes. "Need I say more?"

I grab a piece of bread and slather on some butter. "Well, Phoebe. No matter what kind of man I am, I'm also the kind who's tired of wading through crap."

"Meaning?"

"Meaning I don't intend to spend one second thinking about inviting Marcy back into my life. Just like she wouldn't if I'd Pearl Harbored her!"

"Darius, haven't you ever done something that you were certain was the right thing, only to discover later that it was wrong?"

"Absolutely. Saying 'Hello!' to my ex-wife stands out as a glaring example."

Phoebe frowns. "I'm serious!"

I finish chewing and swallow my bread. "So am I."

"Life is a growth process. That's what happens when people make mistakes. They grow."

"I couldn't agree with you more. And after my ex-wife, Marcy, and those other psych ward escapees, I've grown taller than a giant sequoia."

Phoebe's jaw stiffens. "You're not even going to consider what I'm saying, are you?"

"On the contrary. I'm considering in great detail what you're saying. Would you care to hear my analysis?"

Phoebe huffs and nods.

"Okay. First you suspect that Marcy's merely missing me. Now you're saying she wants a second chance."

"No, Darius. I'm *guessing* that she wants a second chance. And I'm certain that if you made it easier for her, she wouldn't hesitate to make things right between the two of you."

I polish off the last of my bread, flick away a crumb, and sip some water. "No!"

Phoebe blinks. "Huh?"

"*N-o.* No!"

"Can I ask why not?"

"I was hoping you would."

She sits back with one hand in her lap, the other on the table, her fingers slowly drumming.

"It's like this, Phoebe," I begin. "First of all, Marcy showed her true colors and stated her desires the weekend of my, ah, recycling."

"Darius, she could've changed."

"And it could've been for the worse. But it doesn't matter. I'm applying the option women have always exercised and most brothers don't even realize they possess."

"Which is?"

"The *option to choose.* You see, just because Marcy's fine, sophisticated, and alluring doesn't condemn me to defy my common sense and be slain by her charms. That might've happened as recently as two or three weeks ago. But that was then and this is now."

"My, my. Aren't we waxing philosophical."

"You'd better believe it!" I confirm. "And I haven't even gotten to the best part."

"Go on."

"Second, I'm not lifting a finger to convince Marcy to give us another whirl. Beyond the fact that *she's* the one who called it off, I'm not going to be her emotional barometer."

"Clarification, please?"

"When I get involved with a woman, I make certain assumptions. I know it's never good to assume, but there are some that are safer bets than others."

"For example?"

"For example, I assume that I'm getting involved with a fully mature adult. Someone who knows why she's involved with me and doesn't require me performing daily like some court jester to keep her entertained and satisfied."

I pause to gauge Phoebe's reaction and she gestures for me to go on.

"I assume that we're in a monogamous committed relationship and there's no need to worry about what she's doing when we're apart. I assume that she's with me for me and not because I trapped her in my emotional net. And I assume that she stays with me because she wants to, not because I've convinced her."

"And your point is?"

"Everything I've said is the point! Marcy can't be trusted to resist the next guy and his better deal. And from what you've said, even when she has him, she's entertaining better offers. I guess that's okay if it results in happiness and fulfillment."

"Darius, you can't blame someone for wanting to be happy."

"Exactly! Which is why I'm telling you that at this point in my life, my idea of happiness is a world *without* Marcy."

It's also a world without Cookie, but that'll come. In just under two years and that many child support payments from now, I'll finally be rid of her and will reclaim the precious commodity I let her burgle: *peace of mind!*

Phoebe's brow bunches in frustration. "Darius, I know she still has feelings for you. Just like you do for her, and don't deny it!"

"Maybe, maybe not. It doesn't change the fact that Marcy's out, for good!"

"I can't believe you're being so hard-nosed and unforgiving."

"And I can't believe you want me to accept a double standard you'd find insulting."

"What double standard?"

"It's about that business of choice. As long as Marcy wanted me around, I was supposed to be there for as long as she wanted. When she changed her mind, I was supposed to suddenly be a good sport and vanish. If I'd burped a protest, nine-one-one would've been her hammer. But now that *I'm* telling her no, you're calling me hard-nosed and unforgiving."

"So that's it then? You're going to let your pride keep you two apart when a simple phone call could put you back together the way you know it should be."

The strident edge in Phoebe's tone crosses a line that leaves my jaw tight. The fire dims quickly in her eyes as she gazes into mine.

"Darius, all I'm saying is that you're both such good people. All relationships have their ups and downs. This is a down. This is where you have to be the bigger party and help Marcy see that you need each other."

I slowly shake my head. "And what happens the next time?"

"What're you talking about? There won't be a next time."

"Oh *yes* there will. Just like women are fond of saying that a man who cheats on his wife will cheat on his girlfriend too, the same goes for a woman like Marcy."

"But . . ."

"Sure. I could do as you say and convince her to give us another chance. That'd be good for a season, but it wouldn't last."

"Why not?"

"Because it wasn't her decision! Don't you get it, Phoebe? I don't want a woman who has to be convinced to stay with me. She has to want to be there, of her own free will. She has to decide for herself that I'm the man she wants. Anything else is a formula for failure."

Phoebe looks down at the table and ponders for a long moment. "I guess I can see your point. I've never considered it from a man's point of view."

"*Most men don't consider it from that point of view!* Think about it. Let's say I convince Marcy to fall in love with me on Monday. We have fun and get along on Tuesday. But maybe on Wednesday, I'm having a bad day and not being so lovable. By Thursday, she's looking toward the hills. By Friday morning, I've got either to be playing the court jester again or face the possibility that she'll be leaving town with the next act. That's not the kind of person I want or need in my life."

The server brings our chef salads and we dig in. I make small talk about the size of the tomatoes, the tangy Italian dressing, and the sweet sounds of the Stylistics, but Phoebe's mostly quiet. I've never been good at enduring the silent treatment and cave in quickly.

"Okay, Phoebe," I say, suddenly very glad that I'm not Omar. "Why the pout?"

"I'm not pouting, Darius. I just never knew you were so harsh."

"Harsh!" I blurt.

My impulse is to rush to my defense, but a glance at my watch tells me there's no time to prolong this futility.

So I simply say, "Phoebe, I'm sorry you feel that way."

I wolf down several more forkfuls of salad, beg my apologies for having to rush off, and leave my portion of the bill. Phoebe pushes back from the table, pays her portion, and we leave together.

Out in the parking lot she says, "Well, Darius. Have a good meeting."

"I will, Phoebe. And thanks for inviting me to lunch. It was interesting."

"Yes," she agrees. "It most certainly was."

We hug and I turn toward my car, stopping when she calls me. "Darius!"

She saunters over, waving an envelope slowly back and forth. "I almost forgot. Marcy asked me to give this to you."

I look at the envelope for a long, long moment. For all I know, it could be a summons to appear in civil court about those blasted fish.

"What's this?" I ask.

Phoebe shrugs and hands over the envelope with great ceremony. "I have no idea. Except that Marcy was crying when she asked me to do whatever I could to get you to read it."

I glance at the envelope's front. No doubt about it. That's Marcy's elegant handwriting. And the scent filling my nostrils is the *Next Spring* fragrance she knows I love. On the back seal are two red lip prints, the lipstick so glossy it looks wet. I rub my finger across the pattern and remember the moist, full feel of Marcy's lips. Then I give the envelope back to Phoebe.

"But, but I thought . . ." she sputters.

"What did you think, Phoebe? That I wasn't serious? That my 'no!' meant something other than 'no!'"

She frowns, her eyes filling with pity. "My gosh, Darius. You are truly bitter."

"Bitter!"

I smile, shake my head, and walk away, content to let Phoebe believe whatever comforts her most.

35

I CALL VESEY HIGH ON THE WAY TO THE CLEVELAND
Black Historical Society and check to make sure that Jarrod's there.

"Yes," the attendance secretary proudly reports. "He's in biology class right now and will be going to Dynamics of International Relations next period."

Biology and Dynamics of International Relations. Any stranger observing Jarrod's recent behavior would be hard-pressed to believe that he's enrolled in an honors program. It'll be a temporary "honor" if his grades slip any further. He's like Andre Echols, a mind-boggling case of talent choosing to waste itself. I'll bet that just as I'm doing with Jarrod, there's probably someone pulling their hair out over Andre, wondering what it'll take to slap him into reality. I'm going to talk with him again. He might be content with mediocrity, but the blood of our slave ancestors compels me to demand his excellence.

I'm only a few blocks from the CBHS and shift my thoughts to this meeting with the board. I park and hurry inside. CBHS president Lawrence P. Brockett is pacing and smoking in the nonsmoking lobby of the society's stately mansion headquarters. He sees me, crushes his cigarette into a flowerpot, and hustles over.

"Thank God you're here," he rasps, pumping my hand. "I was starting to wonder."

"I would've been here sooner, but traffic was kind of slow."

He grabs my elbow, pulls me into his office, and shuts the door.

"What's going on?" I ask. "If it's about my almost being late, I'm truly sorry."

Brockett paces a few steps, wringing his hands. "Dr. Collins, er, Darius. We don't have much time, so . . ."

A knock on the door interrupts. "Dr. Brockett," a mature female voice calls, "they're heading into the conference room."

"Okay, Ms. Corwin. We'll be right out."

The worry and anxiety permeating this atmosphere get the better of me and I suddenly feel very unprepared for this meeting.

"Look!" Brockett declares. "I'll get to the point. El Bornu's here."

My mouth falls open. "Osmani el Bornu! Of the New Black Movement?"

"The same."

"But . . . I thought this was a meeting with the board."

"Use your head, Dr. Collins. The man just gave the society one-point-two million dollars. He *is* the board."

"Well then, am I meeting just with him?"

Brockett answers with an emphatic negative head shake. "No. The other members are here. He'll be sitting in as an observer. It seems you've earned yourself a generous degree of ill will from the New Black Movement. Something about your opposing el Bornu's speaking at your university."

"What? How could he know about that? El Bornu's never even flown over the campus, much less set foot there."

"Well, he has now. Call it bad timing, but after he made that dona-tion he started sending disciples here to recruit. And, well, you're a smart man. Add his people fanning out over the city to that campus controversy and it equals *you* getting surprised in my office."

"But that's a separate issue. And I'm not directly opposing him. I only pointed out that he's bringing a lot of baggage the university doesn't need."

Brockett grimaces. "So you criticized him?"

"The man's an anti-Semitic viper. Of course I criticized him. Just like the First Amendment gives me the right to do."

"That amendment also gives him the right to his opinions, Dr. Collins."

All this cowering before el Bornu and his $1.2 million angers me. "Dr. Brockett," I say, struggling to control my tone. "I appreciate the clout that's implied when someone donates a huge sum of money to the CBHS. But since when did we allow big-donor sensitivities to take prece-dence over the objective historical study, analysis, and interpretation of African-Americans in Cleveland?"

Brockett literally grabs his hair and pulls. "Don't you get holier-than-thou on me!" he growls, glancing nervously at the door. "I know how cor-rosive this can be. I also know that el Bornu's 'gift' pulled us back from the brink of economic ruin."

The news hits me like a fastball between the eyes. "Did you say 'economic ruin'?"

"That's *exactly* what I said."

Brockett gets up and starts pacing again. "The CBHS was backed into a fiscal corner and I had to make a choice. I've regretted it ever since, but it kept the organization solvent. It also bought some time for you and, if necessary, the next president to devise a strategy for getting rid of that slug."

At least Brockett and I are on the same page in our opinion of el Bornu. But our mutual agreement only serves to heighten the hypocrisy of having cut a deal with him.

I sit riveted as Dad's admonishing echo says, *"Darius, what does it profit a man to gain the whole world if he should lose his immortal soul?"*

There's another knock, harder and more emphatic. "Dr. Brockett! They're waiting."

"On the way, Ms. Corwin."

He hurries behind his desk and pulls out a folder, a writing pad, and two pens. "You're not the only one with something to lose, Dr. Collins. I've applied to take over as chief archivist at the Tubman Library of Slave Culture and History in Washington, D.C. The CBHS's financial dissolution wouldn't have been a welcome addition to my résumé. A philosophic slugfest between you and el Bornu is just as unwelcome. You get my drift?"

I don't answer one way or the other. It's disgusting, seeing Brockett scurry around like some field hand preparing to run up to the big house. And although I need his support, the underhanded smell of this scenario is stoking my anger.

"So how long have you known?" I ask, watching him head for the door.

"Known what?"

"That I was being set up?"

Brockett stops dead in his tracks and faces me slowly. When he's turned completely around, his face is bathed in an angry glow. "It's only because you're a fellow historian and I paid too much for this suit that you'll get away with that insult."

"It's only an insult if it's not true."

Brockett's nostrils flare. "Look! We don't have time for this. So let me tell you what I know. You can choose to believe it or not."

"I'm listening."

Another knock. "Dr. Brockett!"

"I'm coming!" he snaps, glancing at the door.

He looks back at me and speaks quickly. "I didn't know about el Bornu's coming any more than you. When the board pushed me to have this meeting, I thought they just wanted to get all this nomination business over with. As you can see, I was wrong!"

The more Brockett talks, the smaller I get.

"We've both been set up," he says. "My guess is that you've been targeted because of all that confusion at your university and some of the board members being offended by your presentation."

"Offended? But I thought they loved it."

Brockett smiles like he's in the presence of a well-meaning idiot. "You've got a lot to learn about politics, Dr. Collins. Even at this low level."

"Obviously," I respond.

"As for me," he continues, "I think they're after my scalp for supporting someone whose perspective on African-American history amounts to heresy."

"Heresy! Everything I said was rooted in historical fact!"

Brockett shrugs. "My relatives in Youngstown would call it killing two birds with one stone."

He steps quickly to the door, grabs the knob, and looks at me. "Acquit yourself well, Dr. Collins. Both of our necks are depending on it."

36

I FOLLOW BROCKETT INTO THE CONFERENCE ROOM. It's normally one of my favorite places but right now feels more like a gathering place for Romans to watch Christians being fed to the lions. I bolster my courage with the legacy of black excellence filling the room. A stern but loving portrait of Sojourner Truth stares down from over the doorway leading outside to a well-manicured garden. A captivating picture of Frederick Douglass in his later years hangs over a display case containing some of his original letters and notes. A few feet away stands a statue of an African-American Civil War soldier, holding his rifle at the ready. His implacable expression communicates his grim understanding that his only option was victory, since defeat meant certain enslavement and death.

Brockett takes his seat at the far left end of a semicircular table and gestures for me to take my position at the wooden podium, facing the grim-faced board members. Sitting beside Brockett is the slim, regal Erin Driscoll, president of the Freedmen's Insurance Group. Her management style's been described as "slice and dice." She's never said much on previous occasions, and I'm hoping she'll follow that pattern today.

Beside her is jowly Festus Valentine, CEO of Valentine Systems, Inc. He's a talented, obnoxious computer engineer who's discovered a latent love for history and knows just enough to be a frequently erroneous nuisance.

Next to him is corpulent Quincy Poltis, distinguished professor of anthropology at Sunderland Theological Seminary and alleged descendant of David Walker, a free black who disappeared "mysteriously" after his 1829 publication of *Walker's Appeal*. Since Walker was urging slaves to seize their freedom through insurrection, it's likely that his only descendant was the dust cloud billowing behind him as he fled town.

And then there's the lovely muckraking Wylene Narmer, publisher and chief editor of *Pulse Cleveland*, a small but highly influential African-American newspaper. She left the *Herald* after one too many disagreements over its persistent refusal to report anything but the worst concerning black people.

I place my notes on the podium, making sure they're arranged in the same order they were in when I previously delivered my allegedly scandalous presentation. I look to Brockett, who looks to the board, who look to the entrance as Osmani el Bornu swoops into the room and walks along the dimly lit rear wall. Following him are two trim, powerful-looking escorts dressed in dark uniformlike outfits. Their quick, confident steps, scanning eyes, and pantherlike movements indicate they're his bodyguards.

Something in me recoils at the thought that someone so closely associated with the CBHS needs bodyguards. But when that someone has made a career of selling hatred and division, bodyguards are to be expected.

Whatever else can be said of him, el Bornu's impressive. His lean, tall body moves with the grace of someone who's spent much time training as a gymnast, skater, or dancer or in the martial arts. I'm guessing the last. He's shunned his usual garb of the motherland, opting instead for a nicely tailored dark double-breasted suit, a pair of sharp shoes that, in another life, probably swam in the Florida Everglades, and diamond-studded pinkie rings on both hands. He keeps on his trademark sixties-era Black Power shades, which, along with his neatly trimmed Afro, emphasize the militancy he likes to project.

"Sorry I'm late, my brothers and sisters," he says, his voice softer and more inviting than the thundering invective normally blasting through the sound bites.

"Think nothing of it," Brockett fawns. "We weren't going to start until you arrived."

I roll my eyes as Larry kisses el Bornu's butt as he lowers it into a plush chair. He's seated off to the side and slightly to the rear of where the board members are. The bodyguards stand to either side of el Bornu like two-legged Dobermans. And now that they're in full view, I see that one of them is LaThomas Patterson and the puzzle's complete. He sneers a smile at me and silently mouths an obscenity.

"Go right ahead," el Bornu says, gesturing for us to continue. "Just pretend that I'm not even here."

Which is clearly not his intent, since his separation emphasizes rather than diminishes his presence.

Brockett, Erin, and Valentine smile full-toothed smiles while Wylene and Quincy simply nod and look back at me. Brockett's happy face freezes over when he turns toward me.

"Dr. Collins, the CBHS executive board has called this special meeting in hopes of clarifying some points addressed during your recent presentation."

"I'm delighted to answer any questions the board has," I respond, glancing at el Bornu from the corner of my eye.

"Please be assured," Brockett continues, "that we're here as colleagues and not detractors. But the board felt it necessary to get a better understanding of your historical perspective before considering your nomination to the presidency. We sincerely hope this hasn't been an inconvenience."

"Not in the least, Dr. Brockett."

Brockett smiles like his face is cement. "Very well. The floor's open for questions."

I grip the sides of the podium and get ready. El Bornu crosses his legs and arms and watches with intensity. LaThomas and the other Doberman, whom I now recognize as MPC chairman Mubarak Kwanju, are expressionless, but their eyes are filled with interest.

Festus Valentine gestures and I acknowledge him, "Yes, Mr. Valentine."

He nods and clears his throat. "Dr. Collins, let me first say how much I respect you and your achievements. But during your presentation, I was disturbed by your asserting that blacks in the U.S. were afraid to throw off the shackles of slavery."

I dig my fingernails into the sides of the podium, supremely irritated with the manner in which Valentine has casually mangled my point.

"Mr. Valentine, I'm certain that you've misinterpreted me," I say, my tone filling with ice. "I've always stressed that blacks in North America fought slavery's oppression at every opportunity, and with every means at their disposal."

Valentine glowers. "Let me refresh your memory," he persists. He flips through his notes. "Ah! Here we are. You said: 'Slave rebellions in the U.S. were flash points of discontent when compared with similar events in South America and the Caribbean.' Do you still maintain that position?"

I look over at Brockett, who's practically cringing. El Bornu's unchanged. The rest of the board members are like hounds straining at their leashes. This is my moment of truth.

Being CBHS president could open doors for me. There'd be more money and time to research and travel. There's the annual African Diaspora conference in Geneva, Switzerland. I'd come in contact with the best of the best, perhaps maybe even be invited to the White House to lend some advice on "black stuff." And I'd meet plenty of like-minded, similarly interested, equally trained, intelligent *women*! All I have to do is give the right answer.

So I stare directly into Valentine's eyes and say, "I absolutely maintain that position!"

Brockett grimaces and palm-slaps his forehead. Wylene smiles as her muckraking pen goes into action. Quincy taps his chin in contemplation. Erin and Valentine whisper between themselves, Erin glancing at the smoldering el Bornu.

The commotion dies down and Valentine continues. "So then, you *do* believe that blacks in the U.S. were too meek to fight."

"No!" I snap. "I *do not* believe that."

I take a moment to compose myself. Valentine's statement is as insulting as it is stupid. And combined with this board's collective subterfuge in orchestrating this public flogging, I'm starting to wonder if I want to be even a CBHS member, let alone its president!

"Let's clear this matter up once and for all," I command. "Asserting that slave rebellions in America didn't succeed to the extent that they did in South America and the Caribbean *does not* equate with a lack of desire to resist. If anything, it underscores the degree to which America's racist system of human bondage and oppression sought to crush the will of black people. Given that reality, the slaves who rebelled at Stono, South Carolina, in 1739, those who fought alongside Gabriel Prosser in 1800, Denmark Vesey in 1822, and Nat Turner in 1831, are to be considered nothing less than *heroes in the cause of freedom*."

"And yet you insist that their heroism achieved anemic results," Erin observes.

"No, Ms. Driscoll. I only insist upon the facts. There's simply no evidence of a North American slave rebellion succeeding to the same degree as, say for example, the one led by Toussaint-Louverture that established the world's first black republic in Haiti."

I address the rest of the board members. "And I reiterate, lack of similar success *is not* to be misinterpreted as a lack of willingness or courage to try. We know for certain that slaves daily exercised their power through thousands of small acts of defiance. No matter how hard whites tried to snuff out their humanity, they fought tenaciously to retain their dignity."

"That's an interesting spin you've put on it," Valentine observes. "But it still sounds as objectionable as your alleging the existence of elitism within the black community."

"It's objectionable only if you reject the historical reality of African-American economic progress," I counter. "Or do you, like so many whites, prefer to assume that all blacks either live in or come from some drug-infested, crime-ridden hood?"

Brockett slumps in his chair and starts speaking in tongues. Dr. Poltis smirks. Wylene looks me up and down then continues taking notes. Erin and Valentine glance at each other, el Bornu, then zero back in on me.

Valentine balls his fists and narrows his eyes. "Dr. Collins, if you don't mind, we'll ask the questions."

"Ask anything you wish," I encourage. "But don't expect me to bend historical fact to fit your politically correct truth." I smile, surprising myself that I don't mind destroying my chances for being CBHS president.

Dr. Poltis gestures to get my attention. "Dr. Collins, we appreciate your pluck and candor, but all the same, would you clarify your point?"

"Gladly," I answer, nodding. "By most socioeconomic measures, blacks still lag behind the rest of society. But there have also been a lot of African-Americans who have moved into the middle and upper classes. That movement has in too many cases separated them from their less fortunate brethren and fosters lines of division that can't be bridged by mere appeals to likeness of skin color."

"I resent that!" Erin snarls. "We're all in the same boat and you as a professional historian should know better."

"Ms. Driscoll, it's because *I am* a professional historian that I make the observation. And while you're correct in that we're all in the same boat, it's also true that some are below the deck rowing while others are in the grand ballroom, dining on lobster."

"Well then," Valentine billows, "physician, heal thyself. As a well-educated college professor you're also part of that elitist problem."

"It's not a problem, Mr. Valentine. If anything, it's a wonderful testament to the record of black progress in this country that's spent most of its history trying to keep us lower than dirt."

I step to the side of the podium and stare hard into each face. "Look,

FREDDIE LEE JOHNSON III

there's no doubt that African-Americans are a unique and remarkable people. Our history is replete with instances of our successfully conquering one obstacle after another. I daily celebrate that we've gotten to a point where more of us are gaining access to wealth, which means that we're participating more fully in the nation's economic life."

"I'm not just participating!" Valentine protests, swelling up with indignation. "I'll have you know that last year alone Valentine Systems earned . . ."

"Let 'em finish!" el Bornu commands, sitting tall and alert, his shades off and eyes boring into me.

I nod to him and look back at the board members. "All I'm saying is that we have to do a better job in making sure that no one gets left behind. Our progress as a community will never be complete until we're all succeeding individually."

Erin starts to comment, but el Bornu cuts her off. "Wait!" He puts his shades back on and scowls. "Am I hearing you say that the racism which for centuries has demanded the blood and tears of our people is no longer a problem? Am I hearing you say that the poverty and misery we've suffered is our fault and not the oppressors'?"

"What I'm saying and what you're *choosing* to hear are two different things," I retort. "But if you're asking whether I'm declaring racism in America dead, the answer is a categorical, ironclad *no*!"

"And this celebration of the few who've become wealthy among us is the best you can offer to fight it?"

"That's ridiculous!" I snip, knowing that I've just sunk my presidential ship. Brockett, apparently convinced of our mutual demise, mutters. "But I'll tell you this much," I continue. "I'm not interested in all the repetitive bellyaching about the myriad crimes committed against us during our time in America. What I want to do is expose the social and institutional racism that's mutated and gone underground, hiding in the shadows as it continues to plague our people."

El Bornu grunts and sinks back into his chair.

For the next forty minutes the board fires questions and I shoot back answers. The attempted tarring and feathering finally ends when el Bornu announces, "I've heard enough!"

Brockett hoists himself up from his deep slouch and looks at the other board members. "Are there any other questions for Dr. Collins?"

Everyone glances at the glowering el Bornu and concludes that, no, they don't have any more questions.

"I have one," Wylene says, her eyes fixed hard on me.

Brockett licks his lips and cuts his eyes nervously at el Bornu. "Ah, Wylene, I think we've heard enough, so why don't . . ."

"Be quiet, Larry," she softly commands, still looking hard at me.

El Bornu grumbles and shifts in his chair.

"Please ask your question," I say, staring back hard into Wylene's unblinking eyes.

"Dr. Collins, are you aware that you might've just cost yourself the CBHS presidency?"

"Yes. I am."

"And that doesn't matter to you?"

"On the contrary, Ms. Narmer. It matters quite a great deal. But if being CBHS president requires me surrendering to the *are-you-black-enough* culture police, *I don't want the job!*"

I glance into the faces of Brockett, the other board members, and el Bornu, stuff my notes into my folder, and stride swiftly to the door. El Bornu whispers to LaThomas, who catches up and taps me on the shoulder.

"Yes, Mr. Patterson. What is it?"

He scowls. "My new name is Kozi Nkushay."

"Okay, Cozy Mushy. What is it?"

His eyes narrow. "Leader el Bornu says he'll be seeing you soon."

I glance at el Bornu, sitting smug in his chair, then back at LaThomas. "Tell him that Leader Collins says he'll need to make an appointment."

37

I SHIFT MY CAR INTO DRIVE, STOMP ON THE GAS, AND head home. I should be pissed, but for some reason I'll better understand later, I'm relieved. Maybe it's the freedom of not having to kiss up, fawn, and "yassah, boss" Brockett and the board anymore. Either way, what's done is done and I'm hungry. Since I survived the attempted drubbing of that kangaroo court, I'm going to reward myself with a big, juicy steak, a bag of microwave popcorn, and an unspecified number of brewskis.

I turn into the apartment parking lot and see a candy apple red Corvette in my assigned parking space. Standing beside it, smiling and holding a rose, is *Chloe*! Hers is just the face I need to see right now. I park behind her, get out, and we hurry toward each other.

"Hello, Dr. Collins," she says, handing me the rose.

"Hello, Ms. Brown. Is this for me?"

She smiles and nods, wrapping me in her arms. The wonderful feeling of her pressing against me is compounded by the pleasant scent of her perfume.

She pulls back and says, "Are you okay? You seem kind of tense."

"I was. Seeing you has taken care of that problem."

She strokes my cheek tenderly. "You're sweet."

I kiss her. "Would you like to come inside?"

"I'd better. I can't let all this food spoil."

"All what food?"

She opens her trunk. There's a huge picnic basket in the center, wine chilling in a bucket of ice, and the most exquisite-looking chocolate cake I've ever seen.

"A picnic?" I ask, smiling.

"Call it Chloe's Catering," she answers with a wink.

I hug her tight, almost picking her up. "This is wonderful," I say, whispering into her ear.

We gather up the food and stroll inside. I almost start to tell her about my el Bornu incident but decide against it. He's not important enough to let him ruin such a rare, wonderful moment. So I listen closely while Chloe tells me about her day.

"I stopped by Black Heads this morning," she says. "You won't believe what's still going on."

"Knowing Blake and those knuckleheads, I probably won't. But tell me anyway."

Chloe laughs softly. Her voice is like a warm breeze blowing over my ears. "Parker and Otis are still doing the dozens," she says.

"That's got to be a world record," I chuckle.

We get to my apartment and I stick my key in the door. Just as I'm about to turn it I freeze as I suddenly remember: *Player!*

"Darius, is something wrong?" Chloe asks.

"Huh? Ah, no! Nothing's wrong. It's just this key. Sometimes it sticks."

I open the door, step inside, and glare at Player. He's scratching his head with a claw.

Chloe enters and looks around. "This is nice and cozy," she says.

Player looks up and moves along his perch in our direction. I swear if I didn't know better, I'd almost believe that he was trying to get a better look.

Chloe steps over to my poster of Sitting Bull. "My gosh," she says, her voice filled with awe. "He was a beautiful man."

She moves over to Frederick Douglass, looks at him for a long moment, then turns to me smiling. "He was the best."

"A giant among men, *then and now,*" I assert.

I glance at Player. He's just a stupid bird, but it actually looks like he's craning his neck to better check out Chloe. I consider moving him into the bedroom but reject the idea. That might set him off, and then I'd have to kill him.

I set the basket on the dining room table and start setting up for us to eat while Chloe surveys the contents of my bookcase.

"Is there anything you want me to do?" Chloe asks, still looking over my books.

"Yeah, baby," Player squawks. "Come sit on my face."

"What!" Chloe exclaims, spinning around.

I whiz over to the birdcage. "Player! Be quiet!" I command.

I look at Chloe. "I'm sorry, Chloe. This isn't my . . ."

"Baby, you got some *serious* boobs!" Player jabbers, looking at Chloe, who's speeding toward us.

I rattle the cage. "I'ma wring your neck, you scrawny little . . ."

"Darius, you know you wanna get some'a that booty."

"Is that true?" Chloe demands, punching me in the shoulder.

I open the cage and reach for Player, but he nips my finger. "Bend over and lemme spank it!" he says, hopping onto his perch.

"Darius, how could you?" Chloe asks, her voice trembling.

"Chloe, listen to me. This isn't my bird. My friend Nash asked me to . . ."

"Oh yeah, baby! Ride that rod!"

"He couldn't know to say these things unless he'd heard them from *you!*" Chloe accuses.

I grip her shoulders. "Wait right here. I can explain everything. Just wait. *Please!*"

Her angry eyes say no, but she nods anyway. "Hurry!"

I grab Player's cage off the bird-stand hook and dash into my bedroom. I slam the door and lift up the cage so that Player and I are looking eye-to-eye.

"Listen to me, you feathered pimp!" I whisper hoarsely. "If you say another . . ."

"C'mon, D. Help a brother out," Player implores.

"Will you shut up?"

"You're just like the white man, keeping a brother down."

"Player! I swear if you . . ."

"You're only doing this cuz I'm black."

I point a rigid forefinger at the cage. "One more word and you'll be rooming with a *cat*."

Player opens his beak, but instead of talking, he just blinks. He makes a noise that sounds like bird grumbling and turns his back to me. I set the cage on the floor, step quickly to the door, and look back at him.

"Any more trouble and you'll be listed in tomorrow's barbecue obituaries."

He shoots a long stream of crap onto the cage paper and says, "You're just a Player hater."

"Screw you."

"Yo' mama."

If I didn't have to get right back to Chloe, I'd throw Player's sorry butt into the microwave. It'll have to wait. I've got to get Chloe to understand what's really going on here. I hurry out and know immediately from her expression that no amount of explaining is going to help.

"How can you stand to own that horrible bird?" she asks.

"But, Chloe. He's not . . ."

"And how does he know that you want to *get some'a that booty?*"

"If you'll just let me explain. Player belongs to . . ."

"And he's named Player!" Chloe says loudly. "How fitting. Do you have other pets, Darius? Maybe a hamster named Mack Daddy? A turtle named Cool Breeze?"

"C'mon, Chloe. You're blowing this all out of proportion."

"You're right. I should see it for exactly what it is. And I should see *you* for exactly what you are: a player!"

"Chloe, if you'll only listen I can clear . . ."

She whirls around, grabs her purse, and storms out. I stand in the creeping silence, my anger building into a rumbling volcano. It erupts when I hear Player in the bedroom singing Melanie Franklin's new hit, "You Been Busted."

I step slowly toward the bedroom, open the door, and stare down at Player. He stops singing and says, "C'mon now, D. Why you wanna be like that?"

38

"JUST CALM DOWN!" NASH URGES THROUGH THE PHONE. "I'll be right over to get him."

"Calm down!" I shout. "I'll do that after I've finished stuffing that idiot feather duster down the garbage disposal."

Player's glaring from his cage over by the bookcases. "I ain't scared'a this punk!" he squawks.

I slam the phone down into the recharging cradle and stomp over to Player.

"C'mon, D," he says. "You know you're my boy."

I grab the cage and drag it, stand and all, onto the balcony. Player screeches his displeasure as he flaps and flits back and forth across the cage. I slam the sliding glass door shut, hurry to the phone, and call Chloe's cellular. She doesn't answer, not that I'm surprised. I let it ring and ring until her answering service activates.

"Chloe! Listen," I say. "I know you're upset, but I can explain everything. Please call me."

I hang up, lean against the wall, and glance outside at Player. That scandalous bird has jeopardized what I hope will still be an enjoyable budding relationship. It's almost fitting that an incident so stupid would jeopardize something I was coming to value so highly.

I sit down at the computer and try to find refuge in working on my book, but Player's managing to ruin even that by singing Drew Porter's "Hard Luck Is My Lover." I turn and look at him. He's staring straight at me. I know I'm hallucinating, but I swear, it looks like his powerful beak has twisted into a smile. Nash had better hurry and come get this bird!

39

NASH AND I SIT IN HIS SUV FORD EXPLORER, RIGHT OUTSIDE the front door of Chloe's company, Motherland Hair Care & Beauty Supply. The receptionist inside said that Chloe was due back before the end of the day, although she couldn't (or wouldn't) say specifically when. It doesn't matter. Whenever Chloe arrives, we'll be here!

"D, I'm really sorry," Nash says for the millionth time. "Player's been acting really crazy lately."

"Lately!" I growl. "Nash, he's been crazy for as long as I can remember. Where are you getting this 'lately' crap?"

He shrugs. "What can I say? Player likes the ladies."

"He'd better stick to his own species," I warn. "I've never heard of a cockatoo lynching, but that's not to say it can't happen."

"I'm sorry, Chloe," Player squawks from the truck's rear storage area. "I can explain everything. This isn't my bird."

I don't believe it! This bird is actually mocking me. I whip around and point a rigid forefinger at him. "Shut up, Player! You're starting to be more trouble than you're worth."

"Suck my tail feathers."

"Okay. That's it!" I say. Before Nash realizes what's going on, I've grabbed his keys, jumped out of the SUV, and am speeding toward the back. Player rotates his head, following my movements as I open the back hatch.

"Awwww, shucks!" he warbles. "This fool is mad."

I snatch the cage from the truck and march toward a Dumpster where there just happens to be a colony of cats, sitting around and looking bored. Until they see Player. The moment he sees them, he goes into megasquawk.

"Honest, baby!" he screeches. "I was thinkin' of you the whole time!"

Nash jumps out of the truck and dashes to catch up with me.

"You's a lie!" Player challenges. "That baby ain't mine!"

The cats start circling and mewling, their noises sounding like a collective call for snack time.

"It wasn't my fault!" Player defends. "The crack made me do it!"

Nash grabs my arm and jerks me to a stop. "What're you doing?" he asks.

I wink and force more exasperation into my voice. "I'm teaching this little maggot a lesson."

Player hides his head beneath a wing. Several cats stroll over to us, meowing and looking up at Player in his cage with anticipation.

A candy apple red Corvette pulls into the parking lot and parks. "That's her!" I blurt.

Chloe gets out and starts for Motherland's front door, glances at me, Nash, and Player, keeps walking, then stops and does a double take.

"Darius, is that you?" she calls.

I grip Nash's arm and pull him toward her. "Chloe, give me two minutes!" I plead. "That's all I ask and everything will be made clear."

She looks from me to Nash to Player, scowling at him. She looks back at me, crosses her arms, and starts tapping her foot. "Two minutes."

I nudge Nash, who's standing mesmerized as he visually digests her beauty. "Oh!" he says, snapping into the moment. "My name is Nash Ayers," he says, extending his hand.

"Never mind the introductions," I say gruffly. "Tell her about Player."

Nash explains everything, being careful to avoid mentioning that I'd been watching Player so he could run a scam on Eileen. Chloe listens intently, her hard expression gradually losing some of its tension.

"And so Player talks like that from being around me," Nash stresses. "He's my bird and that's the truth."

Chloe narrows her eyes. "So I guess you're the one Player heard saying, 'Darius, you know you wanna get some'a that booty'?"

Nash gulps and nods. Chloe looks at me. "And so, Darius, how did you respond to that statement?"

Sweat boulders pop onto my forehead. "Ah, I, well . . ."

"Never mind!"

Chloe purses her lips and glares at all of us. "This is the most ridiculous story I've ever heard," she blasts. "It's so ridiculous that it has to be true," she finishes, smiling.

I toss Player's cage to Nash and sweep Chloe up into my arms for a tight, spinning hug. By the time I've put her down, we've got a date for dinner.

40

CHLOE'S STEPPED AWAY TO USE THE BATHROOM, ALLOWING me to sit and enjoy a moment of reflection in the soft light of the Moroccan Breeze restaurant. It's been a great evening so far, and Chloe looks lovelier than ever.

After that debacle with Player, it's a minor miracle that Chloe and I are here together. But that just goes to show the kind of wonderful person she is. Her willingness to give us a second chance reinforces my initial thoughts of her gentle nature, quality of character, and resilience. If I'd had any idea that women like her were walking around free, unattached, and looking for the love I was starving for, I might have flushed Cookie and her king cobra attitude years ago.

But this is no time for reminiscing about the turbulent past. Chloe's returning from the bathroom and I don't want thoughts of Cookie dousing romance flames that are burning bright.

Chloe glides up to our table and I pull out her chair. "Why, thank you, Darius," she says, smiling as she sits. "It's so nice to be with someone who has such impeccable manners."

"My mother drilled them into me."

"Well then, my compliments to her as well."

I move swiftly and smoothly back into my seat and focus *all* my attention upon Chloe's high-cheekboned, almond-eyed, smooth dark brown face. I reach across the table and take gentle hold of her hand.

"You're stunning," I say.

"Thank you, Darius. You're quite handsome yourself."

What a boost! A compliment like that from someone this wonderful quenches the yearning I once endured waiting for similar expressions from Cookie.

Chloe and I bring our wineglasses together until there's a soft *clink!*

"To a wonderful evening," I say.

"And many more to come," she adds.

She sips her wine, savoring the taste with a slight sexy pucker of her lips. They're wonderfully full and perfectly shaped for long, passionate kisses.

I extend my glass for another toast. "To cleared-up misunderstandings and much-appreciated second chances."

She laughs, touches her glass to mine, and says, "To *never* owning a pet like Player."

We laugh, drink our wine, and I pour some more into our glasses. The candles on our booth table are burning low but bright, and the few couples who were sitting nearby have left, their absence enhancing the warmth and intimacy of our cozy bubble.

We talk about everything, our antics growing up, professional aspirations and challenges, our favorite movies, music, and books, and even though it's supposed to be a dating no-no, we share some past-relationship war stories. I'm brief in my comments concerning Cookie, knowing how easy it is to slip into a diatribe about the virus she's been in my life.

I take a sip of wine and Chloe says, "So, Darius, do you think you'll ever get married again?"

The wine I'm swallowing turns to sand, making me cough. "Um, well, I don't know. I mean, I suppose so. Right now I'm just trying to find a stable relationship."

"That's understandable," she says. "Especially since you're just coming out of a marriage."

I'm glad she feels that way. It's comforting to know that I won't be subjected to the "Where is this relationship going?" third degree anytime soon.

"What about you?" I ask. "Do you plan on getting married again?"

Chloe's answer is quick and certain. "Yes! I still believe in marriage even though my first one didn't work out."

"Do you mind if I ask what happened?"

She sighs softly. "We just grew apart. It's amazing that we didn't see it at first, but after we got married we found out that we really didn't have much in common."

"I know the feeling," I say, almost grumbling. I raise my glass and say, "To better choices in the future."

We *clink!* again and keep talking. Chloe really is beautiful and smart, talented, gentle, and so very feminine. I can appreciate her ex's wanting out if things were rough, but he's one grade A, supercharged, all-time galactic idiot for letting her get away. Then again, maybe I shouldn't be so hard on him. There's probably some unsuspecting schmuck staring dreamily into Cookie's eyes right now, reaching the same conclusion about *me*.

Chloe runs her fingers along the hairs on the back of my hand. "Darius, do you think you'll have any more chil . . ."

"Absolutely not!"

I kick myself for answering so fast. But why play games? This is one subject about which there must be *no* misunderstanding.

"Wow!" Chloe says, withdrawing her hand from mine. "You sound pretty adamant."

"I am."

It's not that I don't love kids. I adore them. But if I fall in love with another child and one day lose them as a result of Mommy's suddenly not wanting to play house anymore, I'll collapse emotionally.

"Well, I'd like to have kids," Chloe announces, the brightness in her eyes dimming. "I want a family."

"But, Chloe, wouldn't it still be a family with just you and your husband?"

"It's not the same, Darius. A child is the ultimate expression of love between a man and a woman."

Children are also great bargaining chips to use for leverage during divorces. I flash back to a discussion I once had with Marcy on this subject. It was the closest we ever came to arguing.

It started with the usual hypothetical, "What if we got married and . . ."

Marcy simply couldn't understand my worry that a future hypothetical wife of mine might awaken one morning no longer satisfied with being my wife. She couldn't understand that such a decision would slam me twice, once with the loss of a spouse, the second time with the loss of my child. She thought it preposterous that I was prepared to endure life alone rather than risk another emotional lobotomy.

With Marcy not understanding any of that, there was no point in telling her that I also never again intended to participate in spousal arguments over discipline strategies, hassle through adolescent rebellions, or play second fiddle to the powerful mysteries of motherhood.

"You're letting one bad relationship ruin your outlook on life!" she accused.

"My outlook on life is healthy, happy, and whole!" I defended myself. "It's also convinced that paying child support once in a lifetime is enough."

"That's bogus! Another marriage and child could be the most fulfilling experience you ever had."

I calmed myself down and collected my thoughts. "I've got a question for you, Marcy."

She rolled her eyes. "What is it?"

"How do you expect me to believe that a child who's actually *here* will make life better when I'm already catching grief about one that's *not even conceived*?"

Marcy didn't answer, and I don't suspect that Chloe would if I asked her. Rather than argue the point, she just smiles. It's a soft, gentle smile that says, I understand, I'm glad we met, and, *Good-bye!*

"Darius, I've got to be honest," she says. "I really want children. Anyone who truly loves me will understand and want to share love with me in that way."

I nod gravely, wishing that I could change my feelings. But I refuse! When Cookie moved out with Jarrod, I thought my heart would explode. And I'm well aware that I'm letting old baggage derail a potentially tremendous relationship, but so what! With all the bags I've tossed aside, I intend to keep this one.

The server brings our food and Chloe and I spend the rest of the evening sharing the kind of small talk that time and experience have taught me to recognize as the beginning of the end.

41

I SHOVE THE FRUSTRATION OF THE PREVIOUS EVENING'S dinner with Chloe to the back of my mind when I see Gina.

I wave to her as she walks down the exit ramp from the secure portion of the airport terminal. She waves back, but for all the effort she's exerting, she might as well be fanning a lazy fly.

Once she's closer, we hug and I take her carry-on. "How was it?" I ask.

She shrugs. "The dig was nice. The conference okay."

Something's definitely wrong. Gina normally gets as excited about archaeological digs as I do walking across hallowed battlefields like Gettysburg and Antietam. And for her to merely describe the conference as "okay" is equally out of character, especially since many of the speakers were giants in their fields.

We walk in silence toward baggage claim. I grab her bags, give her some of the smaller ones, and we carry them to my car in the short-term parking deck. I stow her luggage in the trunk, open her door just like Momma taught me, then get in and start for Gina's home. I see a Bob Evans restaurant, whip out of traffic, and pull into the parking lot.

"Why are we stopping here?" Gina asks.

"So we can talk," I answer, parking. "Haven't you heard? People are generally in a better mood to discuss things when they're stuffing their faces."

Gina smiles softly. "That's sweet of you," she says, her eyes misting.

I reach into my glove compartment, grab some tissues, and, rather than handing them to her, dry her eyes myself. "I want you to tell me what's wrong," I say, softly dabbing her cheeks.

She nods. "Okay. But really, Darius, I'm not hungry. Let's just go, okay?"

I finish drying her eyes and cheeks. "All right. But I'm not kidding, Gina. I want to know."

She sniffles and smiles. "Okay, okay. I'll tell you. Who'd have known?"

"Who'd have known what?"

"That you could be so persistent."

We laugh, hug, and get back on the highway, going to her house. I'm dying to find out what's bothering her, but only when she's ready. After my recent experiences, I can certainly appreciate her wanting a moment of peace.

I pull up to her house, park, and grab her bags from the trunk. She offers to help, but I tell her to just go inside and get relaxed.

"You've been lugging too much as it is," I say, feeling her heaviness of spirit.

She doesn't resist, goes and unlocks her door. When I get inside, she's sitting on her couch with her shoes off, knees drawn up, and feet tucked beneath her. She's holding one of her big couch pillows like it's a bulging square teddy bear. The sadness in her eyes digs a wound into me and I want to hold her. But Gina's not mine and no matter how much I comfort her, she'll eventually migrate back to Bruce. And while she's with him, I'll be alone in my apartment, curled up on the couch, holding a pillow and wiping egg off my face.

But I can't resist the urge to hold and comfort her, so I do. Minutes pass and I rock Gina back and forth as she sobs away her pain. After a while, she pushes me away, sits up and sniffles, wipes her eyes with her palms, and starts talking.

"Bruce was supposed to be at an auto show in Detroit while I was in Nicaragua," she says.

I vaguely remember Gina saying something about that but not enough to matter, so I just nod.

"The night before I left, he gave me a, um, gift."

"Something from Victoria's Secret?"

She looks at me, surprised. "How did you . . ."

She correctly remembers that I'd heard her and Bruce talking and sighs. "Yes, Darius. It was from Victoria's Secret. Anyway, he said that he'd bought it at Chelsea Hills Mall just outside of Cleveland."

Tear diamonds collect in the corners of her eyes. "When I looked at the receipt the next morning . . ."

"He didn't wrap the gift?"

"Bruce never wraps his gifts. He says keeping them in the bag makes it easier to return items to the store, especially if it's clothing."

I fully remember what kind of "clothing" it was, so there's no need to ask.

"Anyway," Gina continues, "when I looked at the receipt the next morning, it showed that he'd bought the gift at Willow Creek Plaza in Detroit."

I can understand Gina's being disturbed by Bruce's bending the truth, but a little white lie about where her gift was purchased doesn't sound so horrible.

She senses my puzzlement and answers my unasked question. "It wouldn't matter, except that Bruce told me that he's never been to Detroit."

Okay. Now it's starting to sound bad.

"And worst of all," Gina continues, "the auto show being held in Detroit is for tractor trailers. *Not cars.* That one's being held in Chicago."

She purses her lips, damming up a sob. "He's been lying to me, Darius."

I pull her back in to me. "C'mon now, Gina," I soothe, rubbing her back in slow circular motions. "I'm sure there's been some misunderstanding."

"There's no misunderstanding!" she angrily responds, shoving me away.

"But how can you be certain your information's correct?"

"Because I called the main office in Detroit!"

Her answer is stunning. It's so simple that it possesses an element of genius. It also demonstrates Bruce's shrewdness. He probably fed Gina the more complex crap, betting that she'd never do the obvious and make direct contact with his corporate overseers.

"Either way," Gina says, "something's not right. And the way I see it, if Bruce lied about where he bought the gift and the location of the so-called auto show, then he's been lying about other things."

She gets up and gets herself a glass of water. "He's been lying and I'm going to find out about what!" she declares.

She finishes the water and sits back on the couch, scooting far from me and collapsing into the corner. The water she just drank comes pouring from her eyes, and I want to rush over and hold her. But why should I?

I'm tired of being the "friend" who helps heal broken hearts only to later watch someone else enjoy the fruits of my labor. I'm good enough to commiserate with but not good to enough to love. So let Gina find another rich pretty boy. It's not like I didn't warn her that Bruce was a snake.

I glance at my watch. I need to call and check on Jarrod before heading to campus for this emergency meeting Dr. Kurozawa's called concerning

Avi's swastika incident. It's anybody's guess what's going on over at Cookie's now that Candace is there. Between her and Jarrod's girlfriend, Reesie, I almost trust Reesie more. The thought of her sends a chill through me and I get up to leave. But there's no way I can leave Gina alone and crying.

I sit back down, gently pull her in to me, and rock her to sleep. I cover her up, kiss her forehead, and pad over to her door. She looks so sweet and delicate, sleeping her troubled sleep.

"If only you knew," I whisper. "If only I had the courage to say."

I ease out and head for my meeting.

42

"WHERE'S JARROD?" I DEMAND.

I grip the phone tight as my skin crawls from the sounds of Candace's chewing in my ear with loud smacks and grunts. She washes her food down with a sloshing, swilling drink of something (most likely alcoholic) that's probably dribbling along the sides of her face.

"Did you hear me?" I press. "Where's Jarrod?"

"I'on't know. Prob'ly with that Fields fella again."

"Fields!" I yell. Of all the things Cookie and I might disagree upon, we're united in our belief that Fields is the *last* person Jarrod should be associating with, especially while bad political blood still exists between him and Cookie.

"What's he doing over there?" I ask.

"I'on't know. He said something about Fields helpin' 'em."

"Did he say when he'd be back?"

"I'on't know. I guess he'll be back sometime."

"For Chrissake, Candace! Didn't you bother to ask?"

"Jarrod's sixteen years old. How I'ma make him answer if he 'on't wanna?"

I grit my teeth, trying to contain my hostility. "Worthless pig," I grumble.

"Whutch-you say?"

"You're a worthless pig!" I explode.

I slam the phone down and try to clear my mind before going to this departmental meeting. This crap is wearing my nerves thin. What's irritating me most is that I haven't asked Jarrod to perform some complex, energy-sapping task. All I want is a simple phone call so I can know that *he's safe!*

My mood doesn't improve when Chloe crosses my mind. Our budding relationship might not be over, but I'm not naive. Her desire to have children is a hurdle I can't jump. Hassles like the one I'm currently enduring with Jarrod reinforce my unwillingness.

I grab my tablet, weekly planner, and pen and trudge off to the departmental conference room. Esther Kurozawa, department chairperson, walks in with me, a good thing, since I can't be late if we're arriving together. Avi Silberberg, Julian Steinmetz, Reba Gordon, Harold Mills, Dorothy Hanner, and Presley Booth are already talking, getting coffee, or grading test papers.

"Darius, word's gotten around that you actually met with el Bornu," Julian says.

"That's sort of correct."

"Well?"

"Well what?"

"What happened?"

I ponder for a moment. "Let's put it like this: He'll never be mistaken for a protégé of Martin Luther King Jr."

Esther calls the meeting to order and we get started. I glance at my watch, wondering where Jarrod is and what's he doing. As soon as I'm through on campus today, I'm going to introduce his hardheaded butt to some Soviet-style gulag parenting.

"All right," Esther begins. "I'm sure you all have heard about the incident of anti-Semitism that recently occurred."

We answer with grim nods. "Okay," Esther continues. "The Provost is going to have a conference call with the entire Humanities Division in just a moment or two, including our department."

"And then what?" Avi asks.

"We'll know that as soon as we get the call," Esther answers. She smiles softly at Avi. "But just so you'll know, if I had my way, the perpetrators would suffer all the fear, pain, and punishment they've ever inflicted upon ethnic and religious minorities."

Avi offers a slight smile of thanks. Then the phone rings. Esther punches the speaker button and says, "We're here, Dr. Lamchek."

"Ah, excuse me. Is my dad there?"

I grip the table and gasp.

"Who is this?" Esther inquires, frowning.

"Jarrod Collins. I need to talk to my dad."

"I'm right here, Jarrod," I say, leaning toward the phone.

He babbles through his tear-filled voice, "Dad! You've gotta come and get me."

"Huh? Where? What's happened?"

"I'm down at the Leifler Juvenile Detention Center. Hurry!"

I fly out of the room, zooming past Andre Echols on the way. "Hey, Dr. Collins," he says. "I've been think . . ."

"It'll have to wait!" I holler.

Minutes later, I'm speeding toward the grim facility where Judge Lucas "Lock'em Up Luke" Newton presides as zookeeper.

43

ON THE WAY TO GO SEE WHAT'S HAPPENING WITH
Jarrod, I call Reverend Boxwell and ask him to meet me. He's preparing
for the Warrior Passages kickoff but drops what he's doing. Having him
on hand should ameliorate the sting of whatever happens, especially since
he and Judge Newton are good friends.

The reverend turns into the parking lot and I follow him into a space
next to his car. I park, look up at Leifler, and wipe my eyes. Somewhere in
that imposing gray building behind the high fence with its triple-strand
barbed wire spiraling along its top, my son's sitting in the cell I'd urged
him to avoid. And now it's too late.

I rest my forehead on the steering wheel and watch as tears drip onto
the horn.

Reverend Boxwell knocks softly on my window. "Darius, c'mon, son.
I called the judge before I left. He's fixed it so's you can see Jarrod, but we
gotta hurry."

I get out and he hands me some tissues as we start toward the building. Its forbidding austere, functional layout and bulky construction emphasize its punitive purpose. Memories of the barracoon holding pens
where African slaves were held for weeks, months, and sometimes years
before shipment fill my mind, weakening my knees.

Reverend Boxwell catches me as I stagger. "Whoa! Are you okay?"

I nod and take a moment to will the wobbles from my legs. "I'm fine.
Let's go."

We pass through an inner gate, are searched, go inside the building,
and are searched again. A glum-looking guard unlocks a door leading into
a cramped section of hallway, then locks it once we're inside. She unlocks
another door leading to a smaller room, orders us in, and stands aside as
we enter.

"Someone'll be wit'cha in a moment," she says.

She closes the door and locks us in, my ears ringing with the sound of
multiple locks and bolts turning and slamming into place. The room's

probably bigger than a cell, but it still feels like the walls are closing in. I talk to Reverend Boxwell to distract myself from a creeping claustrophobia.

"This better not be a mistake," I grouse. "Jarrod's had his moments but nothing that demands this kind of treatment."

"Why don't we just wait and get the details."

"I don't care about the details!" I snap. "Jarrod doesn't belong here and if this is some bureaucrat's bungling, I'm going on the warpath."

Reverend Boxwell grabs my shoulder and jerks me around till we're face-to-face. His jaw is firm and eyes as hard as the CBHS's Civil War soldier statue.

"Son, maybe you oughta shut your mouth! This is the judge's domain and he doesn't tolerate no smart-mouthin' from kids *or* their parents." He gestures in an arm-sweeping motion. "Take a look around. I'd say that whatever Jarrod's done, it's straddling onto being illegal."

Keys rattle from behind a heavy metal door across the room as locks turn and bolts slide back. It opens and Detective Pullen, who interviewed me on campus just yesterday, steps through.

"Thanks, Officer Grant," he says, passing a husky key-wielding giant.

"No problem. Tell his parent there ain't much time, so it'll have'ta be quick!"

The door shuts and Detective Pullen and Reverend Boxwell shake hands. "Good to see you, Reverend."

"You too, Sergeant. Too bad it's not under different circumstances."

"And what circumstances are we talking about?" I demand.

Detective Pullen looks at me and purses his lips. "Dr. Collins, there's no easy way to say this, so I'll make it plain. Your son's been accused of rape!"

The news hits me like a punch to the solar plexus. "It's a lie," I say, gritting my teeth. "That Cuppersmith girl's lying. Her mother just wants money."

Detective Pullen steps toward me and speaks softly. "I didn't mention the Cuppersmiths."

My eyes connect with Detective Pullen's and I know he's got me. "According to what you told me and Ms. Watsburg, your son barely knows the girl," he says.

Jangling keys bang up against the heavy metal door as locks and bolts are released and it opens. "Okay, Detective," Officer Grant says. "They're bringin' 'em up."

Detective Pullen heads for the door, talking to me over his shoulder. "Dr. Collins, come with me. Reverend Boxwell, I'm sorry, but . . ."

"No need to apologize. I'll wait here."

I follow Detective Pullen into a still smaller room and sit down as he gestures toward an ancient metal folding chair leaning against a battered card table. A rickety wooden chair sits on the other side.

"Who told you to move!" booms a voice, echoing from somewhere in this first level of Dante's juvenile hell. "Move again and I'ma jump in your chest!"

Keys clatter against the door across the room until it opens. And there stands Jarrod, his eye blackened and lip swollen, clothes rumpled, and hair a mess.

"Get in there!" a wiry-muscled guard barks, shoving Jarrod inside.

Jarrod lurches in and staggers up against the table.

"Hey!" I shout, springing up from my chair.

Detective Pullen shoves me back into the chair. *"No!"* he commands, his voice urgent and rasping. "Interfering will only make it worse."

The wiry-muscled guard glares at me and I return my own, communicating with all my might that whatever Jarrod suffers in custody the guard will pay for in court!

The guard glances at Detective Pullen. "Five minutes, Detective. This is breakin' up the routine."

"Thanks, Officer Nelson. It's much appreciated."

The guard glares at me, then slams the door. Detective Pullen releases his hold on me, then talks fast.

"Listen up! Both of you!" he says, looking from me to Jarrod. "This is *not* the outside. *Understand!* Whatever rights you think you had, whatever privileges you enjoyed, whatever comforts you experienced, it's over! This may be juvenile detention, but it's still prison. And don't either of you forget it!"

We nod and he steps aside. Jarrod reaches out to me and I rush around the table and hug him, squeezing him so tight my arms ache.

"Jarrod, what happened?" I ask.

"I don't know."

I grip his shoulders and hold him at arm's length. "What do you mean you don't know?" I shout. "This isn't some game! You don't get sent here without knowing why!"

"Why won't you believe me?" he shouts back. "I wasn't doing anything. Me and Reesie were watching TV at Uncle Milton's when the police crashed in, threw me on the floor, and accused me of rape."

I look at Detective Pullen. "How can he be held on a mere accusation?"

"It's the law, Dr. Collins. Different charges get different responses. If he'd shoplifted bubble gum, you'd be talking to him in your living room. For rape, you talk to him here!"

"Alleged rape!" I correct him. I look back at Jarrod. "What happened to your eye? Your lip? Your hair?"

"They beat me up."

My collar's sizzling. I look at Detective Pullen and say, "By the time I'm through, the cops responsible for this won't be able to get jobs policing garbage!"

Detective Pullen glowers. "Before you launch your crusade you should know that your angelic son resisted arrest. He earned the eye and lip by punching out one officer and slamming his knee into the groin of another."

"What's the matter with you?" I yell, shaking Jarrod.

"As for the haircut," Detective Pullen continues, "when the arresting officers tackled him outside Councilman Fields's residence, they crashed into a wooden fence, leaving a nasty gash at the back of his head and splinters dug deep in his scalp. The docs had to shave his head to give him the necessary first aid."

I let go of Jarrod, plop into the rickety wooden chair, and shake my head. "What a mess," I mumble. "What a royal, out-of-this-world mess!"

Jarrod's voice quavers. "I'm, I'm sorry, Dad."

I look up at Jarrod for a few long silent seconds, watching as the tears gather, then fall from his eyes.

"Don't be sorry for me," I say. "You're the one who's in custody."

"You don't care!" he whines. "And it's not even my fault! I'm being set up because *you* pissed off Bell's mother."

Detective Pullen looks from Jarrod to me, hanging on to our every word. And it suddenly strikes me that he's gathering information. It also strikes me that I'm too tired to care. But mostly, I'm disgusted by the futility of it all. After all my talking and teaching, warning and worrying, encouraging and correcting, pleading and preaching, there stands my son, just another chained black male statistic.

I get in Jarrod's face and speak with a calmness belying my seething frustration. "You just don't get it, do you? *I'm* not the one who's in jail. *I'm* not the one who's accused of rape. *I'm* not the one whose father doesn't know whether or not to believe him about being Bell's baby's father. *I'm* not the one who's looking pitiful and puzzled, wondering why Mommy's powerful friends haven't already made this go away."

Keys clatter against the door and the wiry-muscled guard throws it open. "Time's up!" he yells, his eyes locked on me, hoping I'll give him an excuse to clown.

"Dad!" Jarrod cries. "Do something!"

I steady my voice, hoping my steadfastness will bolster Jarrod. "I will, Son. But I need for you to be strong."

The wiry-muscled guard grabs Jarrod and jostles him toward the door. "C'mon, cupcake. Time to find you a boyfriend."

"It's not my fault," Jarrod whimpers. "I don't belong here."

He's shoved into a dimly lit hallway and the metal door slams with a resounding *clang!* The door leading back to Reverend Boxwell opens and I follow Detective Pullen through.

Reverend Boxwell hugs me. "Be strong, son. The Lord's eyes aren't shut to what's happening."

Something inside me tells me that he's right. It also tells me that no matter how things might appear, everything's under control. But something else argues against the logic of these events. It wonders how the so-called King of the cosmos could peer into all this agony and insist that He's in "control."

My questions of doubt overshadow Reverend Boxwell's assurances of faith and I fall back into the arms of the one person who's never let me down: *myself!*

I look at Detective Pullen. "If it's possible, I'd like to see the judge. Please?"

44

JUDGE NEWTON'S ADMINISTRATIVE ASSISTANT HOLDS up her index finger, telling me, Reverend Boxwell, and Detective Pullen that she'll be off the phone in just a moment.

Detective Pullen glances at his watch. "Gentlemen, I've gotta finish up some paperwork or risk facing the judge's wrath."

I extend my hand and we shake. "Thanks for your help. I hope you'll overlook my earlier behavior."

Detective Pullen's granite expression softens. "Dr. Collins, I understand. You're a parent fearing for his son. I'm here to help, so if there's anything I can do, don't hesitate to use my card."

"I will. I promise."

He exchanges some brief comments with Reverend Boxwell and hurries off. The administrative assistant holds up her finger again, her apologetic expression asking us to bear with her a bit longer. We nod and smile, me making sure mine is wide and ingratiating.

As long as Jarrod's here I can't afford to alienate the judge, his assistant, or anyone else! Now that I've witnessed this dungeon's cruel potentials, I'm glad Detective Pullen kept me from shooting my mouth off to that guard. That would've put Jarrod at greater risk and I'd have been tortured by the thought of being responsible.

The administrative assistant laughs. "Don't worry, Congresswoman Woolford. I'm sure the judge understands that he'll owe you one."

I lean close and whisper to Reverend Boxwell, "Do you think she's talking to Congresswoman Priscilla Woolford?"

"That'd be my guess."

I try listening for more details, but the administrative assistant hangs up. And right on cue, the judge bursts in and storms past us toward the door adjoining their two offices. Two fast-talking, harried-looking lawyer types follow close behind, arguing in their legalese.

"Gus, you know it's not right!" the first lawyer asserts. "The Supreme Court struck that down in *Michelson versus Pettit*."

"Exactly!" Gus counters. "And that's why the Congress modified the legislation empowering schools with the necessary policing authority."

"What about the Fourth Amendment? Aren't you at all bothered by attempts to end-run the Constitution's prohibitions against illegal search and seizure?"

Judge Newton spins around so fast that the quasi-attentive lawyers almost run him over. "Look!" he shouts. "Stop with the redundant dissections of constitutional law. Prior storage of the weapon is ancillary to the commission of the crime. We've got a dead thirteen-year-old and a sixteen-year-old mugger who witnesses saw pull the trigger. I want you two servants of the people to focus on *that* and find me the legal tools to nail him. Now go!"

"Yes, Judge," the lawyers answer.

They respond with such quaking deference that for a moment I wonder if they'll bow before departing. The administrative assistant watches in bemused silence, her eyes following the hoarsely whispering lawyers as they carry their subdued debate out of the office. The judge finally notices me and Reverend Boxwell and grimaces.

"I've been expecting you, Dr. Collins," he rumbles. He looks at Reverend Boxwell. "It's good you came too, Hez. I've got some news for you." He turns to his assistant. "Ms. Gunther, did you contact Priscilla?"

"Yes, Your Honor. Here's the information." She holds a manila folder out to him.

He takes it, reads over the contents, and shakes his head. He turns away and starts toward his office, speaking over his shoulder to Ms. Gunther: "No calls. No visitors. No nothing!"

"Yes, Judge."

Reverend Boxwell and I quickly follow the judge into his chambers. "Wait there, Dr. Collins," he orders once we're inside.

I stop immediately and watch quietly as the judge and Reverend Boxwell saunter side by side off to a far corner. The judge's office is a miniature law library of stupendous quality. The walls are lined from floor to ceiling with shelves containing books of every size, topic, and thickness, leaving my historian's sensibilities panting. It's hard to believe that this sanctuary of intellect is located in a distant corner of the same building housing so much hostility and despair. But then, maybe that's why it's located in a distant corner.

A huge portrait of Justice dominates the wall behind the judge's shiny mahogany desk and high-backed leather chair. Her image stands graceful and full of power, one delicate hand holding the scales that weigh the law against the acts of the accused. In her other hand she grips her sword, its double edges sharpened and prepared to render judgment. And she's resolutely oblivious behind her blindfold, shielded from visions that could influence and compromise the unbiased performance of her duty.

The powerful symbolism of truth, fairness, and equality emanating from the portrait is enough to leave one drunk with idealism. But my idealism is tempered with the historical knowledge that Justice has often lifted her blindfold to view the contents of a wallet, turned a deaf ear to the cries of the oppressed, and mistakenly used her sword to imprison and execute the innocent.

The tomblike acoustics carry Reverend Boxwell's and the judge's subdued voices over to me.

"And you're sure nothing can be done?" Reverend Boxwell asks.

"Hez, there's no mistaking the law on this. She tried selling crack to an undercover."

"But what about entrapment?"

"It's not entrapment when the dealer hounds the buyer into making a purchase."

Reverend Boxwell looks down at the floor and sighs. "Brother and Sister Powell will be heartbroken."

"Hez, so were the parents of the kid who overdosed on the crack she sold."

Reverend Boxwell nods. "Well, you know I had to try."

The judge claps him on the shoulder and escorts him to the door. "I understand. Just like you know I've got to enforce the law."

The judge glances at his watch and tells Reverend Boxwell he'll make it to the Warrior Passages kickoff if he can get through his last court appointment. They say good-bye and the judge turns to me.

"Have a seat, Dr. Collins," he says, stepping lively back to his desk.

I sit down and watch in mounting suspense as he takes his seat and reexamines the contents of the manila folder.

He shakes his head, closes it, and looks at me. "Tell me about your son's relationship with Councilman Fields."

"Huh?"

"Councilman Fields! What's the connection?"

"Forgive me, Judge, but what's this got to do with Jarrod?"

He stands and strolls over to a huge picture window and clasps his hands behind his back. "Milton Fields placed the call that led to the arrest of your son."

I gasp and fall back. "What! But . . . I mean . . . how? Oh, for crying out loud!"

"There's not much time, Dr. Collins. Anything you can offer will be helpful."

I massage my forehead to slow the spinning world. "Jarrod told me that his mother, my ex-wife, Cookie . . ."

"Deputy Tranportation Commissioner Hargrove?"

I nod. The judge mercifully doesn't ask about her difficulties. "She and Fields had a fling that went sour. But things apparently stayed good between him and Jarrod. He even calls him Uncle Milton."

"Go on."

"We had a fight the other night. I was frustrated, Judge, so I put him out. Well, not exactly. I took him to his mother's house, just to let him cool his heels till morning, when I was going to go get him. But he'd made up his mind to seek refuge with Fields, who'd promised to help him out if he ever got in a jam."

"And what jam is that?"

I lower my eyes and sigh, contemplating whether or not to tell everything. But what's there to lose? I had been going to seek the judge's help anyway. He'd have asked the same questions. And since Jarrod's already in custody, it's obviously too late to avoid disaster.

So I tell him everything from Cookie's late night visit up to the slanted responses I'd given Detective Pullen and Ms. Watsburg. And all the while, he stares out the window, listening intently and nodding every so often.

"You've got to believe me, Judge. Jarrod's not guilty of rape."

"We don't know that."

"Why not just ask the girl?"

"It doesn't work that way. There are protocols that have to be observed to protect the alleged victim's privacy, identity, and fragile mental state."

"Privacy! With all due respect, Judge, my son's been locked up on hearsay!"

The judge retakes his seat, steeples his fingers, and bores his eyes into mine. "It's hearsay strong enough to keep him here until the mess is cleared up."

"What about Bernice Cuppersmith's attempted extortion. Isn't that against the law?"

"It's your word against hers."

I feel my eyes bulging. "But . . . doesn't that fall into the same category as the charge against Jarrod?"

"No. There's evidence."

"What evidence? No one's proven . . ."

"The girl's pregnant, Dr. Collins! If DNA testing shows a link, well, you can fill in the blanks."

I slump down into my chair. "This is hopeless."

"Not really," the judge counters, tapping the manila folder. He opens the folder, looks at me, and narrows his eyes. "What's said from here on stays in here, got it?"

I nod hurriedly.

"I'm serious. If I get wind that . . ."

"Judge, *please*! I won't say a word. I just want my son back!"

He searches my eyes for several long seconds, then opens the folder. "I assume you've heard of Congresswoman Priscilla Woolford?"

"Somewhat. Mostly due to her being one of the few truly honest politicians I've ever heard about. No offense intended."

"None taken. And not everyone has always been so generous as you in their opinion of her. Losing out to your ex for that deputy transportation commissioner's post changed all that."

I shrug. "I'm not following you."

"Let me enlighten you."

He sits back comfortably in his chair and folds his hands across his flat midsection. I reflexively suck in my expanding gut and wait for his revelations.

"Priscilla Woolford was next in line to head that department when Rob Jarovitz stepped down. But Milton Fields challenged her qualifications, going so far as to claim that several projects she'd overseen had been plagued with waste, fraud, and abuse."

"Yes," I say, nodding slowly as I recollect the news stories. "There was an investigation. Congresswoman Woolford was cleared, but I remember it got ugly."

"As most things political will, Dr. Collins. While Priscilla's name was being dragged daily through the mud, Fields was tugging on Mayor Tyne's sleeve to name your ex to the post. The mayor balked initially, knowing that bypassing so many others in favor of a district maintenance director would elicit questions."

"But he did it anyway."

"Thanks to Fields, whom the mayor needed to support his tax hike."

"One hand washing the other?"

"Something like that. It didn't help that your ex is quite a stunning woman, something that weighed heavily in her favor with the mayor, who, despite all his public posturing, has something of a roving eye."

I clear my throat and make sure my tone is deferential. "Judge, this is all very interesting, but I still don't see . . ."

"I'm getting to that!" he snaps.

I clamp my mouth shut and listen as the judge continues.

"Commissioner Hargrove hadn't even warmed her chair when Fields approached her about granting a contract to his son's construction company for a street-widening project in his district."

"Fields and Fields Construction? Wouldn't that have been a conflict of interest?"

"Dr. Collins, the world is a conflict of interest!"

With viewpoints like that, the judge could've been a historian. I'm liking him better and better.

"Commissioner Hargrove turned him down and since she was getting politically cozy with the mayor . . ."

"So then, the word was out about them after all?"

The judge purses his lips and scowls, and I shut up!

He says, "Since she was getting close to the mayor, Fields found himself having to do an eggshell walk. But even with that, he wouldn't back off."

I glance up at the portrait of Justice, who appears to be smirking.

"Fields needed the money," the judge continues. "His son's company was on the skids, and since he'd sunk so much of his own cash into it, he needed a major project win. But having gotten snuggly with the mayor, Commissioner Hargrove didn't feel any need to play Fields's game and turned him down, then froze him out."

I shake my head to dispel the vision of Justice flipping up her middle finger.

"The kid's company went belly-up," the judge adds. "The creditors and banks demanded their money. He started drinking. His marriage blew apart. And he took off, becoming a fugitive owing his current ex-wife thousands in child support added to what he owed for twins he'd had out of wedlock years before. Fields lost his shirt and will probably lose his shorts by the time he settles up."

The judge was right. I've been enlightened and it's a scene engulfed in darkness.

"Let me guess," I say. "Cookie's ultimate act of betrayal was her announced intention to challenge Fields in the upcoming election."

"That's right," the judge confirms, nodding. "A loss in this election will strip that pompous crook of any power he's retained to weasel the funds he'll need to stabilize himself." He punches an intercom button and leans toward the speaker. "Ms. Gunther, how much time till the next case?"

"Twenty-five minutes, Judge."

He looks back at me. "The irony is that Commissioner Hargrove might've won. Fields has lots of enemies who'd like to see him suffer. But the mayor has his share too, and with all the rumors now flying about his relationship with the commissioner, there's enough power players who view the scandal as an opportunity to clobber them both."

I hear myself speaking, but I'm not aware of my mouth moving, the shock of this woven web leaving me numb and mentally depleted.

"And by using Jarrod, he not only ruins Cookie's chances but gets his payback. A son for a son."

The judge nods gravely. "You're comprehending city politics, Dr. Collins. You have my condolences."

A lightbulb of inquiry goes on over my head. "Judge, how is it that Fields knew of Jarrod's . . ."

"You said it yourself. Jarrod sought him out. He spilled the beans, Fields saw his opening and took it."

I glance at the manila folder, then look at the judge. He follows the movement of my eyes and answers my question before I ask it.

"No, Dr. Collins. I told you, nothing discussed here leaves this room."

I hold out my hands, imploring him. "Please, Judge. Congresswoman Woolford has knowledge that could call Fields's motives into question."

"No! Congresswoman Woolford survived that investigation, but it dogged her throughout her campaign. There's nothing stopping Fields from calling a new one, and that's not the kind of exposure a politician, even an honest one, needs."

"But . . ."

"We're better informed because Priscilla and the loyalists she still has in city hall would love nothing better than to see Fields's career buried. They confided in me with the understanding that I'd forget the sources."

"But once the facts are known . . ."

"They'll do nothing to change the reality that Bell Cuppersmith's pregnant and your son's accused of being the father by means of rape!"

"And what about Jarrod?" I ask, my voice quavering despite my efforts. "Doesn't your precious law take into account the possibility that such an allegation could be false?"

"Dr. Collins, I'm sympathetic to your cause, but you're trying my patience. Forcing that girl to prove what happened would victimize her twice and condemn your son twice. As for Fields, even if he was suckered, he still comes out smelling like a rose. He becomes the noble politician who risked public humiliation to defend the victim of a heinous crime."

I inject steel into my voice. "Judge, you know this is wrong. How do you expect me to stay silent while my son's sacrificed for Cookie's stomping on the wrong toes?"

The judge gets up, glides over to his window, and clasps his hands behind his back once more. "Before you stomp on my toes let me inform you that I'm not some judicial monster. I've spent far too much of my career punishing diamond-in-the-rough black males like your son."

He turns from the window and faces me, his hands still clasped behind his back, giving him the profound authority of an Olympian jurist. "But all that aside, Jarrod's an unruly, undisciplined, incorrigible loud-mouth who needs a major attitude adjustment."

I'm taken aback by the assault upon Jarrod's character and get indignant. "Look, Judge! I know he's not perfect, but . . ."

"Let me finish!"

The judge marches over to a small closet, opens the door, and pulls out a fresh robe. "That boy's behavior needs to be recalibrated before it destroys him. There was absolutely *no* reason for him to tussle with those officers today. And don't even fix your lips to give me any of that white-officers-in-the-black-community crap! Color had nothing to do with his refusal to follow instructions that were politely given and efforts made to subdue him that would've been considered tame by standards of even five years ago."

He puts on the imposing black robe and shakes out the flowing sleeves, flapping his arms like a huge bird of prey.

"And based on the changes you say he's been putting you through, I'm betting that you wouldn't mind seeing a lightning bolt of reality shot up his butt."

The judge checks his tie and hair in the mirror. "I'll take your failure to challenge my assumption as proof that we're in agreement," he says.

He steps commandingly over to his desk, grabs a thick green folder, and scans the contents. He shakes his head and grunts in frustration.

"Him again," he grumbles. "Well, today he's gonna find out that fat meat is greasy."

He slams the folder shut and looks at me, his eyes clear, full of purpose, and lit bright with judicial fire.

"Dr. Collins, you were correct in deducing that the information I shared with you might help to mitigate your son's case. But mitigation's not exoneration."

He crosses his arms over his chest and drills his eyes into mine. "I won't mince words with you, sir. That boy's in big trouble, and I mean up to his neck. Understood?"

I nod.

"Good! Now, depending upon how a certain investigation goes, it could get better or it could get worse. Much worse. Is *that* clear?"

I nod again.

"Jarrod strikes me as a decent-enough young man. But he's got a burr up his butt and is begging for someone to yank it out. It's time to grab hold and pull. Are you with me?"

"Yes, Judge."

"I much prefer saving a black man to sending him to jail. But if the law says I must, then I must. You follow?"

"Yes, Judge."

"No matter how things turn out, Jarrod needs a course correction. You agree?"

"Yes, Judge."

"Now listen closely. After much hassle and maneuvering I've finally established a boot camp to help disruptive juveniles mend their ways before they wind up as disruptive inmates. Some kids graduate as transformed saints. Others fail and go on to the state pen."

The thought of Jarrod being sent someplace worse makes me shudder. "Judge, I can't let that happen."

"I understand. But it's not your decision. Jarrod's the one who has to decide which side of the bars he'll live life on. We can only try to help him make the right choice."

"Tell me what I have to do."

The judge studies my face hard, one of his eyes narrowing slightly. "Very well then. Here's the rules of the game. First of all, *I'm in charge!* I'm going to see to it that Jarrod understands that the law is real, has teeth, and can turn him out! But I need for you to let me do what I know works and not interfere. Are we clear?"

"Yes, Judge."

"Second, while my drill instructors are giving your wanna-be-a-tough-guy son a rude awakening, you're going to cooperate fully and *truthfully* with Detective Pullen and Ms. Watsburg, ask no questions, and be available whenever they need you."

"But, Judge. I have classes and . . ."

"One hand washes the other, Dr. Collins. What'll it be?"

I answer with a sigh, "Okay. I'll do it."

The judge nods and juts out his jaw, emphasizing his victory. "Third, under *no* circumstances are you to try to contact Milton Fields. Nor are you to attempt contacting Bernice Cuppersmith or coercing her into making a deal. If my suspicions are correct, she and Fields'll be twisting from the same rope before it's all over with. Got it?"

"Yes, Judge."

"And last, you're to be back here in three days at midnight for . . ."

"Midnight?"

"Don't be alarmed, Dr. Collins. It's all part of my special program. Our guests are usually a lot more pliable when they're hauled into court at midnight for their trial."

"Court? Trial? But I thought . . ."

"You thought *what?*" says the judge, getting loud. "That our personal connection would influence me into letting an alleged rapist walk without further investigation? Tell me that's not what you were hoping, Dr. Collins."

I gulp and answer respectfully, "No, Judge. It never crossed my mind."
What does cross my mind is that if Jarrod's going to trial, I need to call
my lawyer, Oliver. ASAP!

Ms. Gunther's voice speaks from the intercom: "Ten minutes, Judge."

"Thank you, Ms. Gunther."

The judge locks his hard eyes back onto me. "I'm glad you weren't entertaining such foolishness. Now, do we have a deal?"

I ponder for a long moment. "Yes, Judge. But . . ."

"No buts! This is a onetime offer. I can work in Jarrod's behalf as a
guide and benefactor or later as his judge and officer of the court. What'll
it be?"

I gulp and nod.

He extends his hand and we shake. "Good choice," the judge says.
"Now please leave so I can pray."

"Pardon me?"

"Don't be surprised, Dr. Collins. It takes more strength than I've got
to tell a seventeen-year-old he'll be turning fifty the next time he breathes
free air."

45

BY THE TIME I GET HOME, THE WARRIOR PASSAGES KICK-off has just started. I should do a quick change and go, but I'm just too exhausted. Reverend Boxwell's fully informed as to why I won't show, so that alleviates the necessity of calling him and explaining.

I drop my briefcase by the door, loosen my tie, grab a diet soda, and plop onto my lumpy couch. I take a swig and consider all the loose ends, all the angles and web strands, of this mess. No matter what perspective, dimension, or distance from which I view things, the catalyst repeatedly asserting itself as the center of turmoil is Cookie! And from the bottom of my heart, I'm truly sorry that I ignored Momma's warning about her: "You got her by breaking Laura's heart, didn't you?"

"Momma, Laura doesn't love me the way Cookie does."

"Darius, don't take me for a fool. I was born at night but not *last* night. You're with her to satisfy your flesh."

"Momma, our relationship's more than physical."

"No, it's not, baby. Just remember: *God doesn't like ugly and He's not too particular about pretty.* Something starting out bad rarely ends up good."

I'd always doubted those fakers who stood up in church and prophesied "this" and prophesied "that," like they had some special fiber-optic link with God while the rest of us were reduced to "waiting for a sign." But the lesson of this moment is that Momma's prophecy from the past concerning my present was correct!

I miss her and Dad so much. And I wonder, Did they ever feel as despondent about me as I do about Jarrod? I wasn't the model son, but I never ran afoul of the law. I was too terrified of the stares, hallway whispers, and finger pointing that would've resulted from my getting someone pregnant. That's why by the time I got to college, I hadn't done anything more than squeezed a breast. It's also why I became a wild sexual adventurer. If my parents hadn't been so strict I'd never have . . .

Reality hits me like a brick slap. I sound just like Jarrod, sniveling and blaming someone else for my behavior. The truth is that my parents' strictness saved me from Jarrod's nightmare. The thundering Sunday morning assurances that such wicked acts would put me on a bullet train to hell were true after all. If only I'd known that those sermons were also referring to the hell of my present!

Almost as though she'd been waiting for me to have thoughts of a hellish present, Cookie calls. Just hearing her voice leaves me feeling so very weary, worn-out, and drained.

"What is it, Cookie?" I ask.

"Where's Jarrod?"

"In jail."

She coughs, sputters, fizzes, and babbles before finally screaming, "*Jail!*"

"That's right. As in slammer."

"For how long?"

"I don't know."

"Aren't you even trying to get him out?" she rails.

"I'm doing everything in my power, Cookie."

"Ha!" she blurts, sounding so scornful it singes my eyebrows. "*Your* power," she says. "You don't have any power, Darius. Which means that Jarrod won't be freed before I get back."

I almost start to ask when she's coming back, but I don't care.

"I never should've left him with you," Cookie sniffles. "And now I'm stuck here in Rome until after they get through investigating this stupid bomb scare."

I almost start to ask why Cookie's in Rome, but I don't care.

"Darius, I swear, if anything happens to Jarrod, I'll make you pay."

I sigh. "Cookie, knowing you has been suffering enough."

She spires off into a new level of invective and I hang up, unplug the phone, grab the TV remote, and cut on the tube. One second, the screen's blank. The next, sour-faced news anchor Grady Stiles says, "And this was the scene earlier today at the home of Councilman Milton Fields."

The screen bursts alive with a mob of shouting reporters, bright lights, and numerous cameras, jockeying for position like a rioting school of one-eyed monsters. And there, in the center of it all, is Jarrod, his head down, hands cuffed behind him, and elbows gripped by two rumpled policemen, jostling him along as they're jostled by the newshounds.

The commentator says, "This was the scene just moments after

Councilman Milton Fields placed the call that led to the arrest of alleged rapist Jarrod Collins, son of Deputy Transportation Commissioner Cookie Hargrove . . ."

Tears sting my eyes as the cameras show Jarrod being jammed into the back of a police cruiser. The scene switches to the front steps of Fields's home. He's standing there answering questions, his chest puffed out and righteously indignant gaze burning into the camera lenses.

Question: "Councilman Fields, how did you learn of the rapist's identity?"

Answer: "He came to me and confessed that he couldn't live with himself."

Question: "Why you?"

Answer: "Commissioner Hargrove and I are competitors, but we're cordial. I guess my record of truth and integrity left him comfortable with the idea of approaching me."

Question: "Aren't you concerned that this'll look like an act of betrayal on your part?"

Answer: "What about the act of betrayal against the victim? If he feels slighted, I'm sorry for that. But I'm a public servant and sworn to protect my community. I did what was right for the people."

I spring up from the couch, grab the TV, and hurl it across the room. It lands with a nasty plastic-and-glass-shattering thud and trundles across the floor. I ball my hands into fists, raise them over my head, look at the ceiling, and let loose a rage-filled scream.

46

I MADE IT! THREE LONG, AGONIZING DAYS HAVE passed, but tonight I finally go down to the courthouse for Judge Newton's special meeting. I'm still not sure what he intends to do, but since it's designed to salvage my son, I'm willing to play along.

I've kept my phone unplugged most of the time to spare myself more of Cookie's long-distance hassling. When I last talked with her two days ago, she carried on about Rome's airport being closed indefinitely. There had been two more bomb scares, and the Italian police weren't taking any chances. They shut down border crossings, ship and airport facilities, international automotive traffic, and anything else that could give fanatics access into or out of their country.

I glance at my watch. The honey golden rays of sunlight beaming through the windows of Room 4 of the CBHS's private research area have turned from dusky gray, to light purple, to dark charcoal. I've been here since early morning, conducting research. After that attempted reputation hijacking by the board, I'd considered resigning my membership. Jarrod's crisis forced me to reconsider that option, and as of this moment, I'm glad.

If the judge knew I was looking into any- and everything having to do with Fields, he'd be pissed. But I'm technically not violating his instructions. He said that "under *no* circumstances," was I to "try to contact Milton Fields." And I'm not. I'm just trying to dig up any dirt, scandal, or tendril of evidence that'll help me crush that worm when the time is right. I haven't found anything yet, but not to worry. There's always something. Just like Robert Penn Warren wrote in *All the King's Men*: "Man is conceived in sin and born in corruption and he passeth from the stink of the didie to the stench of the shroud. There is always something."

I stretch and keep working. I pull the short chain on the desk lamp and finish scouring through the latest box of materials, folder-by-folder, document-by-document, line-by-line. The information I've gathered thus far is disjointed, but the glow in my researcher's gut tells me that I'm on a trail that will expose Fields for the rodent he is. It could also be wishful thinking, but even if it is, I'm feeling good about the possibilities.

I glance at my watch. There's just over three hours before I pick up Reverend Boxwell and Nash. They're riding down to the courthouse with me as a show of solidarity for both me and Jarrod. I initially insisted that they not come, but Nash fussed me out for trying to deny his godson his support. And Reverend Boxwell indignantly cut to the chase, pointing out that while Jarrod was a concern, his larger worry was *me*!

A knock on the door jolts me out of my preoccupation. "Yes. Who is it?"

"It's me, Dr. Collins," Ms. Corwin answers. "Will you be staying past closing again?"

I get up and open the door. "No, Ms. Corwin. Not tonight. Thanks for asking."

She nods and leaves. I keep plugging away. Time passes and I stay as long as possible until there's no choice but to leave. I put all the records back in their appropriate folders and boxes, gather up my notes and other materials, and leave. On the way out I'm both surprised and pleased to see Augusta Baylor.

"Why, hello, Dr. Collins," she greets me, smiling broadly.

"Hello, Augusta. What has you working so late amongst the dead?"

Her smile disappears. "Two things, actually. My project and you."

Mention of the project almost sends my eyes into rolling until she mentions me as a reason for research. She answers the question forming on my tongue.

"I heard about your son on TV," she says.

I feel like diving under a rock. If one of my students has heard about this mess (and with the way it's been splashed all over the news, how could they not?), then the rest of campus is buzzing with talk. The faculty and administration certainly must be.

"Once I heard that there was a connection to Councilman Fields, I started digging deeper," Augusta informs me. She grips my elbow. "Dr. Collins, I think we can help each other."

I grip her elbow. "I'm listening."

She starts talking, and after a few seconds I tell her to stop. Her information is too important to try to digest on such short notice. I suggest going down to the Wired Tight Coffee Shop. I'm still squeamish about being seen with a student in public on what looks like a date. But Augusta's news is too compelling to allow my paranoia to overrule on this occasion. If gaining Jarrod's freedom requires my having to battle misinterpretations of this meeting, then the fight will be worth it.

We pull up to the Wired Tight in our separate cars, go inside, and get a table. The lanky puffball from the day Cookie and I were here is gone, but I chuckle at the memory of his wide frightened eyes. We order our coffee, and Augusta shares the essential investigative nuggets of her treasure.

"And this is what I found," she says, her voice urgent. "Fields years before didn't own the building where the roof collapsed onto my family. He was a building inspector for the Cleveland Metropolitan Housing Authority, and was paid by private contractors to keep the complaints invisible, or, at a minimum, from showing up in front of someone who could take action."

"What a slime," I observe.

She answers with an emphatic nod, then continues. "I've gone back to my old neighborhood several times and the shelter where Marqueen and I were staying for a little while. Some of the people in both places put me in touch with some local thugs Fields had paid to keep people quiet."

"How did you get them to talk to you?" I ask. "Whenever I've tried to conduct research in that demographic, all I ever got were doors slammed in my face and dogs sicced on me."

Augusta purses her lips, then clubs me with her answer: "Dr. Collins, they talked to me for two reasons. First, they still see me as one of them. And second, I didn't treat them like a demographic, but people."

I'm shrinking in my seat but acknowledge to Augusta that she's made her point and that I'm sufficiently chastised. She's satisfied with my contrition and keeps talking.

"I've got reams of records," she says. "I've been to the county clerk's office, the open police files, the local Housing and Urban Development office, and other places, putting it all together, one piece at a time."

I shake my head both in admiration of Augusta's work and in disgust with Fields. "Fields is no different from the Africans who sold their brethren into slavery," I say. "And as bad as the collaborators selling drugs to their own people today."

Augusta nods. "No argument there," she says. "But whatever he is, he's cunning. When the case went to court, Fields was found not liable, testifying that he'd tried to get the contractor North Coast Properties to fix up the building. They were socked with a crippling fine. He parlayed his role into a seat on the city council. And when North Coast went bankrupt, he bought them."

"Let me guess: That was the start of Fields and Fields Construction Company?"

She nods again. We keep talking. By the time I go to pick up Reverend Boxwell and Nash, I'm feeling better than I have in days. Until I remember that no matter how much proof can be gathered regarding Fields's treachery in the past, my son is in a cage *now*! My mood sinks back into darkness.

47

I TAKE A SEAT ON THE COUCH IN REVEREND BOXWELL'S study and look around while he finishes his last few tasks before we leave to pick up Nash. It feels like I'm trespassing on sacred ground, sitting in this cozy room with its Cross hanging on the wall, scriptural quotations etched into several gleaming bronze plaques, and a pair of black marble praying hands on the desk.

I read the plaque inscription on the far wall. It's from John 3:16, probably the most quoted verse in all of New Testament Scripture. It says:

> For God so loved the world that he gave his one and only Son,
> that whoever believes in him shall not perish but have eternal life.

From the corner of my eye I spot Reverend Boxwell staring at me, and I turn quickly away.

"You're really going through it, aren't you?" he asks.

I nod, letting that suffice as my answer. But after so many days of keeping my feelings suppressed, I need to talk.

"If only Jarrod had listened to me," I say. "Things would've been so much easier."

Reverend Boxwell smiles with compassion. "That's how the Lord feels about us."

"What do you mean?"

"C'mon, Darius. You're too smart to not know what I mean. Remember the story of the prodigal?"

I nod and try to swallow the lump expanding in my throat.

"The prodigal had everything," Reverend Boxwell begins. "His wealthy father would've given him even more. But he wanted things *his* way, went off and got himself into trouble."

I recall how passionately Dad taught this story, his voice always rising when he described how the prodigal's wild ways eventually reduced him to poverty.

"He got so low he was ashamed to go home," Reverend Boxwell continues. "The one place where love and riches were his for the taking."

I look away. Reverend Boxwell leaves briefly and returns with a cup of tea. "Here, son. Drink this. It's some of Sister Boxwell's herbal blend. She says it's supposed to be soothing. I just think it tastes good."

"Thanks," I say, carefully taking the hot cup. I take a few sips and relax. "Sister Boxwell's right. This is wonderful."

"I'm glad you like it."

Reverend Boxwell sits down and leans forward, placing his elbows on his knees and folding his hands.

"Darius, you and Jarrod aren't so different. You both have a Father who loves you and wants you to come home. All you have to do is let Him help you."

I sip some more tea and return Reverend Boxwell's stare, his earnest expression dimming when I glance at my watch and suggest we leave.

48

I'M BETWEEN NASH AND REVEREND BOXWELL AS WE take our seats directly behind and diagonal to where Jarrod will be when he's brought in. My lawyer, Oliver Brady, fumbles nervously with his bow tie. When I first asked him to represent Jarrod he said, "Darius, ah, don't take this the wrong way, but, I'm not a, um, criminal lawyer."

I wasn't angry but definitely irritated. "Jarrod's not a criminal! And you won't actually be representing him. You'll be there to give things a proper feel."

"Give *what* a proper feel?"

"Oliver! Will you do it, yes or no?"

Oliver chewed his lower lip, told me what it would cost per hour, then agreed.

Nash looks wide-eyed around the somber courtroom, its severe atmosphere accented by the late hour and general uncertainty.

"What a creepy joint," he says. "This is gonna scare Jarrod half to death."

I try to ignore Nash, absolving myself with reminders that dire circumstances and Jarrod's recklessness have left me no choice.

"When this starts, y'all better be absolutely quiet!" Reverend Boxwell cautions. "The judge doesn't like talking in his court."

A door opens to the left of the judge's bench and Detective Pullen hurries in, a thick brown folder tucked in his armpit, freeing his hands to carry several law books. A minute or so later the door opens again and Jarrod steps into the entrance.

I can scarcely believe my eyes. He's dressed in a blue denim shirt, gray utility trousers, and black combat boots. He's standing tall at the position of attention, not moving a muscle or blinking an eye. The ratty patchwork haircut he had three days ago has been shaved into a smooth baldness. His once soft, spoiled eyes pulse with the heart and strength of a survivor.

The wiry-muscled guard who drew my ire the other day whispers into

Jarrod's ear, then draws away. Jarrod marches stiff and erect to the table, positions himself in the front of the chair next to Oliver, and waits. Oliver looks at me with bewilderment. I shrug and nod for him to face front before the judge enters.

A bailiff strides over to the right front corner of the judge's bench, assumes a rigid posture, and shouts into the cavernous courtroom.

"All rise!"

We stand quickly. A door to the right of the judge's bench whips open and he erupts into the courtroom, filling every corner with his authority as his jet-black robe billows and swishes behind him. He steps up to the bench, grabs his gavel, and bangs the event into official existence.

"Hear ye! Hear ye!" the bailiff announces. "This hearing is now in session! The Honorable Judge Lucas Newton presiding!"

Judge Newton takes his seat and bangs his gavel again. "Order!"

The bailiff follows with, "Take your seats!"

We sit as quickly as we stood. Jarrod scoots close to the table, places his arms just so on it, and interlaces his fingers.

The judge looks over at Detective Pullen and scowls. "What's so important that you felt it necessary to roust me out of bed in the middle of the night?" he growls.

I'm somewhat puzzled that Detective Pullen and not a lawyer is serving as the prosecution, but decide that it must be one more peculiarity of the judge's special "court."

Detective Pullen stands and starts to answer but is cut off by the judge. His brow bunches into knots of anger and he points his gavel.

"Detective, I'm warning you. This better be more than some snot-nosed thug wanna-be refusing to have his diapers changed. I'm already ticked about being dragged down here, and this flu bug has killed whatever good mood I had left. Present your case!"

Detective Pullen points to Jarrod. "Your Honor, I have the misfortune of once more coming before you to announce that the people have been forced . . ."

"I *and* the people want you to hurry!"

Detective Pullen strides across the court and points directly at Jarrod. "The accused, Jarrod Collins, has been charged with rape!"

Jarrod remains stone-faced but starts wringing his hands.

"Rape!" the judge booms. He fixes his narrowed smoldering eyes onto Jarrod. "Boy! I'm gonna grind you up and spit you out!"

Jarrod works his lower jaw back and forth. The judge looks at Detective Pullen and gestures for him to hurry up. "Go on!" he commands. "We don't have all night!"

"Very well, Your Honor. We have a confession that the accused—*of his own free will*—gave to Councilman Milton Fields regarding his crime."

I swear by all that lives in me, Fields will pay for this! Detective Pullen and the judge keep talking. And the more they talk, the more Jarrod's resolve melts.

"Do you have the evidence prepared?" the judge asks.

"Er, we have preliminary submissions, Your Honor."

The judge rolls his eyes. "Oh, all right then! That'll have to do."

"Thank you, Your Honor. The state feels it'll be more than enough to convict."

Oliver rises to speak and is blown back into his chair. "Sit down, Mr. Brady!" the judge blares. "I'll let you know when I want your opinion!"

Jarrod starts muttering to the table. "Shut up!" the judge shouts. "Who gave you permission to speak in my court?"

Jarrod's head snaps up. He locks his gaze onto the judge and quickly wipes his eyes.

"And stop that crying!" Judge Newton orders. "I'm sick'n tired of you gangsta-rappin'-droopy-pants-homey-G-hood rats turning into sissies once you're staring into the eyes of my dragon." He leans forward and glares. "That dragon is the law, son. And he's a mean fire breather with only one purpose in life—*one*! Can you guess what it is?"

Jarrod shakes his head no, but that's not good enough.

"Speak up!" the judge booms. "I know you don't have any trouble fatmouthing your parents, so answer me! What's my dragon's purpose?"

"I, I don't know," Jarrod quavers.

Judge Newton mockingly whines Jarrod's answer back to him: " 'I, I don't know.' " He slams his fist onto the bench and speaks in a low, menacing rumble. "My dragon's purpose is to set the guilty aflame. And, son, he loves his job!"

Jarrod lowers his head and sobs.

I stir and say, "Okay, that's enough."

Nash grips my forearm and whispers hoarsely, "Hold on, D."

"But . . ."

"Jarrod can handle it! You've gotta believe in him!"

"I do! But this is going too far."

Judge Newton bangs his gavel and glares at us. "Is there something you two want to say before I throw you out?"

Nash and I shut up, sit back, and slouch down. Judge Newton harrumphs, loosens his collar, and focuses back onto Jarrod.

"Look at'cha, sitting over there whimpering," he attacks. "You thought you wouldn't get caught, didn't you? Betcha don't feel so slick now, do you?"

Jarrod precedes his answer with a sniffle. "No."

"No *what*?"

"No, sir."

"That's better."

Jarrod starts to turn toward me but stops when Judge Newton roars, "Look at *me*, boy! This isn't between you and your daddy anymore! It's time for you to feel the heat of my dragon!"

"But I didn't do anything."

Judge Newton rolls his eyes with obvious skepticism. "Of course you didn't. But what else could we expect you to say?" He looks at Detective Pullen. "Go ahead! It's late and I'm tired. If we hurry, I can still make it home for breakfast."

Detective Pullen hurries back to his table and shuffles through a stack of papers, making a great show of finding "the" document.

"While I'm still young, Detective!" the judge growls.

After a few more seconds of rummaging and shuffling, Detective Pullen finds "the" document. "Here it is!" he exclaims.

Judge Newton snaps his fingers several times with exaggerated impatience. "*Well!* Let's see the blasted thing!"

Detective Pullen hustles to the bench and hands it over. Judge Newton snatches it, slaps it facedown onto the bench, and locks a withering glare onto Jarrod.

"I don't need this!" the judge rumbles. "Because *nobody* comes into *my* court unless they've earned an appointment. And, son, I guarantee this is one appointment you'll be sorry you kept!" He glances at the bailiff. "Bring in Herk."

I lean over to Reverend Boxwell. "Who's Herk?" I ask, whispering.

He shrugs and nods toward the bench. I follow his gaze into the flaming eyes of Judge Newton's, zip my mouth, and slouch lower. The bailiff disappears out a side door and moments later enters behind a bald, muscle-bound roughneck dressed in a bright orange prison jumpsuit, his hands cuffed, ankles shackled, and wearing flimsy slippers that barely cover his feet. He shuffles in, the clank and rattle of his chains jangling louder each time the bailiff jabs a billy club into the small of his back. He hobbles in front of the judge, stands ramrod-straight, and looks down at his feet.

"How ya been, Herk?" the judge asks, sounding like he's addressing an old acquaintance.

Herk answers with a voice pulled from a canyon. "I been better," he says.

"Take a look at that crying pile of turds."

Herk wobbles around and glares at Jarrod, who lowers his eyes.

"Get your eyes up!" the judge commands. "And take a hard look at your future!"

Jarrod lifts his head so that his gaze meets Herk's.

"Whatcha think?" the judge asks.

Herk's face clouds with disgust. "He won't last long, but," he winks and puckers his lips, "he sure is pretty."

Jarrod shivers and shuts his eyes tight. "Please, God!"

"You'd better call God!" the judge meanly advises. "Because He's all that's between where you're sitting and Herk's standing!" He sits back and relaxes. "Herk, how long you been a guest of mine?"

"I been in and out'a your jail since I was nine, Judge."

"Since you were nine! You've been busy. What were you doing in so much trouble?"

"First time, I got busted for stealin' car radios. When I was about eleven, I was spottin' the po-lease for drug dealers. At fourteen, I was dealin' myself. At sixteen, I pulled some armed robberies, messed up, and shot a dude."

"Don't be modest, Herk. You didn't just shoot that old white salesman, now did you?"

"Naw, Judge. I, I kilt 'em."

The judge shakes his head. "That must'a really pissed off my dragon."

"It put 'em in a bad way."

"Tell us whatcha mean."

Herk's voice tightens. "When I turn eighteen in two months, I'm goin' to the pen."

"Because'a that murder, huh?"

Herk gulps, shuts his eyes tight, and nods slow.

"Speak up!" the judge demands.

"That's right, Judge. Cuz'a what I done."

"You blame me for sending you up there, don'tcha, Herk?"

"You the man, Judge."

"Tell this pissant whatcha think of me."

Herk's canyon-deep voice sinks lower, emphasizing his sincerity. "I ain't got no love for ya, Judge. And besides bein' born, meetin' you's the worsest thang ever happened to me."

Tears collect at the bottom of Jarrod's chin and fall in huge drips. Judge Newton shakes his head sadly and nods at the bailiff. "Take him back and have him wait on his new cell mate!" he orders, glancing at Jarrod.

"Wait, Judge!" I yell, springing to my feet. "I thought you . . ."

Nash and Reverend Boxwell each grab an arm and yank me down into my seat.

The judge bangs his gavel. "*Dr. Collins!* One more word and Herk'll be getting to know you instead!"

"But . . ."

"That's it!" he booms. "Get him out'a here!"

"No!" Jarrod cries. "Dad! Don't go!"

"Order in this court!" Judge Newton hollers. "*I want order!*"

A bailiff grabs my elbow and jostles me down the aisle. I struggle to face the judge and talk to him, reason with him, but it's to no avail. The bailiff shoves me out the heavy double doors into the cold, empty hallway, then stands guard, his legs apart and arms crossed, scowling.

"Please," I beg. "My son, he can't . . ."

"He can't what?" the bailiff challenges me. "The judge believes he *can!*"

I pace back and forth, my imagination torturing me with images of Jarrod cowering in a dark corner as Herk approaches. I approach the bailiff with caution.

"Can I at least listen to what's going on?"

"Look, Dr. Collins. The judge'll have my . . ."

"I'll keep quiet. I promise. *Please!*"

Judge Newton's voice filters through the doors, taunting me with its closeness.

The bailiff snorts in frustration. "Okay, Dr. Collins. But I'm warning you . . ."

"On my word. I only want to listen!"

The bailiff maintains his guard but gestures for me to move forward. I pad closer, the judge's booming voice becoming more intelligible with each step.

"That's close enough," the bailiff firmly cautions, snapping up his palm.

I lean forward and bite my tongue as Judge Newton incinerates Jarrod with combustive abilities rivaling those of his dragon.

"Between you and Herk, *you're* the bigger waste!" he rails. "At least Herk had an excuse! He grew up in a war zone. His momma loved her crack pipe more than him. And his daddy! That sucker better hope I *never* find him!"

"Tell 'em straight, Judge," the bailiff grumbles.

"You disgust me!" Judge Newton hollers. "More than Herk ever could! He never had someone to come be afraid for him in the middle of the night! No one ever cared enough to *not* want to see him locked up! No one ever cared enough to plead with him about staying in school, doing right, and avoiding my dragon!"

"Be strong, Jarrod," I whisper.

"But you've got a father out there sweating bullets about your future!" the judge flames. "He's probably stayed up nights, beating his head against the wall, because you just don't get it! He's probably wondered what it would take to finally get your attention!"

The gavel slams with resounding fury. "Well, son! I'd say your attention's been properly focused. You defied my dragon and now it's gonna turn you into barbecue."

Jarrod sobs loud and hard.

"Reverend Boxwell! Mr. Ayers! I'll have to ask you to leave," the judge says.

Seconds later, Reverend Boxwell and Nash hustle out the double doors. "How's Jarrod?" I ask quickly. "What's going on? What's the judge going to do? Where's Oliver? What about Detective Pullen?"

Reverend Boxwell grabs our hands and bows his head. Nash's eyes widen in momentary surprise; then he grabs my free hand and closes his eyes.

"Stand up!" the judge orders. "You've been strutting around, pretending to be a man. Well, a man has to stand on his own two feet. So *get up!*"

Reverend Boxwell tightens his grip and begins praying with an urgency I haven't heard since the prayers of my dad.

"Our Father, Who art in heaven . . ."

The judge launches into Jarrod with a new tirade, the rage in his voice whipping into a tidal fury. Jarrod tries to get a word in edgewise, insisting upon his innocence, but the judge shuts him down every time. And finally, I can't stand it anymore.

I jam my eyes shut and join Reverend Boxwell as he says, ". . . and deliver us from evil, for Thine is the kingdom, and the power, and the glory, forever and ever. Amen!"

49

NASH DRIVES MY CAR HOME, SINCE I'M STILL SHAKING
with too much rage. Reverend Boxwell rides in the rear while I sit in
the front passenger's seat.

Immediately after the "trial" Detective Pullen strode up to me in the
courthouse lobby and shoved some papers under my nose.

"What are these?" I asked.

"Papers needing your signature for the final phase of Jarrod's boot
camp experience."

I started to tell him that there would be no such thing, but he cut me
off before I could fix my lips to argue.

"Remember," he began. "As rough as the judge's methods might
appear at this moment, it's nothing compared to what Jarrod would be ex-
periencing if he were going through regular channels." He paused and
leaned forward, as if to ensure that the words sank in. "Do you follow me,
Dr. Collins?"

I understood *exactly* what he was talking about. And I still didn't like
it. But I also knew that, just as the judge had stated days earlier, Jarrod
needed to be rescued. I felt angry and inadequate that I hadn't been able
to do it as his father. I was so very pissed at Jarrod's refusing my attempts
to be effective in his life. But this wasn't about me. It was about saving my
son, and if it took me, Nash, Reverend Boxwell, the judge, and anyone
else, that's all that mattered.

I signed the papers, guaranteeing that whatever Jarrod had been going
through would continue, and hoped that he'd forgive me. If not, I'd find a
way of living with his anger, just as my father had found a way of living—
and dying—with mine.

We get to Reverend Boxwell's house and he starts to get out, grabbing
his forehead and wincing just as he opens the car door.

"Are you okay?" Nash asks.

"I'm fine," Reverend Boxwell answers. "I've just been having some
powerful bad headaches. I guess it's time for another visit to the doctors."

He gets out and looks at me. "Darius, will you be okay?"

"Yes." I don't mean to be short, but I'm still too ticked off for prolonged pleasantries.

Reverend Boxwell grips my shoulder and squeezes tenderly. "Have faith, son. It might not look like it, but Jarrod's in the center of the Lord's protective palm. He'll be all right."

I glare at Reverend Boxwell. He smiles, winces, rubs his forehead, and turns away to his house. Nash pulls off and heads to his place so I can drop him off and finally go home.

"I love the way he calls you son," Nash says.

I nod and keep scowling. Nash scores points by staying quiet the rest of the way to his house. We get there and he gets out of the car.

I get into the driver's seat and look up at Nash. "Thanks for coming."

"No problem, man. I wouldn't have been anyplace else."

He smiles. I nod and take off. A little while later I pull into my assigned space, park, and just sit, trying to grasp everything that's happened. Minutes pass. A car comes flying into the parking lot and whips into one of the visitor spaces. What maniac is this? Seconds later the driver gets out and I see that the maniac is . . . *Gina?*

She hustles over to my building until I get out and call her. She stops, squints to see if it's really me, and hurries over. Once we're close enough, she grabs me and pulls me in to her for a tight desperate hug.

"What's the matter?" I ask.

She steps back and holds my shoulders. "Shouldn't I be asking you that?"

I frown. "Huh?"

Gina purses her lips. "Nash called me and explained what happened tonight with Jarrod. *Why didn't you tell me?*"

I shrug. She hugs me, then pulls me toward the building. "C'mon," she says. "Let's go in and talk about it."

I stop and pull my arm from her grip. "I don't feel like talking."

She steps directly in front of me and looks deep into my eyes. "Please?"

I nod and we walk arm-in-arm up to my apartment. Once inside, I shuffle over to the couch, plop down, and lean forward, holding my head in my hands. Gina kneels down in front of me, gently pushes me back until I'm reclining, removes my shoes, and starts massaging my feet.

"Gina, you don't have to do this," I say.

"I know. I'm doing it because I want to."

I look over at her. She smiles and, despite my sour mood, I can't help smiling back.

"So tell me what happened," Gina urges.

And I do. Everything. From the moment Cookie delivered the news of Jarrod's troubles to the last echoing blast of Judge Newton's voice.

"Gina, I'm scared for him," I say. "I almost sometimes wish that I could just shut off my emotions and not care. Just long enough to give myself a rest."

"That might be possible for someone else, but not you."

I look at her. "Oh, really. And why's that?"

She stops rubbing my feet and locks her gaze with mine. "Darius, you're the kind of man who once you really love someone, you love them hard. You can't just shut that off."

Gina's statement contains a hammer of truth that strikes too close to home. "You sure seem to know a lot about how I love," I say, chuckling nervously.

Gina moves slowly up beside me until we're face-to-face. "I should," she says huskily. "It's the way you've been loving me."

I keep my gaze steady with hers. "And what about you?" I ask.

She softly strokes my cheek. "Why are you asking a question that you already know the answer to?"

I open my arms and Gina melts into my embrace. We hug and snuggle, gradually moving our faces closer together until our lips join in a long, tender kiss. Gina's breathing deepens and I open my legs slightly as my erection expands. I gasp and shudder when she reaches down and squeezes my hardness. She does the same when I cup her breast, slowly moving my thumb back and forth along the thin material of her blouse, stroking her nipple to hardness.

I sit up, pull Gina in to me, and we kiss again, this time with fire. We stand together and she grinds her pelvis against my throbbing erection. I grab her hips and grind back, *hard*! We break the kiss and stare hard at each other, our chests heaving. Millions of unspoken words are communicated through our intense shared gaze. She slowly unbuttons her blouse, each freed button exposing more of the smooth, soft roundness of her beautiful brown breasts. I bend down and kiss them, gradually moving up along her neck to her shoulders. Gina exhales a soft, low moan when I slip my hand down to her crotch and start slowly massaging, rubbing slightly harder as her wetness increases its warmth. She grabs my head and kisses me hard, her tongue exploring the inside of my mouth with passionate urgency.

We're still kissing when I pick her up and carry her into my bedroom.

50

IT'S THE NEXT DAY. AND GINA'S GONE. SHE LEFT A note:

> Darius, last night, you let me into your world when you were hurting. Because you did, I know you trust me with your heart just as I trust you with mine. With the other people in our lives we've had convenient excuses to not face the reality of our feelings. Things have obviously changed. We should talk.
>
> Gina

I reread the note and smile, my body warming all over. I lay it off to the side and head for the shower, amazed at how in the midst of so much going wrong, something wonderful has finally gone right!

I finish showering, get dressed, and head for campus. I try analyzing every detail of what happened in Judge Newton's courtroom, wondering over and over if I should've agreed to his plan. Either way, I hope it blasted some sense into Jarrod. I love him and will agree to worse if it finally gets through to him. What's at stake is nothing less than *saving his life*.

I get on the road to the campus, turning my mind more toward the challenges there with each mile traveled. I try to not think about the pro and anti el Bornu rallies being held today. But of course, the harder I try, the more I do, heightening my frustration for not possessing the mental discipline to simply banish the thoughts. And it's not like I need new anxieties, especially with Jarrod still in Judge Newton's draconian clutches and that investigation going nowhere fast.

I get to my office, check my voice mail (mercifully, there's nothing from Cookie or Marcy), review the little bit of writing I've done for my article on racism in the academy, then head off for my African-American history class. I'm anxious to see the smiles on their faces when I tell them of the great job they've done.

Moments later I'm standing in front them and make the announcement. "Your tests were outstanding!" I say. "You've made your professor very happy."

"Likewise, Dr. Collins," Mr. Arrati quips. "This grade'll keep my dad off my back."

Laughter ripples through the class and I direct the students to applaud themselves. Once the mass congratulations are over I start questioning them on today's reading assignment, *The Souls of Black Folk* by the late Dr. W. E. B. DuBois.

I call on Augusta Baylor first. "Ms. Baylor, in the chapter 'Of Mr. Booker T. Washington and Others' cite one of Dr. DuBois's criticisms of Booker T. Washington."

She clears her throat and projects, "He disagreed with Washington's soft emphasis on achieving African-American suffrage and social civil rights."

"And tell me, Mr. Padrewski, what major speech did DuBois reference to illustrate the deficiency of Washington's solution to race relations in the country?"

"Um, I think it was . . ."

"You think or you know?"

His face reddens. "It was Washington's 1895 Atlanta Compromise speech."

"Excellent! Ms. Finwahl, why was it a compromise?"

"Because Washington stated that blacks and whites could live separately as the five fingers, but still be united in pursuits of national mutual progress."

"Mr. Verheusen, was this revolutionary, regressive, or a surrender?"

"I think it was regress . . ."

Ross Verheusen's mouth hangs silently open as LaThomas Patterson barges in and swaggers across the front of the room toward me.

"Mr. Patterson, what do you think you're doing?" I ask, my voice rising.

He pulls out a slip of paper. "I'm dropping this class and need your sign-off."

I snatch the paper from him, sign it, and throw it back. "There! Now get out!"

He scrambles and catches it before it hits the floor, then steps toward me.

"Be careful," I warn, gesturing with my head toward the class. "This many witnesses will definitely ruin your football career."

He glances around the room and sees every eye glued to him. He forces a nonchalant chuckle and backs away. "Forget you, sucka! You're just mad cuz you can't be me."

Hallway snickers draw my attention to a couple of female groupies who've accompanied Mr. Patterson to enjoy the fun he's having at my expense. I can barely maintain my temper and decide to have a little fun of my own. But I've got to remember that I'm supposed to be shaping young minds, teaching them to consider perspectives that'll prepare them for success in an increasingly diverse, rapidly changing world. These are duties I cherish and take seriously, even when it comes to louts like LaThomas Patterson. So I turn to the board and draw a confusing mass of squiggly, crisscrossing lines, arrows, Xs, and Os, face him, and smile.

"You're right, Mr. Patterson. I can't be you. That would require backwards evolutionary movement, robbing me of an ability to answer several questions about you."

"Check 'em out, y'all," he laughs nervously. "He's tryin' to cover up his sorriness by usin' big words."

"Yes, Mr. Patterson," I agree, sighing with a smile. "I suppose that to you, any word beyond *yo* would be considered big."

A shimmer of laughter floats up from the class till he glares them into silence. He balls his hands into fists and hurls a series of vulgarities that challenge me to reconsider his creative abilities.

"As far as your recommendation for me to self-copulate, I'll take it under advisement," I say, "after I've finished analyzing you."

"Suck my nuts! You ain't qualified to analyze me!"

"Right again, Mr. Patterson," I respond, tapping my messy drawing. "I'm grossly unqualified. And I know this because I can't explain how it's possible for you to understand confusing football plays, but not complete a simple reading assignment."

I gesture toward the class. "I can't explain the insanity that's allowing you to sleepwalk through college to afterwards be paid millions—*for playing a game!*—while your classmates are condemned to entry-level oblivion."

I grab *The Souls of Black Folk* and fan it back and forth. "I can't explain why you don't feel guilty for squandering the education our ancestors purchased with their blood."

I fan the book faster and talk louder. "I can't explain why you don't realize that it takes a powerful, trained mind for a black man to survive America, just as it takes a powerful, trained body to survive the gridiron!"

Mr. Patterson's shaking with rage. If he could breathe fire, his nostrils would probably shoot flames. He starts toward me and I'm suddenly very sorry for having pushed him so far.

"Augusta!" I shout. "Get campus security!"

She bolts to the door and is stopped by the groupies. "Where you think you goin', Miss Goody-goody?" Groupie One shouts.

Augusta punches her square between the eyes and she drops to the floor. Groupie two watches, stunned, giving Augusta time enough to slap her and rip open her shirt. The girl shrieks and zooms away, doing her best to cover herself.

Mr. Arrati and Mr. Padrewski rush in front of me and try to reason with Mr. Patterson, the three of us slowly moving backwards as LaThomas approaches. The rest of the class sit like a herd of mouth-gaping deer caught in headlights, too startled to move.

"Tom, c'mon, man," Mr. Arrati tries to reason, gulping. "This won't solve anything."

Mr. Patterson grabs him and flings him into a wall, his narrowed smoldering eyes locked on me the whole time. I move Mr. Padrewski aside, order him to help Mr. Arrati, and step toward Mr. Patterson. These are *my* students and I'm not letting anyone harm them!

Mr. Patterson's taken aback by my forward movement and slows. But he recovers quickly and closes in. "I'ma rip out your lungs," he growls.

I roll up my sleeves and crack my knuckles. "You should've brought help. *Punk!*"

"Tom!" a voice shouts from the doorway. It's Andre Echols, the most talented and sensible of the clown triumvirate. He enters quickly but cautiously. "C'mon, man," he says, his voice firm but steady. "Dr. Collins has got his ways, man, but he's a brother trying to do his job."

Mr. Patterson glares at him. "Whutch'you been doing?" he asks threateningly. "You been letting 'em pump you up the butt? Zat why's you defendin' this sorry chump?"

Andre's eyes harden into ice. "Man, you're lucky I've got your back."

"Or what?" Mr. Patterson challenges. "Whutch'you gonna do?"

"Freeze!"

Everyone's eyes snap over to the doorway, filled with the imposing presence of a black campus security policeman. He speaks into a microphone just above his left breast pocket.

"Send backup!" he barks. "LaThomas Patterson's assaulting one of the faculty."

Mr. Patterson spins around and the officer pulls out his baton. "Better think twice. Fool!"

"You ain't no better than him!" Mr. Patterson protests, pointing back at me. "Both'a y'all's just the white man's flunkies."

The officer shakes his head. "You're pathetic. The white man ain't got *nothing* to do with you harassing one of the few black profs we've got on this campus."

Moments later, several other officers rush in, force Mr. Patterson to the floor, and cuff him. They're quickly followed by Augusta and several other professors, students, and staff who've heard all the commotion. They start peppering me with questions, making sure I'm okay while the rest of my students rush forward, clapping and cheering.

"You should've seen him!" Ms. Finwahl says. "Dr. Collins has some big brass balls!"

Everyone laughs until Coach Wofford dashes in. He sees Mr. Patterson lying facedown on the floor and grimaces. The officers pull LaThomas to his feet and he looks at Coach Wofford with big, sad eyes.

"Coach, it ain't my fault."

The coach scowls. "I don't wanna hear it." He gestures to the officers. "Take 'em." He nods to me and exits. I direct some students to help the still-dazed Mr. Arrati.

"Darius! Come quick!" shouts my department chairperson, Esther Kurozawa. She's staring, frightened, out a nearby window.

"What's the matter?" I ask, hurrying over.

A gaggle of security officers, students, and staff follow, all of us lining up along the windows.

The cause of Esther's alarm escapes me until I see Dr. Avi Silberberg, huddling in his car as a growing circle of yelling black students closes in on him. I hustle out of the room, sharing nods of mutual respect with Andre Echols as I race past him.

51

I FOLLOW SEVERAL SECURITY OFFICERS AS THEY FORCE their way through the shouting, chanting students. The officers position themselves near Avi's car door and order the unruly crowd back, drawing withering glares and grumbled epithets. I ease over to Avi's window and tap several times. He looks at me with the terror-stricken eyes of a man who's been tongue-kissed by the Grim Reaper.

I spin around, elbow one of the security officers aside, and bellow, *"Why?"*

The students closest to me stagger into those behind them, filling the air with babbled curses and complaints.

"Why what?" Mubarak Kwanju (aka, Garland Poole) shouts. Julie Cranshaw's also here with a few MPC members of questionable sincerity. There's Barton Wheeler, a dud who's using the MPC to slobber after Savannah Murcine, just like he slobbered after her through my lectures during his sophomore fall semester. Cathy Bivvins, who'll be involved for as long as it takes her to sign up everyone as a *Soul Tones* cosmetic and skin care distributor. And wealthy Keith Kline, whose father wants his "too white" acting son to get "more black," which better happen if he wants to keep getting his monthly allowance.

"Why are you all doing this?" I shout.

"Because we're tired of, of . . ."

"The man keepin' us down!" an anonymous voice finishes.

I point at Avi and step toward the crowd, making them step back as one body. "What's Dr. Silberberg done to keep you down?"

"He's part of the system!"

"What system? The one you're participating in to get an education? The one preparing you for life? The one that'll help you as much as you're willing to help yourselves?" I step forward again. "*I'm* also part of that system!"

"Which means you're worse than him!" a voice shouts from afar.

Everyone turns toward the response, a confused murmur working its way through the crowd. The sea of people slowly parts, opening for the swaggering, decked-out-in-his-African-garb-Sunday-best Osmani el Bornu. And of course, behind him follow a train of reporters, cameras, microphones, and tape recorders.

"That's right!" he booms, turning his head so everyone can hear. "He's a sellout!"

Ugly murmurs and shouts of agreement follow. "Yeah! Traitor!" Mubarak Kwanju booms. "Collaborator!" Julie Cranshaw shouts. Others join in. "House nigger!" "Don't worry, boss! I'se be a good *boy*." "My massa treats me good!" "O-R-E-O!"

El Bornu thrusts his hands skyward, demanding quiet. He climbs atop a car and looks out with the smug gaze of a conqueror.

"My brothers and sisters, *this*," he says, pointing down at me, "is why we suffer oppression."

"Yeah!"

"*This* Judas has been co-opted by the system!"

"Yeah!"

"*This* wolf in sheep's clothing feeds on our blood!"

"Yeah!"

"*This* white man's dog wants to hunt you down!"

"Yeah!"

"And *that*, brothers and sisters, is why I've come to give you the truth!"

Spontaneous applause erupts. El Bornu looks around, nodding and smiling with approval. I glance behind me to check on Avi. His lower jaw's trembling and he grips the steering wheel like a man clutching a ship railing in a storm.

Visions flash before me of Jew-crowded trains arriving at Nazi death camps and African-crowded slavers arriving in the Americas. Film footage of corpses being bulldozed into mass graves intersperse with still photos of slave mutilations and lynchings. Charges of crimes against humanity echoing from Nuremberg blend into the forlorn voice of Fountain Hughes, an ex-slave who lived long enough to have his story recorded live:

"If I ever thought I'd be a slave again, I'd take a gun and end it all. Because you're just a dog. You're not a thing but a dog."

I whirl around and point up at el Bornu. "What do *you* know about truth?" I shout.

The crowd's noise chops into silence, everyone stunned by this rare challenge to the self-appointed "leader."

El Bornu's eyes widen, then narrow. "I know this system's denied us long enough! I know it's rotten to the core! And I know that we need a land of our own!"

"And from whom do we take that land? Do we take it from the Native Americans like the whites did? Do we take it from Africans like ex-slaves did when they settled in Liberia?"

Heads turn back and forth, watching me and el Bornu volley statements like verbal tennis players.

"And how could *you* know more about denial than Olaudah Equiano?" I ask. "Or Phillis Wheatley, Sojourner Truth, Frederick Douglass, and Fountain Hughes?"

"They were slaves the system kept down!"

"Who fought all their lives for you to be free!"

"This system's too corrupt to achieve real freedom!"

"And yet you stand here exercising your right to free speech!"

"Fool! You've let a legal trinket blind you to your own oppression."

"Your fixation with oppression has crippled your own liberation."

"True liberation can happen only in the motherland!"

"Which makes you an accomplice of the white supremacists who want us to leave!"

El Bornu balls his hands into fists as his nostrils flare, our point-counterpoint exchange having stalled the crowd's gathering hostility.

He turns to the slightly subdued students and extends his arms, beckoning. "You see, my brothers and sisters. There exist among us agents of darkness."

"Like him!" I say, pointing up at el Bornu.

I climb atop Avi's car and make my own open-armed appeal. "Young people!" I shout. "Don't let his twisting of the truth turn you into his pawns!"

"I'm liberating their minds!" el Bornu blasts.

"And what is that truth, young people? That Dr. Silberberg's the ancestral child of former slaves, *just like us*! That his people have been chased around the globe and welcomed nowhere, *just like us*! That throughout their history his people have been marginalized, demonized, and brutalized, *just like us*! That they have good and bad amongst them, *just like us*!"

El Bornu waves his arms excitedly. "My brothers and sisters . . ."

"Let him finish!" someone shouts.

I look for the voice's owner and see Gina, working her way through the throng.

"Shut up, woman!" el Bornu commands. "Nobody told you to speak!"

Every female jaw I can see stiffens. "Who're you telling to shut up?" an indignant young woman demands.

"She doesn't need no *man's* permission to speak!" says another.

Grumbles of support get louder, the suddenly ill wind driving el Bornu into silence.

Gina steps around the security officers and looks up at me. "Darius, I'm so sorry," she says.

I climb down to help her coax Avi out of his car. "Come on out, Avi," I say softly. "No one's going to hurt you. I promise!"

Avi's eyes are filled with distrust. Gina taps softly on the window. "Avi, come out. We won't let anyone harm you."

She turns to the crowd. "Move back!"

And they do, stepping away and making a path. Avi looks from me to Gina, then to me, and gets out. I hold him by his shoulders and stare hard into his eyes.

"Avi, you needed me and I wasn't there. But I promise you, *never again!*"

Gina and I link elbows with him and slowly plow our way through the crowd. El Bornu seizes the moment to castigate me, Gina, and other fake blacks, then turns toward the cameras, microphones, and tape recorders to spew his poison into the afflicted heart of America.

52

WHEN I RETURN TO THE RELATIVE PEACE OF MY OFFICE, there are two messages lying on my desk. I almost dread reading them but do so anyway. I grab the one closest and see it's from Andre Echols. It says: *Dr. Collins, I'd like to stop by sometime and talk to you about being my adviser.*

Sweet satisfaction washes over me, and I can feel the ancestors smiling. The second message says: *Dr. Collins, you're needed down at the Leifler Juvenile Detention Center. ASAP!*

My smile vanishes along with those of the ancestors. I wish whoever called had just said, "Meet me downtown," or used some other kind of coding that would've denied the campus rumor mill new grist to grind. But it's too late, so I whirl into motion and blur out of the building to my car.

For once, the perennial lousy Ohio road construction isn't too bad, and I get to Leifler in decent time. I check in and Detective Pullen comes and gets me from the lobby.

"What's going on?" I ask.

"The judge says *he* should be the one to tell you, Dr. Collins."

Ms. Gunther looks up when we enter the office and points to the judge's door, her rigid index finger, wrist, and arm forming a giant arrow.

"He's been waiting," she says, her tone full of admonishment.

"Hurry!" Detective Pullen urges. "Patience isn't one of the judge's strong points."

We rush to the door, me following on his heels and almost running into him when he slows and knocks softly several times.

"Judge? It's Detective Pull . . ."

"Come in!"

We enter quickly, Detective Pullen gesturing for me to take the seat in front of the judge's desk while he stays by the door.

The judge is standing with his back to us, his hands clasped behind him as he stares out his picture window. Long seconds pass and he doesn't move or speak. I look over at Detective Pullen for a sign, but he stares blankly ahead.

After a few more moments, the judge finally speaks. "Show it to 'em, Detective."

Detective Pullen opens a folder on the judge's desk and hands me a photo.

"Do you know this girl?" the judge asks.

I stare at it for a long time. And then it clicks. "Yes. This is Jarrod's girlfriend. Her name's Reesie."

"Her full name is Rechelle Gartner," the judge corrects me. "What do you know about her?"

"Not much, Your Honor. Except that she's no good for my son."

"You're bull's-eye correct there. Tell 'em, Detective Pullen."

He takes the picture and explains, "This Reesie is the leader of a gang called the Mantises. They're very, very bad news."

He sticks the photo back in the folder and continues. "They allegedly staged a brutal attack upon Bell Cuppersmith."

I jam my eyes shut, purse my lips tight, and pound my fist into my knee. "Please don't tell me Jarrod had something to do with this."

"He's clean on this one," the judge answers. "It's fortunate he was in our good care."

"The paramedics reported her as having received a couple of broken ribs," Detective Pullen continues. "She also suffered a dislocated shoulder and fractured ankle."

He pauses, creating an extended silence until the judge says, "Tell 'em the rest!"

Detective Pullen sighs and shakes his head. "She also lost her baby."

"Which means," the judge continues, "that given the extent of the assault, when we find this Reesie and her crew they're going away for a long time."

"This is unbelievable," I mutter.

"There's more," Detective Pullen says. "Bell told the paramedics that Jarrod wasn't the father. It was her mother's loser boyfriend. We'd suspected him, but couldn't amass any proof until now."

"So we're fairly certain he's the rapist," the judge adds, still looking out his window. "The little girl, Brittany, has been questioned and confirms that he's been molesting them. Both girls are now in our custody."

"How?" I ask, my open, upturned palms accenting the question. "How could he have been doing this without the mother knowing?"

"Don't be naive!" the judge scoffs. "You saw the terror she exercised over those girls. Which of them do you think was willing to risk her wrath for making such an accusation?"

"Well, what're you gonna do about it?" I ask, irritated. "After all this and the grief Bernice Cuppersmith put me through, you guys can't just let her walk."

The judge turns from the window and glowers at me. "Put a lid on your indignation, Dr. Collins. Bernice and her true love aren't going anywhere. Not with charges of molestation, negligence, child endangerment, conspiracy, and a few choice others hanging over them. But first things first. We still have to make certain that Jarrod's not the father."

"But the boyfriend? I thought you said . . ."

"What I said is that we're *fairly* certain!" the judge corrects me. "Being named as perpetrator put him in county lockup. But I want scientific proof. Don't you?"

I swallow the knot of embarrassment in my throat. "Yes, Your Honor."

Detective Pullen shares more details. "Blood samples were already taken from Bell, the baby, and the suspect. Initial results show that the child was definitely his. We've got a rush on the DNA tests which should doubly confirm our conclusion."

The judge turns back to his window. "All things considered, Dr. Collins, it looks like you're taking Jarrod home."

"But we'd like for you to be prepared to offer testimony," Detective Pullen adds. "Especially after we round up Reesie and her thugettes. And of course, we'll need Jarrod's assistance as well."

I collapse back into my chair and tremble as crisscrossing winds of relief, happiness, guilt, and anger blow over me. I feel guilty and dirty for being relieved that the death of Bell's baby has freed Jarrod from premature fatherhood. I'm happy that Bell found the courage to tell the truth and, in doing so, set Jarrod free. But I'm angry that we were thrown into the path of all this fury by Jarrod's following through on a stupid bet.

"Why me?" I mumble.

"What's that?" the judge inquires, still staring out his window. "What did you say?"

"I was just asking, 'Why me?' "

The judge sighs. "Don't go signing up for sainthood or therapy, Dr. Collins. This Lane Younkin was a waste the day his mother excreted him. He's run this scam before, the last time hooking up with a pregnant woman in Tuscon and extorting money from some married guy she'd been screwing."

He glances at Detective Pullen and nods. Detective Pullen leaves and the judge keeps talking.

"You take someone like him, put him with a maternal snake like Bernice Cuppersmith, target a troubled black teen who's more likely to be condemned before being believed, have his mother be a Who's Who, and you've got yourself a nice payday."

The door opens and Jarrod marches in, followed by Detective Pullen, who holds the door. Jarrod looks fit and powerful, but it's come at a price. His eyes no longer sparkle with the light of youth but instead seem vacant, like the thousand-yard stare of combat soldiers who survived their ordeals by retreating to a deep inner sanctuary. That explains the aura of solemnity surrounding Jarrod and piercing me with the knowledge that his last remnant of exuberant childhood has been extinguished.

The judge faces Jarrod and stares into his hard, expressionless eyes. "You got anything to say?"

"No, sir!"

"Will I ever see you again?"

"No, sir!"

"And why's that?"

Jarrod's eyes water as he tightens his jaw, flexing his temples. "Because I hate this place and everyone in it."

The judge stomps over to Jarrod and gets in his face. "I don't care what you do or don't hate! What I wanna know is, *Do you respect my dragon?*"

Jarrod lowers his eyes and his voice. "Yes, sir."

"Good!"

The judge steps over to his desk, picks up his phone, and punches a button. "Ms. Gunther," he growls. "Get me the head guard in pod seven." He waits a few moments, pacing impatiently back and forth. "C'mon! C'mon!" he growls. "Crime's not taking a holiday and neither am I."

I don't doubt that whatever the judge is doing is official, but it has the feel of the dramatic. And knowing him as I now do, I wouldn't be surprised if he was simply adding a reinforcing layer to Jarrod's dark experience.

The judge stops pacing and stares directly at Jarrod as he speaks into the phone. "Is this Officer Mevoychek? . . . Okay. Listen closely. I'm authorizing the release of Jarrod Collins. . . . That's right. Our recent night court case. Here's my instructions. I don't care how you do it, but make sure that his cell remains empty. *Until further notice.* Just in case he decides to defy my dragon, or refuses my next instructions. Hold on."

He pulls the phone away from his ear and scowls. "There's a program called Warrior Passages that you're required to attend. They're having a father-son retreat this weekend. If you complete the program, you walk. If not, Officer Mevoychek will gladly return you to your cage. What'll it be?"

"I'll attend," Jarrod answers quickly.

The judge's eyes narrow and nostrils flare.

"I'll attend, *sir*!" Jarrod shouts.

The judge speaks back into the phone. "Okay, Officer Mevoychek. That'll be all for now."

He hangs up and looks Jarrod up and down like he just bubbled up from a scuz pond. He steps over to his window, turns his back to us, and clasps his hands behind him. "Dr. Collins."

"Yes, Judge."

"Get him out'a my sight!"

53

ON THE WAY TO MY APARTMENT, I DETOUR OVER TO
Cookie's so Jarrod can get some of his belongings. According to what the
judge and I agreed to, Jarrod can stay with me for the next few days. I've
already consulted with his teachers and the administration at Vesey High.
They've been gracious enough to work with me, giving me his homework
and reading assignments for the next few days so that he doesn't fall too
far behind.

The plan is to have Jarrod start adjusting to his reclaimed freedom before I take him to the Warrior Passages weekend retreat at West Branch
State Park. Like other fathers, I'll be there to help out in any way I can.
My main focus, though, will be to simply let Jarrod know that I'm near
and available if he needs me.

I pull into Cookie's driveway and am relieved to see Candace's battered minivan gone. Jarrod opens the front door while I go check the
mail. I'm astonished by all the letters from Holly. I wonder how she knew,
but then, how could she not? Someone as popular as Jarrod was bound to
be missed. And with all the blabbing in the news, it would've been hard to
not know where he was and why.

There are letters postmarked for every day that Jarrod's been away,
some of them showing that Holly wrote twice a day. I gather them up
along with the rest of the mail and amble toward the house. Jarrod's
standing in the open doorway, staring blankly inside.

"What's the matter?" I ask.

I walk up beside him, look inside, and my jaw drops. Cookie's once
immaculate palace is a pigsty. Various pieces of furniture have been shoved
out of place or toppled. Bowls and plates with dried food remains are
stacked high in the kitchen sink. Papers and magazines are strewn everywhere, and a small swarm of gnats is swirling over the kitchen trash can,
filled with stinking discarded diapers.

The stench is overpowering and I step past Jarrod into the kitchen to
open up some windows. Candace has left a note on the refrigerator:

Cookie, June Bug was down at Jaxson's Bar & Grill the other day and say he seen his daddy and got the po-leases. I'm sorry for leaving the place like this, but got called by the court saying I had to get home right quick for my back child support hearing. Maybe I'll get lucky and they catch Naynay's, Reggie's, and Lenrietta's daddies so's I can finally start getting money. Love, Candy.

I reread the note and want to punch myself again and again. It's bad enough that my stupid marital judgment joined me with Cookie's demented clan. But poor Jarrod. He's related to them by blood and carries their genes. He'll someday pass those genes on to my grandchildren, guaranteeing that future generations of Collinses are tied to the Neanderthal Hargroves.

I sigh, take the plastic bag full of stinking diapers out to the trash, then come in and help Jarrod straighten up. He's on his hands and knees, rooting through a pile of junk. He pulls out two shattered halves of a metallic circle and groans.

"They broke my *Snoop Dogg's Greatest* CD," he says, his voice shaky.

I kneel down beside him and rub his back. "Don't sweat it, Son," I say gently. "We'll get another."

We finish putting the house into some semblance of order, and I wait while Jarrod gets whatever he thinks he'll need for the next few days. I look around the still destroyed living room and imagine Candace sitting on her fat butt in front of the wide-screen TV, stuffing her face with chips, cookies, and candy while zoning out on game shows, soap operas, and mind-numbing infomercials. She undoubtedly stayed rooted to the same spot for hours, looking up every so often to yawn and tell her brats, "All right now. Y'all behave."

But why am I getting ticked off about what happened? Cookie's the one who called Candace to come watch over her son and her treasures. Like so much else, she brought this particular mess upon herself.

I go to the steps and holler up. "Jarrod!"

"Yes, sir."

Yes, sir. I like that. I'm sorry about the way he's been conditioned to say it, but it sounds good.

"I'll be out in the car."

"Okay."

Jarrod comes out a few minutes later, locks up the house, and gets in the car. We ride in silence over to my apartment, Jarrod sitting calm and quiet, staring out his window with an active serenity that's almost enviable. He seems to be savoring every breath, lingering over every sight, and tuning into the nuances of every sound.

We approach the Rapid Shop and I slow down. "Do you want to get some popcorn and fruit punch?" I ask.

"No, sir."

"It's no problem, Son."

Jarrod continues staring out the window and blandly repeats, "No, sir."

A wave of fresh guilt washes over me as I realize that the Jarrod I once knew is truly gone, replaced with this subdued, more contained Jarrod. But I want him to be excited again about staying up late, munching bowls of popcorn and sloshing down liters of fruit punch. I want him to bother me about extra change to buy some useless gadget that's caught his eye. I want him to pout and get on my nerves for being too spoiled to realize that money doesn't grow on trees. But he just sits quietly, not wanting or needing anything other than to be left alone and unharmed.

My eyes mist and I wipe them quickly, knowing I'm partly responsible for killing the spirit of my son's childhood. I'm also filled with a sad pride that his manhood has truly awakened.

We get inside the apartment and Jarrod heads straight for the bedroom, then stops.

"Dad?"

"Yes, Son."

"May I sleep in the bedroom?"

"By all means. You want something to eat?"

"No, sir."

He starts to turn away but stops. "Dad?"

"Yes, Jarrod."

"Did Reesie call?"

Like an iron pan to the face, I'm smacked with the reality that *he doesn't know*! And I don't have the heart to tell him, not yet. Why didn't they tell him downtown? But why would they? Judge Newton and his staff have their hands so full trying to salvage young people, tending to offender romances hardly rates as a priority.

I can't look directly at Jarrod and lower my eyes. "No, Son. She didn't call."

"She didn't leave any messages?"

I shake my head no. "Sorry, Jarrod."

Jarrod nods and goes into the bedroom. What a mess. Sooner or later, he'll find out. It'll be worse if he discovers I knew and said nothing. So I go in the bedroom and find him sitting on the edge of the bed, his bag tossed off to the side and him leaning forward, elbows on knees, staring at the floor. I sit down beside him and tell him everything I know about Reesie, Bell Cuppersmith, and the likely resolution to follow.

Jarrod listens passively, his only communication being an occasional blink. When I finish, I hug him tentatively around his shoulders. "Are you all right?"

He nods.

"And you're sure you're not hungry? I can fix something. It's no problem."

"No, thanks. I'd just like to get some sleep."

I get up and leave, stopping when Jarrod calls. "Dad?"

"Yes, Son."

"Would you close the door, please?"

"Certainly."

I close the door and get just a few steps away when I hear Jarrod sobbing.

54

JARROD SLEPT THROUGH ALL OF THURSDAY AND HAS barely stirred through the middle part of this Friday afternoon. After my classes, I came straight home from campus, wanting to be close by in case he wanted to talk, go to a movie, or whatever. As hard as he's been snoozing there's not much chance of that, so I've used the rare free time to bring my book project closer to completion. All things considered, with all the distractions that have compounded the difficulty of my research and writing, it's turning out quite well.

Speaking of distractions, this ringing telephone has done more than its share. I snatch it up and answer sharply. "Hello!"

"My, my. Aren't we in a bad mood," says Phoebe.

"Sorry, Phoebe. I was just writing about the Southern debate over whether to use slaves as soldiers during the Civil War."

"Understood," she offers. "That topic's bound to put any black person into a less than lovable frame of mind."

I chuckle and Phoebe says, "Since we're talking about writing and books, I was wondering if you wanted me to bring anything for this evening's book club?"

"This evening?"

"Why . . . yes. You volunteered, remember?"

"That's right!" I say, suppressing a groan. I make a loose fist and softly punch myself in the head. "Ike's getting his place remodeled and asked me to host it."

"Unh-hunh. And you asked everybody to meet this Friday since you and your son are supposed to be attending some kind of weekend retreat."

"Warrior Passages."

A long period of silence passes until Phoebe says, "Do you want me to call and tell everyone it's been rescheduled, time and place to be determined?"

"Hold on," I say.

I put the phone down and hurry into the bedroom where Jarrod's sleeping. I hate to wake him, but this shouldn't take too long. I gently open the door, tiptoe in, and see Jarrod lying quietly in bed, reading.

"How long have you been up?" I ask.

"A while."

"You should've let me know. I could've fixed you something to eat."

"Wasn't hungry."

I inhale deep and shake my head. "Jarrod, are you sure you're okay?"

"Yeah, Dad. I'm just sorting some things out."

I glance at the paper he hasn't stopped reading since the moment I entered. Lying beside him is a stack of envelopes, addressed from Holly to him. I want to smile and jump up and click my heels, but showing that I'm aware of what he's reading would constitute an invasion of privacy, so I stick to my mission.

"Jarrod, I'm having my book club over this evening. Will that be a problem for you?"

He shrugs. "It's cool."

"Are you sure? Be straight with me, Son. You've been through a lot recently and . . ."

Jarrod looks at me, smiles, and says, "Dad! It-is-cool."

And that's good enough for me. I go grab the phone and tell Phoebe it would help if she brought some French onion dip and some paper plates. We hang up and I start getting ready for my company.

Four hours later, the apartment's presentable. The food's arranged on the dining room table. I've repositioned furniture for the greatest utilization of space. I'm shaved, showered, and dressed clean and in a far better mood when the phone rings this time.

"Hello?"

"Aren't your phones working?" Cookie asks. "I've been trying to get in touch with you."

I don't bother pointing out that she's currently talking to me on the allegedly nonworking phone.

"What do you want, Cookie?"

"Why haven't you called me? Do you know how worried I've been?"

"No. But I'm sure you'll tell me."

"Keep being a comedian, Darius. When I get back . . ."

"When exactly are you coming back?"

"Now! I'm on the train from Paris to London and will fly out of

Heathrow into Detroit to catch a commuter to Cleveland. It's the fastest way I could get there."

"No need to rush. Everything's being handled."

"That would be a rare surprise. I know you, Darius, and . . ."

"I know about you too, Cookie. Especially the part about your affair with Milton Fields."

Cookie sounds like she's choking. "What do you know?"

I take the cordless and go into the bathroom. "I know enough. And let me be the first to tell you that your idiot decisions have had as much to do with all this confusion as Jarrod's poor judgment. But at least he had an excuse. He's not, I mean, he wasn't an adult."

"He's still not."

"Oh, yes, he is! After what we and the system have put him through he's *much* man."

"We'll see about that."

"Yes. You will. And once you see how he's matured, maybe you'll do the same."

She starts snarling and sniping. And because I hate just hanging up on people, I tell her good-bye, click off the phone, and finish getting ready for the book club.

55

THIS HAS BEEN ONE OF THE BEST BOOK CLUB MEETINGS we've had in a while. Gina's deciding to come has added a special treat for me. The sparks that have been flying during the discussion have everyone pumped up and at the top of their analytical game. The big spark flying at the moment is Ike's indignation that Naomi, the heroine, in Josette Green's *Forbidden Treasures*, concluded that no black man could ever give her healthy love.

"Look at'cha!" Kiva says. "Whenever one'a y'all goes sniffing after some white woman, it's okay. But if a sister falls for a white man, you have a hissy fit."

"See! That's what I'm talking about!" Ike retorts. "For the brothers, you say we're just sniffin' after booty. But for y'all, it's all about love."

"But it *is* all about love," Egypt insists. "Riley and I aren't with each other as part of some exotic adventure into taboo territory. We truly love each other."

Silence hangs in the air like a pregnant elephant. Everyone except Phoebe, who's known all along, (and me, who's suspected) is staring open-mouthed at Egypt.

"You hooked up with Mr. Charlie?" Ike asks.

"You make it sound like an indictment," Gina observes.

"You go, girl!" Kiva declares.

"Would you say that if it was a brother?" Omar asks.

"I would," Phoebe quickly responds. "If you were happy and having your needs met, I'd celebrate with you."

"But that's you!" Nash counters. "Ike's got a point when he says that most of y'all would look at us like we'd sold our mothers."

"Nash, aren't you exaggerating just a bit?" Gina asks.

"Get a grip!" Kiva demands. "Black men get those looks because we know you can't handle the power and pride of a black woman."

"Which must mean," Omar says, "that when you hook up with a white man it's because he can. Is that what you're saying?"

"Yeah!" Ike grunts. "Y'all're always so sure that the brothers are messed up and don't have no good job. But when it comes to a white dude, you assume just the opposite."

"Which means," Nash continues, "that whether you realize it or not, you've bought into that whole white man superiority thing."

"Do you honestly believe that?" Gina asks.

"Don't even try playing that reverse reasoning game," Kiva asserts. "Y'all do the same thing when it comes to white women. When you assume they're more feminine and loving, you're assuming that the sisters aren't."

"Which we clearly are!" Phoebe adds. "But we haven't had the luxury of living lives where docility was rewarded and strength and independence weren't needed."

I clear my throat. "Are you saying that white women are deficient in those areas?"

Kiva shrugs. "Hey. If the shoe fits . . ."

"That's the point," I say. "It doesn't fit historically."

"Run it down," Nash encourages me.

I brace myself for the possible back blast that'll follow my comments. "Look. We know that black women have had to demonstrate tremendous courage, strength, and determination to make it in America. But broad, sweeping statements about white women being weak are no more accurate than those about black women being wild, willing sexpots."

"And y'all *know* that ain't true!" Ike chuckles.

The men cringe and the women remain stone-faced. I talk fast to divert the group's attention from Ike's bad humor.

"Just like black women have had to tend to family, hearth, home, and job, so did white women on the frontier who hacked out a life for their families right alongside their men. The black *and* white women who fought for the right to vote weren't weak. Nor were World War Two's black *and* white Rosie the Riveters who provided the home-front muscle that made victory possible."

Kiva's eyes narrow. "Darius, if I didn't know any better, I'd say you had a white woman on the side and were trying to justify your choice."

"No offense, Kiva, but you don't know any better."

"C'mon, y'all," Gina cautions. "Don't get personal."

"I'm not getting personal," I defend myself. I look directly at Kiva. "And I hope you don't take it that way. But think about it. Your assumption about what's motivating my comments proves Ike's point."

FREDDIE LEE JOHNSON III

Which is what?" Egypt asks.

"That if a black man has a white woman, it's merely to satisfy carnal curiosity. But if it's a black woman with a white man, it's because brothers couldn't match or deal with her income, success, title, yak, yak."

"Which is essentially the same lame excuse Naomi gives in the book," Nash observes.

"It's insulting," Ike adds. "Telling the brothers that kinda stuff ain't no different from brothers saying y'all're carrying too much attitude and baggage. It validates America's assumption that we're too messed up to love each other."

"What difference does it make?" Jarrod asks. He's been sitting quietly off to the side, staring intensely into all our faces as the conversation maneuvered through its many stages.

Everyone turns toward him. "What do you mean?" Nash queries.

"Just what I said, Uncle Nash. What difference does it make if two people are black or white just so long as they get along and love each other?"

Omar shrugs. "I guess it doesn't."

Jarrod looks at me and I nod. "Go ahead, Son. Your opinion counts as much as ours."

He lowers his eyes for a moment of contemplation, then looks up. "I know everyone here has more experience than me. But, well, it seems kind of stupid to reject somebody just because they're a different skin color."

He balls up his paper plate and stands. "Finding love is hard. Finding decent love is even harder. When we do, we should tell anyone who can't accept it to kiss off."

He tosses his paper plate into the kitchen garbage can and goes into the bedroom. Every eye in the room follows him out until the bedroom door closes.

"Well!" Phoebe exhales. "I guess he told us."

"Out of the mouths of babes," Egypt philosophizes.

"That wasn't a baby talking," Omar corrects. "What you just heard came from a man."

"So what's y'all's excuse?" Kiva asks.

"The same one you've got!" Ike answers.

With that, they're off and at it again. The rest of us take a break to use the bathroom and refill our plates.

Jarrod comes out of the bedroom and pulls me off to the side. "Dad, can I borrow your car?"

"Huh? For what?"

"Holly and I wanna go down to Henley Park."

I look hard into Jarrod's eyes. Ever since he's been home, nothing has happened that's required an exercise of trust in him. But with this request, he's asking to not only move beyond my direct supervision but also take my only means of transportation. More than that, he's asking about Henley Park, where there's no shortage of nooks and crannies for a copulating couple to do their business.

Jarrod lowers his eyes. "Never mind. I guess it was a bad idea."

I grab my keys off the counter, take his hand, and force them into his palm. "Take the car, Son. Stay as long as you want and be care—I mean, have fun."

He stares at the keys, looks back up at me, smiles, and leaves. He's not gone too long when the door buzzer rings. I'd go see who it is but am busy putting out some more chips, dip, ice, and other goodies.

"Nash, get that for me, will you?" I say.

"No problem."

He saunters over to the intercom to see who it is. Seconds later, he gestures wildly for me to come to the door.

"Gina, would you finish this for me?" I ask.

She agrees and I start toward Nash, stopping when she takes my hand, gives it a tender squeeze, and lets go. I smile and go see what's bothering Nash.

"What's the problem?" I ask, approaching.

He grabs me, pulls me close, and, whispering emphatically, says, *"It's Marcy."*

56

MARCY'S ARRIVAL HAS HAMMERED ME INTO THAT
miserably narrow space between the proverbial rock and a hard place.

"Whatcha gonna do?" Nash whispers.

I glance at Gina, refilling a snack platter. She looks up at me, winks, and smiles. The buzzer rings again. I press the intercom button and talk directly into the speaker, my mouth barely an inch away.

"Okay!" I snap. "Hold on for a second!"

A burst of laughter erupts from the dining room. Everyone's gathered around the table, talking and snacking. Ike's gesturing wildly as he tells one of his inexhaustible supply of funny stories.

The buzzer rings again and Gina looks over at me. "Darius, what're you and Nash doing over at that door?" she asks. "C'mon and let's get back to the book."

"Yeah!" Ike agrees, wiping his mouth with a napkin. "Let's finish up so we can select a book for the next meeting that'll be more friendly to the brothers."

"Do you want fairness or the truth?" Kiva challenges.

Everyone gets quiet as the latest round of the Ike-Kiva snipe-a-thon begins.

I grab Nash's forearm. "Keep them busy!" I order.

"Doing what?" he asks hoarsely.

"Anything!"

"But . . ."

"Pretend that you're lying to Eileen."

Nash grins. "Now *that* I can do."

I check for my keys so I can slip back in without having to ring the buzzer and draw unwanted attention. I have *no* idea what I'll tell Gina if she asks what this weird disappearance was all about, but I'll deal with that later. I hustle downstairs and explode out the door. Marcy blurts an abbreviated scream and hugs the wall.

"Darius!" she huffs, exasperated. "What's the matter with you? You act like you're being chased by a ghost!"

"It's funny that *you* should mention that," I respond, forcing myself into calm composure. I cross my arms and lean against the wall. "Marcy, why are you here?"

She offers a coy pout. "Honestly, Darius. Can't you be just a little cordial?"

Loud laughter filters down from the general area of my apartment and I glance up at my balcony. The curtains are wide open, so I take Marcy by the elbow and firmly escort her to a place alongside the building that better obscures us from curious eyes.

"Look, Marcy," I say, keeping my voice cool and calm. "I've got company, so this is really bad timing."

Her slight smile dims. "I see you lost no time replacing me with a new love."

"You weren't replaced. You were forgotten!" Marcy gasps and I add, "And I at least waited until *after* we'd broken up."

She casts her eyes downward, looking truly dejected. And so beautiful, more than I ever recall seeing her. Her *Next Spring* perfume that she knows I love fills my nostrils, waging guerilla war on my senses. She's wearing a slacks-blouse combo that's not only in my favorite dark blue but also tailor-cut to accentuate her many curves.

"You're right," Marcy sighs. "Coming here was wrong." Her voice cracks when she says, "I'm sorry, Darius. I didn't mean to disturb you."

She pulls a tissue from her purse, dabs a tear, and turns away. My eyes lock onto the firm mounds of her sexy swaying butt, igniting a fire in my crotch that whooshes higher when the memory of our past couplings is poured onto the flames.

"Marcy! Wait!" I call.

She stops but keeps her back to me. I walk softly up behind her, take gentle hold of her shoulders, and turn her toward me. "I'm sorry," I say. "I shouldn't have been so mean, but," I look directly into her eyes, *"you've really pissed me off."*

She sniffles and wipes her eyes. "I know, Darius. And I'm so very sorry. That's all I was trying to tell you when you wouldn't answer my calls." She smiles slyly. "Well, that's what I wanted to tell you after I got over being angry about my fish."

We stare at each other for a few seconds, then laugh. It feels good, just like before, and I want it to last. Until I remember Stan.

"So why are you here, Marcy?" I ask, my humor evaporating quickly. "I'm sure this visit wouldn't sit too well with Stan."

She frowns and pouts. "Stan was a total loser," she declares. "My sister Ariel came to visit me and he was trying to hit on her."

I frown. "Ouch! That truly sucks."

She nods emphatically. "What's worse is that Ariel didn't resist. Can you believe it? My own sister!"

I momentarily ponder her question. "Considering the Twilight Zone confusions of my own recent love life, yes! I can believe almost anything."

Marcy cuts her eyes away, correctly interpreting that I'm including *her* as one of those recent confusions.

"Darius, I'm really sorry for hurting you," she says. "It was a huge mistake and I understood that you probably never wanted to see me again."

"There was no 'probably' in it."

She winces, as though the statement were a literal dagger strike. I shouldn't be rubbing her nose in it like this, but I know she wouldn't hesitate to stuff my nostrils if the situation were reversed.

"I can't blame you for harboring resentment," she says, pulling an envelope from her purse. "But I want you to know that I realize I've been a fool. You were good to me, Darius. And I know that you sincerely loved me."

My jaw hardens, but I maintain my silence.

She takes my hand and puts the envelope in it. "This is a plane ticket to Aruba. You can use it at the end of the semester when you have a few weeks off. I'll be there, Darius, waiting to show you how much I've missed you and how much I want you back in my life."

She steps forward and kisses me lightly on the lips. This is one of the crossroads that I've been preaching about to Jarrod. It's one of those places where I should eliminate trouble before it starts. I should give this ticket back to Marcy, who, after all, is responsible for some of the turmoil of my recent past. I should give it back and rush upstairs to Gina, who offers a more enjoyable, harmonious future.

I glance at the envelope, look at Marcy, and wave the envelope angrily under her nose. "I'll think about it."

Her expression is serious, but her eyes are hopeful. "That's all I can ask of you, Darius." She hugs me, pressing her ample breasts and *(fates of destiny, help me!)* warm crotch firmly into me. Then in a low, husky voice she says, "Take your time, but I hope you'll decide to . . . *come.*"

She steps back, slowly drinks me in with her bedroom eyes, then turns away. I watch the pendular swing of her hips, eventually pulling my eyes away before I melt into a gurgling puddle of goo.

57

GINA MEETS ME AT MY APARTMENT DOOR. I LOOK
quickly around the living room and see everyone hustling to put on their
coats, grab their books and other belongings, and leave. Everyone except
Nash. His sheepish expression proves that the trouble I smell is no imagi-
nary figment.

Everyone files out, quickstepping. "Darius, we'll see you later," Omar
says, holding Phoebe's hand and pulling her along. She looks concerned
for me but quickly follows Omar.

"Later, D," Ike almost whispers, slinking out.

"Hmph!" Kiva grunts, passing by without so much as a glance.

Egypt hurries to the door, stops, starts, grips my arm, looks at me
with sad, earnest eyes, and vanishes.

I close the door and face Gina directly, preparing myself for the blast.
"Okay," I say, glancing from her to Nash and back. "What's going on?"

Nash gathers up his materials and answers first. "I told her, D."

"What! I thought you were going to . . ."

I stop myself, remembering that Gina's standing right in front of me.
Whatever she's angry about, she certainly won't be in a better mood if I
hassle Nash about not lying to her. That hassle is *nothing* compared to the
one I'm going to give him later for, well, not lying to her.

He heads for the door, stopping to whisper, "You owe me."

I'd tell him of the many ways I intend to pay him back but need to
stay focused. The door closes and I summon all my willpower to keep my
eyes firmly locked with Gina's.

"Nash told me everything," she finally says. "Thank you for instructing him to tell me the truth."

"The truth!" I repeat, stunned. "Oh, yeah! The truth! I told Nash to
just lay it out there and that whatever happens, happens."

Gina smiles. Nash is right. I really and truly do owe him.

I bolster the strength in my legs. "Well, since he told you everything,
you know that I had no idea Marcy was coming."

She nods. "He said she's been calling and calling."

"That's right. She's not used to people giving her the blow-off she gave me."

"That 'blow-off' must not have been bad enough for you to shut her out completely."

I frown. "What're you talking about, Gina?"

She glances at the envelope in my hand. My first impulse is to hide it behind my back, but that would only add to any suspicions she might harbor. I hand it to her. She hesitates to take it, but I shove it toward her. She takes it, looks inside, and hands it back to me.

"Aruba," she comments. "Sounds nice."

"Listen, Gina. This is just Marcy's way of pulling out the big guns. Do you really think that . . ."

"Darius," she interrupts, collecting her belongings. "After what I've been through lately, I don't know what to think about a lot of things anymore."

"But . . ."

"I appreciate your telling me the truth, but it looks like you've got some decisions to make. And so do I."

"Huh? What do you mean? If you're talking about us, there's nothing to decide."

She starts toward the door, stopping in front of me and stroking my cheek the same way Laura did all those many years ago. "My sweet Darius," she says. "There's more to decide than you realize."

"Gina, please tell me what you're talking about."

She takes the ticket. "You have to decide if you want to use this, and I," she hands the ticket back and grabs the doorknob, "I have to decide if I want to be with someone who didn't immediately tear it up."

58

AS WAS THE PLAN, NOW THAT THE BOOK CLUB IS OVER
it's time for me and Jarrod to go to the Warrior Passages retreat. Jarrod's
waiting out in the car while I hold my phone, trying to decide whether or
not to call Gina. I certainly want to and definitely need to. But what
would I say?

I hang up, slouch out to the car, and get going. I ask Jarrod how
everything went with him and Holly and he answers in short, almost
monosyllabic responses. I know he's not being rude but, like any good
teenager, is just keeping his parent out of his business. Not knowing his
business has been a major part of what's kept me off balance and constantly playing catch-up during his ordeal. I'd address the issue, but I'm
just too frustrated at the moment.

We turn into West Branch State Park, drive to the retreat area, park,
and get out. Muscle-bound Wilson "Willie" Strayhorn hustles toward me
and Jarrod as we stroll into the main camp. I extend my hand to shake,
but Willie ignores it and grips my shoulders tight.

"Man, where have you been?" he asks, agitated.

"On the way here," I answer, wincing. I wriggle free and look around,
wondering at the emptiness of the campsite. "Where is everyone?"

"They're down at the lake fishing. *But forget that!*" Willie commands.
"You've gotta go see Reverend Boxwell."

"Just tell me where he is, and I'll . . ."

"He's at home," Willie interrupts. "He's been calling for you."

My throat tightens, and I almost croak when I ask, "What's wrong?"

Willie shakes his head. "Don't know, man. One minute, he was full of
energy, pointing here and there, giving instructions and organizing. The
next, he was lying on the ground, unconscious."

I grab Willie's shoulders in my own viselike grip. "Unconscious! What
happened? Did something fall on him? Did somebody hit him?"

Willie shrugs. "They rushed him to the Cleveland Clinic. Mrs.

Boxwell called on the way and said he was asking for you. We tried to get you on your cellular before you came all the way out here."

I'd tell Willie that I had turned my cellular off so there would be no interruptions if Jarrod had wanted to talk. I'd tell him that I had turned it off to guarantee myself more Cookie-free moments. But telling him all that would take time, and I've got to get to Reverend Boxwell.

I look at Jarrod. "I'm sorry about having to leave like this, but . . ."

Willie taps me hard on the shoulder.

"*What?*" I say, almost snapping.

"Mrs. Boxwell said that if Jarrod was with you to bring him along."

I'd ask why but decide against it. Reverend Boxwell's making this request and that's all the explanation I need.

I grab Willie's hand and shake. "We'll be back."

"Tell 'em that we love 'em, man. Tell 'em that we're praying for 'em."

Willie shouts the words to my back as Jarrod and I run to my car.

59

ON THE ROCKET ROAD TRIP OVER TO REVEREND BOXWELL'S house, I talk nervously to Jarrod, sharing with him old stories about the antics of me and my teenage friends and our good times with the man we affectionately called Rev. B.

"He was the only elder I knew who was truly a *man of God*," I blather.

"What about Grandpa?" Jarrod asks. "Wasn't he all into God?"

Even now, the anger of past struggles prevents me from once and for all acknowledging Dad as the faith-filled leader he was. Instead of answering Jarrod's question, I tell him about the time Dad and Reverend Boxwell tag-teamed Cincinnati's city council into funding the church's midnight basketball program. I revel in the story of them standing toe-to-toe against Klansmen in a bruising snowstorm, eventually shouting them back into the hole from which they'd crawled. I recount how Reverend Boxwell sold his rare stamp collection to pay Phylander Corbett's senior year tuition at Ohio State after a hit-and-run driver killed his dad.

"It sounds like Rev. B and Grandpa were the real deal," Jarrod observes.

I reflect for a moment, then simply say, "Yes. They were."

I turn onto Reverend Boxwell's street, zoom into his driveway, and park. I dash to the front door and pound a few times. Jarrod hustles up beside me.

"Please be okay," I mutter, still knocking. *"Please be okay!"*

The door opens and I stare into the supremely calm face of Mrs. Boxwell. I check for the slightest hint of distress, discomfort, or despair, but there's only peace. Either I misunderstood the urgency of Willie's message or Mrs. Boxwell's colder than any fish I've ever seen slabbed on ice at the market.

A distant thunder from one of Dad's sermons echoes through time: *"She possesses the peace that surpasseth all understanding."*

Mrs. Boxwell looks from me to Jarrod, then back at me, and smiles. "Hello, Darius."

I rush in and hug her. "Are you okay?"

"I'm doing fine," she answers softly, patting my back. "I'm doing just fine."

She gently pushes me away and opens her arms to Jarrod. "You must be Jarrod," she says, her voice as serene as her expression. "I'm so glad to meet you."

Jarrod shoots me a puzzled glance, then folds into Mrs. Boxwell's embrace. She smiles and closes her eyes, squeezing out tears I didn't see.

"Now listen," she says, taking hold of Jarrod's face with both hands. "*You pay attention.* Hez has been praying for you." She pulls him closer and speaks in an emphatic whisper. "There's a purpose for your life, and a destiny for you to fulfill. So open your ears, mind, and heart and *listen!*"

Jarrod swallows and nods. "Yes, ma'am," he answers with a reverence and respect I've never heard before.

Reverend Boxwell calls from inside, "Precious, is that Darius?"

"Yes, Hez," she answers, turning toward his voice.

"Wonderful! Tell 'em to come on in."

"Okay. He'll be there in just a minute."

Mrs. Boxwell grips my shoulders. "Darius, I'm going to need for you to be strong," she says, blinking back tears. "Hez is in a bad way, but he's calm and ready to go home."

"Go home! But . . ."

She plants a firm index finger over my mouth. "Ssh!" She's sniffling and staring at me from behind a veil of tears. "You mind yourself and wait till Hez explains everything. That's the way he wants it."

"Yes, ma'am," I answer, my voice a shaky rasping whisper. But I want to know *right now* so I say, "Is he going to . . ."

"Darius, come on back, son!" Reverend Boxwell calls. "I ain't got much time!"

Mrs. Boxwell covers her mouth, muffling a sob. She closes the door, then hurries away. I look at Jarrod. He looks at me.

"Jesus," I gasp. "If this is what I think it is, I don't know if I'll have the strength."

"Go ahead, Dad," Jarrod says. "I've got your back."

Our eyes lock together for a long moment, me drawing from Jarrod the willpower I need to walk the several million miles across the living room to the sunroom where Reverend Boxwell awaits. Each step is like lifting an iron ball, and I concentrate extra hard to maintain my balance and keep moving forward.

Jarrod follows close behind as we slowly and quietly enter the sun-room. It's full of plants and flowers. The air is thick with a pleasing, rich earthiness, mixed with light, sweet odors from flowers and evergreens. Reverend Boxwell's sitting in a comfortable-looking high-backed chair with his back to the door. He's leaning forward, doting over a big, beauti-ful magnolia shrub, slowly turning its pot and spraying it every few sec-onds with a light mist from a water bottle.

"Darius, come on in," he says.

I stifle a gasp upon hearing his voice. It sounds like audio sandpaper. What's worse—*and terrifying*—is the total absence of the vibrant energy that once resonated in every word he spoke. It's as though Reverend Box-well has been hollowed out into a shell of his former self.

"Is Jarrod with you?" he asks.

I nod to the back of his head. "He's right here, Pastor."

He stiffens and stops spraying the shrub. After a few seconds he chuckles softly and says, "Lord, Lord, Darius. Do you know how long it's been since you called me Pastor?"

"Too long," I answer, swallowing a boulder-sized lump.

He chuckles, waves Jarrod and me forward, and continues spraying. We move up beside him, me standing to his right while Jarrod stands to his left.

"Y'all come on and have a seat," he offers, gesturing to nonexistent chairs.

Jarrod and I look around for folding chairs or maybe stools, but with no luck. Jarrod keeps searching while I look at Reverend Boxwell and start to ask him where we might find some chairs, but my question's crushed into silence by shocked surprise. Reverend Boxwell's eyes are open and looking ahead, but his gaze is the blank, vacant stare of the blind.

"That's right, son," he says. "I'm as blind as a bat."

I glance at Jarrod. He's trying not to stare but can't help it. Mrs. Boxwell steps into the room and hands us each a folding chair. We take them and nod our thanks.

"Hez, do you need anything?" she asks, clenching her jaw.

He reaches back for her and she takes his hand. He pulls her close and kisses the center of her palm. "All I've ever needed, the Lord and you provided."

Mrs. Boxwell smiles a broad, soft smile as her eyes brim with tears. "I'll be close by," she says.

"I know, precious. Just like always."

She kisses his forehead, smiles at Jarrod and me, then leaves. We sit on either side of Reverend Boxwell and he gestures for us to move close.

"Darius?" he calls.

"I'm right here, Pastor. To your right."

He takes my hand and squeezes tight. "Thanks for coming," he sighs.

Reverend Boxwell looks so small in his chair, so weak, a wisp of what he'd once been. My eyes blur, and I sniffle.

"Pastor, what's the matter?" I ask. "What's going on?"

He reaches for my face and I move close, making it easier for him to find me. He softly strokes my cheek and says, "Darius, son . . . I'm dying."

I jam my eyes shut and grit my teeth. My throat rattles with sobs, but I choke them down, refusing to succumb to this newest pain in what's been a season of too much hurt.

"There, there, now," Reverend Boxwell soothes me, stroking my hair. "Don't be sad, Darius. It's just my time, that's all."

"This doesn't make sense," I protest. "How could this have happened so quickly?"

He laughs softly. "It's not all that quick. I asked for more time and the Lord answered my prayer. The brain cancer went into remission fifteen years ago, but now it's back and it's time to go home."

I shake my head, utterly confused. Reverend Boxwell senses my anxiety and keeps explaining.

"Do you remember the Old Testament story of King Hezekiah?"

"Yes," I answer. "It was one of the Scriptures Momma was forever quoting to sustain her faith in God's power to heal."

"What was it about?" Jarrod asks.

I glance at him, then look quickly away in shame. Jarrod would already know the answer to that question and the details of that story if over the years I'd been doing my job. But that would've required my being in right spiritual alignment, and I haven't been for a long, long time. It's painfully clear why Jarrod is the way he is, especially since I'm the tree from which his fruit has fallen.

Reverend Boxwell reaches for Jarrod and they loosely hold hands as he explains. "Jarrod, in chapter twenty of the Second Book of Kings, the Word speaks of a king named Hezekiah who one day *became ill and was at the point of death.*"

"He *'turned his face to the wall,'*" I interject, "*'and prayed to the Lord,*
saying . . .'"

"*'Remember, O Lord,'*" Reverend Boxwell continues, "*'how I have*
walked before you faithfully and with wholehearted devotion and have done
what is good in your eyes.'"

"*'And Hezekiah wept bitterly,'*" I add.

Reverend Boxwell relaxes into his chair, still holding our hands. "And
then God, speaking through His Prophet, Isaiah, said to Hezekiah, *'I have*
heard your prayer and seen your tears; I will heal you . . .'"

"And *'add fifteen years to your life,'*" I say.

My eyes widen. Reverend Boxwell turns his nonseeing eyes toward
me. "That's right, son. Fifteen years ago I was diagnosed with brain cancer. And just like King Hezekiah, I pleaded with the Lord to give me more
time."

He reaches up and strokes my cheek again. "You see, Darius, your
daddy asked me to look after you. Even though you two didn't get along
too good, he knew you minded me, and asked me to watch over you if
something ever happened to him."

This time I can't hold the sobs. This time I don't even try. Reverend
Boxwell pats my shoulder as I try to regain some measure of control.

"You don't have to die," I insist. "There's got to be something we can
do. What about radiation treatment? What about chemo?"

Reverend Boxwell takes gentle hold of my chin. "No, Darius," he says
softly. "The docs looked at the X rays and said that the cancer's taken the
whole brain. It's too far gone, son."

"Don't tell me that!" I snap, shoving his hand away. "Your still being
alive and sitting here talking calmly about this is totally inconsistent with
your condition. If the cancer was that bad, you'd have lost more than your
sight. You'd be brain-dead, or howling in pain."

Reverend Boxwell sits up, pulls me in to him for a hug, and says,
"Isn't God good?"

60

NO MATTER HOW MUCH OR HOW LONG I PROTEST, IT *will not* change the fact that Reverend Boxwell will soon be joining our ancestors. His departure will be the latest in a series of wrenching losses, but unlike my other setbacks and tragedies, he's not leaving me high and dry.

"Darius, there's no time to beat around the bush, so listen close," he says. "There's things you've gotta know to finish maturing into the man God wants you to be."

He turns toward my son. "Jarrod, are you listening?"

"Yes, sir."

The reverend squeezes our hands, sits back, and casts his blind eyes onto me. "Darius, you've experienced some things that have left deep scars. You're searching for answers, but don't know where to look."

His vacant eyes seem to come alive and he grips my hand tight. "Son, *a man finds his way, if he lets God light his path with Christ's glory.*"

Jarrod recognizes the statement and glances at me. I glance back at him, then refocus onto Reverend Boxwell. He continues sharing the insights of a lifetime spent serving the Author of Wisdom. His words settle deep into spiritual soil that's been tilled by much trouble, soil that's been broken up and made ready for planting.

"Let me tell you how special you are," he says, facing me. "Before you were formed in the womb, He knew you. Before you were born, He set you apart."

Reverend Boxwell urges me to understand that although being set apart is good, it's pointless without wisdom. "Wisdom, like an inheritance, is a good thing," he stresses. "It preserves the life of its possessor."

On and on he goes, dispensing ancient knowledge to help me navigate the storms of my modern chaos. A critical tool for the journey is *love*.

"Not just any old kind of love," he declares. "The love I'm talking about is patient and kind. It doesn't envy, or boast. It's not proud, rude, self-seeking, or easily angered. It doesn't keep a record of wrongs. It rejects evil and celebrates truth. It always protects, trusts, hopes, and perseveres."

He lets go of Jarrod's hand and takes mine into both of his. "Darius, you've got to make peace with Cookie."

I snort, scowl, and look away. He feels along my face, finds my chin, then lifts it slowly with his index finger until I'm staring into his oblivious eyes.

"You bear a Cross," he says, "but it's nothing like the one Jesus hung from when He looked out across time and forgave us."

I shake my head. "It's hard, Pastor."

"I know," he softly responds, patting my shoulder. "But you've got to do it for Jarrod."

He turns to Jarrod and retakes hold of his hand. "You're young and rebellious, but what you don't realize is that you're already being held accountable for the way you live."

Jarrod doesn't move a muscle as Reverend Boxwell throttles him with truth. "I'm old and you're young, but death could still take you before me," he declares.

He quotes the Book of Ecclesiastes, imploring Jarrod to " 'Remember your Creator in the days of your youth, before the days of trouble come and the years approach when you will say, "I find no pleasure in them." ' "

He grips Jarrod's shoulder. "And, Jarrod, those days *will* come. Just as I'm sitting before you now, sightless and with my life draining with every breath, your looks, strength, and life will also leave. It might take years, or could occur in the next few hours or minutes, but it'll happen. Do you understand?"

"Yes, sir."

"The words I spoke to your father also apply to you. If you value your life, if you want to find your purpose, if you want to find your way, stop being the *world's child* and grow into *God's man.*"

"I, I'll try," Jarrod responds.

Reverend Boxwell smiles and nods. "You'll have to do more than try, son. You'll have to see yourself through God's eyes so you can know what He expects of men."

"Do you mean not getting into any more trouble?"

"That's a good start, but it's not all. It's everything you do, the way you talk, think, and conduct yourself. It's the quality of your character, the value of your word, the compassion in your heart, and your willingness to obey the Master."

He leans forward and speaks emphatically. "You have to see with new eyes, hear with new ears, and think with new thoughts. You have to be that person in First Corinthians Thirteen who said, *'When I was a child, I talked like a child, I thought like a child, I reasoned like a child. When I became a man, I put childish ways behind me.'"*

One hour stretches toward two as Reverend Boxwell pours more love, wisdom, and truth into Jarrod and me. More and more of his strength leaves with each uttered word.

He pauses and I say, "Pastor, you're tired. Maybe you should get some rest."

He smiles. "I will, Darius. Soon and for all time."

"That's not what I mean," I counter. "I'm just concerned that all this activity will . . ."

"Hush up and listen," he gently commands. "I'm almost done."

He relaxes into the chair, waits for a moment, then speaks with an odd overwhelming strength, like the power of eternity is already filling the space where he once lived. He squeezes our hands with a grip that can't belong to the shell sitting before us.

"Give your lives to the Lord," he urges. "And above all, remember this: *'Fear God and obey His commandments, for this is the entire duty of man.'"*

61

JARROD WATCHES AS I BEND DOWN AND HUG REVER-
end Boxwell. "Y'all be sure and have some fun," he says. "Warrior Passages is supposed to be about having a good time too."

"We will," I answer.

He reaches out for Jarrod, who offers his hand. "Jarrod, it was good
meeting you," Reverend Boxwell says.

"Likewise," Jarrod responds.

They shake hands and Reverend Boxwell slumps back into his chair.
"Boy, am I tired," he sighs. "I could sure use some sleep."

"I was just about to suggest that," Mrs. Boxwell agrees from the doorway. Her tone communicates clearly that the shorter our good-bye, the
better.

I hand Jarrod my car keys. "I'll be out in a sec," I say. He nods, says
bye once more to Reverend Boxwell, hugs Mrs. Boxwell, glances at me,
and leaves.

I kneel down beside Reverend Boxwell. "Will you be okay?"

"I'll be fine, Darius. You go on and tend to Jarrod."

I lean over and hug him again. "I love you," I say.

"I love you too."

I turn to Mrs. Boxwell and hug her. "If you need anything, *anything
at all,* don't hesitate to call."

"I will."

I start for the door, stopping when Reverend Boxwell calls. "Darius?"

"Yes, Pastor."

"Good-bye, son."

62

JARROD AND I RIDE BACK TO WEST BRANCH STATE PARK
in an awkward silence. He stares out his window, pretending not to notice
the tears washing down my cheeks. I blow honking snorts into napkins
I've collected from fast-food restaurants, pretending to battle a sudden
cold.

I park and we gather our gear and check into our cabin. Night is
falling and the smell of burning wood fills the air.

"Everyone's supposed to be gathering on Horizon Hill in a little while
for some stargazing," I say. "Are you interested?"

"Not really, but I'll go."

I sit down on the edge of the pseudocot that'll be my bed, lean forward, elbows on knees, and stare down at the floor. The tone of Jarrod's
answer sounds depressingly similar to the same jerk attitude that's brought
us to this point, and I simply don't have the stamina, patience, or inclina-
tion to put up with it.

I'm just about to launch into him when he says, "I was gonna stick
around in case you wanted to talk, but you probably want to be alone
right now."

I look slowly up and stare at him for a long moment. "You're right,
Jarrod. I would like to be alone."

He nods, gathers up some articles for the outing, and leaves. I watch
him go, eventually staring out the window as night finishes pulling its
blanket across the sky. Hours pass and I emerge from my brooding to discover that I'm sitting on a log several feet from a blazing fire burning in
the center of camp. Willie Strayhorn, Kingston Garvey, and a few other
men sit with me, all of us staring silently into the flames. When the fire
dies down, one of us throws on another log, causing ash and sparks to
swirl up into the night.

Hours pass. I nod off but am startled awake when I almost fall back
off the log. Some of the men have retired to their cabins. Most are still up,
keeping the vigil. We sit here as though Reverend Boxwell will come

strolling into our midst at any second, filling us with the joy that was—
is—his pure love of life.

My cell phone rings and I answer it with lightning speed, my throat
constricting with the fear that it might be Mrs. Boxwell.

"Hello?"

"Tell me where you are so I can come and get Jarrod," Cookie
demands.

I spring to my feet and speed-walk to the far edge of the campsite.
"Cookie, he's safe with me. I'll bring him home by the end of the weekend."

"Darius, either bring Jarrod home now or tell me where he is, or
you're going to be listed as one of America's newest kidnappers."

Her threat is so outrageous, wicked, and conscienceless that I know
she's serious. "All right, Cookie," I sigh. "You win."

I tell her where to meet me, then get myself together for our ren-
dezvous. Before I leave, I make a couple of phone calls that defy Reverend
Boxwell's admonition to "make peace with Cookie."

I feel bad about rejecting his words, but by the time I get to my car,
I've gotten over the guilt.

63

I SIT IN A BOOTH AT THE LONG-HAULER'S TRUCK STOP, waiting for Cookie and slowly flipping through the pages of the *Cleveland Plain Dealer*. The police have found a little girl who's been missing for over a week. A corporate executive who's made a career of separating people from their jobs has just been fired. And the government is seriously considering classifying domestic terrorists like Klansmen into the same threat category as the foreign kooks. If I weren't about to have this meeting with Cookie I could almost feel good about this corner of the world. But since I'm about to do battle, I'll save the good feelings for later.

"Can I freshen up your coffee, hon?" a smiling platinum blond blue-uniformed waitress asks.

"Sure. Why not?"

She fills my cup to just below the rim and sashays away. There's plenty of action happening beneath her skirt, and I'd love to enjoy the wave motion. But it's not wise to engage Cookie unprepared, so I refocus on my purpose for sitting here in a smoky truck stop, enduring the sidelong looks of burly cowboy-boot-wearing truckers, who soak up the twangy country music while consuming vast quantities of mashed potatoes, meat loaf, and apple pie.

I add some sugar and cream to my coffee, check the door, and keep flipping pages. I don't know what Cookie hopes to accomplish by staging this drama, but I *do* know that she's not going to usurp the link between Jarrod and me.

I keep checking the door every few moments until it swings open and Cookie storms in. She looks around, spots me, and stomps over. Several of the truckers follow her with their eyes, the tight fit of her painted-on jeans and black leather jacket offering them a voyeur's delight.

She pulls off her black leather gloves and stylish black mink hat as she slides into the booth.

"Where's Jarrod?" she demands.

"At the father-son retreat."

"Why isn't he here and ready to go with me?"

"Because he's *not* going with you."

"We'll see about that."

She pulls her cell phone from her small thin-strapped silver purse and starts dialing. I snatch the phone from her, sit back, and relax.

"Give me my phone," she orders, her voice even and menacing.

"Cookie, you're not needed or wanted here," I say. "Do us all a favor and take your stuck-up, bourgeois, self-centered, mean-as-hell, high-yellow butt back to Cleveland."

She glances at a nearby pay phone and starts to get up. I zip out of my seat and block her.

"Get out of my way!" she demands.

I slide in next to her, shoving her over. "This is your last chance, Cookie. Either leave or I call in the cavalry."

She fumes and glowers but after a few moments slides back to her original position. "Okay, Darius," she says, her voice dripping with malice. "Have your small victory. It'll be one of your last."

I sit near her for an extra moment, then move back to my side of the table. I shouldn't trust Cookie to not get up, but I can't stand being so close to her. The blue-uniformed waitress walks by.

"Oh, miss!" Cookie calls, snapping her fingers like she's calling a dog.

The waitress glares, then forces a smile. She holds up a finger, telling Cookie to wait while she takes an order. She finishes, then hurries over.

"What can I getcha?" she asks. Her eyes are smiling, but her lips are a grim thin line.

"Coffee! Black!" Cookie orders.

The waitress looks at me and beams. "You wanna fresh up, hon?"

"No, thanks."

She winks at me, scowls at Cookie, and switches away.

"When this is over," Cookie says, "I'm going to make your life miserable."

"You mean like when we were married?" I chuckle.

"Oh, no," she answers, her face settling into its typical Cookie cockiness. "It won't be nearly so pleasant as that. First I'm going to destroy you financially. Then I'm going to fix it so that your visitations are limited to *over the phone*."

I clench my jaw. "Don't threaten me, Cookie."

"That's not a threat, my dear, dim, dull, despicable Darius. *It's a promise!*"

I lean forward and speak calmly. "Be careful," I warn her. "Before you find yourself standing beneath the bomb you intend to drop on me."

Her eyes narrow. "You can kiss my . . ."

"I have been, Cookie. I've been kissing it ever since we met. But I'm through. My lips are chapped, the smell is bad, and the taste is worse than ever."

She leans forward and hisses out her invective. "We'll see how big and bad you are once we're in court."

I sit back and casually cross my arms. "Cookie, for the last time: *don't threaten me.*"

She relaxes and looks me up and down, taking her time to paint me with the fullness of her contempt. "Darius, you're way out of your league. I've taken on opponents bigger and smarter than *you* and left them smoking piles of garbage."

I pull out my cellular and start dialing but am struck by an idea of majestic irony. I put my phone away, take Cookie's, and dial. She opens her mouth but stays quiet, apparently content to let me have my way since I'm as good as toast.

The call goes through and I say, "Now!" Then I hang up.

Cookie's expression is still smug and confident, but her eyes have lost some of their cocky certainty.

"What was that all about?" she asks.

"Figure it out," I answer, smiling. "Someone as bright as you are should have no trouble divining the intentions of a despised dim dullard like me."

Her eyes flash and narrow, like she doesn't quite know what to make of things. Then she starts chuckling.

"What's so funny?" I ask.

"You," she chortles. "You're so pathetic, sitting there like you're the cat's meow."

I smile. "Actually, Cookie, I don't even qualify as the cat's kitty litter. *You,* on the other hand, are about to be one of the lumps the cat left behind."

Her laughter dies quickly into a scowl. "I'm going to enjoy crushing you," she says.

"Allow me to introduce myself," says a voice.

Cookie looks up and into the face of a man standing over her. He slides into the booth next to her and says, "I'm Judge Lucas Newton."

Cookie looks from me to the judge and back to me. She's not frightened but definitely off balance. "What's going on?" she asks, her haughtiness deflating.

I get up from the booth and step aside so that Oliver Brady, my attorney, can slide into my seat.

"Allow me to explain," Oliver says. "What's going on is that you're being served with papers."

"Papers!" Cookie gasps.

"As in child custody," I add.

Cookie looks at me with so much hatred, it hits like a force beam. "You bastard," she sneer-snarls, her voice shaking with rage. "I'll get you, Darius. So help me, I'll . . ."

"Young lady, you'd first better figure out how you're going to deal with *me*," Judge Newton commands.

"Don't be ridiculous," she challenges him. "I haven't broken any laws."

"No, you haven't," the judge agrees. "But you have been involved in activities that have exposed your son to influences that, to borrow the language of my colleagues over in domestic court, 'could be considered harmful to the welfare of the child.' "

Cookie's eyes snap from side to side, an old telltale sign that she's searching for some high ground. Seconds later, her eyes darken and she looks at me and smiles. "Nice try, Darius," she says. She cuts her eyes at the judge. "But since Judge Newton presides over juvenile court, so much for your cavalry charge."

Judge Newton chuckles and shakes his head. "You're correct to assume that I don't have direct jurisdiction in custody matters. But as I am a senior officer of the court who's gotten well acquainted with your son and the circumstances and influences that landed him in my jail, my testimony should be quite powerful, wouldn't you say?"

Cookie's face finally registers fear. "You're reaching for straws," she says, somehow still defiant. "Whatever you try," she says, looking at me, "it'll never stick."

"Maybe. Maybe not," I respond, yawning. "But just think, Cookie: *What if it does?*"

"I'll sue!" she threatens, looking at Judge Newton.

He laughs softly. "You may have friends down at city hall, but I've got friends in Washington. When you're ready to sue, give me a call."

He slides a card toward her and stands. Oliver tosses the papers over to her and gets up. We all shake hands and they leave. Cookie stares down at the papers, then looks up at me, her angry eyes swimming in tears.

"I hate you," she sniffles. "I'm sorry I ever met you."

"Yes, Cookie," I say, stepping off. "That was a bad day for me too."

64

IT'S BEEN A WEEK SINCE REVEREND BOXWELL PASSED away, but it feels like I've aged a century. I've cried so much that, at one point, I wondered if I was going to weep myself into dehydration. My tears flowed from two rivers of sorrow. The first was anguish over losing Reverend Boxwell. The second was a torrent of guilt for the years I'd stubbornly withheld my love from my father. I'd made him wonder about it, yearn for it, and suffer its denial. I'm so ready now to give him the affection, honor, and respect that were his due but will never have that opportunity. It's by my own meanness that I'm denied the opportunity to share that part of myself with him.

It's the price I pay for disrespecting time, arrogantly assuming that there'd always be moments available to put things right. I won't make that mistake again, especially with what I have to do now.

I straighten up my desk, cut off my computer, get in my car, and drive off campus into downtown to city hall, where Wylene and Augusta are coming to meet me. I park and go inside, looking up and around at all the ornate sculpture and architectural design. It's like an imposing medieval cathedral, housing a profound but somber atmosphere of power and the burden of responsibility. I wait a few seconds until Wylene and Augusta pull into the parking lot, then saunter up to the receptionist.

"Can I help you?" she asks, yawning.

"Yes. I'm here to see Councilman Fields."

"Do you have an appointment?"

"No."

She frowns. "Well, sir, I'm sorry, but you can't . . ."

"Tell him that Dr. Darius Collins demands a moment of his time."

She scowls. "Sir, if you don't have an appoint . . ."

"Tell him that I'm Jarrod Collins's father," I interrupt. "Tell him that *I am not happy*. Tell him that I want to see him *now*!"

Her droopy disinterested eyes slowly widen with comprehension as the rusty half-used gears of her bureaucratic brain lurch into motion, connecting who I am with recent events.

She quickly grabs her phone and punches the appropriate numbers. "Vernice, the councilman has a visitor. . . . I know he's in a meeting. Trust me, he'll want to make time for this one. . . . Darius Collins. . . . That's right. His father. . . . Well, let's just say that he's not happy."

She hangs up and points down the hallway to her right, her movements suddenly crisp and full of professional pride. "Dr. Collins, go down to the first intersection and take a left. You'll see some elevators on your right. Go up to the fourth floor. You'll find him in Suite Four-twelve."

"Thank you," I say.

"You're welcome."

I walk a few steps away, wait until the receptionist turns away, and gesture quickly to Wylene and Augusta standing by the entrance. They hurry across the big lobby and we zip onto the elevators.

We get to the fourth floor and I lead our small group into Suite 412. Directly ahead of us is a door with a large brass nameplate on it. The nameplate reads: MILTON S. FIELDS, PRESIDENT, COUNCIL, CITY OF CLEVELAND, OHIO.

I glance over my shoulder at Wylene and Augusta and say, "C'mon!"

I march past a woman sitting at a desk in the outer office. The sign on her desk says: VERNICE TROYHILL, ADMINISTRATIVE ASSISTANT. Vernice stands quickly and rushes from behind her desk, blocking my path.

"If you'll just have a seat, the councilman will see you in a few . . ."

"I don't want to sit, and I don't feel like waiting."

I try to sidestep her, but she matches me movement for movement. "If you don't take a seat, I'll be forced to call . . ."

Augusta rushes forward and shoves Vernice aside. She staggers backwards, bounces off the wall, boings against her desk, and falls back into her chair. We burst through the door of Fields's inner office, stride commandingly up to his large oak conference room table, and level our gaze past everyone sitting around it and onto him.

Vernice hustles in after us, snorting and fuming. "I'm sorry, Councilman," she huffs. "I tried to . . ."

"That's all right, Vern," he says, casually waving her into silence. "This won't take long."

"You've got that right," I confirm.

Fields scowls. "Let me guess. You're Dr. Darius Collins," he says, glancing around the table to make sure he has everyone's attention. "You're the father of alleged rapist Jarrod Collins."

Some people gasp; others widen their eyes; they all glare at me. "You all excuse us for a couple of minutes," Fields says. "We'll get right back to work after I've finished humoring Dr. Collins."

The glowering group get up and file past us, some sneering, most scowling, as they depart. Once they're gone and the door's shut, Fields pours himself a shot of liquor from his small wet bar and sits back down at the head of his conference room table.

"All right," he says, taking a sip and glancing at his watch. "Whaddya want? I'm a busy man."

I gesture to my two companions. "Councilman, allow me to introduce my colleagues. This is Wylene Narmer, chief editor at *Pulse Cleveland* . . ."

Fields's eyes bulge and he starts hacking and coughing up his liquor.

I turn to my other companion. "And this is Augusta Baylor, a former tenant of the Euclid Gardens housing project that *you* were managing the winter its roof caved in."

Layers of pure fright paint Fields's face. His mouth hangs open slack-jawed and his eyes dart from Augusta to Wylene, then to me.

"And you of course know me through my son," I say. I place my palms flat on the table and lean forward. "You know, it really upsets me that you've been so instrumental in his being labeled an 'alleged rapist.' "

Wylene pulls out a pad and pen and takes a seat next to Fields on the left side of the table. Augusta sits down opposite Wylene and to Fields's immediate right.

"My daughter has brain damage because of you," Augusta says, her voice tight with anger. A tear rolls from her eye. "You made her suffer, and now it's your turn."

Fields gulps the rest of his booze, sneers, and gets up to fix himself another. "You're wasting your time," he retorts, forcing a chuckle. "That Euclid Gardens accident was investigated and declared no-fault."

He finishes fixing his drink and leans back against the bar counter, his expression a portrait of victorious gloating. "So much for your attempted shakedown." He looks at all of us with contempt. "Now get out of my office before I have you thrown out." He looks at me and says, "And wouldn't the press just love to see you incarcerated. It would explain how Junior got his delinquent tendencies."

"Before we leave," Wylene begins, "perhaps you could explain these."

"Explain what?" Fields growls.

Augusta pulls a thick folder from her shoulder bag. She slides it over to Wylene, who opens it and pulls out a document. "This is a report written by one Martin Hammerskold," she says. "It says that the Euclid Gardens roof cave-in resulted from criminal negligence on the part of the unit supervisor, *you,* and the building contractors."

Fields's cheeks sag. His hand trembles, sloshing some of the liquor out of the glass.

Augusta pulls out another sheet of paper. "And this is a sworn statement from Mr. Hammerskold, who was fired when he alleged that his original report had been destroyed and replaced with a false one absolving you of responsibility."

Vernice rushes in. "Councilman! Councilman! Oh, my God. A TV news crew is on the way up," she babbles.

Fields staggers over to the conference room table and lurches into his chair. Wylene starts peppering him with questions, demanding explanations over and over for his lousy treatment of the disadvantaged "brothers and sisters" he's always claimed to care so much about.

Vernice hustles out to manage the chaos that's burst upon the scene with the news crew. I glance at my watch. I've got to go meet Nash. I start maneuvering toward the door and I look into the eyes of Augusta Baylor. She smiles. I nod and smile back, then ease out past the news crew. I back slowly away, taking a last moment to savor the doomed expression on Fields's face, then leave.

I get on the highway and hurry off to meet Nash. My thoughts wander to Reverend Boxwell. He'd probably be saddened that I stooped low to get some payback. He'd look at me with dismay, stirring up the guilt in my gut for preferring to get even instead of choosing to forgive. He'd admonish me, saying, "Darius, son, don't you remember when the Lord declared that *'Revenge is mine. I shall repay'*?"

And I'd feel bad for failing to be a better man. But I'm also a father, a father who almost lost his one and only son. A son I love and adore. That near loss helps me better understand the anguish God must've felt when Jesus was nailed to the Cross. It helps me better understand why there'll be literal hell to pay for those rejecting the salvation won through His sacrifice.

I need to acquire the Lord's forgiving spirit. I need to squelch my hostility for losing Jarrod to Cookie through divorce. I need to harness my hatred for nearly losing him to jail through the manipulations of "Uncle Milton."

I'll be a better man tomorrow.

65

THE SERVER AT THE ERIE EATERY DISTRIBUTES DESSERT
menus, then clears away our dinner dishes. I suppress a chuckle as I spot
Nash glancing once more into the cleavage of his date, Yalinda. He's done
it so often that his eyeballs are probably burning their imprint onto her
boobs.

Yalinda's friend, Charisse, is built and nice enough, but she's no
match for Gina. No one is. And just as I have so many times over the last
few days, I'm wondering why I didn't tear up that ticket when Marcy gave
it to me. More to the point, why did I take it in the first place?

I've tried over and over to apologize to Gina, but she's kept her distance. I understand that she's hurting and not in the mood for explanations, but she's not the only one who's been dealing with the pain from
love's battlefield. After the past few weeks, the last thing I felt like doing
was going through the begging for forgiveness routine. But Gina's valu-
able to me, so I did it. Her refusal to hear me has revealed a stubborn side
that I hadn't noticed before and is, frankly, kind of disturbing. After
Cookie, I'm *very* disinclined to deal with someone possessing such charac-
teristics, no matter how slight or remote. But still, I miss her.

Gina's silence has left me with plenty of time to reconsider some
things Phoebe said during our lunch date: "Marcy's missing what she had
with you. . . . She wants a second chance. . . . If you made it easier for her,
she wouldn't hesitate to make things right between the two of you. . . .
All relationships have their ups and downs. . . ."

I'm still pissed about the way Marcy rolled me for Stan, but we all
make mistakes and maybe she deserves another chance. If nothing else, I'll
get a nice trip to Aruba and some fantastic lovemaking out of the deal.

My introspection is disturbed by Yalinda's and Charisse's laughter.
Nash is laughing also, but his laughter sounds forced and weak.

Yalinda casts a lingering glance at Nash, then says to Charisse, "So I
make sure my man knows I like to be pampered. If he's not willing to do
that, then we don't have a future."

"Say *that*, sister-girlfriend," Charisse agrees.

They reach out and give each other a high five. Nash puts his arm around Yalinda, pulls her close, and kisses her cheek.

"Well, baby, we're gonna do just fine," he says. "Because I love pampering a woman."

She smiles sweetly and snuggles close. "I'm glad to hear that," she purrs. "Since you like doing that, do you think that maybe next time we could go to a better restaurant?"

Nash's eyes widen with alarm. He glances at me, licks his lips, and says, "Ah, no problem, Yalinda. I only agreed to come here because *Darius* recommended it so highly."

He looks at me hard, his eyes begging me to do my part. I shrug sheepishly. "Nash is right," I quickly confirm. "Coming here was all my idea."

Nash almost wilts with relief, maintaining enough strength to glance again into Yalinda's cleavage.

"So, Darius!" Charisse calls. "Are you like Nash?"

"How do you mean?"

"Do you believe in pampering a woman?"

"I believe in treating the woman in my life with dignity, decency, kindness, respect, and love."

Yalinda and Charisse glance at each other, their eyes communicating that while they appreciate the answer, I've missed the point.

"But what about taking her places?" Charisse presses. "Buying her things? Taking her out? Showing her a good time?"

"All that's important," I answer. "But I think the depth of someone's heart is what truly matters."

They blink at me like I just spoke in Martian. Nash forces a laugh and says, "Y'all have to excuse Darius. He's something of a romantic idealist."

Nash must be describing another Darius Collins, but I let his comment pass. I only came on this double date to help him make Yalinda happy, which she appears to be and should help smooth the way for him later this evening. And judging from the slight frown that passed over Charisse's face, she's already concluded that I'm not her type.

The server glides up to our booth all smiles and goodwill. "Are you all ready to order dessert?"

Everyone makes a selection, but I pass, ordering some coffee instead.

"Have y'all heard the latest news about Councilman Fields?" Charisse asks.

Nash and I glance at each other. "I caught a bit of it on the radio," I answer.

"He's going down," Yalinda says.

Charisse nods in agreement. "And to think he used to be a church deacon. If he loses the next election, he'll have to go back to doing that."

"How are you connecting the possibility of his losing the election with being a church deacon?" I ask.

Charisse looks puzzled, like the answer should be obvious. "C'mon, Darius. You know Fields is a man who loved being seen and throwing his weight around."

Nash sits up tall. "Charisse, you've got me confused too. What's any of that got to do with being a deacon?"

"Stop playing ignorant," Charisse admonishes. "If Councilman Fields loses, the only place he'll be able to exercise his little bit of remaining power is in the church."

Nash and I blink and glance at each other.

"Why do you-all look so surprised?" Yalinda asks. "You know that black men have always used the church to get the respect and authority they often can't get in society."

The utter sincerity of her statement fills me with despair, and I start doodling on my napkin.

"That's not true," Nash challenges. "Lots of brothers go to church purely for worship."

"Lots of brothers?" Charisse chuckles. "Check out any church on Sunday morning and you'll always see more women than men."

"That might be true where *you* attend," Nash persists. "But that's not all churches."

"Nash, you know she's right," Yalinda counters. "Women are the ones who've always held the black church and family together."

Charisse leans over to see what I'm doodling. Yalinda cranes her neck, can't see, and gesturing to Charisse asks, "What's Mr. Antisocial drawing?"

"Sixteen-nineteen," Charisse answers. "The whole napkin's covered with the number sixteen-nineteen."

Puzzle lines bunch up on Yalinda's brow. "What's that all about?"

I ball up the napkin. "Sixteen-nineteen was the year twenty Africans were brought by a Dutch ship to Jamestown, Virginia, marking the beginning of what eventually became North American chattel slavery."

Charisse and Yalinda both say, "What?"

"Since then we've been waging an ongoing struggle to defeat slavery, segregation, and stereotypes."

I look hard at Charisse and Yalinda. "Including the kind you two have been perpetuating."

"Stereotypes?" Charisse sneers. "That's a matter of opinion."

"You're absolutely right," I say. "And I'm of the opinion that you two are no different from bigoted whites who believe that blacks are lazy, stupid, and criminally predisposed."

Charisse snorts and her eyes harden. "Don't blame us if you can't handle the truth."

I stand and put on my jacket. "I can at least understand bigoted white people. They're motivated by fear, ignorance, and racism. But you two! You're part of the family."

"Oh! I get it," Charisse snarls. "We should know our places and be quiet. Is that it?"

I look at Nash, now slouching in his seat and looking glum. "I'm sorry, Nash. I can't do this anymore."

"Can't do what, D?"

"I can't fight America, and them too," I answer, jerking my thumb at our "dates."

Nash pouts, then stands. "Me neither."

We ignore the scene erupting behind us and stroll out to the parking lot. "You owe me," Nash says.

"For what? Saving you from certain disaster?"

"No! For making me leave a cleavage like Yalinda's."

"I didn't make you do anything," I chuckle. "You left because we want the same thing."

"What? To be celibate?"

I roll my eyes. "To be loved, you nut!"

"That's what I'm talking about!" Nash jokes. "I would'a been gettin' some lovin' if you and that slave ship hadn't messed up my action."

Nash's comment is more profound than he realizes. "Nash, that slave ship messed up a whole lot of people's action."

The smile drops from his face. "You're right, D. I'm sorry."

"Don't be sorry, black man. We're here, black, free, and employed. The ancestors survived."

We shake hands, hug, and go our separate ways.

66

I STEP ONTO THE OBSERVATION DECK AT CLEVELAND-
Hopkins Airport and inhale the pungent odor of aviation fumes wafting
on the brisk, crisp night air. A jet roars down the runway, its wing, tail,
and landing gear lights illuminating the powerful beast as it launches itself
into the brilliant starlit sky.

A few days ago, in a rare calm moment in the midst of all this recent
confusion, I was out one evening strolling through the woods of West
Branch State Park. I was deep in thought, trying to analyze how my life
had gone so far off course, when I bumped into Tyler Underwood, an old
grad school acquaintance who was home, visiting from Pittsburgh. Seeing
him made me realize that my life hadn't just gone off course. It was lost on
another planet.

There he was with his wife, Nell, fourteen-year-old son, sixteen-year-
old daughter, and, yes, even the obligatory Golden Retriever. Tyler and
Nell were walking hand-in-hand behind the kids, who flanked either side
of the dog. I could've puked.

I wanted to dive into the bushes until after they passed, but events
happened too quickly. I turned the corner of the narrow walking path and
boom. There they were. Tyler and I navigated our way through the usual
awkwardness of old acquaintances suddenly and unexpectedly reunited.
Then there was the torture of being introduced to his perfect wife, perfect
kids, and perfect dog.

I vaguely remembered Nell. She'd been one of those women whose ge-
netics had made her wait until full adulthood before allowing her to completely blossom, and blossom she had. She was gorgeous, and the tender,
sweet personality emanating from her left my back sweating, knees buck-
ling, and insides sloshing green with envy. She'd taken her bleeding heart
desire to help people, added some latent business wizardry, and founded
ProJob, one of the fastest-growing job placement firms in Pittsburgh.

Tyler had just finished up his second year as chairman of the history
department at Carnegie-Mellon University, a premier institution that I'd

once drooled after. That is, until I slammed into the reality that the world had far more historians than jobs available for them.

Tyler and Nell's kids were doing wonderful things also. Fourteen-year-old Carl was already drawing the attention of Ivy League schools that were salivating at the chance to recruit a black math-physics prodigy. Sixteen-year-old Erika had in her spare time published a small collection of poetry, was headed to the national long distance–running championships, and had been voted Teen Mentor of the Year by her Sunday School. Even the Golden Retriever, Harmony, and had been selected as "the" dog representative for a national dog food advertising campaign.

I was happy for Tyler. Truly I was. I also wanted to snatch him by the collar and beat him to a pulp for having the life, wife, and kids that should've been mine. I wanted to spit on him for having evolved from the dull joke of grad school into a mover and shaker of the black upper middle class. I wanted to get Cookie and Jarrod and slap them silly for using their crushing selfishness and juvenile self-destructiveness to deny me a better marriage, family, and life.

But even as my heart ballooned with jealousy, it was punctured by the truth that I, and only I, had denied myself a better reality. I had constructed my nightmare of the present through a series of consistently bad decisions made over the course of many years. *Turning my back on the truth of God had been my first and worst mistake.* Marrying Cookie ranked as a just-as-bad second. The attempted futile mixing of that oil and water had produced Jarrod, a realization that nearly crushed me with remorse.

When I think of Jarrod, my heart swells with more love than it has room to hold. But there are times when I'm nearly overwhelmed with despair and disappointment, not in him but in myself. At those moments, I wish desperately that he'd been born to someone other than Cookie. I condemn myself for not having loved him enough to be more cautious and discriminating in choosing the woman who'd be his mother. I'm sickened knowing that my lust doomed him to his parental combination. But that's the rub.

Jarrod wouldn't be Jarrod without me *and* Cookie. His being born to someone else might have produced a great child, but a hypothetical great child could never be as wonderful as the real Jarrod. I lament helping drag him into the insanity that is his family but am glad that he's insane with *us.* So there's nothing I could, or would, do to change his being here or who he is. But I've still got to warn him about people like Cookie, people who seem to be born only to rain havoc and misery into other people's lives. I've got to teach him to be alert and beware, or one day he'll be standing in my shoes, wondering why he didn't leap out of the path of an oncoming train.

For the moment, Jarrod seems to be doing fine. He's dating Holly, who he finally made more than a friend, especially after seeing Reesie in that police lineup and realizing how close he'd been to standing in one himself. It hurts that he doesn't call more, but this man-in-training is still a teenager, living a teenager's self-absorbed life. At least now when he calls sometimes it's to ask how I'm doing and not just for money. Chitlins refused when Jarrod asked for his job back. That must've hurt, since even with Cookie's lavish indulgence, Jarrod's never had enough cash. To his credit, he didn't ask me to use my puny influence to get Chitlins to change his mind but found himself another job.

As for Cookie, she's fighting my attempt to get custody with her usual feistiness, promising that I'll pay dearly, yak, yak. Judge Newton assures me that there's nothing to worry about.

"The system's a giant screw," he said recently, grinning. "Every now and then we get to hold the screwdriver."

My biggest prayer is for the quick arrival of the day when I *never* again have to hear Cookie's voice or look upon her face. It's a petty, bitter prayer but will have to suffice until I learn to pray better. It's a prayer that would draw many a disappointed "Tsk, tsk," from those who think I shouldn't be so small but let bygones be bygones and just get on with life. They're right, and I eventually will.

In the meantime, if any of my objective, large-minded critics ever find themselves subjected to the storm I've endured, I'll be available to help comfort them. I'll know that their petty, bitter inability to instantly "get over it" isn't rooted in immaturity but in their struggling to heal. I'll tell them that our nightmare experiences were launched by our own decisions and that in the future we must . . .

Be as wise as serpents and harmless as doves, Dad whispers.

Wisdom. Dad always said that even though I should avoid evil and be on good terms with all people, I should be mindful and watchful. He emphasized that the world was full of nice-looking, sweet-talking people whose sweet words were as rotten as the hearts beating within their chests. Over and over he said, "Darius, choose wisely, Son."

I pull from my jacket's inner pocket the airline ticket Marcy gave me.

I run my fingers along the edges, tracing the lipstick outline of her kiss imprint. I bring it to my nose and inhale deep the lingering scent of her perfume, closing my eyes as its goodness electrifies my senses.

I'm looking forward to lying beside her on a warm beach, sipping an exotic drink, and slowly getting soused before going back to our room to make love. I'm excited about working my tongue along every curve, indentation, and orifice of her body, sending her into stratospheres of pleasure. I'm going to enjoy squeezing her jiggling breasts as she closes her eyes and moans while riding me.

Darius, listen to me, Son: "Guard your heart . . . I, wisdom, dwell together with prudence; I possess knowledge and discretion . . . My fruit is better than fine gold; whoever finds me finds life . . . whoever fails to find me harms himself."

I glance at the ticket, tear it into tiny pieces, and let them flutter away on the wind. Gina's the one I need, and I'm going to do all in my power to help her understand that. But no matter what happens, I won't feel noways tired. I finally see a lighted path and know for certain that even if I have to walk it by myself, I won't be walking alone.